Jaybird

M.A. FOSTER

Jaybird

ISBN: 13-9781543299335
ISBN: 10-1543299334

Cover design: Robin Harper, Wicked by Design

Interior Design: Angela McLaurin, Fictional Formats

To my mom who's a true rock star. Not everyone gets a second chance at love. So, to my dad, Frank, thank you for stepping into the madness and embracing our craziness with your patience, love, and most of all, your bravery. Thanks for always having my back. You're an amazing dad and pop.

And to my dad in heaven, I hope I've made you proud.

Jaybird

INTRO OO:

THEY SAY THAT right before you die your whole life flashes before your eyes. Like photographs on shutter speed. But as I drift in and out of consciousness, it's not my life that flashes before my eyes; it's the faces of the people I love, and the fear of leaving them behind.

And regret for everything I've taken for granted.

TRACK 1: DADDY'S GIRL

Jayla

"I'M HOME!" I announce as I open the front door. "Daddy? Mom?" I call out, dropping my bags in the foyer. The house is unusually quiet for the middle of the afternoon, and that has me feeling a little uneasy. A few seconds later, Bass—pronounced 'Base'—my bodyguard, comes through the door with the rest of my bags. "How's he doing, B?"

"He's hanging in there, Princess." He jerks his chin toward the stairs. "They're upstairs."

I race up to my parents' room and find them on their king-size bed. My mom is lying on her side with her head resting on my dad's chest, arm curled around his waist, and leg hooked over both of his thighs, holding onto him as if he's being pulled away from her. My dad croons their favorite love song, "I Love You," while running his fingers through her hair.

This right here is what true love looks like.

It's beautiful. And heartbreaking.

Most kids would probably be horrified at the sight of their parents being affectionate with one another, but I'm not most kids. I think it's amazing that, after twenty years of marriage, they're still in love.

Maybe it's because I'm still swooning over Zach, my longtime childhood crush. The same boy I just spent two of the most amazing weeks of my life with in St. Thomas.

Maybe it's because I believe in fairy tales and that every princess gets her prince... or princess.

Hey, I don't judge.

But if I've learned one thing in the past two years, it's that fairy tales don't always end with a happily ever after. Because, in this particular real-life fairy tale, Emerson's prince—my dad—is dying.

It's been two years since the doctors discovered my father's inoperable brain tumor. My parents have accepted his fate. I, on the other hand, have not.

"Hey," I say, pulling their attention to me before pushing off the doorframe and making my way over to their bed. Bending down, I give both a kiss and perch on the edge of the bed.

"How are you feeling?" I ask, running my fingers through my father's short, dark hair.

He reaches for my hand and brings it to his chest, placing it over his heart, and covering it with his other hand. "Just a little tired," he answers with a wink.

My father, Marcus King, lead singer of the rock band, Royal Mayhem, is loved by all because he's charismatic and talented. His Latin charm, handsome features, and tattoos give him that bad-boy rock star image, making him popular with the females. He's my dad, but I'm not blind; he's a good-looking man. But he's no bad-boy.

As a celebrity, he's one of the most down-to-earth and genuine people in the industry. He's even earned the nickname "The Gentleman of Rock 'n' Roll" in the tabloids. As the front man of Royal Mayhem, and America's favorite judge on *America's Voice*, he has a wide fan base.

However, his number one fan is and will *always* be me.

"Did you have a good time?"

I always have a good time in St. Thomas, and recently, it's become one of my favorite places. *"You're my girl, Jay,"* Zach's whispered words have been on constant replay in my head since I boarded the plane back to California.

I was just a few months shy of turning six, the first time I met Zach and his brother, Logan. It was the beginning of an annual summer tradition, my first vacation, with my grandparents and cousins, Dylan and Cole. Zach and Logan came with their grandparents, who happen to be my grandparents' closest friends.

Unfortunately, I couldn't go every summer because my life revolved around concerts, tours, interviews, award shows, and all the other fun stuff that comes with being the child of a rock star.

However, I looked forward to those vacations where I got to be a normal kid, and hang out with my grandparents, cousins, and their friends. No bodyguard. No looking over my shoulder for cameras. Not that there would be cameras since no one really knows who I am, but still....

Just normal.

Turns out this summer, it was just Zach and me. My cousins, Dylan, Cole, and Aiden, stayed in Heritage Bay, and Zach's brother, Logan, was wrapped up in summer college classes. Our vacation couldn't have been more perfect. For two whole weeks, our days were spent either lying on the beach, swimming, fishing, sailing, snorkeling, shopping, golfing, or just exploring the island. And our nights were spent sneaking into each other's rooms and doing things my parents would not approve of.

"Of course, Daddy," I say with a smile. "You know how much I love it there." I pull my phone from my back pocket and tap on the photos app before passing it to him.

Of course, I made sure to delete anything questionable.

Now, Marcus King, my *dad*, is as overprotective as they come. And for most of my life, he's kept me on a short leash. Wherever he goes, Mom and I go. And if my parents go somewhere without me, I hang with Bass. My mom has been homeschooling me since day one, and when I'm not studying, I'm writing music or practicing. My friends are limited to the few I grew up with. And boys? Out of the question until I'm thirty.

Mom reaches for my phone. "Is that Zach?"

"Yes." I smile. I can't help it.

"Wow. I can't believe how much he looks like his father." She looks over at me. "He's gorgeous, Jayla." She winks.

Zach *is* gorgeous with his dark blond hair, bright blue eyes, and perfect smile.

He's perfect.

My parents know I've had a crush on Zach for like *ever*, but as far as they know, it's innocent—just like me. And we'll leave it at that because it would crush me to see them disappointed. Luckily, having a mom in PR, I've learned to keep my facial expressions neutral.

When my dad's eyebrows skyrocket to his hairline, I know it's because he's found the picture of me kissing Zach on the cheek. And yeah, he's not happy.

"Daddy, stop," I say softly. "I'm sixteen, not six. And it's just a kiss on the cheek."

"Doesn't mean I have to like it." He narrows his eyes. "It doesn't matter if you're six, sixteen, or twenty-six. You're beautiful and sweet and I worry about boys taking advantage of you. I was his age once, and I know exactly what I was thinking *and* doing." *Gross*. "Tell me he kept his hands to himself."

"Oh my God! Daddy, it wasn't like that," I lie.

He smirks, giving me that "you're so full of shit" look. "There isn't a boy in this world good enough for you. Not even Zach."

"Stop it, Marcus," Mom says, playfully smacking him on the chest. "My dad said the same thing to me about you after we eloped. *You* proved yourself and now I'm pretty sure they like you more than me."

My dad chuckles. "They do."

Taking my phone back, I say, "You guys never gave me this much crap about Zach before."

"You didn't have boobs before," Mom teases.

I hold up my hand. "Please stop."

Dad groans. "Yes, Em. For the love of God, please stop. My heart can't take it."

"Get over it, Marcus. And Jayla, stop lying. You have the same love-struck look on your face every time you come home after spending time with Zach." My mother's bullshit meter is on point today. "You're in love. It's written all over your face," Mom says with a laugh.

My dad jerks his face down to hers. "She better not be."

"I am not!" I lie again. *I totally love him*. "Yes, he's gorgeous." I roll my eyes. "I'm not blind. But we're *friends*." That is the truth. Being anything more than friends right now isn't an option. "Zach and

I were talking, and we were wondering what happened between you and his mom, Elizabeth?"

Mom's smile disappears. "Why?" she snaps.

Wow. Okay.

"Because the Parkers are family," I explain. It's true.

My Mimi and Zach's grandma, Kate have been friends for nearly sixty years. The Parkers are not only my grandparents' closest friends, but they're godparents to my mom and her two brothers, Max and Liam.

Growing up, my mom and Zach's mom, Elizabeth, were best friends all the way through high school until they got into a fight and ended their friendship. Even after twenty years, neither of them will say what their fight was about.

However, my mom's youngest brother, Liam, and the Parker's youngest son, Cam, have been inseparable since they were babies and somehow ended up on the same MLB team. *How does that even happen?*

"Settle down, Em." Dad chuckles. "It's a valid question. I'm surprised it hasn't come up sooner."

Mom blows out a breath. "Sorry. I try not to think about my life before I moved to California and married your dad. Elizabeth and I were best friends—sisters, basically. We had a misunderstanding, and it turned out that she wasn't the person I thought she was. Elizabeth got pregnant with Logan right after we graduated high school, married Mike, Logan and Zach's father, and started her family. I moved to California for college and a fresh start." She shrugs. "We both moved on with our lives and never looked back. It's been over twenty years and nothing's changed. She still hates me. She's never wanted me around her boys, which is why I've never met them and why your father and I don't come with you on vacation. It's also the reason why the Parkers have never brought Zach and Logan to our home. If your grandparents and the Parkers hadn't kept their friendship going all these years, you probably would have never met Zach and Logan."

Thank God for long-lasting friendships.

"I'm sure Mimi and Grandma Kate would've helped you and Elizabeth work it out. Maybe if you had, we'd all be spending our summer vacations together."

Mom shakes her head. "I love my mother, and Kate, but it was between Liz and me. I'd never let our drama cause a rift in their friendship. Too many people would be hurt by that. Besides...." She tilts her head and smiles up at my dad. "If Mimi and Kate had gotten involved, I never would've met this guy."

True story.

My parents met on the plane the day my mom left Heritage Bay for California. They spent the whole flight talking, and, it wasn't until they landed at LAX that she realized she'd been talking to *the* Marcus King the entire time. My dad said it was fate that brought them together, and he knew, without a doubt, he was going to marry her. And less than a week later, he did.

My grandparents were pissed that their only daughter had run off with a rock star and eloped. Luckily, things worked out because my grandparents absolutely love my father. Not because of his celebrity status, but because he's a good man, and he loves the hell out of my mother. And me.

I shift my gaze to my dad. "I told Zach about you," I admit. His brows pull inward, and a confused expression crosses his face. "Not about the cancer," I quickly clarify. "He told me his dad was a lawyer and wanted to know about you." I shrug. "I told him you were a rock star." I snort, remembering the look on Zach's face. "He thought I was kidding. You should've seen the look on his face when he realized my dad was *the* Marcus King of Royal Mayhem."

"I assumed he already knew."

I shake my head. "You told me I wasn't allowed to talk about our family."

Dad laughs. "I meant to the media."

"It probably would've never come up if the other boys had been there. All they talk about is football and girls."

"It's fine, Jay," Mom cuts in. "It's not like people don't know who you are. The media just hasn't figured it out yet. Hell, for the first three years of our marriage, everyone thought I was just your dad's PR rep. They had no idea we were a couple until the paparazzi snapped a photo of us holding hands while I was pregnant."

That's when my dad hired Bass as his head of security. Mom and

Bass met freshman year at UCLA, and after he was injured playing football, which took him out of the game, Dad hired him as a bodyguard for Mom. He's been with us ever since. Bass has always been more than just a bodyguard; he's my mom's best friend, and my dad's right-hand man. He's family.

"I'm gonna go unpack." I lean over and kiss my dad once more before standing up from the bed and heading for the door. "Weenie's on her way over."

"Evangeline," he chides. "You two are too old to be using those ridiculous nicknames." *Ha! Never.* I've been calling Evangeline, my best friend, "Weenie" since I was seven because I had a hard time pronouncing Evangeline. My dad hates it. Obviously. I do it more out of habit now than anything.

"Jaybird," my dad calls. I pause at the door and turn around. "Before I forget, I scheduled an interview for you next month with Miles Townsend from *Rhythm & Riffs* magazine."

"Why?"

"The album," he drawls out slowly like a smartass, as if I'd forgotten.

Off the top of my head, I can name six things I inherited from my dad: his height, his eyes, his olive skin, his talent, his sense of humor, and his quick wittedness, which sometimes borders on the side of smartass.

Did I mention he's a smartass?

Like I'd ever forget. The new Royal Mayhem album, *Jaybird*, which I co-wrote with my dad, and named after me, is expected to release sometime in the early spring of next year. We spent the last year and a half working on that album. I'm still recovering from the long, agonizing hours working in the studio.

"I figured that much, but why are you letting him? I thought I wasn't allowed to talk to reporters."

"You're not. Miles is a writer, and he interviews all my new artists at King Records. He's also an old friend. I trust him with you."

"Okay." I shrug. "If you trust him, then so do I."

"And we're not done talking about Zach," he quickly adds.

I scoff. "Yes, we are. Bye. Love you. Mean it."

TRACK 2: TOO LATE FOR REGRETS

Zach

"HEY, JAY, IT'S Zach. Just checking to see if you made it home okay. I hope you were serious about coming Labor Day weekend because I'm already counting the weeks until I get to see you again. Anyway, I'm on my way to my friend Brad's house for his annual end-of-summer party. I'll call you tomorrow. You're my girl, Jay. I miss you. Bye."

I haven't stopped thinking about her since we parted ways at the airport in St. Thomas. I missed her the second she boarded her father's private jet, heading home to California while I went back to Heritage Bay.

I still can't believe the girl I've known all these years is the daughter of *the* Marcus King.

I'm in love with Marcus King's daughter.

I'm shaking my head in disbelief right now; I couldn't make this shit up if I tried.

It makes sense now why she didn't come on vacation every year with the rest of us.

I'll never forget the day my older brother, Logan, and I met Jayla for the first time. She wore a white T-shirt with a hot pink princess crown printed on the front, denim shorts, and hot pink Converse with the tops covered in tiny crystals. I remember wondering if they were real diamonds. Before you judge me, I was six, and going through a pirate phase. Logan kept teasing her and calling her "Sparkles," so Jay kicked him in the shin and called him a punk.

I think I might have fallen in love with her right then. If I knew what love was.

When my grandparents told me that we were going to St. Thomas this summer, and that Jayla would be there, my only thought was *when do we leave?*

Before St. Thomas, it'd been two years since we'd last seen each other. Two years since we shared our first kiss. I'd always been a little shy with girls, so I considered myself a late bloomer. It took everything I had to get the courage up to kiss her. I remember being nervous as hell, heart racing, and palms sweaty. I wasn't sure if I'd ever have another chance, so I went for it.

I remember everything, from the smell of mint on her breath when she gasped, to the softness of her lips against mine.

The kiss was perfect, and sweet, just like her.

It changed my life.

I thought I was the shit after that kiss, even though my friends had already made out with half the school. Then I met Gabby, my first girlfriend. Sweet and innocent. She reminded me of Jay in that way. We weren't together long before Gabby's dad got a new job, and she moved with her family over Thanksgiving break. I haven't had a girlfriend since.

Even though I'm not that shy kid anymore, I'm not good at talking to girls; most of the time I come across as an asshole. I have zero experience when it comes to relationships, and, to tell you the truth, girls scare the shit out of me. They're pushy and loud and full of endless drama.

Except my friend Evan's girlfriend, Lexi. Of course, she can be all the above, but she doesn't scare me. She's cool.

And there's my best friend, Chelsea.

Chelsea scares me sometimes. She's loud, annoying as shit a lot of the time, and the queen of drama. But she has her moments. She's still my best friend, and she's always got my back. So, that makes her tolerable.

And then there's Jayla.

Easygoing, laid-back, sweet, funny, and sassy as hell.

With her, I'm just me. She doesn't scare me or make me feel awkward. She makes me feel like I can say anything.

She hangs on my every word.

She laughs at my dumb jokes.

She gets me.

She loves me.

And she calls me "Z."

God, I sound like such a pussy.

I knew I was in trouble when she climbed out of the pool wearing a white bikini, her drenched raven hair cascading down her back, and her jewel-colored eyes pinned on me.

She looked good.

No.

She looked smoking hot.

And when she smiled at me, I knew right then that it was going to be the best. Summer. Vacation. *Ever*.

And it was.

"Zach!" I turn my head at the sound of my name and see Chelsea running toward me. I brace for impact when the little fireball slams into me, nearly taking us both to the ground. *Oomph!*

"Finally!" Chelsea squeals, her arms tight around my waist. "Did you have fun building sandcastles with your little girlfriend?" she teases, but I hear the jealousy in her voice.

Chelsea is jealous of any and every girl who isn't her. Although she denies her jealousy, claiming it's because she's protective of me, I know better. She's jealous. Our mothers have been trying to marry us off since we were babies. Don't get me wrong, I love Chelsea, but in a sisterly way. I have some great memories of the two of us growing up. She really is my best female friend, but she'll never be my girlfriend.

Chelsea doesn't know Jayla, but she's been jealous of her ever since she found out that Jay, from California, and my best friend's, cousin—who vacations with us over the summer—is actually Jayla. A *girl*.

Then all I heard for weeks, months, years, was "What does she look like, Zach?" "Is she pretty, Zach?" "Do you like her, Zach?" "Do you have any pictures of her, Zach?" "Does she have a Facebook, a

Twitter, an Instagram, or a Snapchat, Zach?"

You get the idea.

I can't help the stupid grin that spreads across my face when I deliver my answer, "Hell yeah, I did," with a wink.

Because I've known Chelsea my whole life, I know every single one of her expressions, and what they mean. This one means she didn't get the usual "she's not my girlfriend" response she was expecting. The one she usually gets when she teases me about a girl. Her expression morphs into shock, but she quickly recovers by plastering on a fake smile. I call it her cheer smile. It's the one she uses to rile up the students at the pep rallies or people in the stands during a game.

I hate when she smiles at me like that.

"Well, I'm glad you're back," she says, giving my waist a squeeze. "I missed you."

I chuckle, and curl my arm around her shoulders. "I missed you too."

"Chelsea!" someone calls out from the crowd, drawing her attention.

She waves, and then turns to look up at me. "See you later, Zach."

"Later, Chels."

"DUDE, YOU TOTALLY got laid," Brad says with a laugh, a little too loud, as he slaps me on the back and passes me a plastic cup.

I jerk my head to the side and glance over my shoulder to make sure no one heard Brad's declaration before I grab his arm and lean in. "Shut the fuck up," I growl through gritted teeth, steering him away from the bonfire and the nosey fucks lingering nearby, pretending they aren't listening. "What are you talking about?"

"You've got a perma-grin a mile wide." He laughs again. "What's got your panties in a twist?"

"Nothing." I look around again. "Just don't let Cole hear you."

His eyebrows dip in confusion. "What's Mackenzie got to do with you getting laid?" he asks, lowering his voice. "Come to think of it, Mackenzie strikes me as the jealous type," he deadpans.

I snort. "Shut up." Brad has always been the clown in the group. He and I have been friends since kindergarten, and our fathers are law partners.

"So, you *did* get laid?"

I smirk and that's all the answer he needs.

"You did, you slick motherfucker. Was it one of those island chicks?"

"No." I pause. "It was Cole's cousin, Jay."

Brad gives me a confused look. "The dude from California?"

"Jay is a girl," I clarify. "Her name is Jayla."

Brad's eyebrows go up, and his mouth forms an O. "No shit," he says with a grin. "Don't you two have some kind of bro code? Like no banging each other's moms, sisters, cousins...."

I smile and shake my head.

"Dude, are you insane?" he exclaims. "Mackenzie will kick your ass if he finds out."

Don't I know it.

"He's not gonna find out." *Not unless Jay tells him. And she won't.*

"Secrets never stay secrets for long, my friend. Remember that."

"I guess he'll figure it out when she comes down Labor Day weekend."

"Can't wait." He grins. "So, tell me about this chick. Is she hot? What's her name again?"

"Jayla, and she's more than hot. She's beautiful."

"Nice." Brad nods. "I can't believe all this time I thought his cousin Jay was a dude."

I chuckle. "He's protective of her. He probably wanted you to think that." I pull my phone from my front pocket. "I mean it, Brad. You can't say anything to anyone."

Brad gives me a "get real" look. "I won't... but if Mackenzie finds out, don't tell him I knew."

"Pussy," I tease, shaking my head, as I tap the photos icon and pull up the first picture of Jay and me. It's of us on the beach with our cheeks pressed together, smiling. I look like a love-struck idiot, and I don't care.

Brad smirks at me as I pass him my phone, then drops his gaze to the screen. "Ho-leeeey shit, bro." He glances up at me quickly with wide eyes, then back to the phone. "She's gorgeous."

Brad also has a flare for the dramatic, but at this moment, he's right—Jayla King *is* gorgeous.

"I know." A smug grin stretches across my face.

"How is this goddess related to Mackenzie, exactly?" He slides his fingers across the screen to scan the rest of my pictures.

"Her mom is Emerson Mackenzie."

"Ah, the black sheep," Brad says knowingly. "Yep, I can see the Mackenzie resemblance. Good-looking bastards," he mumbles. "So, you got your cherry popped by a goddess?"

"Fuck off." I laugh and punch him in the shoulder.

I'm far from being a virgin. Cole and I lost our virginity, freshman year, to a couple of college girls during a party we went to with his brother, Dylan.

"So, are you guys doing the long-distance thing?" Brad asks, passing my phone back to me.

"We didn't really talk about it." I shrug and stare down at the picture. Jay doesn't do social media, which is fine since neither do I, so we'll stick with texting and FaceTime.

"You should've locked that shit down. Marked your territory. Stamped 'Property of Zach Easton' on her ass. Something. We don't grow girls like that around here."

Truth.

I chuckle. "It's not like we won't see each other again. I told you, she's coming Labor Day weekend."

"So... what? You just see each other on holiday weekends? What if you want to hook up with someone else? What if she does?"

I hadn't considered that. I guess it could happen. Not me, but her. Although, she said her dad is pretty strict about her dating.

Brad picks up on my internal struggle. "Aww, my boy Zachy is in love," he singsongs, hooking an arm around my neck. I hate that stupid nickname. I hate it as much as Jayla hates Sparkles. *Fucking Logan.*

"Does this mean your obsession with Reagan is over?" Brad asks.

Ah, yes. Reagan Vaughn.

I wouldn't say I was obsessed.

Reagan *was* the object of my affection last year. She was the new girl. She'd had my attention ever since the day she pranced her hot little ass into Mr. Jones's first period Marine Biology class and sat down at the desk in front of me. She teased, and all but tortured me with flirty smiles, a touch here and there, or by flipping her strawberry-scented hair over her shoulder. She was the girl of my dreams, until she wasn't.

"I wasn't obsessed with Reagan," I lie. Kind of.

"So, you wouldn't care that she's been asking about you all night?" Brad chuckles, bringing his cup to his lips, and eyeing me over the rim.

I shrug. Honestly, I don't know what to think. Reagan has dated a lot of guys and has never shown any interest in me.

I'm... intrigued?

Why me?

Why now?

Reagan is no Jayla, that's for sure. Comparing any girl to Jayla would be unfair. And I'm not saying this because I just spent the last two weeks with her. It's just a fact.

The two couldn't be more opposite. Reagan is pretty, in a wholesome kind of way, petite, and blonde with a heart-shaped face, big, brown, doe eyes, and soft, pink lips.

Jayla is more exotic-looking. Tall and thin, with legs for days, black hair, olive skin, full lips, and captivating, blue-green eyes.

Some people are just born beautiful, only to become even more beautiful over time. Jayla King is one of those people. I'm not just talking about her face or her body; I'm talking about her heart. She's sweet, and kind, and when she smiles, you can't help but smile too. She's infectious that way.

I miss her.

"I say stick with the goddess," Brad advises.

I huff out a laugh. "It's not that easy," I remind him. "High school relationships hardly work out. How is a long-distance relationship supposed to work? I've got football, and I'm sure she's doing her own thing. I guess we'll just have to see how things go."

"Well, you better figure it out." He gestures with his cup, prompting me to look over my shoulder to see Reagan making her way toward us. "I'm gonna go find Hannah." He slaps me on the shoulder. "Be careful, bro," he says before walking off, lifting his cup in a mock toast, and nodding to Reagan as they pass each other.

Famous last words.

"Hey, Zach," Reagan says, smiling up at me with those big, doe eyes.

"Hey."

TRACK 3:
PIECE OF ME
Jayla

"So, tell me everything," Evangeline says, as she plops down on the opposite end of the sofa, and tucks her legs to her side. "And don't leave anything out." Propping her elbow on the back of the sofa, she rests her cheek in the palm of her left hand, gesturing with the right for me to hurry up and start talking.

I laugh quietly. *This bitch loves her some gossip. Damn drama queen.*

Evangeline Skye, aka Weenie, is my best friend, and keeper of my secrets. I've known her my whole life. She's four years older than me, and my only true female friend. If it weren't for her—and Tumblr—I'd know nothing about the opposite sex. However, judging by the look on Mom's face earlier, I'd say "the talk" is coming soon.

Evangeline has no filter; she tells it like it is. If she doesn't know you, she doesn't like you. And if she doesn't like you, she'll tell you. She's a bitch most of the time, but in our world, it's how we protect ourselves. However, she's *my* bitch, and I love her just the way she is.

Evangeline has been modeling since she was thirteen. Recently, she's become quite popular, gracing the cover of almost every fashion magazine over the last few months.

"Come on, asshole." She unfolds her long legs and kicks me in the shin, making me laugh harder. "You've been in love with this kid for like *ever.*" She rolls her eyes. "Why are you laughing? Are you embarrassed or something?" She pauses to study me. "Aww," she coos. "Va-jay-jay, you *are* embarrassed."

I cover my face with my hands. Best friend or not, this is still embarrassing. Joking about sex is one thing, but having to talk about it, in detail, is not as easy as I thought. And, honestly, I'm not sure I want to share something so personal.

I jerk my head away from my hands. "You know what I just realized?"

"What?"

"This is the first real conversation we've ever had about sex."

Her eyebrows pull inward. "Not true."

"It is. Yeah, we've joked about it before, but we've never had a real conversation about it. You never told me about your first time. Maybe if *you* shared, it would be less embarrassing for me to tell you about mine. Was Alex your first?" Alex is Evangeline's hot-as-hell boyfriend, who also happens to be my cousin, Dylan's, friend. She and Alex met when Dylan and Alex interned for my dad at King Records a couple of years ago.

They've been together ever since.

She drops her head and suddenly becomes very interested in the frayed holes in her skinny jeans. "I wish... but no. There was one guy before him," she murmurs, and my heart sinks from the sadness and regret in the tone of her voice. She sounds nothing like my tough, tell-it-like-it-is, smartass, best friend.

"Holy shit, you *were* holding out on me, bitch." I stretch out my leg and kick her back. "Who was he? Tell me," I demand.

"I wasn't holding out on you. It just wasn't worth talking about. He was a dick."

"Give me a name, and I'll get Bass to kick his ass."

She snorts at my ridiculousness and shakes her head. "I'm fine, Jay. I was young and dumb. I thought I was in love and that he cared about me, but I was wrong. I didn't know any better." She shrugs. "He cheated on me with another model and broke my heart."

"I can't believe you never told me." I pout. "We promised to never keep secrets from each other."

She holds up her hand. "Don't be mad. I wasn't keeping it a secret, I swear. I didn't want to make a big deal about it until I knew for sure it was going to work out. Obviously, it didn't. And, thank God, because when I met Alex, I fell hard. He's got that whole brooding, alpha-male thing going on. It's hot. He's sweet to me, and he loves my crazy. It wasn't too long after that I realized Alex is the one I'm supposed to be with. I can't wait to marry his sexy ass, and pop out a bunch of his little, blue-eyed babies." She lifts a shoulder in a half-shrug and smiles. "That's all I got. Your turn."

Alex and Evangeline's relationship is what has me holding out hope that things will work out for Zach and me. Alex lives in Heritage Bay, where he and my cousin, Dylan, manage my Uncle Max's restaurant, Mac's, while Evangeline travels all over the world for modeling.

It doesn't escape my attention that she totally avoided telling me the name of the asshole who broke her heart.

I'll let it go. For now.

For the next hour or so, I tell Evangeline all about Zach and me, and the most unforgettable summer vacation ever.

"Do you think we'll still be friends when we're in our sixties?" she asks, referring to the longtime friendship between my Mimi and Zach's grandma, Kate.

I roll my eyes. "God, I hope not," I tease, dodging the throw pillow she whips at my head.

AFTER A LONG hot shower, I slip on a pair of sleep shorts and a tank top before crawling into bed with my iPad. My cell phone pings on the nightstand with a text from Lucas, and, when I reach for it, I notice there are two missed calls and two voicemails from Zach.

I tap the message icon and pull up Lucas's text first. ***Sorry I didn't make it over tonight. Still in the studio. Be over tomorrow. Promise. Luv U, little sis.***

Lucas Wild is my brother from another mother. His father is Andrew Wild—I call him Uncle Drew—my dad's best friend, and the drummer for Royal Mayhem. My dad and Andrew formed Royal Mayhem together when they were still in high school. Andrew hooked up with Lucas's mother while they were on tour, and, when Lucas was three months old, she abandoned him. My mom and dad were already married by then, and both of my parents helped Andrew raise Lucas. To this day, my mom is the only mother Lucas has ever known.

A couple of years ago, Lucas formed his own band, LAW—Lucas Andrew Wild, or Lucas, Ace, and Wes. *Insert eye roll.* I'll admit, it's catchy, and it works for Lucas and his bandmates. LAW is currently in the studio finishing up their first album and will be touring next summer.

Another text from Lucas comes through. ***Drew is driving me nuts. Whose idea was it to make him our manager?*** I laugh out loud. I totally get where he's coming from, and I sympathize. I've been there.

It wasn't that long ago that I was spending long hours in the studio with my dad and the rest of the guys from Royal Mayhem, working on the *Jaybird* album. Working with my dad was fun, but frustrating at the same time. Let me just say that I love my dad more than anything; I would give my life to save his. I know he's sick, and it sounds wrong, but the truth is, sometimes he pushes me too hard, and it pisses me off. I feel guilty for all the times I got angry with him, wishing he'd back off.

For Lucas and me, music is our rite of passage. We've both been given a talent people pay tons of money for, writing and performing since we were kids.

I'm glad Lucas didn't come over tonight; I'm so not in the mood to be grilled over Zach, again. Lucas plays the protective big brother role pretty well, so as much as I love him, I could never tell him about Zach and me. I don't trust that he wouldn't tell my dad, or worse, Bass.

No worries. Weenie wore me out today lol ;)

Hahaha! You're not right.

Going to bed. See u tomorrow. Say hi to the guys and give Ace a kiss for me. xoxo

I snicker, picturing Lucas scowling at his phone right now, as he reads my text. Ace is the drummer for LAW. He's hot and a total flirt.

I think he does it to piss Lucas off. Even if I were allowed to date, I wouldn't date a musician. Sounds crazy, I know, considering I'm surrounded by them, but I've seen and heard enough in my life to conclude musicians—rock stars—are not for me. I'd even go as far as to rule out athletes, too, but since Zach is a football player, I'd make an exception.

Stay away from Ace. You're gonna get his ass kicked.

I laugh out loud again as I text back ***xoxo***, before switching to my voicemail.

Butterflies flutter in my stomach as I pull up the first from Zach. It's from earlier today.

"Hey, Jay, it's Zach. Just checking to see if you made it home okay. I hope you were serious about coming Labor Day weekend, because I'm already counting the weeks until I get to see you again. Anyway, I'm on my way to my friend Brad's house for his annual end-of-summer party. I'll be sure to tell the boys you said hi. I'll call you tomorrow. You're my girl, Jay. I miss you. Bye."

I'm grinning hard right now. I've never been in love before, but if this is what it feels like, I never want to feel any other way again. I just wish we could be together, not three thousand miles apart. It's unfair. And forcing a long-distance relationship isn't fair either.

The second message is from thirty minutes ago. When the message begins, I press my free hand flat against my stomach and take a deep breath, calming the butterflies that are my nerves. After ten seconds of nothing but music and the muffled sound of voices in the background, I realize Zach must have accidentally pocket-dialed me. Just as I start to pull the phone away from my ear to delete the message, I hear something that has me bringing it back to my ear.

The sound is muffled, but the heavy breathing makes it pretty clear what's happening. Then I hear his voice.

What did he just say?

My stomach flips and bile rises in the back my throat.

And those butterflies from earlier? They burst into flames and fall to their ashy death.

I don't bother pausing or deleting the message before pressing the callback option, which immediately dials Zach's number.

His phone rings three times before it clicks, and a female voice says, "Hello?"

My heart shatters into a million pieces as my eyes well up with tears. I can't speak past the lump in my throat.

"Hello?" she says again.

Swallowing past the lump, I finally choke out, "Uh... I think... Is this Zach's phone?" I don't even recognize my own voice.

"Yes. He's asleep. Who is this?"

"You answered his phone, so I'm sure you already know who this is. Who are you?"

"I'm his girlfriend. And, let me guess, you're the skank he hooked up with in St. Thomas, right?"

The most significant moment of my life has just been reduced to a hook-up. And now I'm pissed.

"Excuse me? Skank? You don't know me," I bark into the phone.

"I know enough." She huffs out a breath. "Look, Zach and I broke up over the summer, but we're back together now. He still loves me, so I would appreciate it if you stopped calling him."

Click.

Did that just happen?

Zach has a girlfriend?

A fucking girlfriend!

I feel like I'm gonna throw up.

And I do.

Splashing some cold water on my face, I make my way back to my bed, flopping on the mattress, and pressing my hand over the gaping hole where my heart used to be. My chest heaves and tightens with every breath until I can't hold back anymore.

I burst into tears.

I AWAKEN TO the sounds of heavy footsteps and muffled clipped conversations on what sounds like two-way radios, and my phone still clutched in my hand. I realize I must've cried myself to sleep. Blinking, I clear away the haze and dried-up tears from my eyes, and check the time on my phone—2 a.m. It sounds like an army is invading my house on the other side of my bedroom door.

What the hell?

Then the sound of sirens breaks through my sleepy, confused brain.

Oh my God, Daddy.

Leaping from the bed, I rush to my bedroom door and yank it open, and see at least half a dozen paramedics filtering in and out of my parents' bedroom.

I sprint down the hall and push past the crowd of firemen lingering outside their doorway. I freeze just inside the room, taking in the scene of paramedics loading my father's unconscious body onto a stretcher. My eyes immediately seek out my mom, who's perched on the edge of the bed. Grace, our housekeeper, is beside my mom, with her arms wrapped around her, comforting her.

Before I know it, I'm in front of them, dropping down on my knees, my hands flat on my mom's thighs. "Mom, what's happening?" I ask through a sob.

She shakes her head and cries harder into her hands. I jump to my feet and turn toward my father, still unconscious with an oxygen mask over his nose and mouth.

"Daddy!" I take a step toward him, but am stopped by strong arms embracing me from behind, holding me back as the paramedics wheel my father past me and out of the room. "Daddy!" I cry hysterically. Mom stands and follows the paramedics out with Grace still at her side. "Mom? Is he gonna be okay?" *Why won't she look at me?* "Let me go, B! I need to be with them. I need to know he's okay."

"Princess, let them get him to the hospital," Bass says, holding me tight.

I fight against his hold on me, kicking and clawing, but it's pointless; the man is built like a brick wall. My chest heaves as I struggle once again to catch my breath.

"Please don't let him die," I whisper as the noise around me fades.

And my world goes black.

TRACK 4: SYMPATHETIC

Zach

"HELLOOOO." CHELSEA SNAPS her fingers in my face. "What are you thinking about?"

"Nothing," I lie, shaking my head. I'm thinking about Cole. Two days ago, he and his family left for California because his uncle Marcus, Jay's dad, is dying.

Apparently, he'd been sick for some time, but Jay left that part out when she told me about her dad. According to Cole, the night Jay returned from St. Thomas, Marcus King's health took a turn for the worse, and he was given a few months at best.

I guess that explains why I hadn't heard from Jay. It's been six months since we said our goodbyes at the airport in St. Thomas. However, it doesn't explain why she blocked my calls.

"Yo!" Justin Phillips, my friend and teammate, calls out, pulling me from my thoughts, as he drops down in the empty chair beside me. "You coming to my party tonight?"

"Of course, he is," Chelsea says at the same time Reagan says, "Of course, we are." They sneer at each other.

My eyes flick between the two of them before I shake my head and tell them to grow up. Reagan and I have been officially dating for a few weeks now, against Chelsea's protests. Chelsea thinks Reagan isn't good enough for me, and, apparently, Chelsea also thinks she's my mother. I turn to Justin. "We'll be there." Reagan smiles triumphantly at Chelsea, and I inwardly roll my eyes.

Perfect example of why I've avoided relationships.

It all started the night of Brad's end-of-summer party—the night I came back from St. Thomas.

"Hey, Zach," she said as she walked up, holding a red Solo cup in one hand and using the other to play with her hair. "How was your summer?"

All I could think was Holy shit, she's finally talking to me.

No. Scratch that.

She was flirting with me.

"Good. Yours?" My voice came out a little high-pitched, so I cleared my throat, and took a sip of my drink in an effort to calm the hell down and have a normal conversation with her.

"Boring till now." She winked.

Yep, she was definitely flirting.

When the party was over, I crashed in the guest room. A few minutes later, Reagan came in and crawled in the bed beside me. We talked for a little while about nothing important. Then she leaned over and kissed me.

I won't lie. I kissed her back.

I'd always wanted to kiss her.

But then guilt settled in the pit of my stomach, forcing me to pull away.

Jayla.

I couldn't tell Reagan the reason we had to stop was because I was in love with my best friend's cousin and risk Cole finding out what happened in St. Thomas. Instead, I told Reagan I didn't have a condom. Which wasn't exactly a lie. The next morning, I woke with a feeling of dread. I felt sick with guilt, like somehow I'd betrayed Jay. I needed to clear my conscience, so I called Jay to come clean about what happened with Reagan, but every one of my calls went straight to voicemail, and my texts went unanswered. This continued for two weeks straight. Until I realized all my texts were undelivered.

She'd blocked me.

Not just from her phone but from her life, as if I didn't exist. As if nothing had ever happened between us. I told her I loved her, and she said she loved me, too. If we were nothing else, I thought we were at least friends. But instead, she crushed me, and broke my damn heart. I know I sound like a little bitch, whining over a girl, but she isn't just some girl. She's supposed to be *my* girl.

Football season had started, and, surprisingly, Reagan was still interested. I wasn't. I hadn't touched her since that night at Brad's. I was too messed up over Jay, wondering what went wrong, and why the hell she blew me off. When Labor Day weekend finally came, I still secretly held out hope that Jay would show up.

She didn't.

The following weekend, Reagan and I hooked up. And we continued to hook up for months. I wasn't sure I wanted more with her. She was cool and good at sex, but she was a flirt and a little self-centered. I find that to be the norm with most girls, but I didn't trust her. Maybe it wasn't just her I didn't trust. Maybe it was all girls. I blame Jay.

Either way, my heart was off-limits.

If that makes me an asshole, well....

Reagan was fine with it. "It is what it is. It works for us." Her words.

"Wear something sexy for me," Justin says to Chelsea with a wink. Chelsea rolls her eyes, brushing him off. Justin's been chasing after Chelsea for years, but either she doesn't realize it or she doesn't care. I offered to talk to her, but Justin said, "No, I want her to figure it out on her own." Justin's a good dude, so, hopefully, Chelsea will figure it out before it's too late.

"You and your brothers are only throwing this party as an excuse to gawk at tits and asses all night," Lexi chides, narrowing her eyes.

"Will yours be there?" Justin asks, jerking his eyebrows up and down.

"Watch it, Phillips," our friend, Evan, and Lexi's boyfriend, warns, picking up a french fry from his tray and chucking it at Justin's head.

THE PHILLIPS BROTHERS' annual "CEOs and High-class Hoes" Valentine's Day party is basically a Halloween party on Valentine's Day, with a slutty theme. It's just another excuse to throw a party. And like Lexi said, to gawk at tits and asses all night.

The house is littered with dudes in half-buttoned dress shirts and loosened ties, alongside girls dressed in anything from short dresses to skimpy lingerie.

Reagan looks hot in her pink and black lace corset top, paired with a short black miniskirt that shows off her thigh-highs and pink and black lace garter belt. She had to change in my car because Judge Vaughn would die if he saw his little girl in this getup.

Reagan grabs my arm, and I bend down so she can speak into my ear over the loud music. "I'm gonna go find Ashton," she tells me before she disappears into the crowd.

Evan and Lexi are in the media room watching a car commercial on the TV. If there's a TV on somewhere, that's where I'll find Lexi, and Evan by default, because they're attached at the hip. Lexi is obsessed with the entertainment channels. I'm sure it's has something to do with her mom being some big-time movie star.

I make my way to the sofa and drop down on the end. "What are we watching?"

"*Entertainment News*," Lexi tells me. "Marcus King died."

"What?" I knew it was coming but I feel like someone just reached into my chest and squeezed my heart. I could cry. Poor Jay. And Cole. I can still picture the devastation on his face the day he left for California.

Lexi nods to the television, picking up the remote, and turning up the volume.

Video footage of Marcus King performing during a Royal Mayhem concert plays on the TV, as a male voice filled with sadness filters in over the sound of the video. The words "I can't believe he's gone" pop up on the screen, the person speaking noted as entertainment attorney Jack Reynolds.

The female correspondent opens with her typical dramatic drawl. "Heartbreaking news tonight for Royal Mayhem and *America's Voice* fans. Forty-five-year-old Marcus Alexander King has died. A representative for the family, Attorney Jack Reynolds, confirmed that the singer, and America's favorite judge on the reality TV show *America's Voice*, passed away peacefully this morning at his Malibu home with his family by his side. The details surrounding King's cause of death are still unknown at this time, but a source tells us that he had been battling cancer for over a year. While we are all shocked and saddened by the news, our hearts and prayers go out to King's family, friends, and, of course, his fans. The King family also released a statement: 'It is with great sadness that we announce the passing of our beloved son, husband, father, brother, and friend, Marcus Alexander King. On behalf of the family, we would like to thank everyone for their love, support, and prayers. We also ask that you respect our privacy during our time of grief.'"

TRACK 5:
LIFE IS BEAUTIFUL
Jayla

"TODAY WE GATHER to celebrate the life of Marcus Alexander King," Pastor Solomon begins.

"I'm sorry," my dad said through a shaky breath. I was curled up beside him in his bed with my head on his chest. His arm wrapped around me while he stroked my hair with his free hand.

"For what?" I asked.

"Since the day you were born, I've done everything I can to protect you from anything that might hurt you, but I can't protect you from this."

"It's not your fault. I don't want you to leave me, Daddy, because I won't be able move on from this."

"You will, baby girl. You're a King. You're strong."

"I love you so much, Daddy." I tightened my hold on him.

"I love you too, Jaybird." He squeezed me gently and kissed the top of my head. "Do you remember what I told you?"

I nodded. "To trust my gut, follow my heart, and never, ever settle for anything less than I deserve."

"Always."

Lucas gives my hand a gentle squeeze, bringing me back to the present, and I turn to look at him. He jerks his chin to the large screen on the wall behind the pastor displaying photos of my dad. "Marcus was..." Pastor Solomon continues as I take in each picture.

Dad with Andrew when they were teenagers. Andrew in a faded black Motley Crue T-shirt with his arm draped over Dad's shoulder, a pair of drumsticks in his hand. Dad in a gray Guns N' Roses T-shirt with his arm draped over Andrew's shoulder. Both wore wide grins. So young and innocent, completely clueless to what fate had planned for them.

"How did you know you wanted to be a rock star?" I asked him.

"Music was my first love, my true love, and, at certain times of my life, my only friend," he said. "Music was my escape from the reality that was my crappy childhood and parents who barely remembered I existed. They didn't abuse me physically—they just didn't take care of me. We moved around a lot and never stayed in one place long enough for me to make any friends. I had this little Walkman with headphones that I took with me everywhere. Every time we moved, my Walkman was the first thing I grabbed. My parents didn't mind because it kept me out of their way. Sometimes they'd hook me up with a cassette tape or batteries or a new pair of headphones."

A photo of my parents on their wedding day appears. Just the way they're looking at each other, you can feel their love.

"How did you guys meet?" I asked my parents one night, out of the blue, after we had just finished watching a movie about soul mates. Mom's eyes darted to Dad and she blushed.

"We met on the airplane the day your mom left Heritage for California," my dad answered with a knowing smile. He'd always claimed that he fell in love with her from the first moment she turned her emerald-green eyes on him. "We've been together ever since."

The next picture is one of my favorites of my dad and me. A black-and-white from when I was about five years old. I was sitting on his lap. His arms wrapped around me from behind, and he was pressing a kiss to my cheek while smiling. My eyes were closed tight, my nose scrunched up because I was giggling.

I'm still lost in my memories when Pastor Solomon calls my name. I jerk my head up to see him smiling down at me. With a nod, he says, "Whenever you're ready."

Evangeline squeezes my hand and whispers, "I love you, JJ," while Lucas squeezes the other and kisses the side of my head. Evangeline, Lucas, and I have had our share of arguments and fights over the years, because that's what siblings do. And though we're not related by blood, they're my family.

Right now, in this moment, they're my strength.

Taking a deep breath, I stand, and make my way up to the stage. Pastor Solomon wraps me in a hug, then moves to the side, as I stand in front of the podium. I'm a little stunned when I look out to see so many sympathetic faces blinking up at me. Hundreds. Maybe a thousand. I didn't realize so many people were here, and it warms my heart to know that so many people cared about my dad. Mom wouldn't allow them to be here if she didn't believe they did.

The front row is filled with the most important people in my life—in my parents' life—my family. And, of course, Dr. Ramos, the woman who made it possible for me to stand up here in front of all these people and talk about my dad.

I clear the lump from my throat and begin. "Thank you all for coming this morning, and for your continued love and support throughout the last few months. It means a lot to me and my family.

"I could stand up here for hours and talk about Marcus King, the incredibly talented musician, singer, songwriter, producer, and headstrong business man. But if you're here today, then you already know those things about him.

"So, instead I want to tell you about Marcus King, my dad." A smile pulls at my lips as so many memories come to mind. "Before he passed, my dad said to me, 'People come into our lives for a reason, no matter how long they stay. It's fate.' Now, I'm not going to lie. I'm upset with God for taking him away from me—from us—but I'm also thankful to God for choosing Marcus to be my father, and I'm grateful for every single day he was in my life. I'd give anything for one more day, one more minute, but that's not how God works. I ask God every day, 'Why him?' It's not fair, but the saying is true. 'Life isn't fair.' I'm sure every one of you has had those thoughts if you've lost someone you love. Sometimes I feel like this is all just a bad dream that, any moment now, I'll wake up to the sound of him strumming his guitar. I keep expecting to find him in the kitchen, dancing in his boxers, and singing about making pancakes and bacon." A mixture of laughter and sniffles drifts from the pews. "He was funny and entertaining. He was always happy. Music was his remedy for everything. If I was sleepy, he'd grab his guitar and sing me a rock-a-by. That was his version of a lullaby. If I was moody, he'd crank up the music, grab me by the hands, and we'd dance until we were breathless and laughing. There was never a dull moment in the King house. I still remember the day I wrote my first song. I'll never forget the prideful look in his eyes, or the smile that stretched across his face when I performed it for him and my mom. That look inspired me to embrace my talent. And, in return, I was rewarded with that look often." I pause to breathe through the knot tightening in my chest.

Movement in the back of the church draws my attention. A woman is leaning over to speak to the man beside her, but it isn't her I'm focused on. It's the glimpse of dark blond hair slightly curled at the ends. My chest tightens at the thought of the boy who broke my heart nearly seven months ago. *That can't be him.*

My gaze moves to Dr. Ramos because she's my anchor. When I look to the back once more, the woman has righted herself in her seat, and I can no longer see the person behind her. The person who looks a lot like Zach.

I take a breath and continue. "Marcus King was just a man who loved his family. Music was his life, but family was his everything. He was an amazing father and husband. I can only hope that one day I'll be lucky enough to have a man love me as much as my dad loved my mom. What I've learned from this experience, this loss is, that at the end of the day, we're all human. Our titles, our social status, our money—none of that stuff matters when it's our time to go." Understanding crosses some of the faces staring back at me.

"I know he's in a better place, and he's at peace. I'm relieved that he no longer feels pain. Call me selfish, but that doesn't make me miss him any less, nor does it dull the pain I feel of having to let him go. A pain so fierce it hurts to breathe because my heart is broken." I feel the first tear roll down my cheek and pool between my lips. Soon, there are more. I don't care.

Dr. Ramos stands from her seat and moves to the steps, but I give her a slight shake of my head and turn to my mom. I can barely see her through the tears in my eyes. I struggle to swallow past the lump in my throat, my chest heaving as I fight to catch my breath. "I speak for my mom as well when I tell you that my dad was the moon in the night sky. The sun on a cloudy day. He was our life. Our world. He was our everything. I'll miss you, Daddy," I choke out the last words, and Dr. Ramos is immediately at my side, wrapping her arm around my shoulders, and guiding me back to my seat.

"That was beautiful, Jayla," she whispers in my ear. "I have no doubt that your father is very proud of you, because I know I am."

TRACK 6: BROKEN

Zach

"THAT WAS THE saddest thing I've ever seen," I say to my dad as we enter our hotel room. Tossing my suit jacket, I loosen my tie before falling back on the sofa and propping my feet up on the coffee table.

"I know." My dad sighs, making his way over to the mini bar and pulling out two beers. "I think we both could use one of these, don't you?"

"I think yes." He passes me a beer before dropping down on the sofa beside me and propping his feet up, mimicking my pose.

Before today, I can't remember the last time I cried. I'm not ashamed to admit Jay's eulogy shredded me. I doubt there was a dry eye in that church by the time she was done. I'm surprised she was able to speak and even more surprised that she held it together for as long as she did. There's no way I could get up in front of all those people and talk about losing one of my parents. When she went on about being heartbroken and described her pain as "so fierce it hurts to breathe," that's when I lost it. That kind of heartbreak is a whole different kind of pain.

I feel like a giant douche for whining like a little bitch, for the past six months, over my own heartbreak. It feels so insignificant compared to hers. Just the thought of losing someone I love makes me tear up all over again.

"You want to talk about it?"

"About what?"

"Whatever's on your mind."

Exhaling deeply through my nose, I say, "I feel so bad for her. For the whole family. The Kings. The Mackenzies. Grandma and Pop. Uncle Cam. They were all close to him. We should've been sitting up front with our family, showing our support. Mom, too. Whatever her issues are with Emerson, they should've been set aside long enough to pay her respects."

"I agree, but it isn't up to us to decide that."

"Have you ever met Marcus King before?" I ask.

He nods. "Once."

I raise my brows, intrigued. "Really? When?"

"A few years ago. He had a friend who needed some legal advice, so Mimi sent him to me."

"What was he like?"

"He was exactly the way Jayla described him. He was a great guy. Laid-back, kind, genuine. And he loved the hell out of his girls."

"I think Jay hates me," I blurt out. *Shit. Why did I say that?*

"Why's that?" He chuckles.

I shrug, picking at the label on the beer bottle.

"Look at me, Zach," he commands. I do. "Why do you think she hates you?" He raises his eyebrows. "Did something happen?"

I turn my focus back to the label. "Yeah," I breathe.

"Did you—"

"Yes," I answer honestly, before turning to look at him. "Please don't say anything to Mom."

"I won't." He nods slowly. "But why do you think she hates you?"

"Because she hasn't answered any of my calls or texts since we got back from St. Thomas. Then she blocked me."

His brows shoot up to his hairline. "Wow. Sounds like she *does* hate you," he says with a laugh. "What did you do?"

I drop my head back against the sofa and blow out a breath. "I have no idea. That's what pisses me off the most. We've known each other since we were kids. Jay's not the type to let something go without having her say. If I did something, she would've called me up and told me what I did and given me the chance to make it right."

"Maybe she wasn't the one who blocked you. Maybe it was Marcus or Emerson. They're pretty protective of her."

I hadn't thought of that. I figured if they ever found out the truth about Jay and me, most likely Cole would too. And if he knows, then either he doesn't care or he's just waiting for the right time to punch me in the junk. Knowing Cole, I'd say it's the latter.

"Can I tell you something?"

"Of course."

"I've been trying to move on for the past six months, but I can't. Seeing her again has brought all those feelings back. I'm not over her. And I'm not ready to be over her." My dad just nods in understanding. "I know it sounds crazy and stupid because I'm only seventeen, but she was my first love, and I'm still in love with her."

"I don't think you're stupid, Zach. Your mom was my first love. I've loved her since we were in elementary school. She was my best friend, and I didn't realize I was in love with her until we were in middle school. I was shy, like you, and I was afraid if I told her how I felt, she wouldn't be my friend anymore, and I'd lose her for good. If anyone understands young love, it's me and your mom."

"I guess it doesn't matter. She lives three thousand miles away. And let's not forget that she blocked me from her life."

"Maybe she did. Maybe she didn't. Talk to Cole. See if he knows anything."

"I can't risk losing my best friend. Jay is like a sister to him. He's very protective of her."

"Aren't you dating Judge Vaughn's daughter?" he asks.

"Reagan, yeah. She's cool, and we have a good time when we're together, but it's not serious. We're fine with the way things are. Does that make me an asshole?"

"No. High school relationships aren't exactly built on love, Zach." He chuckles. "You're teenagers. You're supposed to be dating and having fun, not proposing marriage. But while you're dating her, you'd better respect her. I don't need to be on Judge Vaughn's shit list."

I smile. "I know."

TRACK 7:
RISE ABOVE THIS
Jayla

HE'S GONE.

Today I said good-bye to the man who gave me life.

He was my whole world.

Six months ago, that world was shaken and flipped upside down the night the paramedics came into our home and took him away.

That night the doctors gave him three more months.

He lived for six.

Because that's how Marcus King rolled.

He did things his way.

On his own time.

No exceptions.

When life gave him lemons, he'd exchange them for limes and a bottle of tequila and say, "Who the hell wants lemonade when they can have margaritas?"

And now my world is shattered.

My mom is sitting across the room with my grandparents by her side. She smiles sadly and nods as friends and acquaintances offer their condolences. Her eyes are red and swollen and her face is splotchy, but she's still beautiful.

I wonder if her pain feels different from the pain I feel.

He was my dad, but he was the love of her life.

Her soul mate.

Her best friend.

Her prince.

I wonder if she'll ever find another soul mate.

Another love?

Another prince?

Did she do something so terrible in her life that Karma came to collect?

I thought Zach was my soul mate, but what the hell do I know?

I still love him though. Even though I shouldn't.

Maybe there's hope for us one day.

Hope.

That's something I don't have much of these days.

I could almost swear that was Zach in the pew.

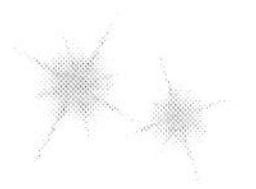

"JAYLA?"

Tilting my head back, I look up at the man standing over me. He looks oddly familiar—friendly face, light brown hair, and kind hazel eyes—but I can't place him. "I'm Miles Townsend." He extends his right hand. *Ah. The writer from* Rhythm & Riffs.

I never did that interview with him about the release of *Jaybird*. More important things and all that.

As we shake hands, my gaze immediately shifts to my mom, unsure of what I'm supposed to do or say. I've never been allowed to talk to reporters and, honestly, I'm not even sure why he's here.

Sensing my discomfort, Miles puts my mind at ease. "Emerson suggested I come over and introduce myself." He gestures to the empty space on the sofa beside me. "May I?"

"Sure." I shift on the sofa to face him, tucking one leg under the other.

"I'm sorry about Marcus," he says, leaning forward and resting his forearms on his thighs, clasping his hands together. "You probably don't remember me. It's been a few years since I last saw you. Marcus and I go way back to the day Royal Mayhem got their first gig."

"Davie's Dive Bar," I add with a small laugh followed by a sniffle.

He nods. "Davie was my father. Marcus and Andrew came into Davie's, heads held high, and asked if they could play. Marcus said, 'You don't have to pay us or anything. We just want a chance to be heard.'" Miles smiles knowingly. "Marcus had no idea how much those words meant to my father. Davie was all about giving chances. If someone hadn't given him a chance, he wouldn't have had his bar, or me. He used to say, 'Life is all about chances. Taking chances. Giving chances. Second chances. Chance encounters. Chances lead to possibilities.' Davie loved those guys like they were his own family. A few months later, my father called his nephew, my cousin Chandler, who was in the music business, asking him to stop by the bar." He pauses to let the information soak in, waiting for me to catch up.

"So, you're Uncle Chandler's cousin?" *That explains why my dad trusted him.*

He nods again. "I also own *Rhythm & Riffs*. I personally interview all of the artists signed with King Records."

"Truthfully, I was surprised when my dad told me he'd set up an interview. He'd always been protective when it came to the media." I think back to our conversation about the interview. "He said you're the only one he trusts with me."

Miles lowers his head. "That means a lot. Those guys inspired me to become a writer. In college, my first creative writing paper was about four kids, barely out of high school, who went from playing for free in a dive bar to becoming one of the biggest rock bands in the world. Needless to say, I got an A-plus." He smiles. "One day I'd like to publish that story."

"I guess they owe a lot to Davie for giving them a chance. If he hadn't made that call, they might not have gotten so lucky."

"No. If he hadn't made that call, *Chandler* wouldn't have gotten so lucky." He laughs. "Those guys were destined for success." *True.* "Well, I really just wanted to come reintroduce myself and offer my condolences. I understand you need time to grieve, but when you're feeling better, I'd still like to do the interview, if you're up to it. Andrew mentioned King Records is pushing back *Jaybird's* release."

"I'd be happy to do the interview, Mr. Townsend—"

"Please, call me Miles."

"Okay, Miles. Just set it up with my mom. I'll be there."

"Great." He rubs his hands over his thighs. "I'll get in touch with Emerson next week. In the meantime, I'll compile a list of questions for you both to review and we'll go from there." He stands up and looks down at me, sympathy filling his gaze. "I really am very sorry about Marcus. I'm still having a hard time believing he's gone, but I can honestly say I understand what it feels like to lose an amazing father."

I gasp. "Davie?"

He nods again. "Nearly ten years ago. There isn't a day that passes that I don't think about him and miss him. He was a good father. I want you to know that I know your pain. What you said about the pain of losing him, I've been there. Right now, it's raw, like your heart has been ripped out. Your chest feels like there's a hundred-pound weight on it and the only way to breathe is by taking small breaths. But even that hurts." He rests a hand on my shoulder. "Everyone grieves in their own way, but pain is still pain. I promise you that the pain will fade and with each day that passes it'll be easier to breathe. You'll always have that dull ache as a reminder of what you lost, but it's okay. Think about him as often as you'd like. Keep him alive in your memories."

Releasing a heavy sigh, I say, "Thank you, Miles. I *really* needed to hear that. If one more person asks me how I'm feeling, I might punch myself in the face."

He laughs. "There are only so many ways someone can offer their condolences before it just becomes awkward. I wish we were meeting under different circumstances, but it's been a real pleasure talking to you, Jayla. You did an amazing job on the album. I listened to it with Marcus the day he and I met to set up your interview. He was very proud of you. You're a sweet girl and I can see why he was so protective." He gives my shoulder a gentle squeeze. "I'll be in touch."

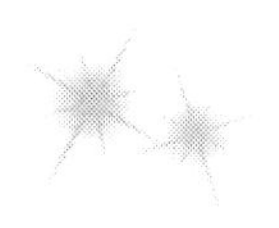

"LET ME TAKE her," Aunt Jessica says, lifting a sleeping eighteen-month-old Willow from my lap. For the past few days, my little cousin, Willow has been an adorable distraction from the hell that is now my life. We've watched *Monsters Inc.*, her favorite movie, at least five times. Well, she watches the movie and I watch her. Her sweet little angelic voice and the way she puts her tiny hands on my cheeks to get my attention soothe my aching heart. I've started calling her "Boo" because she looks so much like the little girl in the movie.

Willow is the youngest child to my Uncle Max and Aunt Jessica, who are also the parents to my cousins Dylan, Cole and Aiden. Honestly, if I didn't know Willow was adopted, I'd say she was born a Mackenzie, with her dark hair and bright green eyes, just like the rest of the family.

"Hey," Lucas says, dropping into the empty spot beside me on the love seat with a plate of food in one hand, setting another plate of fruit on the coffee table. "I didn't think I was hungry but one whiff of Grace's cooking...." He shakes his head before shoveling a forkful into his mouth. "Have you eaten today?" he mumbles as he scoops another forkful from his plate and holds it out to me. I wrinkle my nose and turn my head.

I lost my appetite when I lost my father.

"Jay—" Lucas starts, but I shut him down with a "don't even start" look.

"Don't give me that look," he chides. "You have to eat something or you're going to get sick. I know you don't feel hungry, but I've seen you eat an entire watermelon in one sitting right after you swore you weren't hungry."

I snort as Lucas picks up the plate of fruit from the coffee table and holds it out to me. "Come on. When have you ever turned away from a strawberry?"

I do love me some fruit. It's my second favorite food next to chocolate. Give me some chocolate to go with my fruit—*heaven.* Plucking a strawberry from the plate, I pop it into my mouth and smile.

"See?" Lucas grins.

It had always been Evangeline, Lucas and me. The Three Musketeers. The Three Amigos. And in some situations, the Three

Stooges. But most of the time growing up, it was just Lucas and me. Especially when we were younger and living on a tour bus. Lucas is protective and in some ways, he feels a sense of responsibility for me.

"I'm kind of tired, Lucas," I say quietly as I hand over the barely touched plate of fruit. "Will you cover for me?"

He gives me a hesitant nod. "Yeah, go ahead. I'll be up to check on you later."

THERE'S A GENTLE tap on my bedroom door just before it opens and immediately shuts with a soft click. I don't need to look to know it's Mimi. I can smell her Donna Karan perfume. A moment later the mattress dips as she lies down beside me.

After a few moments of silence, she asks, "Do those things still glow?" We're both lying on our backs, staring up at the plastic stars scattered across the ceiling above my bed.

I blow out a puff of air through my nose.

"Not sure. I remember when Mom put them up there. I was like six or seven, I think. Dad told me they were magic stars, that each star held one wish and the big ones were for special wishes. I don't think I was ever as excited for bedtime as I was that night. I had a mental wish list a mile long by the time I went to bed."

"What did you wish for?"

I smile at the memory. "A pink guitar."

Mimi laughs. "Oh yes, I remember. I have several pictures of you with that little pink guitar. You were already making up your own songs then, too. And you loved everything pink."

"It was my favorite color." I roll my head to the side and smile at Mimi. "Remember my first piano?"

"Of course. First time I'd ever seen a pink baby grand piano."

"I used up one of the big stars for that," I admit with a laugh, turning to look up at the ceiling once more. "I used to try counting them, but I'd always end up falling asleep." I roll my head to the side again. "There are seventy-five total—eight large, twelve medium, and fifty-five small. I finally counted them the day we found out dad was sick. I wished on every single one of them, hoping by some chance that Dad was right, that they were truly magic. I wished for him to get better, but instead he got sicker. He was wrong. They're not magic. They're just stupid plastic stars." I choke out a sob and cover my face with my hands.

"Oh my sweet girl," Mimi coos, shifting on the bed to wrap her arms around me. "Shhh. Honey, he was sick. His fate was in God's hands." She rubs a soothing hand down my back.

Fate.

I'm not a fan of that word.

Karma is a bitch who owns her shit.

Fate is misleading.

Fate paints a pretty little picture of 'meant to bes' and 'happily ever afters.' But what about death?

Fate is a passive-aggressive bitch.

"Nothing can change God's plan. Not a wish. Not even a prayer." Mimi comforts me for a few more minutes before we pull apart and I wipe the tears from my cheeks. When I look up again, she has a concerned expression. "Can I ask you a random question? It's been on my mind for a while now."

"Hmm?"

"What happened with Zach? You two were joined at the hip in St. Thomas." *Not exactly the hip, but close enough.* "He asks about you all the time. Says he hasn't talked to you since our vacation."

I scoff. "He should focus more on his girlfriend and less on me."

"What do you mean?"

"I'll tell you, but you have to promise you won't get mad, and you can't tell anyone. Not even Grandma Kate."

She frowns and holds up her fingers. "Scouts honor."

I burst out laughing. "Mimi that's the shocker. Who taught you that?"

"Aiden. That little shit." She laughs. "What's the shocker?"

TRACK 8:
CAN'T LET GO
Jayla

THE EARLY MORNING light pours through the floor-to-ceiling windows of my bedroom causing me to stir. Subconsciously, I think to myself that I'd forgotten to close the blinds as I slowly wake, and I realize I'd actually slept.

My thoughts instantly drift to Zach. I've been thinking about him a lot lately.

Love isn't something you can just stop feeling. Even if it's not meant to be, you can't just turn it off.

I still love him.

It was hard letting him go when all I wanted to do was call him and tell him everything that was happening. I wanted to hear his voice.

There have been times when I almost asked Cole or Zach's Uncle Cam, about Zach, but I was afraid to hear about him being with someone else.

Someone who wasn't me.

Maybe I should just call him.

A rhythmic knock saves me from inner turmoil as my bedroom door swings open and Cole walks in. "By all means, come in," I say sarcastically.

"Don't mind if I do," he quips before falling on my bed. Rolling to his side, he props his head on the palm of his hand. "You doing okay?"

"Yeah." I smile sadly. "One day at a time, right?"

"I guess." He exhales loudly, rolling to his back and tucking his hands behind his head. "Do those things still glow?" He jerks his chin toward the plastic stars on the ceiling above my bed.

I snort. *What's with everyone and their fascination with plastic stars.* "I have no idea. I doubt it. They've been up there for over ten years."

"Well..." He pushes himself up from the bed. "...I was sent to tell you that your presence is required downstairs for family breakfast."

"I'm not hungry," I murmur.

"Jay—"

"Cole."

He crosses his arms over his chest and narrows his gaze. It's the Mackenzie blood in our veins that makes us so stubborn. "Jay, it's been three days. Get your skinny ass out of this bed and come downstairs. Seriously, Jay, I love you but you look like a Pez dispenser. It's not a good look for you."

I gasp. "I do not!" I probably do but... shit. The stress of watching the most important man in my life, my world—the man who gave me life—spend the last six months fighting for his own life and losing had taken its toll on my body. I can't help it that I don't have an appetite. I'm not starving myself. I eat. Just not as much as I used to.

"You do. You're too skinny and your head looks too big for your body."

"That's pretty harsh, Cole," I say. "Even for you."

"Just keeping it real." Cole sits back down on the edge of my bed, one leg tucked under him and the other on the floor as he shifts to face me. "Listen, Jay. You know I love you. I know this has been hard for you. It's been hard on all of us. I can't imagine how much hurt you feel right now. If I lost my dad...." He lets his words hang in the air and shakes his head. Tears pool in my eyes. "You're grieving and as your family, it's our job to take care of you. And that includes feeding you. Now get your ass up and let us do our jobs."

Wiping the tears from my cheeks, I lean over and pull him in for a hug. "You're such a dick, but I love you."

Cole huffs. "Yeah, well, you can be a butthole sometimes too."

I snort a laugh and pull back. "Butthole? What are you, five?"

He smiles. "I'm trying to curb my language. Willow repeats every fucking thing I say."

"And 'butthole' is an acceptable word for a toddler?" I ask through another laugh. "Oh, my God. Can you imagine her saying 'butthole' in that cute little voice?"

"No." He laughs, standing up from the bed and holding out his hand. "Come on, Pez dispenser."

I slap his hand away.

"With tits," Lucas adds from the doorway. He ducks, laughing when I chuck my pillow at his head.

Falling back on my bed, I poke out my bottom lip. "You guys are so mean."

"It's called tough love," Cole says, grabbing one of my arms. "Bobblehead."

"I hate you both."

"You're still beautiful, Jay," Lucas says, reaching for my foot. Together they pull me from the bed. "Now come on," Cole adds. "Everyone's waiting on you and I'm starving."

"I still think you're both mean, but I'll admit that was a good one. Expect payback, butthole," I drawl, following them from the room. "Hey, Willow—"

"Don't you freaking dare, Jay."

"JAY," LUCAS WHISPERS.

"Hmm?" I hum into my pillow.

"Come on, little sis, you need to wake up and move around. You've been in this bed for a week." *A week?* "Get up. Grace brought you something to eat."

"Not hungry," I mumble. "Too tired."

"Come on, Jay."

I hear the blinds being drawn before sunlight floods the room, making me wince, as the comforter is yanked away from my warm body.

Someone gasps.

"Oh baby girl, what have you done to yourself?" my mom cries, cupping my face in her hands. "Oh, my God. This is all my fault."

"It's not your fault, Em," Bass whispers.

"It is! She's my daughter. I should've been paying attention. Goddammit! I'm calling Dr. Ramos."

"Princess?" Bass pulls me into his lap and brushes my hair from my face. "I need you to open your eyes and look at me."

"No, B, it hurts," I whimper.

"What hurts, Princess?"

"Everything."

TRACK 9: ALL FOR YOU

Jayla

Trust your gut
Follow your heart
And never, ever settle
for anything less than you deserve

I TRAIL MY fingers over the words tattooed on my ribs. They're delicate but rough to the touch. The tattoo hasn't quite healed yet, but then again, neither have I. It's been three months since my dad passed and each day has been a struggle. But I'm getting there one day at a time. Thanks to Dr. Ramos.

Dropping my arms to my sides, I take in my reflection. I can proudly say that the girl staring back at me no longer looks like the walking dead.

Or a Pez dispenser with tits, as Cole and Lucas so kindly put it before.

Jerks.

But they were right. I *wasn't* taking care of myself.

I pretended to be okay, but after everyone had gone back to their lives, I went back to my grief.

To the pain.

I couldn't move on. I missed him so damn much that it made me sick.

I stayed in bed, shutting out the world and everyone in it. My thoughts were consumed with the 'whys,' 'hows' and 'what-ifs.'

All I wanted to do was sleep because being awake made everything real.

I cried a lot.

The grief had taken over completely, forcing me into a dark place.

Days turned into a week.

I lost control.

And before I knew it, I became someone even *I* didn't recognize. A skeleton version of myself.

I was in so much pain, I just didn't care anymore.

That's how I ended up at the Wellness Center with Dr. Ramos for six weeks while I recovered both mentally and physically. Talking with Dr. Ramos, I discovered a lot about myself. Not just as Marcus King's *Jaybird* but as myself, Jayla King. The seventeen-year-old girl who doesn't know who she is without her father or how to move on.

My dad's career was our life. But I was happy to be a part of it because it's who he was. I can write a song and sing with the best of them, but I'm struggling. Now I can't decide if I was doing it for him or for me. Was it because I craved his attention? Maybe. Did I think he'd love me less if I wasn't interested in a music career? No.

I needed to take a step back and work these things out for myself. Set goals. Try new things.

"Baby steps" is what Dr. Ramos told me. "Don't put so much pressure on yourself to be what you think others expect. Just be you."

I set some personal goals. Started exercising and eating more. No skipping meals.

I wasn't trying to hurt myself on purpose or starve myself to death. I have no problem with food. I love to eat. I've always been tall and thin, so I welcome the extra weight. Luckily, I inherited my mom's boobs and ass, which evens out my slimmer body. I'm proud to say that I've gained back twelve of the eighteen pounds I lost.

Bass and I have started working out daily, starting with a morning run. Bass even got me one of those punching bags, which I love and now refer to as a "session"—like a therapy session.

Dr. Ramos got a laugh out of that one.

The punching bag helps me clear my head and ease my anxiety. It's also great for relieving aggression, whenever I feel the need to punch the shit out of someone—I mean something. But mostly it helps me focus. To think clearly.

I'd also like to start writing music again. I haven't touched an instrument or written anything since the day I flew back from St. Thomas.

That was August of last year.

I STEP INTO the beautiful floor-length gown. The gown is amazing, the bodice an intricate gold threading which flows down the shimmery bronze skirt and floats around me like it's made of air. My dark hair is pulled back from my face into a high sleek ponytail. My makeup is minimal, a smoky eye highlighting my light eyes and a nude gloss on my lips. I keep my jewelry simple, just my Cartier diamond studs in my ears, the matching two-carat pendant around my neck and the gold and diamond love bracelet on my wrist. All three pieces were given to me by my parents on my sixteenth birthday.

Evangeline's reflection appears behind me in the mirror, moving closer to zip my dress before taking a step back. Tilting her head, she says, "Wow, Va-jay-jay, you look absolutely stunning."

"Thank you." I do a little twirl before turning back to the mirror to swipe on some lip gloss.

Turning away from the mirror, I say, "You look gorgeous, but, of course, you always do." Evangeline looks gorgeous whether she's in a gown or yoga pants and a T-shirt. Hell, she could rock a burlap sack and call it couture.

"Thank you," she replies with a wink. "Are you sure you don't want to model? I know people."

I shake my head. "Nope, that's all you." Evangeline is in high demand these days as one of the hottest supermodels on the runway. She's been on the cover of every fashion magazine—some twice—over the last year. She's got the charm and the right attitude to make the runway her bitch.

"Drummer boy is gonna cream in his skinny jeans when he sees you," she says, wiggling her eyebrows and I burst out laughing.

"You're so crude, Weenie."

"Drummer boy" is Ace Matthews, the drummer for LAW, who Lucas has repeatedly warned me to stay away from. Ace is hella hot and we've been hanging out a little over the past few weeks. Lucas is not happy about it, of course, but Ace is fun and he makes me laugh. As I've said before, I have no intentions on getting involved with a rock star and I meant it. Right now, it's what I need. This is me figuring things out for myself.

I need more friends in my life besides Evangeline and Lucas.

Evangeline has Alex.

Lucas has his band and girlfriends all over the place.

I've got Bass and my frickin' iPad.

I need a life.

"Eva? Jay?"

"We're in here," I call out to Alex from inside my closet as Evangeline walks out to greet him. Grabbing my cell and the tube of lip gloss, I drop them into my clutch and head into my bedroom.

Alex is standing just inside the doorway dressed in a tuxedo, looking like he just stepped out of a photo shoot for *GQ* with his perfectly styled dark brown hair and bright eyes. The man is seriously hot. I watch the way he looks at Evangeline as she makes her way over to him, a knowing smile curling one corner of his mouth.

Ugh! I know that look.

"All right you two, stop it," I joke. "Don't make me get the hose."

Alex's gaze shifts from Evangeline to me, his eyebrows shooting up in surprise as a low whistle escapes through his teeth. "Wow. You look beautiful, Jay."

"Thank you." I do another twirl.

"She does," Evangeline agrees as her eyes well up with tears. "And she looks healthy."

Here we go.

"Hey. What's with the tears? I'm fine," I reassure her. "I promise. Now stop it before Mom sees you."

Evangeline rolls her eyes as she wipes the tears away from the corners. Schooling her expression, she says, in her best Emerson impression, "Tears aren't for the public eye, Eva. It shows weakness. If you need to cry, do it in private."

The three of us burst out laughing.

Yep. That's my mom.

"Jayla, Eva, and Alex, let's go." *Speak of the devil.* "The car's here."

The three of us file out of my room and head for the stairs. "We're coming!"

I pause halfway down the stairs when I see my cousin Cole waiting for me at the bottom, dressed in a tuxedo and looking as gorgeous as ever.

"Look at you, hot stuff," I wink as I reach the bottom and pull him into a hug. He's my cousin, but he's a good-looking sonofabitch. He's tall and muscular from years of playing football. His black hair is short on the sides, longer on the top and styled to perfection—because Cole wouldn't have it any other way. He takes his hair very seriously. No joke, I think he takes longer to do his hair than most girls. And he has those bright green eyes that Mimi like to refer to as the Mackenzie family jewels.

The guy's got swagger.

"Thanks," he says. "You look really good. Pretty."

"You mean I don't look like a Pez dispenser anymore? Or a bobblehead?" I tease.

He chuckles. "No. I'm sorry, I shouldn't have said that. I was trying to get you out of bed."

"It's fine." I wave him off. "Thanks for coming out and being my date. I just feel bad that you're missing your junior prom."

Tonight is the first charity dinner for the Mayhem Foundation. The charity focuses on putting music back into schools and giving scholarships to kids who want and deserve a higher education but can't afford it. My dad was still in the beginning phase of putting together the foundation when his cancer was discovered. With all his other projects in the works, he was too tired to put any time into the foundation. Mom tried several times to talk him into turning the charity over to more capable hands, but my dad was a hands-on kind of guy; he liked things done a certain way and he liked to be involved in everything. Unfortunately, he didn't get to see it through. Mom and her assistant, Lilly, took over and hired a few people to get things moving.

Cole holds out his hands, palms up as if he's weighing his options. "Hmm. Let's see." He raises one hand higher than the other. "Junior prom with people I see every day?" He lifts the other hand and wiggles his eyebrows. "Or support my favorite uncle's charity with my favorite cousin, an open bar, and hot celebrities?"

I laugh and smack him playfully on the arm. "Behave yourself tonight."

"I'm not making any promises," he states, holding out his arm for me.

"Let's go!" Mom hollers from outside.

"Wow, she's wound up tight tonight," I murmur. Cole chuckles as he escorts me to the limo idling in the driveway. "Someone put a muzzle on that woman," I yell and laughter rings out from inside the limo.

"THERE'S MY FAVORITE girl," Liam coos, curling his arm around my shoulders and pulling me in for a side hug, kissing me on the temple before he reaches for my mom. "And my favorite sister."

"I'm your only sister," she says, accepting his hug.

"That makes me the luckiest guy in the world," Liam replies.

I turn and smile before hugging Liam's date. "Hi, Dr. Ramos."

"Good to see you, Jayla," she says before taking a step back to admire my dress. "You look gorgeous."

"Thank you. You, too."

Dr. Ramos is a beautiful lady, tall and thin, mid-to-late thirties. Her raven-colored hair is cut in a sharp, shoulder-length angled bob with long bangs sweeping over her left eye and she has the most fascinating violet eyes, fringed with long, thick black lashes.

She's the opposite of the women Liam normally dates.

And I use the term *dates* loosely.

"Hello, my gorgeous girls," Cam says to me and my mom, taking my hand and pulling me in for a hug. Cameron "Cam" Parker is not only Zach's uncle, he's also my Uncle Liam's best friend and former teammate from the LA Heat. "How are you doing?" he asks close to my ear. He pulls back to look down at me and I see the concern in his eyes.

"I'm doing really well," I tell him as I wrap my arms around his middle and give a little squeeze. "How's Florida?" Cam left the LA Heat to pitch for the Tampa Bay Tornadoes just before my dad passed. I miss having him around, and I know Liam misses being on a team with him.

"I miss my boy…" He means Liam. "…and my teammates, but I love being back home and close to my family. Have you talked to Zach lately?"

"Um… no," I say, realizing he just gave me an opening, but before I can ask about Zach, I catch the sight of a familiar face over Cam's shoulder. Pasting on the smile that I've perfected over the years, I say, "Hi, Lauren," catching the attention of everyone in our group.

Cam immediately goes rigid in my arms and turns his head to the side to look over his shoulder. Evangeline scoffs as Alex wraps an arm around her waist—most likely to keep her from lunging at Lauren. Liam curses under his breath, Mom rolls her eyes, Cole chuckles and Dr. Ramos looks confused.

Lauren is a model and Cam's ex. The breakup was nasty from what I've heard from Mom and Liam, which is why I'm surprised to see her here. I don't recall seeing her name on the guest list and I'm positive my mother didn't invite her.

Like the rest of us, my mom isn't a fan. So, in true Emerson King fashion, she plasters on her perfected fake smile, says her hellos, and then excuses herself to go find Evangeline's parents.

"It's so good to see you, Jayla." Lauren leans in to give me an air kiss. "I hear you're going to be working with Anna Sizemore. Congratulations."

"Thank you."

"Evangeline," Lauren sneers.

Evangeline rolls her eyes and scoffs. "Whatever," she says in a bored tone, and turns to Cam. "I thought you got rid of her."

Cam sputters, spit-spraying his drink all over the front Lauren's dress.

"Cameron!" Lauren huffs, wiping at her dress before storming off in the direction of the bathrooms.

"Babe," Alex whispers the gentle warning, pressing his lips to the side of her head while attempting to hide his own smile.

Evangeline gives an unapologetic shrug before shifting her gaze to me and winking.

Told you she can be a bitch, but she's *my* bitch.

"Well, that's one way to get rid of her," I quip.

"What is she doing here?" Liam snaps at his best friend, as if Lauren being here is ruining his night.

Cam scowls. "I don't know. Why don't you ask her?"

I roll my eyes. *Men*. "I'll check with the coordinator and see who she came with. I don't need her starting any drama tonight."

"If she's here, there will be drama," Evangeline adds. Something behind me catches her attention and she narrows her eyes. "Just when we got rid of one asshole, another pops up."

I turn around to see Tyge Reynolds, the new hotshot pitcher for the LA Heat, walking into the ballroom with his date. I guess you could say Tyge is a family friend. I've known him since I was a kid. His father, Jack Reynolds, is one of the top entertainment lawyers in LA and one of my dad's good friends. I've always thought Tyge was good-looking but too old for me and he's kind of a cocky asshole.

Tyge scans the room before he notices our group and begins making his way over.

"You look beautiful, Jayla," he says. "You legal yet?" He winks.

And, yes, he really did just say that.

In front of his date.

I snort a laugh as Liam's, Cam's, and Alex's eyebrows go up. "You wanna keep that pitching arm, Reynolds?" Liam asks in warning.

Tyge laughs. "I'm kidding, Mackenzie. I've known her since she was like eight."

After Tyge introduces everyone to his date, I snake my arm through Cole's and say, "Excuse me. I need to go find my mom and check on the Lauren situation." Turning away, I drag Cole along beside me.

"Reynolds is kind of a dick," Cole says with a soft laugh. "He makes me look like an angel."

I pat him on the arm and smirk. "Keep telling yourself that, Cole."

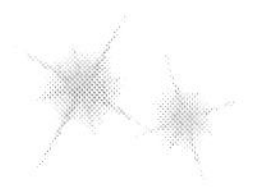

THE REST OF the night goes by without any snags. Turns out Lauren came with one of Cam's former—and Liam's current—teammates. I caught her several times eyeing Cam like a hawk, but she kept her distance.

"Jayla!" Chandler Skye waves me over to one of the round tables where he's sitting with our attorney, Jack Reynolds, and Nikki Fox.

Nikki was last year's winner on *America's Voice* and the song she performed during the finale was written by yours truly.

"Introduce me," Cole mumbles under his breath as we make our way over. He's been bugging me about Nikki since we left the house. I can't blame him. Nikki has an edginess to her that draws people in. Her chestnut brown hair is now electric blue and curled around her heart-shaped face, falling in waves just below her shoulders. She reminds me of a sexy cartoon pinup girl "with lips made for sucking"—Cole's words, not mine.

"Hi, Jayla," Nikki says as she stands from the table to greet me with a hug. "It's so good to see you again. Thank you for inviting me."

"Of course." Nikki and I have only met a few times. We're not friends, but she seems nice enough.

Evangeline can't stand her. *Shocker.*

Nikki's first album, *It Girl*—which features three songs also written by me—comes out next month. She'll be opening for LAW on the "Wet and Wild Tour."

Sweeping my hand toward Cole, I say, "Nikki, this is my cousin Cole. He's a fan." The last part earns me a pinch to my side.

"I was wondering who this hottie was." Her hungry eyes rake over Cole from head to toe. *Well, okay then.* "You're always surrounded by gorgeous men, Jayla. I'm so jelly."

Ugh! I hate that word.

And with that, I leave Cole to it and pull out a chair between Drew and Chandler.

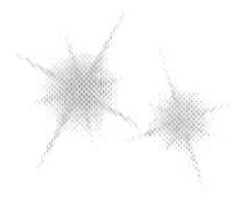

"COME ON, KIDDO." Andrew appears beside the table and extends his hand. "Come dance with your Uncle Drew."

"Okay." I giggle. Taking his hand, I push back from the table and rise from my seat, before he leads me to the dance floor. "Where's Lucas? I haven't seen him much tonight." Actually, I haven't seen much of Lucas or Andrew in the past week.

"He's probably hiding somewhere, trying to catch up on sleep. The band has been rehearsing nonstop."

"I feel like I never see or talk to him anymore."

Andrew gives me a tight smile. "He'll come around. Just give him some time to work through it."

Leaning back, I look up at Andrew, confused. "What are you talking about? Is he mad at me?"

"No, sweetheart, he's not mad. He's just... upset."

"Upset with *me*? Why?"

"No." He sighs. "Sweetheart, you gave us all one hell of a scare. Losing Marcus shattered Luc and me. And then you…." He shakes his head and blows out a shaky breath. "We were just worried about you. That's all."

"I scared him," I finish. "He's been snippy with me lately, but I thought it was because he was mad at me for hanging out with Ace."

"Well, he's not happy about that either," Andrew adds with a laugh.

"I need to talk to him. I'm okay, Uncle Drew. You believe me, don't you?"

"You never have to ask."

When our dance comes to an end, Andrew leads me back to the table. Cole and Nikki have disappeared, but Chandler and Jack are now joined by the remaining band members of Royal Mayhem, Tommy Stone and Chaz Vargas. All of them are eyeing me cautiously as if they know something I don't. Something that could possibly set me off.

"What's going on?" I ask.

Chandler gestures to the empty chair in front of me. "Have a seat, sweetheart. We just want to talk to you."

I pull out the chair and sit with my hands clasped in my lap.

Chandler leans forward with his forearms resting on the table. "I hadn't planned on bringing this up tonight, but with Andrew going on the road with Lucas, and Tommy's baby boy due any minute, I'm not sure when we'll all be together like this again, and we're running short on time." Now that my dad is gone and Drew is leaving to go on tour with Lucas, Chandler has taken over the reins at King Records.

"Oookay."

"I'd like to set the release date for *Jaybird* next May with the first single, 'Piece of Me,' to release the second week of February."

"Okay. Whatever you think. You're the boss." I smile.

Chandler smirks. "We both know that's not true. But that's a conversation for another day." Another day, as in the day I turn eighteen. Chandler's expression changes from serious to uncomfortable as he looks around the table before turning his attention back to me. "I know this is going to be difficult for you—for all of you—but we need to discuss filling the spot for lead vocals."

I feel like I've been punched in the stomach.

I've been preparing myself for this conversation for months, yet somehow, being prepared doesn't soften the blow. The thought of a stranger's face replacing Marcus King's—my father's—as the front man for Royal Mayhem makes me physically ill. Dad and Andrew started Royal Mayhem when they were my age. Although my dad had always been the one in charge, Andrew should still have a say. I can't just hand over his hard work, his blood, sweat, and tears—his *heart*—to a total stranger.

I can't do it.

I won't.

It can only be one person.

Chandler continues, "We could hold auditions in December. That should give us plenty of time to—"

"What about Alex?" I interrupt and every head swivels my way.

Clearing my throat, I continue, "I think Alex would be a perfect fit. He's been a part of our family for a few years now. He knows every Royal Mayhem song ever written and performed. He spent the last two summers interning at King Records and working with my dad. He's already familiar with the new material on *Jaybird*. Other than the people sitting at this table, there's no one more qualified or deserving than Alex. We can trust him. Besides, don't you think he could pass for a young Marcus King? That alone will win over the die-hard fans. They'll eat that shit up."

I look around the table to see everyone smiling at me.

"What?"

"I'm impressed," Chandler says with a small laugh. "You've given this a lot of thought."

I shrug. "I had a lot of time to think while I was on 'vacation.'"

I get nothing but blank stares.

Too soon?

Andrew drops his forehead to the table and groans. "You're killing me, kiddo."

Chandler chuckles at my offhanded joke, cutting through the awkwardness. "Does anyone object or have anything to add?"

Everyone sounds their agreement with my choice. Chandler will schedule a one-on-one meeting with Alex first and, if he accepts the offer, then we'll have a group meeting.

"For the record, Alex was Marcus's choice, too, for the same reasons. But he wanted the decision to be yours," Andrew informs me.

That explains why Andrew hadn't taken over the decision-making for the band. He agreed with Marcus's decision; they were all just waiting for me to make the obvious choice. Huh. "It was the right decision." Chandler grins and I preen. "You're gonna make one hell of a CEO one day, sweetheart."

My stomach sinks.

Suddenly, my dress feels too tight and I begin to squirm in my seat, feeling uncomfortable in my own skin.

Is that a hive?

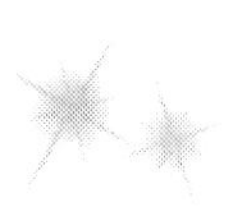

TOWARD THE END of the night, I find Bass, Dylan, Lucas, Evangeline, and Alex sitting around a table watching the band on stage. “Hi, B,” I say, kissing his cheek before plopping down on his lap and wrapping my arms around his neck. After that intense conversation with Chandler and the guys, I need Bass. He’s my security blanket, if you will. I’ll never be too old for cuddles from B. The man practically raised me along with my parents. He’s the closest thing to a father I have now. Sure, I have Uncle Drew and the guys from the band for support, but Bass and I live under the same roof, so he’s with me twenty-four seven.

A moment later, Cole appears at the table with a cat-that-ate-the-canary grin on his face. The front of his shirt is rumpled and his hair is a mess.

It’s blatantly obvious that he’s been off somewhere doing the dirty, presumably with Nikki Fox. Not even semifamous popstars can resist the Cole Mackenzie charm.

I curl my lip and give him a disgusted look.

“What?” He smirks.

“You’re unbelievable.” I shake my head. “Do you ever keep it in your pants?”

“Sure, I do.” He winks.

I roll my eyes.

Alex and Dylan shake their heads. “Mom and Dad would be *so* proud,” Dylan says sarcastically.

“Shut up,” Cole says, scowling at his older brother.

“You’re lucky this is a private affair, Cole, or your face would be all over the Internet. My Little Pony is a superstar and the cameras love her,” Evangeline states.

“Who?”

Evangeline rolls her eyes. “Nikki Fox.”

Cole barks out a laugh. “Did you just call her My Little Pony?”

“Shhh, keep your voice down,” I say, looking around before pointing at Evangeline. “Weenie, knock it off. Your dad will be pissed if he hears you talking shit about her."

Evangeline shrugs.

"I'm not talking shit about her," Cole says. "That sexy little blue-haired freak knows how to work a microphone." He wiggles his eyebrows before laughing at his own joke, slapping the table, prompting everyone at the whole table to guffaw and people at nearby tables to look our way. Even Bass's big body is shaking under me.

"Nice one," Evangeline approves, holding up her hand for a high five as Alex rests his head against her shoulder to mask his amusement.

"You're both crazy," I say, shaking my head.

Dylan is still not amused.

Cole says to Dylan, "Don't worry, *Dad*. I was careful. It was a one-night, one-time special performance."

"Enough you two," I chastise as I stand and hold out my hand. "Lucas, come with me for a minute."

"Why?" he snaps.

"Because I'm asking you to." I wiggle my fingers, urging him to take my hand. "Stop being a jerk face, *Lucas*, and come with me," I demand in a harsher tone, letting him know I'm serious.

Lucas huffs like a child but gets up from the table, brushing past my extended hand and walking out of the ballroom to a private lounge area near the bathrooms. He stops short and I nearly slam into his back. Turning around with his brows raised, he questions, "What's up?"

Fisting his shirt in my hand, I drag Lucas inside the lounge. Turning to face him, I cross my arms over my chest. It's what I do when I'm gearing up for an argument. "I know you're upset with me, so let's do this."

"Not really," he says, shrugging and shoving his hands in his pockets, avoiding my eyes.

Cupping his face, I tilt his head, forcing him to look at me. "Lucas, yes, you are. I'm sorry if I hurt you, but you're acting as if it was personal. I wasn't trying to hurt anyone, including myself. I was sad and depressed. I know you well enough, Lucas Wild, to know that if it were Andrew who'd died, you'd be exactly where I was."

Lucas jerks forward and wraps his arms around me, burying his face in my hair. "I know," he admits, his voice muffled. Pulling back, he stares down at me. "You scared the shit out of me, Jay. You didn't see what I saw that day. I should've just stayed with you until you got better."

"Don't do that, Lucas. Don't blame yourself. Everyone is blaming themselves. It's nobody's fault. It's grief. You know I would never do *anything* to hurt myself on purpose. That's not who I am." I start to cry. "I promise you I'm okay now. But I'd be even better if you'd stop being so mean to me."

"I'm not being mean." He hugs me tighter. "You know I'm not good at expressing my feelings. I know I'm not around much, but you're still my little sister and I love the hell out of you."

"You should've talked to me. All this time, I thought you were pissed because I was hanging out with Ace."

"You're right." He presses a kiss to my forehead. "And I *am* pissed that you've been hanging out with Ace. He knows you're off limits."

It's a good thing Lucas wasn't around earlier when Ace attempted to stick his tongue down my throat. *Dick.* I shut that shit down real quick.

"We're just—" I'm about to tell Lucas that Ace and I are just friends when the bathroom door opens and Ace stumbles out, tucking in his shirt and sweeping a hand through his disheveled faux hawk, followed by a familiar head of blue hair.

Oh. My. God.

Perfect example of why I'd never get involved with a rock star.

"See? You have nothing to worry about," I say with a humorless laugh.

Ace turns his head at the sound of my voice. "Oh, *heeeeey,*" he drawls slowly, squinting. "Jayla, baby. What's up?"

I bark out a laugh because *really*?

Nikki Fox is a big ol' slut. Who knew?

Wonder what Cole would say about his one-time performance giving an encore in the bathroom.

"Looks like that's going to make for an interesting tour. We'll talk more later."

TRACK 10:
IT'S TIME
Jayla

"YOU READY TO go, Princess?" Bass's large frame fills my bedroom doorway. He leans against the doorframe with his hands shoved in the front pockets of his jeans.

"No," I reply honestly, shaking my head and fighting back the tears. "I'm not ready. I know he's not physically here, but he *is* here. He's everywhere in this house. This is where he died, B." I cover my face with my hands to hide the unpreventable ugly cry. "I still feel him. I can't leave him and all of the memories we made in this house behind." Pulling my hands from my face, I wipe my damp palms down the front of my dress. "I'm sorry, B. I can't do this."

It's only been six months since my dad passed and already everything is changing. I know I promised Dr. Ramos that I'd try, but I don't think I'm ready to make this move.

Bass wipes away his own tears as he takes a step forward and pulls me into his arms. I thought I was ready for a fresh start and a chance to be a normal teenager for a while, but I can't leave the only home I've ever known and all the memories it holds.

I can't leave my dad.

Bass pulls back and cups my cheek. "Princess, we're not leaving him. He lives in here now." He taps my chest. "And the memories are in here." He moves his finger to my temple. "We have to move forward. You have to trust Emerson to do what's best for you and you have to trust me to take care of you." He lifts my chin so I'm looking up at him. "Do you trust us?"

With a slight nod and a heavy sigh, I grab my oversized handbag and follow Bass to the door. Grabbing the handle, I glance over my shoulder one last time before closing the door on my past.

"GOOD AFTERNOON, MISS KING," George, our pilot, greets as I step inside the brand-new jet called *The Jaybird*, of course. A gift from my dad.

"Hi, George." I return the greeting with a hug before scanning the interior of my new jet. Cream-colored leather sofa and bucket seats with a shiny wood-grain table between them. A small kitchen and a bedroom with a queen-sized bed and full-sized bathroom, complete with a bathtub and stand-up shower.

It's beautiful.

A bit over the top, but I know his heart was in the right place.

I always had nice things growing up, but I've never thought of myself as spoiled. I knew my parents had money, but they weren't the type to spend it on extravagant material things just to show off their wealth. Our garage wasn't filled with expensive sports cars and toys. My dad had one car, a 2013 Range Rover Sport, which he gave to me when I turned sixteen. We lived in a beautiful house on Malibu Beach and had a couple of vacation homes—a villa in St. Thomas and an apartment in New York City—all of which they considered good investments. They were smart with their money.

My parents taught me early on not to take life or this lifestyle for granted because it could all be gone tomorrow. If I wanted nice things, I had to work for them.

So, I did.

I started earning my own money writing music. I built up a nice bank account for myself, too. I didn't have the kind of money my parents had, but I could get by for a while if I had to. The best part is that it's mine. And I haven't even started earning royalties from *Jaybird* yet.

Just a few days after the charity dinner, Mom and I met with my dad's attorneys, including Jack Reynolds, for the reading of his will.

Yes, it took me three months to finally get there.

When all was said and done, I had more money than I could spend in a lifetime, most it set up in a trust to be disbursed monthly. He also left me the villa in St. Thomas—which used to be my favorite place until a certain someone ruined it for me—as well as the apartment in New York City. Forty percent of King Records—once I turn eighteen—making me the majority shareholder. And my own private jet.

He left *me* everything.

According to my mom, those investments had always been meant for me.

And why would he buy me a jet, when King Records already had two? It's not like I traveled all over the world. When I asked, Jack's eyes shifted to my mom with a look that clearly said "This is where you jump in."

She shifted in her seat beside me. I turned my head in time to see her blow out a breath before she said, "Jayla, we're leaving California. Indefinitely."

Turns out, my dad had this planned all along. Mom wasn't exactly thrilled with his plan, considering it involved us moving back to her hometown, Heritage Bay, the one place she swore she'd never go back to. However, the rest of the family is ecstatic that we're coming home. Mom told me that my dad built us a new home. All I know is that it's in a private gated community only minutes away from my grandparents and the rest of the Mackenzies.

I'll be attending Heritage Academy with my cousin Cole. Mom, along with the Mayhem Foundation, has been in contact with the principal of Heritage Academy, who was more than excited to be the first school to represent the Project Mayhem class. This year, the foundation gave out nine scholarships and, if things go well, the class will expand next year, meaning more scholarships and more teachers. I look forward to being a part of the first Project Mayhem class.

Before leaving California, I had a few loose ends to tie up. I met with Miles Townsend and gave him an interview. The article came out two days ago in the August issue of *Rhythm & Riffs*, which I plan to read during the plane ride to Florida. There's a cartoon version of me on the cover because Mom doesn't want pictures of me floating around on the Internet and risking the chance someone will recognize me. Since the album release has been moved, there's no hurry to expose my identity.

The cartoon version of me came out a little sexier than she'd expected. Personally, I think I look pretty damn hot.

After my interview, Miles and I hung out for a little while. He's a cool guy and he had some interesting stories about my dad, Andrew, Tommy, and Chaz with his dad, Davie. Miles proposed doing a tribute article in next year's February issue, with the whole magazine dedicated to the memory of Marcus King. I loved it and, of course, I bawled my eyes out. Miles agreed to let me read the article before it went to print.

I also posed for Anna Sizemore's "Girl Next Door" fashion campaign in exchange for her assistance in designing some Project Mayhem T-shirts and hats. Working with Anna was an awesome experience and I can now check modeling off my list of new things to try.

Now here we are, Mom, Bass, Grace, and me, on my new jet and heading to Heritage Bay, Florida.

TRACK 11:
SOMEBODY THAT I USED TO KNOW

Zach

BRAD CLIMBS UP on a chair, sticks two fingers in his mouth, and blows out a whistle that can pierce an eardrum. "Yo! Listen up!"

The loud chatter drops down to a low buzz. "A toast." He raises a red Solo cup in the air. "To senior year!" A chorus of whistles ring out from the crowd. "And to my boys." He pauses and stretches his neck. "Where's Easton?" He searches the crowd until his eyes zero in on me and a devilish grin appears on his face. "Ah, there you are, you pretty sonofabitch." He winks as more whistles and catcalls ring out.

Shaking my head, I raise my beer, toasting the embarrassing asshole.

"He's also single, ladies." *I'm gonna kill him.* "Show our QB some love, but not too much. He needs his energy for the field." He raises his cup again in a salute. "Go, Hurricanes!"

"Hurricanes!" the crowd echoes, followed by another round of whistles and catcalls.

"Did he just call you pretty?" Evan asks, coming up beside me.

I chuckle. "I don't know how many times I have to tell the guy that I'm just not into him."

Evan laughs and bumps his fist against mine. If I'm the shy one out of the group, Evan is the silent, broody one. He's good-looking, well-liked, and has been dating the same girl, Lexi, since the tenth grade.

In Evan's world, Lexi is the sun, moon, and stars. He doesn't even look at other girls. Not that I blame him, of course. Lexi is hot, popular, and one of the sweetest girls I've ever met. Unless you piss her off. I'm convinced her temper is a turn-on for Evan; sometimes I think he pisses her off on purpose. It wouldn't surprise me if the two ended up married after high school.

"What's going on out here?" Lexi asks as she snakes her arms around Evan's waist.

Evan throws an arm around her shoulders and tucks her in to his side. "Where ya been, Lex?"

"Inside cleaning and kicking everyone out." She turns her attention to Brad who is now twerking on top of the lawn chair. Lexi shakes her head. "His big ass is gonna twerk himself right through that chair."

Evan and I burst out laughing.

"Oh, hell, no," Lexi growls, eyes narrowed, lip curled in disgust. Turning my head, I follow her line of sight and see Reagan heading our way.

The girl I once considered to be the girl of my dreams turned out to be my worst nightmare.

Reagan and I had only been officially together for two weeks when my dad and I flew out to California for Marcus King's funeral.

When I got back to school a couple of days later, there was a rumor going around that Reagan cheated on me. Reagan blamed Chelsea for starting the rumor because she was jealous and trying to break us up. Chelsea swore it was true and that she was just watching out for me. That is the reason why I hated relationships—drama. I decided to give Reagan the benefit of the doubt and let it go. I told Chelsea that I appreciated her looking out for me, but she had to let it go, too. If Reagan cheated on me, the truth would come out eventually.

Besides, I was in love with Jay and I couldn't help but constantly compare my feelings between the two. Ever since I came back from California, seeing Jay and admitting to myself and to my dad that I wasn't over her, nor was I ready to be, I realized that everything with

Reagan was purely physical. That wasn't enough for me. I was miserable. And, admittedly, I started to pull away.

Maybe Reagan knew that and that's why, three months later, the little bitch cheated on me. At the junior prom after-party, for fuck's sake.

And that was the end of us. I guess that was Karma's way of kicking me in the ass.

"Just ignore her, Lex," Evan says.

Apparently, Reagan sent Evan a few texts the other night, asking him to come over and that no one had to know. Unfortunately for Reagan, it was Lexi who saw the texts first.

And she flipped the fuck out.

I've known Evan since kindergarten and I've never seen him so gone over a girl. Seriously, the guy was almost in tears when he showed up at my house, freaking out because he was afraid of losing her. After I calmed him down, I called Lexi and smoothed things over so Evan could go talk to her. I normally don't involve myself in other people's bullshit, but they're my friends and I couldn't help but feel responsible for what happened. I knew Reagan was messing with my friends to get my attention.

But she's wasting her time and making herself look desperate because my friends don't even like her.

"Fuck that, Evan. Whore!" Lexi shouts when Reagan walks past.

Reagan stops and whirls around to face Lexi. The girl has some brass balls; I'll give her that. Lexi is a little thing, but she's a firecracker. I have no doubts that she'll kick Reagan's ass. "Excuse me?" Reagan tosses back.

"For what? Being a whore?"

She's quick with the comebacks, too.

"How many times do I have to tell you, Lexi? That text wasn't meant for Evan," Reagan explains in her defense. Evan keeps his arm around Lexi's waist to keep her from pouncing on Reagan.

"Oh, really? That's funny since your text said no one has to know. You lying bitch-ass ho!" Lexi leans in and jabs her finger in Reagan's face.

I bring my fist to my mouth to mask my smile. Sweet little Lexi has transformed into ghetto Lexi. I kind of like ghetto Lexi. I watch and wait with bated breath to see if she'll kick off her flip-flops and start taking off her jewelry.

Brad moves to stand beside me, grinning. Shaking his head slowly, he sighs. "Our little Lexi is growing up so fast. Where did the time go?"

I chuckle.

"Get your finger out of my face," Reagan slaps Lexi's hand away. "Before I break it."

Oh, shit.

"Uh-oh," Brad murmurs.

"Oh, really?" Lexi laughs before she lunges at Reagan, grabbing her by the hair.

"Shit!" Evan yells, struggling to pull Lexi away.

"You gonna break my finger?" Lexi presses her index finger into Reagan's forehead. "How about I break your fingers so you can't use them to text my boyfriend or anyone else's, stupid whore."

"Guys, a little help," Evan grunts, jerking his head back to avoid getting clawed to death in the middle of this catfight.

As much as I love watching Reagan get her ass handed to her by Lexi, I reach out and pry Lexi's claws from Reagan's hair as Brad grabs Reagan. Lexi snarls like a wild animal. Evan bends at the knees, scoops her over his shoulder and carries her toward the house, all while Lexi kicks, screams, and slaps at his back.

"Put me down, Evan!" Lexi lifts her head and points at me. "Zach, you traitor!" She moves her finger to Brad. "I just cleaned your kitchen, asshole, and this is the thanks I get. I'll remember that, you guys." Then to Reagan, she shouts, "Text my boyfriend again, bitch, and next time I won't go easy on you. Try me. See what happens."

Reagan's friends gather around to console her and she looks over at me with her big doe eyes.

Yeah, that look doesn't work on me anymore.

Brad wraps his arm around my neck and leads me away from Reagan. "I can't believe she texted Evan. That girl must have a death wish."

"No shit," I reply, grabbing one of my beers from the cooler.

"Hey, Zach," Piper purrs, cocking her hip and twirling her hair around her finger. She's wearing a denim skirt that barely hits her thighs and a belly shirt with her cleavage peeking over the top. Piper dresses a little slutty and she's got a reputation for having fantastic oral skills. I wouldn't know; I try not to go where everyone has been. Doesn't mean I don't like Piper as a person. She's one of the few who doesn't get on my nerves. "Reagan is upset," Piper informs me. And judging by her bored tone, she couldn't care less. My bet is Ashton sent her over.

"So. Why are you telling *me*?"

Piper shrugs.

Ashton walks up and clucks her tongue. "You should go talk to her, Zach."

"Why?" Brad asks.

"Because she still loves you, Zach."

"You guys were together for like eight months," Hannah adds, pursing her lips and making that stupid duck face that girls think makes them look sexy.

These girls drive me fucking crazy. Ashton Grant is a bossy pain in the ass, but Hannah is just a straight up bitch. It's possible she might even be a little crazy.

Hannah and Brad dated for over a year and they only just recently broke up. Brad is one of those guys who everyone likes to be around. He knows how to have fun and never takes himself too seriously. Hannah is anti-Brad; dumping her was the best decision he's ever made. And knowing Brad, it wasn't easy for him.

"She wants him back," Hannah blabs on. Why is she still talking?

"How is it any of your business?" I ask.

Ashton turns to me. "I know you still love her."

Okay, whoa.

Ashton has lost her mind. I never told Reagan that I loved her.

I've only ever loved one girl.

And it isn't Reagan.

"When did we go back to eighth grade?" I ask and Brad chuckles beside me.

Piper shrugs as if to say "Oh, well, we tried."

"Seriously," Brooklyn, Brad's younger sister, cuts in. "This is Reagan's problem. She should've kept it in her pants." She shrugs.

Brad and I chuckle. Brooklyn has never been the kind of girl to hold back her opinion.

"She made a mistake. She's still our best friend," Ashton defends, glaring at her friends—her minions.

Ashton and Chelsea were best friends last year and, for all I know, they still are. But now that Chelsea's gone off to college, Ashton has taken over as the head varsity cheerleader and assumed the role of queen bee at the Academy.

Or she likes to think so.

I'm not a fan of Ashton Grant. She's an annoying pain in the ass and she's done some shady shit to her so-called friends. I have no idea what the hell Cole sees in her.

I never used to be this much of a dick, but a broken heart and a cheating girlfriend can make any guy bitter.

"Like you know how to be a friend," I reply sarcastically, downing the last of my beer before tossing the bottle into the trash.

"What are you talking about, Zach?" Ashton replies in a snotty tone.

"Zach?" a female voice calls out from behind me. I twist around and see Lindsay Miller waving at me from the opposite side of the pool deck. Turning away from the bitch squad, I head over to her.

"Hey, Lindsay." I pull her in for a hug and step back. "I didn't even know you were here. Have you been here all night?" Lindsay Miller is one of the nicest girls I've ever met. She dated Evan's older brother, Grayson, off and on for a couple of years and we all liked her. Even Evan.

Then Grayson crushed her and broke her heart when he hooked up with Reagan—my girlfriend—in a walk-in closet at the prom after-party.

So, there's that.

Lindsay smiles. "I came with some friends. I didn't know you were here either until Brad made that epic speech." She laughs lightly, and gestures to Reagan with her cup. "I see you guys haven't kissed and made up yet."

"No." I smirk, rubbing the back of my neck. "I don't date cheaters."

I haven't dated anyone since Reagan and I broke up. I hooked up with a couple of girls at the beginning of summer, but I spent the rest of the summer training.

"Me, either," Lindsay says. "How was your summer?"

Our traditional summer vacation with my grandparents didn't happen this year—which didn't surprise me—but I'll admit I was kind of disappointed because I was hoping to see Jay. So, I spent the last few weeks of summer at football training camp with Cole, Justin, and Carter.

I shrug. "I trained all summer."

"I see that." She reaches out and squeezes my bicep.

I've worked out hard all summer and it shows. I'm not a small guy, taking after my dad at six foot two, two hundred pounds. I was born to play football, just like him.

"Lindsay!" her friends call out from where they're gathered near the edge of the pool deck, waving for her to hurry up.

She holds up her index finger, gesturing for them to wait. "Kristen's my ride, so I have to go," she says, disappointed. "Will you be here tomorrow?"

I answer her with a smirk and a look that says "Do you really need to ask?"

She laughs. "Okay, so maybe we can catch up tomorrow." She takes a few steps backwards with a flirty smile. "I still have your number, so I'll text you."

"Sounds good."

"Bye, Zach." She gives me a quick wave before turning around and hurrying off with her friends.

"She wants the D," Brad says from beside me as we both watch her fine denim-covered ass disappear around the side of the house.

"Shut up, you jackass." Even if that were true, it's not happening.

"YOU STILL MAD at me?" Evan asks, sticking out his bottom lip and pretending to pout. Lexi ignores him as she furiously flips through one of her celebrity gossip magazines. Her knee bounces frantically and I doubt she's even looking at the pages.

Oh, yeah. She's pissed.

After everyone left the party, Evan, Lexi, and I stuck around to help with the cleanup.

Evan fights back a smile as he brings his beer to his lips.

"She's lucky I didn't rip her fucking hair out," Lexi growls and I chuckle. *She's so feisty, it's adorable.*

"Chill out, Lex. Why are you so pissed? You know I would never cheat on you. Even if I were single, I wouldn't touch her. She's not my type."

"You mean the whore type?" Lexi quips, making us all laugh.

"Exactly." Evan winks. "I think you made your point tonight, so let it go." He chuckles. "You don't need assault and battery on your permanent record." Reagan's father is a judge with a reputation for being ruthless in the courtroom.

"If I go down, I'm taking that whore with me." Her mouth pulls to the side. "I took a screenshot of all her texts and forwarded them to my phone. The next time she pisses me off, I'm gonna send them to the judge."

Brad turns to me and says, "Piper was looking extra busty tonight." His change in subject is less than subtle. "Did she get a boob job over the summer, or does Victoria have new secret?"

I nearly choke on my beer over a laugh. "How the hell should I know?" I say, wiping my mouth.

"What are you laughing at, Evan?" Lexi glares.

Evan's smile falls from his face. "I'm laughing at them," he explains before leaning over to kiss her on the side of the head and shooting Brad and me a pleading sidelong look that says "Will you two shut the fuck up?"

Evan lost his blow job virginity to Piper back in ninth grade before he and Lexi started going out. It was big news around school and, apparently, it still bothers Lexi.

Girls.

"You ever gonna tell us what happened with Hannah?" Evan turns the attention to Brad.

Brad scowls as he leans back in his chair and crosses his arms over his chest. "She tried to hook up with Brice." This time it's Evan who nearly chokes on his beer before barking out a laugh.

Brice is Brad's older brother.

And he's gay.

"No way!" Lexi throws her head back and laughs out loud. "Sounds like someone didn't get the memo."

"I guess not." Brad rolls his eyes. "She swears it was an accident. That she was drunk and thought she was in my bed."

"Maybe she's telling the truth," Lexi says. "It's possible. Your bedroom *is* right next door to Brice's. And if she was really drunk...."

"Maybe." Brad shrugs, picking at the label on his beer bottle. "If it hadn't been for the fact that she grabbed his dick and said, 'Let's find out how gay you *really* are,' I would've believed her."

"Oh, my God." Lexi wipes away the tears from under her eyes with the backs of her hands. "I bet Brice was traumatized."

Brad shakes his head and chuckles. "He told my parents he's suffering from PTSD." He rolls his eyes again. "He's such a fucking drama queen."

"What did your mom say?" Lexi asks.

Brad's mom is the "cool mom" everyone goes to for advice because she's down to earth, and doesn't judge us based on our stupid teenage mistakes. I guess with five kids, you have to be open-minded.

"She said to do whatever makes me happy. Good decision or bad decision, it's still my decision. That's all that matters."

We all say the last part in unison. Her famous words of wisdom. The woman gives good advice. Too bad I never took it a year ago.

"Hannah wasn't good for me," Brad goes on. "Things were awesome at first, but then she turned into a bitch. We fought over the stupidest shit, too." He alters his voice and does his best Hannah impression. "Brad, you hug on me too much. You breathe too loud. You joke too much. You think everything is funny. Oh, my *God*!" He rakes his hand through his short blond hair. "I'm so glad to be rid of her." He picks up his beer and holds it out to me. "This year is gonna be awesome. No Hannah. No Reagan."

"Agreed." We tap our bottles together.

"I saw you talking to Lindsay earlier," Evan says.

"She wants the D," Brad chimes in at the same time as I say, "She wants to hang out tomorrow."

"Meaning she wants the D." Brad laughs and slaps me on the back. "Give that girl what she wants."

Ignoring Brad, Lexi asks, "So, are you gonna hang out with her because you like her or because you wanna get back at Grayson?"

She's insightful, that one.

"My brother doesn't give a shit, Lex," Evan tells her.

Lexi shrugs off his comment and picks up another magazine.

"Neither," I answer. "Lindsay's cool, and as much as I'd love to give your brother a little payback, I wouldn't use her to do it."

"What the hell are you reading, Lexi?" Brad asks, reaching for Lexi's magazine, but she pulls it out of his reach. "Is that a comic book?"

Evan tilts his head to look at the cover. "*Rhythm & Riffs*? Why are you reading a guitar magazine?"

"It's not a guitar magazine, doofus. It's a rock and roll magazine. Like *Rolling Stone*." She flips the magazine around and holds it up so the cover is facing out.

This time I do choke. On my damn tongue.

Aquamarine eyes.

Black hair.

Right there on the glossy cover of *Rhythm & Riffs*. Written across the top, are the words "Meet Jaybird" and below them is Jayla King. *My girl.*

But it's not exactly her. It's a cartoon version of her. Right below her picture it says "The Princess of Rock."

Even as a cartoon, she looks damn hot.

"She's looks familiar," Brad says, leaning forward, squinting at the photo.

"She's a cartoon," Evan says.

"This..." Lexi taps the cover with the red-painted nail of her index finger. "...is Jayla King. Marcus King's daughter."

"No shit?"

Lexi nods. "This is her first interview ever."

I chew on the inside of my lip, hoping Brad doesn't figure it. It's a cartoon, for fuck's sake. He leans forward and studies the picture, eyebrows drawn.

I shift my gaze to Evan, who's eyeing me skeptically. Like he knows. "What's up with you?"

I run both hands though my hair before clasping them behind my neck, as I lean back in my chair. "Nothing. I'm tired. Maybe a little drunk," I lie.

I'm a shit liar and Evan knows it.

I haven't been drunk since prom night.

"When did cartoons become so hot?" Brad gives me a quick sideways glance. "She looks like a goddess," he says, turning to me. "Don't you think?" He winks.

The fucker figured it out.

"She's hella hot," Lexi agrees as she turns the magazine over and begins flipping through the pages. "I'd totally do her."

The three of us just stare at her.

"What?" She shrugs. "I'm just saying if I was gonna bat for the other team, I'd want her to be my teammate."

"It's a cartoon, Lexi." Evan chuckles.

"Damn." Brad shakes his head. "You're a lucky guy, Martinez." He holds up his hand for a high five. "That was awesome, Lexi."

"She is awesome," Evan agrees, punching the palm of Brad's hand in lieu of a high five.

"I'm still mad at you," Lexi says to Evan, but there's a hint of a smile on her lips as she continues to flip through the pages. Closing the magazine, she looks down at Jay's picture. "I'm just saying if she's this hot as a cartoon, imagine how hot she is in person. She's definitely my new girl crush."

"Thank you, Lexi." Brad grins.

"For what?"

"For the visual." He wiggles his eyebrows.

Evan picks up a beer cap from the table and snaps it between his fingers, hitting Brad in the forehead right between the eyes.

"Oh, nice." Laughing, I reach across the table and bump fists with Evan.

TRACK 12: JAYBIRD

Zach

Rhythm & Riffs
Interview of Jayla King
by Miles Townsend

SEVENTEEN-YEAR-OLD Jayla King, daughter of the late Marcus King, also known as "Jaybird," and the title of the latest Royal Mayhem album, expected to release May of next year.

How are you, Jayla?

Jayla: I'm okay. Just taking it one day at a time.

Is it true Royal Mayhem's latest album, *Jaybird*, was named after you and that you co-wrote the album with your father, Marcus King?

Jayla: Yes. It was a side project my dad and I had been working on for a year or so before he decided he wanted to turn it into an album.

What's the significance of Jaybird? Is it a nickname?

Jayla: Jayla is derived from Jay Bird. It also means "one who is special." My mom fell in love with the name Jayla, and my dad loved the idea of calling me Jaybird. It was a win-win, I guess.

Will there be a tour?

Jayla: Yes. Tour dates will be announced before the end of the year.

Will the album be different from Royal Mayhem music?

Jayla: No. Royal Mayhem is devoted to their fans. However, you can expect several covers of songs from some of our favorite bands.

Tell me about your father's charity, the Mayhem Foundation.

Jayla: The Mayhem Foundation focuses on putting music and performing arts back into schools. It works mostly with private and charter schools because public schools are run by the state where funding is only accepted through fundraisers and budget approvals. That could take years and in the meantime, kids are missing out. The foundation provides scholarships to kids who can't afford the hefty private school tuitions. It also provides each school with instruments and the necessities to teach students about music and performance. To quote my dad: "Music has come a long way since high school band class and a five-dollar recorder."

Have you or the band chosen a new lead singer for Royal Mayhem?

Jayla: I appreciate you not using the term "front man" because Marcus King will always be the front man of Royal Mayhem. The band was his and Andrew's. I don't think there's anyone who can ever replace him, but as they say in this business, the show must go on. I do have someone in mind. Someone I feel would be a perfect fit.

I've discussed my choice with the other members of the band. I expect that once a decision is made, we'll make an announcement sometime before the tour. So, stay tuned.

I have a few "getting to know Jayla King" questions. Would you mind?

Jayla: Shoot.

Favorite color?

Jayla: Any shade of blue. Preferably lighter blues.

Guilty pleasures?

Jayla: Oh, um, I have a few. Okay, don't laugh. Chocolate, of course. Fruit, romance books, T-shirts with funny quotes—sometimes I even design them myself—and Pinterest.

You recently did a photo shoot with fashion photographer and designer Anna Sizemore's "Girl Next Door" campaign, correct? It appears you might have a knack for fashion modeling. Ever thought about a career in fashion *or* modeling?

Jayla: Thank you and no. I'll leave the designing to Anna and the modeling to the professionals. I loved working with Anna and I love the photography. It's the perfect combination of innocent, flirty, and sexy. She's a friend of a friend, so when she asked, I was happy to do it. It was fun and someday I can look back and say, "Hey, I did that," but it's not something I'm interested in pursuing. I would like to add that the Mayhem Foundation has teamed up with Anna Sizemore for a special Project Mayhem clothing line, consisting of T-shirts, tank tops, and hats, which are for sale on the foundation's website. All proceeds will go to the foundation.

How old were you when you wrote your first song?

Jayla: Six.

What instruments do you play, and what is your favorite?

Jayla: I play a little of everything. I'm okay on the drums, better on the guitar, but the piano is my favorite.

What's your favorite type of music?

Jayla: I don't have a favorite type of music or a favorite song. There are too many great songs out there to pick from. I grew up listening to everything. My dad liked classic rock and hip-hop. My mom likes anything from the eighties, classic rock, and hip-hop. I do have a preference in my workout routines. Like when I go running, I listen to hip-hop and rap, and when I work out in the gym, I listen to rock. So, there's that.

Have you ever been in love?

Jayla: Yes.

Boyfriend?

Jayla: No.

Hobbies?

Jayla: Songwriting. Reading. I love watching YouTube videos. There's a lot of undiscovered talent on YouTube. Designing my own T-shirts and, of course, whatever cool ideas I find on Pinterest. I love arts and crafts. If my music career doesn't work out, I could always teach arts and crafts.

Tell me something random about yourself.

Jayla: Hmm... oh, I know. I'm addicted to my iPad. It's always in my purse unless I'm at an event. I don't do social media. And one time when I was bored, I nicknamed everyone in my contacts.

Last question, and it's a two-part one. What are your plans? Will you continue making music?

Jayla: Music has always been a part of my life. It's shaped who I am, but, honestly, I don't know what I want to be when I grow up. Like I said before, I'm taking things day by day. I love writing music and I think no matter what I do in my life, I'll continue to write. As far as my plans, the only ones I have are to finish high school and the tour next year. After that, we'll just have to see.

"WHAT'S IT SAY?" Brad whispers over my shoulder, causing me to nearly jump out of my skin and almost piss my pants.

I slap a hand against my chest over my racing heart. "Holy shit, dude, you scared the hell out of me."

Brad laughs. "You didn't think I wouldn't recognize the cartoon version of the goddess, did you?" He smirks. "I knew your ass would be down here reading that article. So, what's it say?"

"Nothing really. It's mostly about the new Royal Mayhem album, *Jaybird*, and her dad's charity. There're some personal questions, but nothing too personal. She did some modeling recently."

"That's it?"

I shrug. "Yeah, pretty much."

"You know, the rumor is that Emerson Mackenzie ran off and eloped with a rock star. I always thought it was just a bullshit rumor."

"It's not but you can't say anything to anyone, Brad."

"Bro, I won't. I swear."

TRACK 13:
WHEREVER YOU WILL GO
Jayla

THE SUN IS just about to set as the *Jaybird* touches down on the private airstrip. Two black SUVs sit idling on the private drive. A smile spreads across my face when I see Uncle Max and Cole climb out of one and Dylan and Alex exit the other. It's exciting and weird knowing I'll be seeing my cousin every day at school, and the rest of my family more than on just holidays and the occasional summer vacation.

And then there's Zach.

How am I going to be able to see Zach every day and pretend like he didn't tear my heart out?

After our luggage is loaded up in the two SUVs, Bass slips behind the wheel of the new Denali and I slide into the passenger seat. Mom and Grace climb in the back.

BASS EXITS THE highway and cuts through downtown Heritage, then over a short two-lane drawbridge. Heritage Bay is actually an island located on the outskirts of downtown Heritage, connected to the mainland by two small drawbridges.

The island reminds me of something out of an old movie set. The buildings and roads are brick-paved and lined with streetlamps, townhomes, small businesses, boutiques, markets, bistros, and coffee shops with apartments above them.

Bass continues past Heritage Bay Golf Club and Beach Resort, Heritage Bay Athletic Club and Spa, and the Heritage Bay Hotel. And, of course, the Heritage Bay Medical Center. It's a private medical facility founded and built by my grandfather. The Mackenzie name is kind of a big deal around Heritage Bay.

We pass a few gated neighborhoods before we finally stop beside a guardhouse that sits in front of a pair of wrought iron gates that are at least twenty feet high. The words "Heritage Lake Estates" are scrolled across the front in a gold font.

Two men dressed in black cargo pants, black T-shirts with "Security" written in bright yellow stretched across their muscular torsos, and combat boots—looking like a couple of sexy soldiers—step outside the door of the small guardhouse. Bass gets out of the car and follows them back inside.

"Well, hellooooo, Joes," I drawl out, jokingly.

Mom laughs. "Take it easy there, tiger," she teases, shaking her head at me as Grace laughs beside her.

Bass comes out of the guardhouse and gets back behind the wheel. The gate opens and the guards wave us though.

"Is this a neighborhood or a military base?" I joke.

Bass smiles knowingly. "The security company is owned and operated by former military. Some of the guards are active in the reserves. You'll be safer here than on any base."

I seriously doubt that, but whatever. I'm safe so I'm good.

"Good to know, but I'm still just the daughter of a totally awesome rock star, not the President." I twist around in the front seat to face Emerson. "Is my life in danger or something? Why all of the security?"

Em gives me a "don't be ridiculous" look. "This was all your father's doing. Your safety and protection *was* and still *is* always a priority. And, no, your life isn't in danger, but I have been getting e-mails and phone calls ever since the magazine came out. No threats or anything, but still, you can never be too careful. Your fan base is building and sometimes fans can be a little overzealous. You're much safer here on this island than you'll ever be in LA. I can promise you that."

"But no one knows who I am."

"No, but they will eventually. For now, we live our lives the way everyone else does. There are a lot of important people who live on this island. Famous people. The residents here respect each other's privacy, but like I said, there are still the overzealous fans and shit stirrers with their cell phones ready. Conduct yourself in public the way I taught you, as if there's a camera on you at all times. Don't give anyone anything worth selling down the road. But for now, you don't have to worry about the paparazzi popping out of the bushes. If you leave the island, Bass goes with you. Be polite. Be kind. Be you."

I can deal with that.

The streets inside the gates are lined with lampposts like the others. Tall bushes obscure the view of the massive multimillion-dollar homes that sit at the end of a long driveway behind another private gate.

Bass wasn't kidding about the security being tight.

The SUV rolls to a stop in front of another set of tall black wrought iron gates at least fifteen feet high. Bass punches a code into the call box, the gate swings open, and he continues up the driveway.

When the house comes into view, I gasp and slap a hand over my mouth at the same time I hear Mom's sharp inhale from the back seat. My dream house.

It's huge. Even bigger than our house in Malibu.

I loved our beach house in Malibu and the villa in St. Thomas, but my dream house has always been something geared to an estate home. Kind of like a modern-day castle.

And since I'm a princess and all...

"Every princess should live in a castle," Bass says as if he hears my thoughts.

And it's the most perfect castle.

Even more beautiful than I could've ever imagined, with stones in various shades of creams and muted grays.

When you don't have a lot of friends and you're banned from social media, you find other ways to entertain yourself. Mine is

Pinterest. I love it. Before setting up an account, I had to get my dad's approval, but after a few minutes he was hooked. We set up an account for both of us with similar boards like Music, Quotes, Tattoos, Dream Homes, Cars. However, he didn't particularly care for my Hot Guys board. He told me to delete it but I hid it instead.

I'd spent too long perfecting that one.

"You guys go in. We'll get the bags," Bass says as he moves to the back of the SUV.

Cole jogs up the steps to the front door and waves me over, seemingly just as excited as I am. "Come on, Jay. Let's go check it out."

I GASP AND cover my mouth again as I step through the front door and into the foyer. I feel like I'm on an episode of one of those home makeover shows. The house is beautiful and spacious with dark espresso wood floors, white walls and hints of color splashed throughout.

Black-and-white photos of our family had been blown up and transferred to canvas to decorate the walls.

To the right of the foyer is a sweeping staircase leading to the second floor and just beyond the stairs is the dining room.

To the left is a small formal sitting area. A hallway leads to an office that connects to a music room with a small recording studio, followed by a master suite for my mom, and two bathrooms at the far end.

Straight ahead is a wall of windows overlooking the pool deck. The patio and the swimming pool are lit up and beyond the pool area is a man-made lake, a dock, and a boathouse.

I hear a gasp from Grace as she steps into the kitchen. Stainless steel appliances, a commercial grade subzero refrigerator, and gas range with a double oven. A large granite-top island—white with swirls of gray and cream—lined with barstools doubles as a breakfast bar. A farmhouse table sits off to the side with a chandelier hanging over it.

The kitchen overlooks the great room, which is spacious and decorated with slip-covered sofas surrounding a coffee table that looks like a tree trunk. A large flat-screen hangs on the wall over a uniquely carved wooden entertainment unit.

Behind the kitchen is another staircase leading to the second floor. There's also a laundry/mudroom, small guest bathroom, a gym, and a door that leads to the garage.

I love it.

The house is big—three stories—but it's cozy.

Tomorrow I plan to look around, but for now I want to see my room—specifically, my closet. My suite is on the second floor, along with five additional guest rooms with adjoining bathrooms, and two additional guest bathrooms. At the end of the hall is a door that leads to a separate apartment over the garage, which is where Bass will live. And on the third floor is the media/game room and another door leading to an additional apartment for Grace.

My king-size bed, piled high with white linens, is centered against the left wall on top of an oversized area rug and flanked by two shabby-chic nightstands topped with lamps. The tufted headboard is made with gray satin fabric, and a matching bench sits at the foot of the bed. The aquamarine silk drapes add a perfect amount of color to complement the room. A small seating area is arranged on the far side of the room in front of the French doors leading to the terrace. I'm tempted to skip the shower and dive right into bed, but first I have a closet to inspect.

A set of double doors opens to a massive closet which resembles a boutique or a small department store, filled with aisles of clothes which are all mine. *I'm a bit of a fashion whore, sue me.* A small seating area is arranged in the corner of the room in front of a three-way mirror.

On the far wall are two separate but smaller closets for shoes, handbags, and accessories. Inside the shoe closet is a built-in dresser, and on top is a large vase filled with fresh ranunculus in shades of light pink and cream.

"You have entirely too much shit," Cole says, coming in behind me.

I scoff. "There's no such thing."

Every square foot of this house is beautiful and perfect.

And suddenly I get the strangest feeling.

Goose bumps cover my arms as a sense of calm comes over me. It's as if my dad is here, with his arms around me, and he's telling me everything is going to be okay.

You're home now, Jaybird.

AFTER EVERYONE LEAVES, I head back up to my room to shower, then shoot a text to Evangeline and Lucas, letting them know that I've arrived and will talk to them tomorrow.

Beside my phone is an envelope addressed to Jaybird in familiar handwriting. A shudder runs through me as I sit on the edge of the bed and reach for the envelope. As I brush my fingers over the letters, I realize my hands are shaking. Shifting on the bed, I scoot so that my back is against the headboard and open the envelope slowly, careful not to rip it.

Jaybird,

Welcome home, baby girl. I hope it's everything you've ever dreamed of because it's all for you. I'm providing you with a foundation, but it's up to you to build the life you want for yourself. Fill it with new memories and remember that no matter which path you choose to follow, it will always lead you back home. I hope I've made you as proud as you've made me. I love you so much, my sweet girl.

Love always and forever,

Daddy

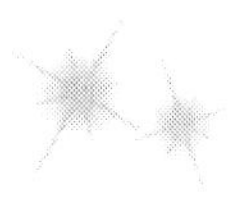

DO I SMELL bacon?

Blinking the sleep away from my eyes, I throw the covers back, roll out of bed, and head to the bathroom, cringing when my eyes meet the mirror. I look like a hot mess. My eyes are red and puffy from crying myself to sleep after reading the note from my father. It makes me sick to my stomach thinking how hard it had to be for him to write that note, knowing his fate had already been decided.

With a fresh face and minty breath, I throw on a pair of shorts and tank, snag my sunglasses from my bag and slide them over my swollen eyes before making my way down to the kitchen.

Cole is sitting at the island messing with his phone while Mimi and Grace flutter around the kitchen. "Good morning, sunshine," Mimi sings from the coffeepot as Grace sets down a plate in front of Cole.

With an excited squeal, I rush toward Mimi and wrap my arms around her petite frame. Pulling back, I look around. "Where's Mac Daddy?"

"Mac Daddy" is my grandfather, Max Mackenzie. Everyone calls him "Mac" but I call him "Mac Daddy" because he's cool like that.

"He had a meeting, but he promises he'll be over later." She frowns. "What's with the sunglasses?"

Shrugging, I turn away from her, snatching up a bacon strip from the platter as I move to sit beside Cole, ruffling his hair as I pass, which he immediately tries to fix. Such a diva.

"I thought you had practice this morning," I say, sliding onto the stool beside him.

Cole eyes my sunglasses, then looks down at his watch. "I do, in about thirty minutes. So, what's with the sunglasses?" he asks, reaching for them.

Leaning back, I swat his hand away. "Stop. I'm fine, Cole."

"What do you think of the house?" Mimi interrupts as she sets down a mug of steaming hot coffee in front of me.

Wrapping my hands around the mug, I look around and say, "It's beautiful, Mimi," before bringing the mug to my lips, blowing on it before taking a sip. "I haven't been in all of the rooms or out back yet, but so far, I love it. Of course, the closet is my favorite room in the house." I smile.

"That closet is ridiculous." Cole rolls his eyes. "I don't get why women need an entire room for their shit."

"Oh, hush, you." Mimi smacks him on the arm, as do I.

I turn my attention back to Mimi. "Seriously, Mimi, you guys did such a beautiful job. I appreciate you and Aunt Jess and I'd like to do something nice for you both. Maybe a spa day or dinner with the whole family."

Mimi winks. "You're welcome, and that's not necessary. You're my granddaughter. I'd do anything for you."

"Speak for yourself, Mimi," Cole says before turning to me. "I helped too. There's a new place that just opened in Pelican Cove. Feel free to thank me by taking me to dinner."

I snort a laugh. "You got it." I reach up and ruffle his hair again. "How much crap do you put in that hair, pretty boy?"

Jerking his head back, he swats at my hand before combing his fingers through his hair.

"Shut up." He laughs and stands to shove his phone into his front pocket. "I gotta get to practice, but I'll be back afterward to pick you up. I'm taking you to my friend Brad's end-of-summer party."

I go still for a fraction of a second, remembering Zach's message, *'I'm on my way to my friend Brad's end-of-summer party.'*

"Okay. Just text me and let me know what time. And don't forget what I said earlier." I'd warned him not to tell anyone—Zach—that I'm in town. I want to surprise him.

Cole shakes head. "Chill out, girl. I won't." He smacks a kiss on the top of my head and another on Mimi's cheek before rounding the island to plant one on Grace's cheek, thanking her for breakfast. Then he's out the door. Cole comes off as an asshole to most people, especially to those who don't know him, but when it comes to family, he's good people.

TRACK 14:
WHAT ARE THE CHANCES?
Zach

"Yo, Mackenzie!" Brad calls out as we walk into the locker room where Cole is sitting on the bench, lacing up his cleats. "Where'd you go last night?" he asks, reaching out to give Cole a fist bump. "Or should I ask, who'd you disappear with? I know it wasn't Ashton because she was still at the party being her usual annoying-ass self." He wiggles his eyebrows. "So, who was she?"

Cole shakes his head. "I wasn't hooking up. I had some family sh—stuff."

I lift my eyebrows, intrigued.

"Yo, I was up at Mac's the other night," Justin says. "Who's the new redheaded chick?" He blows out a low whistle. "She's bangin'."

Cole's brows pull together in confusion before he shakes his head. "No idea. Haven't see her."

Dex closes his locker and turns to face us. "I have and, dude, she's a dime piece," he confirms, nodding. "But don't tell my girl I said that. She'll have my balls. My baby gets jealous."

"Pussy," Justin taunts with a laugh, then dodges Dex's fist. "Scared of his girl."

"Let's go, ladies! Quit your gossiping and get your asses on the field," Coach Morgan orders, passing us on his way through the locker room and out the door. One by one, we all file out and jog toward the field.

Cole and I fall to the back of the line. "I saw Jay on the cover of *Rhythm & Riffs*. Well the cartoon version of her." I chuckle. "Lexi has a girl crush on her."

Cole snorts. "Yeah, I saw it too."

"How's Jay doing?" I ask.

"She's better."

"I can't imagine what she's been through."

Without looking at me, he scratches his jaw and replies, "She took it pretty hard. Harder than anyone expected and she made herself sick."

"Sick how?"

Cole shakes his head. "Just sick. But she's better now."

Before I can push him for more information, Coach Morgan yells, "Easton, Mackenzie! Move it!"

COACH BLOWS HIS whistle before cupping his hands around his mouth. "All right, guys, that's it for today."

"So, Reagan texted me last night after I left the party," Cole tells me when we get back to the locker room.

"Of course, she did," I huff. "Took her long enough. Let me guess. 'Come over'?"

"Something like that."

"She sent the same message to Evan. What'd you tell her?"

"Nothing." He scowls. "I'd rather ignore her. I know you say you don't care, but bottom line, she fucked you over."

I shrug. "Yeah, but it's not like she hurt me. She just pissed me off. Ignoring her will only make her try harder. She loves to play games and you're presenting her with a challenge."

"She needs a dose of reality," he says. "Ashton and I aren't in a relationship, but I think it's pretty shitty of Reagan to be texting me behind Ashton's back."

"I agree. Especially when Ashton stood up for her last night after

Lexi nearly ripped her hair out."

He chuckles. "I wish I'd been there to see that. Evan's got his hands full with that one."

"I saw Lindsay last night at Brad's."

"Miller?"

I nod. "I'm bringing her to the party today."

"She wants the D," Brad cuts in. *Always the clown.*

I shake my head.

"You trying to hit that?" Cole asks me before he turns to smirk at Evan. "I wonder how Grayson would feel about it."

Evan shrugs. "He's the idiot for cheating on her."

"Better watch out, Mackenzie. Our boy Zach is gonna steal your playa card," Dex singsongs and pops him in the ass with his sweat-soaked tank top.

"Zach doesn't have what it takes to be a player," Cole teases, grinning. *What's he doing?* "His conscience won't allow it." *True.*

"That's because I have one." I chuckle. "But I've done the girlfriend thing and we all saw how well that worked out. Besides, I don't need any distractions this year. I've gotta keep my head in the game."

"A hundred bucks says you'll have a girlfriend by the second week of school," Cole challenges with a smirk.

"What?"

"A hundred bucks—"

"I heard you," I say, scowling at my best friend. "Where is this coming from?"

Cole grins and holds out his hand.

"Fine." I clasp his hand with mine and tug him toward me. "Be ready to crack open your piggy bank." I smack him hard on the ass before shoving away from me.

"Hold up!" Evan walks over. "I want in on this."

"Okay, what the fuck is going on?" I say to the ever-growing group around me.

"Something tells me I gotta get in on this," Brad says with a grimace. "Sorry, Zach. Count me in, Mackenzie."

"Me, too," Dex jumps in.

"Are you guys serious?"

"Sorry, Zach, but I gotta get in on this, too," Justin says.

"You guys are dicks." I look around. "Is this a joke? Did you sign me up on Tinder or something?"

"Oh, come on, Zach," Evans says, smacking me on the back. "Having a girlfriend isn't a bad thing. You just gotta find the right girl."

"Easy for you to say, Evan. Your girlfriend isn't a whore," I argue, but they all just stare back at me with stupid smirks on their faces. "Okay, assholes, you better have my money when it's time to pay up."

"YOU FUCKERS READY to party?" Brad shouts, stepping between Cole and me, throwing his arms over both of our shoulders.

"I need to pick something up first. Give me a half hour or so." Cole turns and calls out to Evan. "E, you want me to swing by and pick you up on the way?" It's rare that Cole ever drinks, so most of the time he's the designated driver.

"Nah. Lexi's driving," Evan replies before climbing in his truck.

Cole turns to me. "You need me to pick you up?"

"Nah. I gotta pick up Lindsay."

"All right. I'll see you in thirty." Cole whips his shirt around and pops Brad in the chest.

"Ow! Dick."

"Later, pussies." Cole laughs as he jogs over to his truck.

"I think my nipple's bleeding," Brad hisses, rubbing his chest.

TRACK 15: CHANGES
Zach

LINDSAY STEPS OUT of her house wearing a short yellow dress with the neon green strings of her bikini top tied around her neck and a beach bag slung over her shoulder. Her eyes are hidden behind a pair of oversized sunglasses that take up half of her small face and her long blonde hair is twisted into a side braid and draped over her right shoulder.

Behind the lenses of my own sunglasses, I scan over her features. Lindsay is cute in the whole girl-next-door kind of way and it makes me wonder what it is about her that attracted Grayson. He likes slutty girls, like Reagan. Lindsay is far from slutty.

She's one of the good ones.

It's too bad I'm not interested in her like that.

I've sort of been in a shitty mood all day. No, I've been in a shitty mood since last night after seeing *my* girl on the cover of a popular rock magazine.

But that's not even what pissed me off.

What pissed me off is the hurt I felt.

The not knowing.

My heart still wants her.

I still want her.

I still love her.

But I can't have her.

I PULL UP to Brad's and park in my usual spot while Lindsay texts her friends. I pull off my t-shirt and sunglass and toss them in my front seat before Lindsay and I make our way along the paved walkway and step through the gate that leads to the backyard and the beach. I bump fists with Joe, an old friend of the Mannings, who Brad pays big bucks to guard the gate, watch over things, and keep his mouth shut. I pass Joe my keys, which he tags before tossing them into a bucket with the rest.

Lindsay and I continue up the walkway, rounding the side of the house, and nearly collide into Reagan.

"What the hell?" I bark out.

"Zach, can I talk to you for a minute?" Her eyes flick between Lindsay and me.

"Stalk much," Lindsay mumbles under her breath. Lindsay's got a little fight in her. I like it.

"Jesus, Reagan, I just got here. What do you want?"

"I just need to talk to you for a second." Her gaze moves to Lindsay. "Alone."

Lindsay looks up at me and rolls her eyes. "Go ahead. Kristen just texted me that she's inside. Come find me whenever you're done."

Lindsay walks off and Reagan watches her until she disappears into the sea of bodies before turning back to me with raised brows. "Lindsay Miller, really?" She puts her hands on her hips, cocking one hip to the side. "I always knew she wanted to bang you."

This girl is certifiable. "So, what if she does? It's none of your business. You've got some nerve talking shit about Lindsay when you're the one who cheated on *me* with *her* boyfriend. If anything, you should be apologizing to her for what you did."

"Ugh! Whatever." She waves me off with a flick of her wrist. "Will you please talk to Lexi? I know she's here somewhere and I don't want to spend the entire day looking over my shoulder."

I laugh. *Go, Lexi.* "You invited her boyfriend over to your house. What do you expect?"

"I didn't mean to send that text to Evan. I swear."

"You're so full of shit. I know you've been texting my friends and if you're doing it to make me jealous, you're wasting your time. I don't care who you bang, so get over yourself. If you get your ass kicked, it's your own fault. Stop chasing after guys who aren't available."

Her jaw drops and eyes go wide. "Your friends are the ones texting me."

"Then show me the texts." I hold out my hand. "Show me the texts and I'll tell Lexi to leave you alone."

"I don't have my phone."

"Mmhmm." I'm calling bullshit.

"Zach," she whines, stomping her foot like a toddler throwing a tantrum.

"Reagan," I mimic.

"God, Zach, we've been broken up for three months already. Get over it already. Believe me, if I could go back and change what happened, I would. We were together for nine months."

I exhale a harsh laugh and shake my head. "I was over it three months ago when you cheated on me."

"Maybe I wouldn't have cheated if you hadn't flown out to California to chase after some girl who doesn't even want you."

What the hell? "What are you talking about?"

"The only reason you even asked me out was because your little girlfriend in California dropped you." I flinch. Reagan notices and straightens her shoulders with a newfound confidence. "Chelsea told me you were using me and that you'd never date me seriously because you were in love with Cole's cousin."

What the fuck, Chelsea?

I make a mental note to call Chelsea later and rip her a new one. Chelsea and I aren't exactly friends anymore, but back when we were, I finally broke down and confided in her about Jay. And if what Reagan is saying is true, then Chelsea is a deceitful bitch.

"I'm not doing this with you right now," I say, sidestepping Reagan and heading over to my friends who are lounging around on the outdoor pool furniture, conveniently next to the keg. Pounding a few fists along the way, I step up beside Brad and Justin while Evan works the keg. Evan shakes his head and passes a Solo cup to me.

I huff out a laugh as I reach for it. "Thanks."

Justin curls his arm around my neck. "Please tell me you're not hooking up with that again. Because I'll give you my hundred bucks to stay away from her."

I shake my head. "Keep your money, dude. I'm not interested in going back there. Ever. Been there, fucked that and, apparently, so has everyone else." I hold out my cup and gesture to Evan's brother, Grayson, who's sitting with my other teammates. "The T-shirts are on backorder." Justin and Brad laugh and Evan just shakes his head.

Yeah, I know. That was a dick thing to say and my dad would probably kick my ass if he heard, but Reagan brought all of this on herself. "I'm gonna go find Lindsay."

TRACK 16:
WELCOME TO NORMAL
Jayla

Taylor Swift drifts from the speakers above as I slip on a bikini cover-up before grabbing a pair of sandals from the shelf. Cole texted me that he's on his way, so I expect him to be here any minute.

After Cole left for practice this morning, Mimi and I explored the rest of the house. I love my office and adjoining music room. Both rooms are decorated in the same color scheme. The walls are painted in a shimmery silver-gray color. In the office, a white desk is centered under the window and a teal-blue velvet sofa is centered against the opposite wall with a silver and white coffee table on top of a faux zebra skin rug.

But what I love the most is the beautiful white grand piano in the music room right in front of the floor-to-ceiling window overlooking the front lawn. My fingers were itching to play but I knew if I sat down, I'd be there for hours and I didn't have that kind of time today.

"Taylor Swift, really?"

"Oh, shit!" I yell, my sandals flying out of my hands. Pressing my hand to my chest to calm my racing heart, I turn to face Cole, who's standing in the doorway with his hands braced on each side of the frame, laughing. "You scared me!"

Still laughing, he leans forward and shakes his head, feigning disappointment.

I give an unapologetic shrug as I slide my feet into my turquoise Tori Burch jelly thongs. “Guilty pleasure,” I say with a wink. “It’s catchy.”

“It’s all the same shit about putting her exes on blast.”

“Yet guys are still lining up to date her. Go figure. Besides, all singer-songwriters write about relationships, sex, love, and broken hearts,” I explain. “People can relate.”

Cole zeroes in on my cover-up and whistles between his teeth. “Emerson will never let you leave the house wearing that.”

I look down at the thin, cotton crochet cover-up that falls just below my butt. “She bought this for me, so I think I’m good,” I deadpan as I turn back to the shelf and reach for a tote. “You said the party is on the beach.”

“Just put some shorts on under it, Jay,” Cole says in a firm tone, reaching over my head and pulling the tote from the top shelf before passing it to me. “And hurry up.”

Tilting my head to the side, I say, “I don’t think we’ve met. I’m Jayla King, aka you’re not the boss of me,” before brushing past him and grabbing the denim shorts I’d laid out earlier. I shoot Cole a wink as I slip them over my bikini bottoms.

“SO, WHAT’S GOING on between you and Zach?” Cole asks, waving to a security guard as he passes through the gates of a different neighborhood.

“Nothing. Hey, why didn’t the guard stop you? If this were my neighborhood, there’d be a GI Joe hanging off your hood right now. Are all of the neighborhoods here gated?”

Cole barks out a laugh and points to the sticker in the bottom left corner of his windshield. “I live in this neighborhood, too. And, yes, they’re all gated. You have GI Joes because you live in the wealthiest neighborhood in this town. There are a lot of important people who live in there and they pay out the ass for security.”

"So, whose party is this?" I ask when Cole pulls up to a massive Mediterranean home and parks beside a black Jeep Rubicon.

"His name is Brad Manning. You'll like him. Everyone likes the Mannings. And I'll introduce you to Lexi, Evan's girlfriend. She's a trip. I think you two will get along. But just a head's up, she's a huge Marcus King fan and from what I've heard she has a little girl crush on the cartoon version of Jaybird."

"Great," I mumble, rolling my eyes behind my dark sunglasses. "She's not one of those girls who'll follow me to the bathroom and try to take pictures of me or my lady J, is she?"

Cole looks over at me with furrowed brows and says, "Your what? Oh, my God, Jay. Gross—no! I doubt she'll even recognize you."

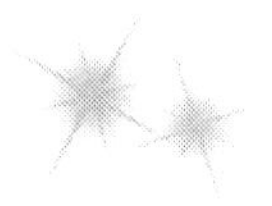

THE PULSING BEAT of The Chainsmokers' "Roses" drifts from the back of the house. Cole and I sing along, bumping shoulders and hips as we make our way down the path running along the side of the house, leading to the back gate.

Brad lives on the beach side of the island. His backyard is a blur of shirtless guys, bikini-clad girls, and red Solo cups. A game of water volleyball is in play, the net stretched across the pool.

I grab hold of Cole's bicep as he leads the way through a sea of people, greeting his peers with a few nods and fist bumps along the way. People are downright staring at us, a mixture of curiosity and disdain. Girls are looking at me as if I'm their competition.

Cole turns his head and says, "They're all wondering who the lucky girl is." He laughs.

I snort and shake my head. *Cocky bastard.*

"Mackenzie!" A blond guy holding a red Solo cup waves us over from under the covered porch. "It's about damn time you got here. Thirty minutes, my ass." He punches Cole in the arm. "That's for earlier, asshole. This shit still hurts." He looks down at his chest and brushes a hand over his nipple, a purplish bruise around it. "What the hell took you so long? Did you stop by the spa for a bikini wax on the way?" He snickers and I burst out laughing.

This has to be Brad. He looks like a Brad, an all-American boy with short, blond hair, blue eyes, and a perfect smile. *He's cute.*

His blue-eyed gaze moves to me as if he's just now noticing me. I lift my hand and offer a small wave. "Sorry. It's my fault. Wardrobe issues," I say, extending my hand. "I'm Jay."

His eyebrows jerk up to his hairline. "Well, shit. You sure are." He takes my hand and glances over at Cole. "I've heard a lot about you, Jay." Brad winks.

"Really? From who?" Cole asks with a smirk.

Brad shrugs. "You?"

"I hope it was all good," I joke, trying to play along.

"Good. Interesting." He grins and turns to a couple standing nearby with their arms around each other. The girl has on a red string bikini and big sunglasses, her caramel-colored hair piled into a messy bun on top of her head. Her guy is also wearing sunglasses and black and red board shorts. His hair is dark brown and he has tattoos on his biceps and chest.

He kisses her on the nose and she giggles.

"Would you two give it a rest," Brad teases and both of their heads swivel our way.

Hot damn.

"This is Evan and Lexi," Cole introduces them. "This is my cousin, Ja—"

"Jayla King," Lexi breathes out in almost a whisper and I'm immediately scanning our surroundings to see if anyone heard. "Holy shit, what are you doing here?" she asks. I frown. "Oh, my God! Evan." She bounces on the balls of her feet and looks up at her boyfriend, then back at me. "I'm sorry. I'm acting like a crazy fangirl." She slaps a hand over her mouth.

I've never had anyone fangirl over me before. It's kinda weird. But she's freaking adorable.

"I think what she's trying to say is it's nice to meet you," Evan jokes. Lexi nods.

I turn to Cole. "You said she wouldn't recognize me."

"It's a cartoon." He gestures to me. "How the fuck was I supposed to know?" He turns to address Lexi, Evan, and Brad. "She's Jay Mackenzie. My cousin from California. Okay?" The three of them just nod.

Maybe I should leave.

Cole sees the worry on my face even behind my sunglasses. "It's fine, Jay. They're my good friends and they know how to keep a secret. Brad's parents are good friends with Mimi and Mac. Lexi's mom is some famous actress or some shit and Evan's dad owns the company for all the security on the island. You can trust them. I promise."

I nod, still processing everything.

"You want something to drink?" Cole asks.

"Just water."

He points to Lexi. "Lexi, you want a drink? Or a valium?" he adds, teasing.

"No, I'm good." She waves him off and turns to me. "I'm so sorry," she apologizes. "I'm a little in shock. I literally just read your interview last night and now you're standing here. I can't believe it." She giggles nervously. "You're even more beautiful than your cartoon."

I laugh. "Thank you. I was just thinking the same thing about you."

Lexi scoffs and waves off my compliment. "Thanks. And don't worry, I won't say anything, Jay Mackenzie." She winks. "I know how this shit works. That's why I live here with my dad and not my mom."

"I can't believe you recognized me from a cartoon picture." I snort. "I can't wait to tell my mom." I scan the crowd, looking for Cole. "Hey, can you point me in the direction of the bathroom?"

"I'll show you," Lexi offers.

She leads the way inside the house, weaving through the crowd. The bathroom is occupied, so Lexi and I make small talk over the music.

"So, are you here visiting?" Lexi asks.

"Actually, no. I live here as of yesterday."

"You're kidding. How exciting! Tell me you're coming to Heritage Academy." She slaps a palm to her forehead. "Of course, you are. You're part of the Project Mayhem class."

I smile and nod. "That's the plan."

"Awesome. Maybe we'll have a few regular classes together. I'll be happy to show you around."

"So, who is your mom?" I ask.

Lexi glances over her shoulder quickly. "Diana Cooper."

My eyes nearly pop out of my head. "No way!" Diana Cooper is a huge movie star and my mom's favorite actress.

Lexi shrugs. "We don't talk much. She's too busy to be a mom. I've lived here with my dad since I was four. I don't really even know her."

"Oh. I'm sorry."

She shrugs again. "It's cool. I'm happy here and I have Evan."

"What does your dad do?"

"He's a real estate developer." She smiles, knowingly and points to herself. "You're looking at the product of a one-night stand." She turns her attention to the bathroom door. "Jesus, what the hell is taking so long?" Lexi bangs on the door. "Hurry up, assholes. Some of us have to pee." Female laughter echoes from the other side of the door. A second later, the door swings open and my heart drops into my stomach.

TRACK 17: HELLO

Zach

IN MY SEARCH for Lindsay, I see Piper peeking her head out the bathroom door and looking around.

"What are you doing, Piper?"

She sighs in relief and waves me over. "Zach! I need your help." She reaches for my arm, pulls me into the bathroom, and closes the door. She turns her back to me, holding her bikini top strings in her other hand.

"Those jerks out there keep pulling on the strings. Will you tie this for me in a double knot? I tried to do it but my hair keeps getting caught in the knot."

"Hold your hair up." I take the strings from her grip and tie them in a double knot. "Is that better?"

Piper turns and smiles. "Much. Thanks."

"You're welcome." I smile back.

"And can I just say thank you for always being so nice to me and not grouping me with the rest of my friends? I know Ashton and Hannah get on your nerves, but I want you to know I don't agree with them. I think Reagan is an idiot. You're a good guy and you deserve better."

I've never been attracted to Piper. Probably because she's friends with Reagan or because of her reputation. But every rumor I've ever heard about her contradicts the girl standing in front of me. She isn't flirting with me or dropping to her knees; she's being genuinely nice.

I smile. "Thanks, Piper, and so do you. Let me know if anyone else gives you a hard time and I'll take care of it."

Someone bangs on the door. "Hurry up, assholes. Some of us have to pee." I chuckle at the sound of Lexi's voice on the other side of the door. She's such a little firecracker.

I tug on the strings once more. "You're all set. This thing isn't coming undone. You might have to cut it off later." I chuckle, reaching for the door and pulling it open. Piper laughs, double-checking her top as she leaves first and I follow. Just as I step into the hall, I freeze.

It takes a second for my brain to register that the girl leaning against the opposite wall with the black hair and aquamarine eyes is Jayla King. *My girl.* "Jesus, Zach," Lexi chides. "The bathroom? You couldn't use a bedroom like everyone else."

"Um...."

Piper scoffs. "Chill, Lexi, he was helping me with my top. We weren't doing anything." Piper looks up at me, then follows my gaze to Jay.

Piper lifts her hand and gives a small wave. "Hi, I'm Piper."

"Hi, I'm Jay." Jay smiles at Piper before her gaze moves to me. "Hi, Zach."

"What are you doing here?" I ask, shocked, my tone harsher than it was meant to be and she frowns.

Piper turns to me. "Thanks for the fix," she jokes with a wink. "See you later." Then just to make things more awkward, she smacks me on the butt and walks off.

Jay points to the bathroom and I move to the side to let her by, catching a whiff of her familiar scent. She always smelled so good. Expensive. Not like that fruity-flowery stuff Reagan used to drown herself in.

When the door closes, Lexi eyes me skeptically. "Piper? Really?"

I give her a pointed look. "I was helping her with her top, Lexi. That's all."

She gives me a look that tells me she's not sure she believes me.

Jay comes out and Lexi steps into the bathroom as Jay moves

back against the wall to wait for her. She's so goddamn beautiful. Her nose is pierced with a tiny diamond stud. Her sunglasses are resting in her dark hair that's piled on top of her head. She's taller than I remember. And thinner.

For some reason, I feel the need to explain myself. "I know that looked bad, but I really was just helping her out with her top."

Jay gives a careless shrug and it's like a stab to the heart. Of course, she doesn't care. Why would she? I feel my shoulders sag slightly.

"How are you, Zach?" she asks, pushing the knife in deeper and giving it a little twist. She hasn't called me Zach since we were six. I've always been Z. I loved it the first time she called me that; it made me feel cool. That was *our* thing. To this day, no one is allowed to call me Z.

Then I come to my senses and remember this girl broke my fucking heart.

"I'm good," I reply in a clipped tone, making her frown again.

"Zach." Lindsay walks up and hugs my arm. Her timing couldn't be more perfect. "I've been looking all over for you."

I smile, lifting my arm and draping it over her shoulders. "You found me." I wink.

I do and say dumb shit when I'm feeling vulnerable or exposed. That's exactly how I've felt for the last five minutes. For the last year.

Lindsay turns to Jay and smiles. "Hi, I'm Lindsay."

"Hi, I'm Jay. Nice to meet you."

"Jay is Cole Mackenzie's cousin," I tell Lindsay, extending the introduction. "We've known each other since we were kids."

"Oh?" she says. "That's awesome. It's really nice to meet you."

The bathroom door opens and Lexi comes out. "Hey, Lindsay."

"Hey, Lexi." Lindsay reaches out and gives her a quick hug.

Lexi turns to Jay. "You ready?"

"Yep," she says, pushing off the wall. Without another word or glance my way, she walks off.

"I'm gonna use the bathroom," Lindsay says, bringing my attention back to her.

"Okay. I'll be outside," I tell her and hurry off to find my soon-to-be ex-best friend, Cole Mackenzie.

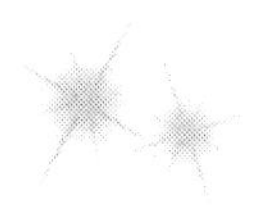

I FIND COLE near the keg talking to Evan, Justin, and Brad. “You okay, Zach?” Brad asks through a chuckle as he passes me a red Solo cup.

“Not really,” I say, turning to Cole with a look that clearly says “I’m fucking pissed.”

Brad raises his brows. “I guess you saw the goddess. I’m sorry I slipped up. Sort of.”

I shoot Brad a pointed look.

Cole holds up his hand to me and turns to Brad. “The what?”

Brad shakes his head and averts his eyes as he brings his cup to his mouth to keep from answering.

Cole turns his attention back to me. “Don’t get pissed at me. She told me not to say anything.” His gaze moves past my shoulders. I look around and notice we’ve caught a few curious looks. “Let’s take a walk.” He jerks his head to the side, gesturing for me to follow.

“You guys aren’t gonna fight, are you?” Brad asks as we turn to walk away.

As I’ve said before, Brad can be a bit dramatic. Cole and I have never fought, much less argued throughout our entire friendship.

Cole shoots Brad an annoyed look before we head to the far side of the pool deck.

Cole stops and turns to me. “What’s going on between you and Jay? he asks at the same time as I ask, “How long has she been here?”

“She got in last night. Why?”

“Why didn’t you tell me she was in town when I asked about her earlier?”

“She asked me not to tell you because she wanted to surprise you.” He shrugs. “I thought you guys were friends.”

“Yeah, well, I thought so too.”

“Why are you so pissed off right now?” He chuckles.

I shake my head. “I’m not pissed off. I’m just.... You should’ve told me she was coming today. She probably thinks I’m the biggest douche bag.”

“Why?” His playful expression turns serious.

"Because I was in the bathroom with Piper helping her with her bathing suit and Jay was standing outside the bathroom door when we came out. She probably thinks I was in there hooking up."

"Why would she care?" Cole narrows his eyes. "You guys hooked up in St. Thomas, didn't you?"

I nod once.

"I knew it." He shoves my shoulder. "I've been trying to get one of you to admit it but you're both too fucking stubborn."

"I'm sorry. You know I would never do anything to hurt her. Everything was good until she went back to California and blew me off."

Cole clasps his hands behind his head and blows out a breath. "She didn't blow you off, Zach. Her dad was dying."

"I know. But that doesn't explain why she blocked me from contacting her. Why did she do that? Or was it her parents."

He shakes his head. "I don't know. If you had come to me, I could've asked her. Look, I get that you're pissed and you have a right to be. But you have no idea what she's been through. They were close. She stayed by his side until he took his last breath. Imagine what that's like. She screamed and cried for days." He shakes his head and tilts it back to take a deep breath. "I meant what I said earlier. She took his death really hard and she's changed because of it. Her whole life has been flipped upside down and she's a little fragile right now, so give her a break. I'm not saying you have to be her friend. You don't even have to talk to her. Just don't be a dick."

I nod. "How long is she here for?"

The corners of his mouth quirk up. "Indefinitely. Oh, and she's Jay Mackenzie now."

"She lives here?" I ask, incredulous.

He gives me a slow nod, eyeing me skeptically. "You should've talked to me."

"I wanted to. I was going to tell you when she came for Labor Day weekend, but then she wouldn't take my calls or answer my texts. And she never showed up, so I figured that was it. It was over, so there was no point in bringing it up. It wasn't worth ruining our friendship over. Plus, I was afraid your family would hate me."

"That's bullshit, Zach. We've been best friends our whole lives.

You don't think I knew about you two crushing on each other all those years? My whole family knows. Even Uncle Marcus knew."

"He did?"

He shakes his head again. "I should punch you in the junk just for being an idiot."

It takes everything in me to fight back the excitement burning in the pit my stomach. Am I surprised to see her? Of course, I am. I wasn't sure if I'd ever see her again. Am I happy she's here? Fuck, yes. I feel like I'm dreaming. And the fact that she's here for good is amazing. But it still doesn't change the fact that she broke my heart and cut me out of her life. I want to know why. She owes me an explanation. I think I deserve that much.

My jaw clenches when I see Evan's brother, Grayson, talking to Jay.

I hate that guy.

"You know he's gonna try to get in her pants," I inform him.

Cole laughs and turns to me. "Watching you sweat over her will be much more fun than punching you in the junk."

"You're such a dick. Why are we friends?"

"Because you love me, Zachy." He laughs again, smacking me on the back, and I punch him in the arm.

Jayla

"JAY, THIS IS Grayson, Evan's brother," Lexi says, and I turn to face Mr. Tall, Dark, and Ha—holy shit! "Grayson, this is Jay. She's Cole's cousin."

"Hi," I say with a smile, holding out my hand.

Grayson smiles and takes my hand. "Very nice to meet you."

"Grayson, are you hitting on my cousin?" Cole says from behind me. Turning, I see him standing with his arms crossed and beside him is Zach, minus his little blonde girlfriend.

He's still gorgeous. Taller. And his body is perfectly sculpted, like he's been in the gym all summer. He's wearing aqua-colored board shorts and a backwards baseball cap with the ends of his wavy hair peeking out along the edge.

Jesus. My stomach flutters.

Glancing at his wrist, I see he's still wearing the leather bracelets I bought him last year in St. Thomas. I lift my gaze to his face and notice he's looking down at my toes, specifically the toe ring he bought me. I wiggle my toe and he jerks his gaze away.

Busted. I laugh to myself.

A group of guys come walking up from the beach and begin filling their cups. "Guys, this is my cousin Jay. Jay, these guys are my teammates, Dex, Carter, Justin, Derek, and, of course, you already know Zach," he says, a mischievous twinkle in his eye. It's unlikely I'll remember all their names. With Zach standing so close, I'll be lucky if I remember *my* own name.

Screw California.

It's like hot guy central around here.

Florida is where it's at, people.

Cole hooks his arm around Zach's neck and opens his big mouth. "Zach was Jay's first love." I make a mental note to kill Cole Matthew Mackenzie.

"Yeah, when I was like six," I say with a careless shrug as if it's no big deal, but inside my heart recognizes its owner.

Zach frowns, but doesn't say anything. He looks almost... crushed.

An older version of Brad walks up to the group and puts his hands on his hips. "Brad, why is Hannah here?"

"Because this is a party." Brad rolls his eyes. "Don't worry about Hannah. She knows your pee-pee is off-limits." A chorus of laughter erupts from the group.

"Yeah, until she gets drunk and tries to grab my dick," he retorts and rolls his eyes. "*As if.* Not even a bottle of liquid curiosity could get me near *that* cat." Another round of laughter rings out as he jerks his head from side to side and pushes out his lips, pretending to pout. His eyes flick over to me and his eyebrows rise high above his sunglasses. "I'm Brice Manning."

"Hi. I'm Jay." I lift my hand with a small wave.

"Oh, I know who you are, gorgeous."

"Zach," Lindsay calls out as she walks up, holding a cup that looks more like a mini-keg with a handle, and a couple of girls trailing behind her. "We're going down to the beach. You wanna come with?"

Zach flicks his gaze to Cole, then to Grayson briefly, and then to me before he says, "Sure."

"I'll meet you down there in a minute," Cole says. "I gotta take a piss first."

Classy.

I'VE BEEN AT this party for close to an hour and so far, no one else has recognized me. If they have, they haven't said anything. It's not like I'm some big-time celebrity. I've caught a few curious glances here and there, but I think it's because these people are all familiar with each other and I'm an outsider. I'm hyperaware of people around me holding up their cell phones, but as I study the groups of girls and some guys, I realize they're too absorbed in each other, posing for selfies and posting them on social media.

Walk the Moon's "Shut up and Dance" plays over the outdoor speakers as I watch Cole through the glass doors talking to a blonde girl inside. She's pushed up against him and he looks annoyed. As if he can feel my eyes on him, Cole turns his head and I quickly look away. "So, Grayson's hot," I say before taking a sip of the frozen nonalcoholic drink that Brice whipped up for Lexi and me. The guys are down at the beach while Lexi and I hang out at the bar with Brice.

"I love Grayson to death because he's Evan's brother, but he's a dog. A major manwhore."

I laugh. I like Lexi, a lot. Not once since she realized who I was has she asked me anything personal about my life or my dad. It's comforting and I feel like I can trust her, which isn't easy considering the lifestyle I've lived. But with Lucas on tour and Evangeline traveling all over the world, I could use some new friends.

And I just know in my gut that Lexi would be a good friend.

"So, you and Zach?" Brice asks with a smirk, leaning his forearms on the bar.

"What about us?" I smirk back.

Brice chuckles. "Sweetie, I could *smell* the tension between you two."

"Ewww!" I smack him in the arm and he laughs louder.

"It's true," Lexi confirms. "I saw the way he was looking at you. I think I might actually be pregnant."

This girl is a trip.

I snort, inhaling the frozen drink and ending up in a coughing fit. *Oh God, brain freeze.* "Zach and I were close until things got complicated." I pinch the top of my nose. *This shit hurts.*

"Girl, there is nothing complicated about Zach. He's a good dude, laid-back and—"

"Unless you piss him off," Lexi cuts in with a laugh.

I want to ask her what she means by that, but Brice keeps going. "He doesn't whore around like Mackenzie—no offense."

I wave him off. "None taken. Cole can be a handful, but he's family and I love him by default. And I've seen Zach with two different girls since I got here."

"Zach wasn't hooking up with Piper in the bathroom. I was just messing with him," Lexi defends. "I saw the expression on his face when he saw you. It's the same one he had on his face last night when I showed him the magazine cover. I didn't understand the look at first because I didn't know he knew you, but now it makes sense. He's got feelings for you."

"What about Lindsay?"

"He's *not* with Lindsay," Lexi says, waving me off. "Trust me."

A tall blonde girl walks around the bar and wraps her arms around Brice's waist. With her is Piper, the girl from the bathroom, and another girl with long reddish hair, pale skin, and a bored look on her otherwise pretty face.

"This is my sister, Brooklyn," Brice introduces and gestures to the other two girls. "This is Piper and Hannah." Brice says Hannah's name with a hint of disgust in his voice and I have to bite down on my bottom lip to stifle a laugh. "This is Jay." Brice gestures to me. "She's Cole Mackenzie's cousin. She just moved here from California."

Brooklyn smiles and I see a flash of recognition on her face before she says, "Hey," while Piper and Hannah exchange a quick glance before Piper says, "we met earlier."

"Where's your little friend Reagan?" Lexi asks.

Brooklyn snorts. "Reagan knows you're out here, Lexi. She's not dumb enough to come anywhere near you after last night."

"That text wasn't even meant for Evan," Hannah adds, rolling her eyes. "She's just trying to make Zach jealous."

Lexi and Brice shoot a glance my way while I sip my drink and keep my expression neutral.

"I don't care," Lexi says. "She shouldn't even have Evan's phone number in her phone. And she needs to get over herself. They broke up months ago and Zach doesn't give a fuck about her."

"Where's Brad?" Hannah asks, moving the conversation along.

"Beach," Lexi answers at the same time Brice gives a snarky reply of "Staying as far away from you as possible."

Hannah rolls her eyes again and stalks off toward the beach.

"Let me go after her before she starts her shit with Brad," Brooklyn sighs, before she turns to me and winks. "It's nice to meet you, Jay." Then she and Piper hurry after Hannah.

"What's up with Hannah and Brad, if you don't mind me asking?"

"She's Brad's ex," Lexi informs me, twirling her finger beside her head, the universal gesture for crazy.

"She's crazy all right," Brice adds. "She crawled into my bed last week, grabbed my dick and said, 'Let's see how gay you *really* are.'"

My jaw drops and I blink in disbelief. "You're *gay*?"

Brice winks. "I'm the rainbow sheep of the family."

I burst out laughing and tap my temple. "My gaydar must be off today."

"Can't really blame the girl, Brice," Lexi adds. "You're a hot piece of ass." She wiggles her eyebrows.

Brice purses his lips and waves a hand in front of him. "Don't I know it."

I laugh. "Who's Reagan?"

"She's Zach's ex. He dumped her for being a whore," Lexi explains.

I can't help but wonder if Reagan was the girl who answered Zach's phone that night.

"Were they together long?"

Lexi shrugs. "A few months. But she'd been after him since the party last summer." *I want to push for more information but I decide to leave it for now.*

"And she was texting your boyfriend, Evan?"

"Yep, and I confronted her ass last night. There may have been shoving and definitely some hair pulling." A satisfied grin stretches across her face.

"Man, I wish I'd been here to see that." Brice grins as well.

"HE LOOKS MISERABLE," Brice says with a laugh, nodding to Zach who is looking in our direction. The three of us are now sitting on the beach, looking out at the water where Zach, Lindsay, Cole, Brad, and a bunch of other people are sprawled out between two oversized floats anchored about twenty feet from shore.

I'm a little ticked off at Cole because he pretty much ditched me for Zach and Brad and the rest of his football friends. If it weren't for Brice and Lexi, I'd probably be sitting here on the beach by myself.

I snort a laugh. "Good." Zach's reaction to me being here wasn't at all what I expected. Oh, he was surprised all right—it was written all over his face when he came out of the bathroom with Piper—but he was clearly not happy to see me. I'm not gonna lie; I'm disappointed and a little hurt. It's only been a year since we've seen each other, but it feels like a lifetime ago. He's obviously pissed at me. Probably for blocking his calls. But what did he expect? He had a girlfriend.

"I don't get it," Lexi says as she picks up a seashell and inspects it before tossing it back into the water. "Why is he still out there with them if he's just gonna stare at you all day?"

I don't get it either. I'm not his girl anymore. Clearly, he's moved on. Lexi swears he's not with Lindsay, but he hasn't left her side all day.

"So, Jay," Grayson begins, dropping down in the sand beside me. He and Evan just finished playing a game of beach volleyball. Evan sits in the sand behind Lexi and pulls her to his chest. "How long are you here for?" he asks.

"I live here now," I reply. "Do you go to the academy too?"

Grayson smiles. "No, I graduated in May. I go to the University." He nods to my tattoo. "What's your tattoo say?"

I'm so lost in Grayson's hotness that it takes a moment to sink in that he asked me a question. "Oh." I lift my arm and look down at my tattoo. "It says, 'Trust your gut. Follow your heart. And never, ever settle for less than you deserve.'" I don't need to look at the tattoo to know what it says. I'll never forget my father's last words for as long as I live.

"What's that from?" Lexi asks.

I give her a sad smile. "My dad." Standing up and brushing the sand off my butt and legs, I say, "I need to check my phone. My mom's probably blowing up my phone," before walking over to my bag and pulling out my phone. Yep, I have eight missed calls. It's nearly four o'clock already, so I shoot off a quick text telling her that I'm heading home. She replies immediately with ***OK***. Then I text Bass asking him to pick me up, to which he replies, ***Be there in fifteen minutes***.

Funny how he didn't even ask me for an address.

"You leaving?" Grayson asks from behind me.

"Yeah, I think so." I pull my cover-up from my bag and slip it over my head. "The sun is kicking my ass and I'm kind of tired."

"Jay, are you leaving?" Lexi asks.

"Yeah. My, um...." *Shit, what do I call Bass without sounding like an ostentatious asshole?* "My ride will be here soon." I yawn. "Sorry, I didn't get much sleep last night."

"Didn't you come with Cole?" Evan asks.

I look out to the water just in time to see Cole with his head back, laughing. As irritated as I am with him, I don't want to pull him away from his friends. "Yeah, but he's having a good time and I already have a ride home." Turning to Brice, I ask, "Do you mind if I grab a water before I go?"

"Of course not," he says, holding out his arm. I like him. "Come on."

I slip my bag over my shoulder and snake my arm around Brice's before turning back to Lexi, Evan, and Grayson. "Are you guys coming?"

Grayson shrugs. "Sure."

Lexi grabs her bag off the chair and holds out her hand to Evan. "Come on, Ev."

Zach

"COLE, I THINK your cousin is leaving," Brad says, looking toward the beach. "Is she leaving with Grayson?" That gets everyone's attention, especially mine.

I lift my head to see Jay walking arm in arm with Brice toward the house. She's wearing her cover-up and her bag on her shoulder. Grayson is on her other side and Evan and Lexi are following them.

Cole shields his eyes with his hand. "What the hell?"

Cole turns to me with an amused expression. "It's killing you, isn't it?"

"You're a dick," I snap and glance over at Lindsay, who's been passed out on the raft beside me for the past thirty minutes.

"You're the dick. You barely said two words to her, yet you've been staring at her all fucking day like a creeper. Man up, Zach." Cole smirks as he pushes off the raft, dropping into the water. "I'll be back," he says as he swims toward the shore.

"What's going on with you two?" Brad asks.

I look over at Lindsay. "Nothing."

"Good to know." Brad laughs. "But I was talking about you and Mackenzie. You guys good?"

"We're straight."

"You should've talked to her," he tells me.

I shake my head. "This isn't the place for the kind of talk we need to have. I have too much to say and there are too many nosey-ass people here for that." I look over at Lindsay again. "Besides, I brought her here." I feel responsible for Lindsay. I've never known her to drink this much, but I'm sure it has a lot to do with Grayson being here. The asshole really did a number on her.

I nudge her awake. "Lindsay, come on. You've been in the sun too long, girl. Let's go get some water before you get dehydrated."

"Okay," she mumbles.

I slide off the raft into the water. Lindsay climbs on my back, resting her cheek on my shoulder. But when her lips graze my neck, I jerk upright, and blame it on the alcohol.

Cole is standing at the bar talking to Jay, who looks unhappy. Brice and Grayson are sitting on either side of Jay facing her, Evan and Lexi take up the remaining barstools. Evan sees me coming his way and stands. I drop Lindsay onto the vacated stool and grab two waters.

Passing one to Lindsay, I ask, "Where's your stuff?"

"Why? Are you trying to get rid of me?" she teases.

"No." I laugh. "It's getting late. I'm ready to head out. I was gonna take you to get something to eat before I drop you off. I'd be an asshole if I dropped you off sunburned, dehydrated, and starved."

As she takes a sip of her water, Lindsay's gaze moves to Grayson and Jay talking a few seats away. I don't miss the hurt expression that passes over her face.

I know how she feels.

"Hey," Lindsay calls out and all heads swivel in her direction. She points to Jay and says, "I don't know you, but I feel like I should warn you. He…" She points to Grayson. "…is a douchebag."

Jay's eyes flick to me and back to Lindsay before she replies, "Aren't they all?" A half smile curls one side of her beautiful sassy mouth. "But thanks for the heads-up."

Grayson laughs. "Ignore her. She's my ex, and, obviously, she's jealous *and* drunk." He jerks his chin to me. "You need to take better care of your girl, Zach."

Jay stiffens at Grayson's choice of words and that pisses me off.

I take a step toward Grayson, but Evan gets in my way, putting his hand on my chest. I don't get into fights. Ever. But I want to punch Grayson in his smug face. "She's not my girl." My gaze flicks briefly to Jay then back to Grayson. "But she is my friend. And she's right, you *are* a douchebag."

"My ride's here," Jay says, hopping off the stool and throwing her bag over her shoulder.

"You should've told me you wanted to leave," Cole says. "I would've taken you home."

"It's fine," she says, waving him off. But it's not fine. She's pissed. *I forgot how cute she is when she's pissed off.* I take a sip of my water to keep from smiling. "Stay and hang out with your friends," she tells him.

Grayson leans over and whispers something in her ear and I have to look away to keep myself tackling him to the ground. Cole watches me with a wicked grin on his face. The fucker.

"Thanks for keeping me company, you guys," Jay says. "Tell Brad I said thanks and that I'll see him around." She bends to hug Lexi. "Call me tomorrow. Maybe we can meet up for coffee. Evan, good to meet you, even though you maybe said three words to me." She laughs, sidestepping me and holds her hand out to Lindsay. "It was nice to meet you, Lindsay."

"You, too."

Jay throws me a glare and says, "Take care, Zach." Turning, she walks off and disappears into the crowd.

I liked it better when she called me Z.

"She seems nice," Lindsay says.

"I think she's a little pissed at you, Cole." Lexi smirks.

"What did I do?"

Brice scoffs and rolls his eyes. "It's a good thing you're pretty, Mackenzie."

Cole scowls. "What does that mean?"

"It means you're clueless," Lexi explains. "You brought her to a party where she knows all of two people and you just left her by herself." Lexi shakes her head at Cole, then turns to me and points. "And *you* acted like you couldn't stand to be near her, but you were staring at her all day."

"I was not," I lie.

"Yes, you were, Zach. You're supposed to be the good guy, but you're all jerks and now I'm pissed off," she chastises before turning to Evan. "Evan, Grayson, let's go. I've had enough sun for the day."

I look over at Lindsay. "You broke her heart, didn't you?" she asks.

I rub the back of my neck. "Actually, she broke mine."

TRACK 18:
SHE'S LOVELY
Jayla

My somber mood is lifted by the sound of Willow's squeals of laughter and the splashing of water. There's an instant smile on my face when I step out onto the pool deck and see Willow's chubby butt jumping off the side of the pool into Uncle Max's arms.

Mom, my grandparents, and Aunt Jessica are all sitting poolside while Uncle Max and Aiden are in the pool entertaining Willow.

"Boo, I didn't know you could swim."

She nods, her eyes wide with excitement. "Watch me." She twists out of Uncle Max's arms and drops face-first into the water. I snort as she stretches her floaty-covered arms out to the side and kicks her little chubby legs for about two seconds before popping her head up and gasping for air. Max pulls her back into his arms and Willow smiles up at me all wide-eyed as she proudly wipes the water from her face.

"Good job, Boo." I clap.

"Come wimmin wif me." She cheers and holds out her arms. There is nothing more adorable in this world than Willow Jade Mackenzie.

"Okay, I'll come swimming with you," I tell her, kicking off my sandals as I pull my cover-up over my head and toss it on the empty lounge chair. Mac Daddy mumbles something about me "leaving the house wearing that" and "hiring more bodyguards." I hold back a laugh and jump into the pool. The cold water feels incredible against my sun-kissed skin.

Aiden is grinning when I break through the surface and reach for Willow. "What?"

"Nothing," he says with a nervous laugh as his eyes zoom in on my chest.

"Eww! You little perv." I swipe my hand across the top of the water and splash him in the face.

"Aiden, she's your cousin," Uncle Max chides.

Aiden shrugs. "They're still boobs."

"Boobs," Willow parrots.

I roll my eyes and splash him again and Willow attempts to do the same.

"So, what are you doing back so early?" Uncle Max quickly changes the subject. "Where's Cole?"

"Where's Co?" Willow parrots again.

"He's still at the party. I didn't want to pull him away from his friends, so I had Bass pick me up. I had fun though. This is just a lot to take in, you know? Besides, I'm kind of tired. I didn't get much sleep last night and then being in the sun all day...." I shrug.

"Yeah." He glances over his shoulder at my mom and then back to me. "You've been living in a bubble for the past year—"

"You mean the past seventeen years?" I joke, even though it's true. It's no secret that Uncle Max didn't always agree with the way my parents sheltered me from experiencing life, going to school, and growing up with kids my own age.

Max smiles. "You're overwhelmed."

"This move." I wave my hand and gesture to the house. "And this house. It's all overwhelming."

Willow swims between us, kicking and splashing water in Max's face.

"Mimi and Jess did good, huh?" he asks, brushing the water from his eyes. "You like it?"

"I love it. They did an amazing job." I lift Willow and set her on my hip. She rests her head on my shoulder. "I really want to do something nice for them. To thank them."

"That's not necessary. We're family."

"How was the party, Jay?" Mom asks.

"It was fun. One girl recognized me," I tell her.

"How?"

I shrug. "She just did. Her name is Lexi. Her boyfriend is Evan. He plays on the football team with Cole."

"Evan Martinez." Max nods knowingly. "His dad is Jason Martinez," he explains to my mom before turning his attention back to me. "Lexi's a trip."

"She's hot," Aiden adds.

"You'll never believe who Lexi's mom is?"

"Who?" my mom asks.

"Diana Cooper."

Emerson's eyes go wide. "No shit?"

"Shit!" Willow parrots and Aiden laughs.

A CLICK AND a flash of light have me opening my eyes, startling me when I see Cole standing over me with his phone in his hand. "Are you taking pictures of me?"

"Of both of you." He turns his phone around to show me the picture.

"She's so cute." I give Willow a little squeeze and kiss the top of her head. "I gave the adults the night off so I could have her all to myself."

"Where's Aiden?"

"Your pervy little brother is spending the night at his friend Smith's house."

"He's a Mackenzie." Cole chuckles and sits on the coffee table, facing me. "Hey, I'm sorry about today."

I frown. "For what?"

"For ditching you. Lexi bitched me and Zach out after you left. I didn't do it on purpose. You and Lexi seemed to be getting along, so I figured I'd give you some space to make friends. And you were with

Brice. I knew he'd make sure no one messed with you. Anyway, I'm sorry."

"It's fine." I wave him off. "I was a little pissed at first, but I'm over it. It's not your job to babysit me. That's why I have Bass." I laugh.

"Did you have fun, at least?"

"Yeah. Brice is hilarious and Lexi is awesome. Evan is... quiet. Grayson is hot. And Zach's a dick, but whatever."

Cole laughs. "Watch out for Grayson. And Zach's just being a little bitch because he's pissed at you for blocking his calls. Why did you? What'd he do?"

"I don't want to talk about it right now?"

"Fine, but you guys need to kiss and make up."

"Yeah, I'll get right on that as soon as I don't feel like punching him in the throat. What time is it, by the way?"

He glances down at his phone screen. "Eight thirty. How long have you been asleep?"

"I don't know. Probably an hour." He raises an eyebrow. "What? I told you I was tired, and this little diva wore me out. What are you doing back so early?"

"Early? I was there all day. Do you have anything to eat? I stopped by my house to shower and change. I realized on the way over here that I hadn't eaten since I got out of practice. I'm starving."

"Grace made lasagna. There's plenty left over in the refrigerator. Help yourself." Willow burrows herself closer and sighs. I lift my head to look at Cole and smile. "She's so sweet. I want my own Willow one day. Do you think your mom would let me keep her for a few days?"

Cole scoffs. "It's not my mom you'd have to convince; it's my dad. Willow runs the show in our house. She's got Dad wrapped around her tiny finger. And you're too young to be thinking about babies." He gets up and heads to the kitchen.

"I said 'one day.' Not now, dork. But one day I want a big family."

He shakes his head and opens the refrigerator. "You're crazy. I hope you brushed her hair after her bath because it gets tangled. She's tender-headed, so she screams bloody murder whenever we try to brush it out."

I stare at his back as he pulls the lasagna from the fridge.

“What?” He quirks an eyebrow as he sets the dish on the counter. “Don’t believe me? Come to my house in the morning and see for yourself.”

I snort as Grace walks into the kitchen and takes the tray of lasagna away from Cole and shoos him out of the way.

“Your mom told me that, so I put some product in her hair which is supposed to prevent tangles and then I braided it. I guess we’ll see tomorrow if it works.” I lift one of her feet. “I painted her toenails. She threw a fit when I refused to paint her fingernails too, so we compromised on nail stickers.”

“You spoil her, but, for what it’s worth, I think you’ll make a great mom one day.”

TRACK 19:
OLD FRIENDS
Jayla

"EMERSON!" A PRETTY dark-haired woman steps out from behind the receptionist's desk and hugs my mom. "I'm so glad you're back. We have so much catching up to do."

"Definitely," my mom says before she turns to me. "Jayla, this is Lisa. She and I went to high school together. Lisa, this is my daughter Jayla."

"She's beautiful, Emerson," Lisa says, taking my hands and giving me a once over.

"And who are these gorgeous ladies?" a smooth voice says beside us.

I look over to see a guy who looks like he's in his mid-twenties with black hair styled to perfection, dressed in a dark grey tapered button-up rolled up to his elbows and tucked into a pair of dark fitted jeans, a black belt, and black Prada loafers.

"Xavier, this is Emerson, an old friend, and her daughter Jayla," Lisa introduces.

He smiles, showing off his perfect white teeth before gesturing to my mom and me. "So, which one of these beauties do I get to play with today?" He winks at Lisa.

Lisa smiles. "Xavier is my second-in-command," she tells us.

"Jayla, from now on Xavier will be taking care of you. Whenever you come in here, you only see Xavier."

I nod and smile at Xavier. "Got it."

Two hours later my hair is trimmed, my nails are manicured, my feet are pedicured, and Xavier is my new best friend. *Love him.*

"YOU ARE NOT taking pole dancing classes, Jayla," Mom argues as she pulls into the parking garage below Mac's. I don't really want to take a pole dancing class, but I love to get her going. *She makes it so easy.*

I turn my head to look out the passenger side window and stifle a laugh. Next door to Lisa's salon is a private dance studio called Juliette's. She teaches everything from ballroom dancing to pole dancing. You must be eighteen or have a parent's consent to participate in her classes. When we walked inside, Juliette's assistant showed us to the waiting room, which consisted of a couple of sofas and a one-way mirror. Juliette was in the middle of teaching a pole dancing class and I joked that I wanted to take that class. Mom's eyes nearly popped out of her head.

I swear, it's like she doesn't know me at all.

We settled for hip-hop classes on Wednesday evenings.

"You're lucky I even agreed to the hip-hop class."

Scoffing, I ask, "Why? I've seen the way you dance, hoochie mama."

"Oh, be quiet," she says and we both laugh.

Mac's is located in Pelican Cove, at the front of the island between the two drawbridges. There are also other restaurants, bars, shops, boutiques, restaurants, a movie theater, a bowling alley and luxury apartments. Everything is within walking distance.

I pictured Mac's to look more like a sports bar with memorabilia plastered all over the walls, but it's nothing of the sort. It's open and airy, giving off an island feel. Floor-to-ceiling windows overlooking the water. Tropical fans hang from the high ceilings. The floors are a shiny polished marble; the walls are light and the doors are a heavy wood with palm leaves carved into them. A circular hostess stand, made of the same wood and carvings, is positioned in the center of the room and behind it are two sweeping staircases leading to a second level. The place is extremely upscale.

"JJ!" Willow screeches, wiggling away from Uncle Max to run to me.

"Boo!" I reach down to scoop her up, settling her on my hip before kissing her on the cheek.

"Wook." She holds up her fingers to show off the nail stickers that I put on her last night.

"Wow! Who put these pretty stickers on your nails?" I ask, feigning shock.

Willow giggles. "You."

"Wow! I did a good job." Willow nods and I move to sit down at the table and settle her in my lap. "Uncle Max, this place is amazing," I say.

"Thanks," he replies. "But I can't take all the credit." He gestures to Mimi. "I'll show you around after lunch."

Willow pulls her thumb from her mouth and points to something over my shoulder. "Dat's Ahpee."

"Who?" I turn my head to see a girl about my age and height with a gorgeous shade of red hair approaching our table with a pad and a pen. She's wearing khaki cuffed shorts and a black three-button polo with "Mac's" embroidered in red on the left side. Her hair is pulled back into a messy bun, showcasing her bright green eyes.

"Harper," Max says before gesturing to my mom and making introductions. "This is my little sister Emerson, my niece Jayla, and this handsome sonofa—"

"Language," Aunt Jess warns.

"—gun is Bass," Max finishes.

Harper smiles. "It's great to finally meet you."

"Harper is new, but she's one of our best servers," Alex adds as he approaches our table.

Harper smiles at the compliment.

"Do you go to Heritage Academy?" I ask.

She nods. "I'm a senior this year."

"Me, too. Maybe we can hang out sometime. I met a lot of Cole's friends yesterday, but most of them were guys. They were nice—"

"Yeah, I'll bet they were," Dylan chimes in. "Harper hasn't met Cole yet," he adds with a smirk.

I snort. "You're kidding? You guys go to the same school."

Harper shifts nervously on her feet. "I know who he is, but we haven't actually met."

"Oh." *How has this girl managed to stay off Cole's radar?*

Harper takes our drink orders, then hurries off to the kitchen. "How has Cole never noticed her before? She's gorgeous," I say to Alex and Dylan.

He will today. Mark my words.

"They don't have the same friends," Dylan says. "Harper's a loner, a bookworm."

"She's a nerd," Aiden chimes in with a laugh. *The little shit.* Uncle Max and Aunt Jessica are going to have their hands full with that one. He's thirteen, gorgeous, and a smartass. *He's a younger version of Cole.*

"Oh, stop it, you guys," Aunt Jessica chimes in. "You're making Cole out to be a shallow jerk. His focus is on football right now, not girls."

Uncle Max shakes his head. Either Aunt Jessica is delusional or in denial.

Mimi lets out a loud laugh and that's my cue. I cup my hands over Willow's delicate ears just as Mimi shakes her head and says, "Jess, honey, he's an eighteen-year-old young man with the libido of a porn star. His penis is like a GPS permanently programmed to direct him to the nearest willing piece of ass within a five-mile radius."

The whole table erupts in laughter just as Cole swaggers in and over to our table.

"What's so funny?" he asks.

"Co!" Willow wiggles off my lap and hobbles over to Cole.

"Baby girl!" Cole scoops Willow into his arms and hugs her to his chest. "Sorry I'm late," he announces to the table as he pulls out the empty chair across from me and settles Willow in his lap. "Have you guys ordered yet?"

"Just our drinks. Why are you late?"

"I had something to do."

"Something or someone?" I joke, just as Harper arrives at the table with our drinks.

"Shut up," Cole mumbles.

I do my best to keep a blank expression, as does everyone else. Cole is distracted by Willow's toddler babble until Harper says, "Cole, do you know what you'd like to drink?"

"A fruit punch," he says and tilts his head to look up at our server. It takes everything I have not to laugh when Cole does a double take. "Who are you?"

Harper narrows her eyes and frowns at Cole's harsh tone.

I open my mouth but Willow beats me to it. "Dat's Ahpee, Co."

Cole chuckles at Willow before he looks back up at Harper. "Sorry. I didn't mean to sound so rude. Are you new?"

"Yes, but we've been going to school together since sophomore year. I'm Harper." She holds out her hand. "Nice to meet you, Cole."

"You too, Harper." Cole smirks, shaking her hand and raking his eyes over her from head to toe. Harper takes our food orders and once again hurries off to the kitchen, with Cole's eyes locked on her ass like a heat-seeking missile.

"What'd I tell ya," Mimi says.

Called it.

TRACK 20: MISSING YOU

Zach

"Brad, you're up," I say, poking him with the pool stick.

Brad, Justin, and I decided to blow off the parties and head over to Mac's for dinner and a few games of pool.

Brad turns away from the railing and says, "Mackenzie just walked in with the goddess."

I look over the railing to see Cole and Jayla heading for the stairs, Evan and Lexi right behind them. "Stop calling her that."

"Yo!" Cole hollers with his hands in the air, making his presence known to everyone as he makes his way over to me.

Cole taps the pool stick just as Brad is lining up his next shot. "Dude, come *on*," Brad growls and tosses it on the table. "I'm done."

"I thought you were going out to dinner?" I ask.

"We did," Cole answers before he turns his attention to a group of girls sitting at the high-top table in the corner and winks. *This fucking guy*. "Jay wanted to see Alex and Dylan play tonight."

Jay walks up and her eyes immediately zero in on the girls—who, by the way, are not here with us. Without acknowledging me, she says to Cole, "Lexi and I are going downstairs to get a table."

Cole nods. "I'll be down in a few."

Jay nods and walks off with Lexi. I watch her until she disappears from my view before shifting my gaze to Cole, who's grinning.

I shake my head.

"I told her yesterday that you two need to kiss and make up."

"Oh, yeah? What'd she say?"

"Something about punching you in the throat." He chuckles and walks off.

Jayla

LEXI AND I find a table near the stage and settle in while Alex, Dylan, and two other guys are setting up the stage." Harper comes over to our table. "Hey, Jay. You want a sparkling water?" she asks, remembering my drink order from lunch.

"Yes, please. With a glass of ice and a lime?" I wave my hand between the girls. "Do you two know each other from school?"

Lexi smiles. "Yes. Harper, right? I think we were in Mr. Fritz's fourth period math class together last year."

"Yes, that's right." Harper nods and smiles. "Would you like something to drink?"

"I'll have what she's having," Lexi says, jerking a thumb at me.

"Sure thing. Be right back."

Harper walks off and Lexi turns to me. "I've always wondered about her. She's so pretty, yet I've never seen her with a guy. She never ate in the dining room with the rest of us or went to any of the parties. I think I saw her a few times at the football games last year, but I don't think she has many—if any—friends." She shrugs. "Not that I have many friends either. All of my friends are Evan's friends."

I frown at that bit of information. "What about the girls you introduced me to at the party yesterday?"

"They're Ashton's friends, not mine."

"Who's Ashton?"

Lexi snorts. "Ashton Grant. She used to be my best friend until she and her gold-digging mother moved into our house and took over my life. Now we barely tolerate each other."

"So, your dad is married to her mom?"

"God, no. My dad is an idiot for moving her in, but he's not stupid enough to marry her. I think he only did it because Ashton and I were close and he thought her mom would be a good fit, but Ashton's mom is a fake bitch. It's funny how people change when they win the lotto."

"She won the lotto?" I'm confused.

"She did when she hooked my dad." She rolls her eyes. "And, of course, he's never around to see the way she really treats me. I can't stand her, so I stay at Evan's a lot of the time."

"That sucks. Have you talked to him about it?"

She lifts a shoulder. "Nah. She makes him happy, so I just stay out of the way."

"Wow, Lexi. I'm sorry. My dad wouldn't go anywhere without me and Mom. That's why I was homeschooled my whole life. And if it makes you feel any better, I only had two friends growing up. Now they're both busy with their own careers, traveling all over the country. I could really use a friend or two." I give her a wink and she smiles. "And I'm sure Harper could use a friend or two."

Lexi nods. "Definitely."

"HEY, EVERYONE," ALEX greets the bar patrons. "Thanks for coming out tonight. I want to introduce you to a member of the Mackenzie family. Come on up here, Jay."

I look over at Lexi and she smiles, giving me a little push. "Go."

I shake my head and look around the table. Evan and Cole are with us, along with Brooklyn, Piper, Hannah, and Ashton, who is perched on Cole's lap, like a queen.

I like Brooklyn. She's a year younger and a grade below the rest of us, but she's much more mature than the company she keeps. And she's down to earth, like all the Manning kids I've met so far. Piper is quiet and seems to go along with whatever her friends are doing. Hannah is an asshole. She's rude and snarky to everyone, as if she just hates everything and everyone around her. Ashton is self-absorbed and only interested in Cole. I keep my thoughts to myself because I'm the new girl and I'm not here to stir up any shit. I don't need the negative attention.

"Go, Jay," Cole urges.

"Fine," I mumble, pushing my chair back from the table and heading to the stage. I hear Hannah say, "Why is she going up there? Can she even sing?"

And Cole replies with, "Shut up, Hannah."

"Everyone, this is Jay," Alex says into the microphone and a round of applause rings out. "Feel like singing something?"

I give a half smile. "Do I have a choice?"

Shaking his head, Alex smirks. "Nope."

I look over my shoulder and wink at Dylan before returning my attention to Alex. "Okay, but I get to pick the song." I walk over to the side of the stage, grab a tambourine, and move back over to the microphone.

Zach

BRAD, JUSTIN, AND I finish our game of pool and head downstairs just as Alex calls Jay up to the stage. Ashton, Hannah, Piper, and Brooklyn are at the table. Thankfully, no Reagan.

Brad takes Jay's empty seat while Justin and I grab two chairs from a nearby table just as Jay taps a tambourine to her side and Alex strums the guitar.

"Oh, my God," Brooklyn squeals at the same time Lexi shouts, "I love this song!" Both girls jump out of their chairs and haul ass to the small dance floor in front of the stage.

"Wait for me," Ashton calls out and Piper follows. Hannah leans back in her chair with her arms crossed because—like I said—she's a bitch. Just about every female moves to the dance floor and begins singing and dancing along with Jay.

"This song sounds familiar," I say.

"It's Adele," Hannah informs me in a snarky tone. "They play it on the radio like twenty times a day." She rolls her eyes.

I hope they get stuck.

Maybe then I'll enjoy looking at her.

"So, does Brooklyn," Brad adds. "She's got it on replay. I heard it four times in a row in the car the other day." Brad smirks at me and says, "Your goddess has a set of pipes on her."

"His what?" Justin asks.

I say, "Nothing," at the same time Brad says, "I meant *the* goddess. Not *his* goddess." He smacks himself on the forehead.

Cole laughs and leans forward with his forearms on the table. "You ain't heard nothing yet. She's really good." He looks over at me. "Goddess. Really?"

I jerk my thumb at Brad, which is all the explanation he needs.

TRACK 21:
IN MY DREAMS
Jayla

I CAN'T SLEEP.

Rolling to my side, I lift my phone from the nightstand and check the time. Twelve thirty. *Ugh.*

Tossing the covers back, I slide out of bed and make my way over to the French doors leading to the balcony. I punch in the four-digit code on the alarm panel and step out on the balcony into the humid air. The air is so thick, it's not five minutes before I feel like I need another shower. And the mosquitoes are no joke.

I spot a familiar figure standing alone on the dock facing the water. Turning around, I head back inside, grab a long-sleeved T-shirt and a pair of yoga pants and slip them on over my tank and sleep shorts. Sliding my bare feet into a pair of flip-flops, I skip down my balcony stairs to the path leading to the dock.

"I guess I'm not the only one around here who can't sleep," I say, snaking my arm around Bass's waist. Bass lifts his big arm and wraps it around my shoulders, tucking me closer to his side. I tilt my head back to look up at him. Even in the shadows of the moonlight, I can see the pained expression on his face. My heart sinks. "What's wrong, B?"

"Nothing, Princess." Bass smiles, but it doesn't reach his eyes. "I was just thinking."

"You're sad."

He nods slowly. "Yeah." He sighs. "I am."

I rest my head against his chest. "I miss him, too." I turn to stare out at the lake. "Do you think he would've liked it here?"

"I do," he says, pressing a kiss to the top of my head before turning us around and guiding us back to the house. "Come on. It's late and you have school tomorrow."

"B, will you do me a favor?" I ask, pausing to look up at him.

"What's that?" He smiles again, but this time it's real.

"Will you get a life?" I smile and bite down on my bottom lip. Bass's eyebrows draw inward. "Just hear me out," I begin. "You've been taking care of us for a long time. It's time you find someone to take care of you. You're still young and handsome. Mom has a pretty friend named Lisa she could hook you up with." I wiggle my eyebrows. "I'm not saying I don't need you anymore because I'll always need you. You're one of the most important people in my life and the closest to a father that I have now, besides Uncle Drew, but he isn't with me twenty-four seven like you are. Now that I'll be busy with school and dance classes on Wednesday nights, you'll have more free time to live your life instead of babysitting me."

"That was a mouthful, Princess." He chuckles. "And I'm not babysitting you. It's my job to take care of you and to protect you," he states in a firm tone. "It's what Marcus wanted."

"I know, B, but we're not in LA. I don't think we need to worry about the stalkarazzi jumping out from the bushes. Besides, I'm not a celebrity."

Bass gives me a look.

"I'm not," I insist. "Not really." He raises his brows. "Okay, fine," I growl. "You mentioned something the other day about hiring additional security. I don't think we need it but if it will give you break, then I'm okay with it."

Bass nods. "Well, if I'm gonna get myself a life, you'll need it." He chuckles. "We'll see how things go first. Come here." He pulls me to his chest. "I love you, Princess, but you're not calling the shots when it comes to protecting you. You'll get your space, but give me some time, okay?"

"Okay."

He releases me and we walk to the house in a comfortable silence, only the chirping of crickets and croaking frogs echoing in the darkness.

I'm completely lost in my thoughts when I hear a fluttering sound, like a helicopter in the distance.

But the fluttering sound gets closer to my ear. Before I realize what the hell it is, something lands on my neck and crawls up the side of my face.

Something with too many friggin' legs.

"*Aaaaah!*"

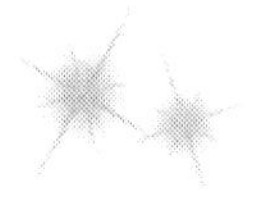

EVERY LIGHT INSIDE and outside the house flicks on at the sound of my scream. Two men appear out of nowhere and come running toward me. *What the hell?* It doesn't escape my attention that they're dressed the same as the GI Joe guards at the security gate.

"She's okay," Bass calls out—more like laughs out—from behind me. I sprint through the back door and into the kitchen, swatting at my neck, hair, and clothes.

"What happened?" my mom shrieks as she runs into the kitchen. Her eyes are bugging out as she reaches for me, grasping my shoulders to look me over.

I can only imagine what she's thinking when she sees my disheveled appearance. Half of my hair has fallen from the hair tie and probably looks like a couple of rats got to it. My clothes are ripped. I've scratched my neck, which I'm pretty sure is bleeding right now. I might've even punched myself in the face; my lip feels a little swollen and I think I taste blood in my mouth.

"She's okay," Bass chokes out through a laugh from behind me. He leans against the island in the kitchen. "She...." Laugh. "A bug...." Laugh.

"It's not funny, B," I pout.

"I'm sorry, Princess, but that shit was *so* damn funny." He laughs again, wiping his eyes. "Em...." Laugh. "I don't even think her feet touched ground."

He's right about that.

I turn to face my mom. "I was attacked by a flying roach," I screech, shuddering. "It crawled on my face and then fell down my shirt." I shudder again. Just the thought of it crawling on me.... *Bwah!*

Mom's lips roll inward between her teeth, clearly fighting back her own laughter. Her eyes sparkle with amusement as she gives me a once-over, taking in my appearance. "It looks like it."

I narrow my eyes in warning but it's too late. A loud laugh rips from her throat as she leans against Bass, prompting his laughter to continue and urging the rest of the people who've joined us in the kitchen to start laughing.

"I'm glad you all find my traumatic experience hilarious." I raise an eyebrow and turn to B. "We'll see how it goes, huh?" I gesture to the two dudes standing in my kitchen who are trying not to laugh. "It looks like you've already made that decision." I'm not sticking around for an explanation. Bass can explain when I'm ready to speak to him again.

I turn on my heels and stomp toward the stairs, pouting like a child. "I'm going to take another shower." *Or three.* "You're all fired," I call over my shoulder, which earns me another round of laughter. "Except Grace," I add. "She feeds me."

I OPEN MY eyes when Justin Timberlake's "Can't Stop This Feeling" starts playing from the small round speakers in the ceiling. My bedroom door swings open and Mom dances her way into the room, holding her cell phone as a microphone. I believe the only way that phone will ever leave her hands is if she has it surgically removed. She dances her way over to my bed, climbs on top of the mattress, and proceeds to sway her hips to the beat, shaking me awake. My mom loves her some JT.

A minute later, Bass dances his way into my room. Of course, he doesn't jump on my bed because his big ass would break it. Mom leaps onto his back and they dance their way out of my room.

Freaks.

I groan as I toss the covers back.

I feel like crap.

I tossed and turned the entire night because I kept feeling like I had bugs crawling all over me. I shudder at the thought. And I haven't forgotten about them all laughing. I mean, come on. It was a flying roach. That's just freaking gross. The only upside to the bug attack was that I forgot about starting my first day of high school.

Until now.

I'm not particularly shy, but I'm out of my element here, my comfort zone. But I'm also nervous and excited to see the work of the Mayhem Foundation.

The school uniforms are the basic navy and green plaid skirt, white oxford, a tapered navy blue blazer—which is only required during the cooler months or special assemblies—navy knee socks and navy spanks bottoms, like the cheerleaders wear under their skirts.

Fridays are spirit days, which means we can wear whatever we want if it's within the dress code.

Dressed in my uniform, I slip my feet into a pair of navy Tory Burch ballet flats and make my way into the bathroom. I keep my makeup minimal, brushing on a coat of mascara and swiping on nude lip gloss. My hair is pulled up into a high ponytail and I finish off with diamond stud earrings and necklace, my watch, and my diamond "Love" bracelet, which never comes off.

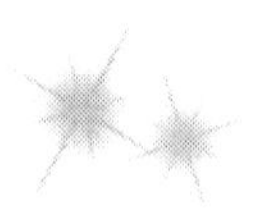

MOM IS AT the counter drinking coffee and looking at her phone. Grace is at the stove, swaying her hips to Shawn Mendes' "Stitches."

"Look at my girl, Grace," Mom says as I walk into the kitchen. "Doesn't she look adorable in her uniform."

Grace turns away from the stove to take in my attire. I give her a little twirl. "Good morning, Grace."

"*Hermosa*," she says with an affectionate smile. Grace speaks fluent English, but every so often when she gets excited she busts out the Spanish.

I drop a kiss to her cheek as I take a coffee mug from the cabinet. I'm not one of those people who needs coffee to function, but after the night I had, I'm going to need the caffeine today.

"Are you ready for your first day of school?" Grace asks excitedly.

"I'm nervous about school, but I'm really excited to see the new Project Mayhem building." I lean back against the counter, gripping my coffee with both hands.

"It's called the performing arts building," Mom corrects me.

Meghan Trainor's "All About That Bass" starts playing and right on cue Bass slides into the kitchen and starts breaking it down. I snort and almost choke on my hot coffee. Morning dance parties used to be the norm for us back in California, before my dad's health took a turn for the worse.

"B, can you believe our girl is going off to school?" Mom asks.

"Good morning, Princess." Bass kisses the top of my head as he reaches past me for a coffee mug.

I roll my eyes and move over to the island. "You guys act like this is my first day of kindergarten or something."

"No, but it's still a big deal. For you *and* for me."

"And me," Bass says, turning to lean against the counter.

"Me, too," Grace chimes in as she sets our breakfast platters in the middle of the island.

I grab a plate and load it up with bacon and blueberry pancakes. *Mmm.*

"It's going to feel weird not having you around for seven hours a day." She scrunches her nose, almost as if she hadn't thought this through. "I'm gonna miss my little girl." She pushes out her bottom lip.

I swear, if she starts crying I'm gonna whip one of these pancakes at her head.

"Are the skirts supposed to be that short?" Bass asks, eyeing my skirt over his mug.

I roll my eyes and stuff a pancake in my mouth as I move over to the barstool.

"That's the uniform, B. She's just got long legs."

"Besides, I'm wearing these." I stand up and lift my skirt to show him the spanks.

"Jayla!" Mom laughs as Bass sputters and covers his eyes.

"Chill, B. These things cover more than my bikini bottoms, and probably my running shorts. These are what the cheerleaders wear under their skirts."

Bass shakes his head and looks down at his watch. "We need to get going, Princess. You're supposed to meet Principal Avery at seven thirty."

I look down at my watch. Seven fifteen. "Crap. I'll meet you in the car." I stuff one last pancake in my mouth and grab a strip of bacon on my way out of the kitchen before heading back upstairs to brush my teeth and grab my bag.

Climbing into the passenger seat, I pull on my seat belt and search for a decent radio station as Bass backs the Denali out of the garage and eases down the driveway. The Calling's "Wherever You Will Go" is playing on one of the local Top Forty stations, bringing an instant smile to my face. I glance sideways at Bass to see him pressing the volume button on the steering wheel. My dad loved this song; he performed a cover on the new *Jaybird* album.

"I was thinking we could go car shopping after school," Bass suggests.

"Is this your way of apologizing for laughing at me last night, after I was attacked by that vicious, flying beast?"

Bass guffaws. "I've never seen you run so fast."

I twist my lips to the side to hide my smile. "How about I make it easy on both of us? I liked driving dad's Range Rover, so if you can find me one in white, fully loaded, with a good radio, I'll be a happy girl. I don't care about rims and all that. I'll leave that up to you."

"Well, that was easy. I'll make some calls."

TRACK 22: NEW KID IN TOWN

Jayla

BASS DROPS ME off in front of Heritage Bay Academy. It's a two-story, red brick building lined with windows across the front. The only way in is through the double doors which lead to the office.

"Do you want me to walk you in?" he asks.

I breathe out a laugh. "You're kidding, right?"

Bass arches a brow telling me he's not kidding and I laugh again. "No, I don't want you to walk me in, B. I told you, this isn't kindergarten." I lean over the console and kiss him on the cheek, before grabbing the door handle. "I'll be fine. See you this afternoon. Love you. Mean it." I hop out of the Denali and pull my bag over my shoulder. Shutting the door, I turn and head for the office.

Principal Avery asked that I arrive early enough to pick up my schedule and parking sticker and to give me a quick tour of the new performing arts building.

I walk into the office and see a petite middle-aged woman, with a short blonde bob, seated behind a desk on the opposite side of the counter. Patty Avery is engraved on the brass nameplate situated in the center of her desk.

"Good morning," I greet her with a smile. "I'm Jayla Ki–Mackenzie. I'm supposed to meet with Principal Avery this morning."

"Oh, my goodness, Jayla," she coos, pushing back her chair to stand. "Come on in." She waves me in through the open space of the counter. "It's so nice to finally meet you." She extends her hand to me. "I'm Patty Avery, Principal Avery's wife, but everyone calls me Mrs. Patty." She cups her free hand over our joined ones. "I've heard so much about you from your grandparents. I feel like I already know you. I don't think there's a picture of you that I haven't seen since the day you were born. I'm surprised Ella didn't throw a parade when you arrived in town."

I laugh lightly. *She's sweet.*

"I'll let David know you're here."

"I can hear you, Patty," a male voice calls out from the office just behind her desk. "Show her in."

Principal Avery stands up from behind his desk and smiles, extending his hand to me. "Good morning, Jayla, I'm David Avery, but everyone calls me Principal Avery," he jokes, repeating Mrs. Patty's words. I laugh quietly. "As Patty said, it's nice to finally meet you. Please have a seat." He gestures to one of the two leather chairs positioned in front of his desk.

"I understand you were homeschooled," he states, clasping his hands together and resting them on top of his desk.

"Yes, sir. My mom homeschooled me."

"Well, you had a good teacher. Emerson was one of my brightest students. Class president, head cheerleader, senior planning committee, and anything else she could squeeze into her schedule. Emerson was a smart girl." He chuckles again.

"Yes, I know."

"So, are you ready to see the new performing arts building where Project Mayhem will come to life?" he asks, standing from behind his desk and moving toward the door. I give Principal Avery an enthusiastic nod and follow him out of his office to the new building.

"As you probably already know, this year we'll start off with a smaller class of ten students including yourself, in addition to the existing students in the marching band," he explains as we make our way inside. "The cheerleading team falls under our sports department, but the dance team will also fall under the umbrella of the performing arts. We hired two additional, extremely qualified music and performance instructors who come highly recommended." He winks.

The performing arts building is located at the back of the school next to the gym. Inside the two-story building is a small common area with hallway on each side and two sets of double doors straight ahead, which lead to an auditorium. One of the classrooms, on the bottom floor, is designed for the dance team, with two of the four walls covered in mirrors, and a locker room at the far end. Another room houses the band instruments with an adjoining room for practice. On the second floor, there are classrooms designated for the drama club, an art studio, and a darkroom for photography.

"I wish my dad were here to see this," I admit.

Principal Avery leads me back down to the auditorium to another set of doors. "I was saving the best room for last." He opens the door and swings his hand, gesturing for me to step inside. "Welcome to Project Mayhem."

"YOU'RE KIDDING ME, right?"

"You can call me Mr. Alex." Alex smirks. "We're not that formal around here."

Alex is my new teacher. *Highly recommended, my ass.* This has Marcus King written all over it.

Principal Avery chuckles. "I'll leave you two to go over the specifics. If you need anything, Jayla, just come to the office. Welcome to Heritage Bay Academy. Enjoy your first day." He nods and leaves.

I turn to Alex. "How come you didn't tell me?"

He laughs. "I wanted to surprise you. I knew you'd probably be a little nervous about your first day, so... *surprise*!" He makes a surprised face, holding up his hands and wiggling his fingers. I burst out laughing because that was *so* not an Alex move. I can't wait to tell Evangeline that one.

This is going to be an interesting class.

Crossing my arms over my chest, I lean against one of the desks in the front row and ask, "Did my dad set this up?"

Alex lifts his shoulders. "He might have put in a good word for me, but I still had to apply for the job, interview, and go through the same hiring process as all of the other teachers."

"Won't it be weird being my teacher? We're practically family. And with us going on tour next year?"

Alex laughs. "We both know you don't need a teacher. Marcus was the best teacher to both of us and Principal Avery knows that too, but you should still be here. Look at it is this way. The Mayhem Foundation was Marcus's baby, and Project Mayhem is yours. Think of it as hands-on research. You get a front row seat to see how this program works and what doesn't. You'll be working alongside your peers, working with true raw talent, and that's the best kind. You might even find a few diamonds in the rough. Just remember that when we're in here, I'm the instructor, so lead by example. This is win-win for both of us."

"Fair enough." I shrug.

Alex smirks. "You're going to give me shit, aren't you?"

I laugh. "Nope. I'm going to be teacher's pet, Mr. Alex."

He huffs out a laugh. "Welcome to Project Mayhem, Miss Mackenzie."

TRACK 23:
BACK OFF
Zach

"*PSSST*. ZACH," DEREK the douchebag whispers loudly from two seats over. Derek is one of my teammates and he gossips more than a girl.

Tipping my chair back on two legs, I look over at him. "What?"

"Lindsay Miller?" He wiggles his eyebrows. "You hit that?"

See?

I shake my head and my attention falls on the girl sitting between us—Kali, a cheerleader, I think—who is looking at me with raised brows.

I frown. "What?"

She winces. "Nothing," she says softly before picking up her backpack and moving to the empty seat in front of me.

I'm an asshole.

"Hey," I say, and she glances at me over her shoulder. "Kali, right?"

"Yeah," she replies before turning in her seat to face me. "I wasn't trying to be nosey, but it's kind of hard to mind my own business when you two are talking over me."

"Sorry." I shrug.

"No worries." She smiles sheepishly and turns back around in her seat.

"Bro, how about Mackenzie's cousin?" Derek continues, shaking his head. "That girl is fine as *fuuuck,*" he drawls. "Mackenzie threatened my balls if I didn't stay away from her."

I laugh under my breath. If Cole hadn't threatened his balls, I would've.

Dex chuckles. "She's pretty. Got a nice ass and titties, but she's too skinny for me."

"You mean she's too skinny for your big ass," Derek says and Dex flips him off.

Mr. Baxter breezes through the door carrying a briefcase in one hand and a Starbucks in the other. "Good morning," he greets us, taking seat behind his desk. "Welcome back. I hope everyone had a nice summer. I expect the announcements will be exceptionally long this morning. Go ahead and make yourselves comfortable, but not too comfortable. I don't want any snoring, or drool on my desks."

"I'M STARVING," COLE says as he sets his tray down on the table and straddles the chair beside me.

"You're always starving," Carter states.

"True," Cole agrees, twisting off the cap of his sports drink. "Has anyone seen Jay today?"

"No," we all say as Evan takes the open seat beside Brad.

"She's the hot topic of the day," Evan tells us as he unwraps his sandwich. "Did you seriously threaten every guy in school to stay away from her?"

Cole smirks and his eyes flick over to me. "Just about."

Evan shakes his head and chuckles before taking a bite of his sandwich.

Cole shrugs, carelessly. "I'm protective of her."

"I don't blame you," Brad says. "I'm the same way with Brooklyn."

Ashton and her crew—Reagan, Piper, and Hannah—sashay their way down to our end of the lunch table. "Here we go," I mumble under my breath, but loud enough for the guys to heed my warning. Brad quickly drops his gaze to his food to avoid Hannah. I can feel Reagan's eyes on me, but I keep my attention on Ashton as she moves to stand beside Cole with her hands on her hips. *Let the shit show begin.*

Without looking up, Cole asks, "What's up, Ashton?"

"Oh, so now I'm Ashton? Not Ash? What's going on with you? You ignored my calls all day yesterday. You promised me you'd wait for me at your locker so we could sit together at lunch today. What's your deal?"

Cole slowly lifts his head and locks his wide eyes on me with a "what the fuck" look before he tilts his head to look at Ashton.

"Holy stage-five-clinger shit! What the fuck is *your* deal?" I bring my fist to my mouth to hide my smirk. "First of all—not that I owe you an explanation—I was busy with my family yesterday, and second, I didn't wait for you at my locker because I was starving." He jerks his chin toward the opposite end of the table. "Go down there and eat with your friends and let me eat my lunch in peace."

"Fine," she huffs and storms off, Piper following her.

"Bro, that was pretty harsh," Carter says with a knowing smirk. Because this is typical Cole and Ashton behavior. She bitches. He snaps. And later they'll be humping like rabbits. It's a sick form of foreplay in their weird relationship.

"She knows better than to come at me like that. She acts like I need permission from her to take a shit. She's not my girlfriend."

I shake my head. Ashton doesn't need a label. She's his girlfriend in every sense of the word. Despite what the others think, Ashton is the only girl Cole messes around with.

"Brad?"

"Not happening, Hannah," Brad says, eating his food while avoiding Hannah's glare. "I'm not in the mood for your crazy shit today either. Move along."

I lower my head to hide my smirk. *Go, Brad!*

And here we go. In five... four... three... two... "Zach, can I talk to you for a minute?"

I lean back in my chair and cross my arms over my chest. "Sure. Talk."

"I'd rather talk to you alone," Reagan says, looking around the table. "Outside."

"I already know what you want to talk about and it's not gonna happen because it's none of your business."

Cole lifts his head. "What?"

Reagan laughs once, rolls her eyes, and crosses her arms. "Whatever." She scoffs as she turns and walks down to the end of the table with the rest of her crazy friends.

"What does she want to talk about?" Cole asks.

"What do you think?"

"What's up with them today, anyway?" Brad asks. "Did they get a double shot of psycho in their Starbucks this morning or what?"

"Seems like it. Reagan's been up my ass lately." I shake my head. "I don't get it. We broke up months ago. I'm not getting back with her. I don't even like her."

"They've got their cheer panties in a bunch because all the new girls are taking the attention away from them," Evan says, picking up three fries at a time and dragging them through a mound of ketchup before shoving them into his mouth. "Like Jayla."

"And Harper," Carter says, jabbing Cole in the side with his elbow.

"You know that Harper has been at this school since our sophomore year, right?" Evan informs them.

"Is she the redheaded waitress from Mac's the other night?" I ask.

"Yeah, but someone hadn't noticed her until now," Carter replies. "Right, Cole?"

"Shut up," Cole says with a laugh.

"You got the hots for Harper, Mackenzie?" I ask.

Cole shrugs. "She's all right."

"She's not your type," I challenge.

Cole smirks. "She's female. She's my type."

"What about Ashton?" Evan asks.

"What about her?" Cole shrugs again. *He can't possibly be that dense.*

"Cole—" I start to say but Brad snags my attention, tapping my thigh under the table and jerking his chin, gesturing to something across the dining room. Following his line of sight, I see Lexi, Jay, and another girl I've never seen before, with wild curly brown hair, heading our way, and my friend Justin trailing behind them. "She's hot in a bikini, but damn, she's sexy as hell in that uniform," Brad murmurs under his breath earning a jab to his thigh. "Damn, who's the firecracker?" he asks.

I shrug. "I think she's new."

"Look at Justin," Brad says with a laugh. "He's like the hot-girl wrangler."

The commotion at the end of our table quiets to a low buzz as they approach our table. Justin takes a seat beside Carter, and Lexi squeezes in beside Evan, as Jay drops down in Cole's lap and throws her arm over his shoulder. Whispers, gasps, and snickers drift from the opposite end of the table.

"What's with all the glares?" Jay asks and then to Brad, she says, "They were all smiles at your party."

"Welcome to high school," Lexi jokes. "Ignore them. They're just a bunch of jealous bitches."

"Where's Brooklyn?" Jay asks Brad.

"She eats lunch with the juniors," he replies. "How's your first day going, Jay?"

"Great." Jay smiles and gestures to the new girl. "This is Cherry. She's in my Project Mayhem class. Cherry, this is my cousin Cole, Brad, Zach—"

"And this is my boyfriend, Evan." Lexi cuts in. "You've met Justin and that's Carter."

"Hey," Cherry says with a small wave. Cherry is pretty and tall, like Jay, with a head full of light brown, spiral curls, bright eyes and skin the color of coffee with extra cream.

Jay stands from Cole's lap. "Anyway, I just came to say hi. We've got to get back to class. We told Alex we were going to the bathroom."

"Aren't there bathrooms in the performing arts building?" Cole asks.

She smirks. "Exactly."

"What exactly is the Project Mayhem class? Is it like the School of Rock or something?" Brad asks.

"Or something," Jay replies. "Alex is no Jack Black. Oh, yeah!" She playfully smacks Cole on the arm. "Thanks for telling me about Alex. I mean Mr. Alex." She rolls her eyes. "I'm calling Weenie after school. I'm sick of that bitch keeping secrets from me."

"Who's Weenie?" Brad asks.

"My lying-ass best friend who lies."

"Alex wanted to surprise you," Cole explains. "Don't be a bitch about it."

"Shut up." She smacks him on the shoulder this time. "I'm not being a bitch. I love Alex. It's just weird having him as a teacher because he's practically family. Come on, Cherry. See you guys later." Everyone says their goodbyes as Jay turns and walks away with her new friend, Cherry.

I look around the table to see everyone watching me. Chuckling, I shake my head as I push my chair from the table and stand. "Will you dump that for me?" I point to my tray and, without waiting for a response, go after my girl.

Jayla

"WHAT'S UP WITH that guy Zach? Is he in love with you or something?"

"No." I snort. "I don't think he even likes me. We—" I start to explain but I'm cut off.

"Jay." I look over my shoulder to see Zach jogging toward us.

"Are you sure about that?" Cherry laughs as we stop and turn around to face him.

"Hey," he says, then looks over at Cherry and nods before bringing his gaze back to me. "Can I talk to you for minute?" His eyes flick between Cherry and me.

I look over at Cherry and smile. "Go ahead. I'll be there in a minute." Returning my attention to Zach, I ask, "What's up?"

“I’m sorry for being an asshole these past few days. You were the last person I expected to see at Brad’s party.”

“Yeah, I could tell by the look on your face when you came out of the bathroom with that Piper girl. You don’t seem all that happy about me being here.”

“Nothing happened with Piper,” he starts to explain, but I wave him off because he doesn’t owe me an explanation. “And you’re wrong,” he continues. “I’m happy you’re here. I think I’m just in shock.”

“Why?”

“Because we haven’t seen or spoken to each other in a year.” He shoves his hands in his pockets. “Why?”

I cross my arms over my chest and huff out a sharp laugh. “Talk to your girlfriend.”

“I don’t have a girlfriend.” The bell rings, indicating that lunch is over. Zach blows out a breath and says, “Listen, I have football practice until six. Do you think we can meet up after?”

“Why?”

“Because we need to talk, Jay. It’s been a year.”

“Fine. Okay. Where and what time?”

“How about Mac’s at seven? That’ll give me time to go home and shower first. Is that cool?”

I nod. “Sounds good.”

“Can I get your number from Cole?”

“It’s the same number.”

His mouth pulls to the side. “Then you’ll have to unblock me.”

The corners of my mouth curl up slightly. “I unblocked you six months ago.”

Zach’s eyebrows shoot up to his hairline. “I’ll see you at seven.”

TRACK 24:
HOW DOES IT FEEL?
Jayla

BASS AND I walk into the kitchen from the garage and find Mom sitting at the island with papers spread out in front of her. "Hi, honey. How was your first day?" she asks.

"Interesting," I reply, heading straight for the refrigerator and pulling out a large bowl of fruit. "What's all that?" I nod to the papers scattered across the counter.

"Work stuff," she says, gathering the papers together to put them in one neat stack. Then she pulls out a small familiar envelope and holds it out to me. "I was told to wait and give this to you after your first day of school."

My stomach bottoms out when I see "Jaybird" in my dad's handwriting once again scribbled across the front. "What are these notes about?"

Mom gives me a sad smile. "They're his way of being a part of the special moments in your life."

Only Marcus King would think to do something like that.

I carefully tear open the envelope and pull out the card inside.

> ***Jaybird,***
> ***I hope you had a good first day at school. I'm***

sure you were surprised to see Alex. I wish you could've seen his face when he found out he'd gotten the job and would be working with you on Project Mayhem. It means a lot that the two of you are working together on something so important to me.

Thank you.

Love always,

Daddy

Sweet, simple words. Yet, because they're my father's, I feel another stitch in my heart unravel.

"You okay?" Mom asks.

"Yeah." Sniffling, I slide the card back into the envelope and slip it into my purse. "The performing arts building is beautiful and I really like my teacher." I smirk.

Mom smiles, accepting my need to move on. "Alex was very excited about the job. He wanted to surprise you. We all think it's great that the two of you will be working together. And look at it this way, you'll get in some additional practice before the tour. It's a win-win."

"Everyone keeps saying that," I say with a smile as I pop a strawberry into my mouth.

"You don't sound too thrilled about it."

"I *am*. It just feels like there's more to it, that's all." I shrug. "I have this gut feeling you guys are keeping something from me."

"You're being ridiculous." She waves off my accusation. "Tell me about the Project Mayhem class."

"There are ten of us split into two groups of five. Today, we did mock auditions. Alex thought it'd be a good way to determine our strengths and weaknesses. He wants us to push ourselves out of our comfort zone to—" Our conversation is interrupted by the doorbell.

"Princess, that's for you," Bass calls out from somewhere in the house.

Mom and I shoot each other a confused look before we both head for the front door.

A man holding a clipboard is standing on the porch and beside him is one of the Joes. "Good afternoon. I'm Steve with Land Rover USA. I have a delivery here for Jayla King."

Peering over his shoulder, I see the brand new white Range Rover parked in the driveway. Squealing like a teenage fangirl, I brush past Steve and run over to the driver's side, opening the door. Sliding behind the wheel, I wrap my hands around the leather steering wheel, breathing in the new car smell as I take in the interior, black on black with a dark gray oak veneer finish.

A moment later, the passenger side door opens and Bass slides into the seat, holding the key. "I had this key custom made just for you. See this button?" He fingers a small red button on the key fob. "This is a panic button. It's connected to your security. If you find yourself in a threatening situation, just hold the button down for three seconds and your security will come to you."

"How very James Bond," I joke.

Bass grins. "So, what do you think, Princess?"

"I think you did good, B. And your timing couldn't be more perfect because I have somewhere to be tonight."

Zach

"HEY, YOU'RE HOME early," my mom says, turning from the sink to look at the clock on the microwave. "How was your first day back?" She picks up a bowl of veggies and shakes the water free before setting them on the counter.

"Fine," I reply, dropping a kiss on her cheek on my way to the fridge to grab a Gatorade. "Coach cut practice early." Twisting the cap off the Gatorade, I toss it into the garbage before chugging half the bottle down in one gulp.

"Oh." She nods as I hop up on the counter and pluck a carrot from the strainer. "I talked to Rebecca today." *Here we go.* Rebecca is Chelsea's mom and my mom's best friend.

"So? You talk to her every day."

"Smartass." She grabs another carrot from the bowl and tosses it at me, which I catch between my hand and chest and shove into my mouth. "And you're wrong. I haven't talked to her much because she's been busy helping Chelsea get settled in at school." She gives me a look.

My friendship with Chelsea took a shit last year after "the incident." It all started at the prom after-party when I caught Reagan and Grayson screwing in a closet. I left the after-party and went to Cam's. Chelsea ditched her date and came with me. Cam was in California—at the Mayhem Foundation charity dinner—so his house was free. I was planning to spend the night there with Reagan after the after-party.

Chelsea and I raided Cam's liquor cabinet and went down to the beach. We talked, laughed, got drunk, and hooked up right there in the sand. Stupidest thing I've ever done. *Besides Reagan.*

I knew it was a mistake and I regretted it immediately afterward. We both did. We agreed to keep "the incident" between us and pretend it never happened. But things were still awkward and tense. Our friendship hasn't been the same since.

"I planned on calling Chelsea this week," I tell her. It's the truth. I need to have a chat with my former best-friend-turned-backstabber. What the *fuck* was she thinking telling Reagan about Jay?

"I'm sure she'd love to hear from you. It's always nice to hear a familiar voice when you're in a new place," my mom continues.

She won't love hearing what I have to say.

"Chelsea is a big girl. I'm sure she's already made plenty of friends."

"Rebecca and I just thought…." She flicks her hand dismissively. "Never mind."

Seriously, Chelsea?

I groan and drag my hands down my face. "You thought because we hooked up one time—which was a huge mistake, by the way—that we'd fall in love or something." I shake my head. "I can't believe Chelsea told you."

"She didn't." She turns to me, leaning a hip against the counter and crossing her arms. "Rebecca did."

"Great." I throw my hands up. "Now Rebecca and Chris probably hate my guts."

"Rebecca doesn't hate you and Chris doesn't know." She turns back to chopping vegetables. "You're not seeing that Reagan girl again, are you?"

I shake my head. "No." I hop off the counter and turn to face her. "I can't force myself to have feelings for Chelsea just because you and Rebecca want us together. Let me worry about my own love life."

"Okay. I'm sorry. I wanted to know where things stood between you and Chelsea and I didn't know how to bring it up. Again, I'm sorry. Honestly, I just want you to be happy." She wraps her arms around me and squeezes me until I can barely breathe. She taps my chest and continues with dinner preparations. "I'm just glad you're not with that little slut anymore. I don't give a shit who her daddy is."

I laugh at her little jab at Reagan, but she's holding something back. "What else did Blabbermouth tell you?"

She raises her eyebrows in that way moms do when they're being serious. "Jayla King."

"Jesus Christ." I tilt my head back and pinch the bridge of my nose before bringing my gaze to meet hers. "I'm not talking about Jayla with you," I tell her, plain and simple.

"Why, not?"

"You know why," I reply, shaking my head as I turn and walk out of the kitchen.

My dad is sitting behind his desk, leaning back in his chair, most likely reading a legal document.

"Hey, Dad." I drop down in one of the two navy leather high-back chairs in front of his desk.

My dad looks up from whatever he's reading. "Hey." He smiles and sets the paper down on top of the open file before closing it. Leaning forward with his forearms on his desk, he clasps his hands together and rests them on top of the file. "Coach let you guys out early today, huh?"

"Yeah, he went easy on us today." I shrug. "First day of school and all. I'm sure we'll pay for it tomorrow."

"How was your first day back?"

"Strange," I say, tapping my fingers on the armrests. "She's here." My dad knows exactly who *she* is.

"I know." He nods.

"Mom knows too. Which is probably why she's trying to marry me off to Chelsea, again." I roll my eyes.

"Probably," he agrees with a laugh, shaking his head. "I never thought you and Chelsea dating was a good idea. Did you talk Jayla at school today?"

"Yeah, at lunch for about five minutes. On one hand, I want to be pissed at her—I am pissed at her—for ignoring me for an entire year, but on the other hand, I just want her. She's so beautiful and I don't mean just her face. Just... everything about her is beautiful. Honestly, I don't know why I bother getting so worked up over it. It's not like I could stay away from her even if I tried."

Dad chuckles as he leans back in his chair and claps his hands behind his head.

"I've been kind of an asshole to her," I admit.

"Don't do that, Zach. Just talk to her. Maybe you guys can be friends again."

"I don't think I can be *just* friends with her. I asked her to meet me later so we can talk."

"That's a start. Do whatever makes you happy. All I ask is that you keep your priorities straight. Your grades and football come before everything else. You got a lot riding on you this year, so keep your head on straight."

TRACK 25:
YOUR DEMISE
Jayla

WALKING INTO MAC'S, I spot Harper at the hostess stand and wave.

"Hi, Jayla," she greets me with a smile. "You by yourself?"

"Zach is supposed to meet me here."

"Okay." She smiles, grabs two menus from behind the counter and heads toward the dining room. "Follow me," she calls over her shoulder.

"How long have you worked here, Harper?" I ask.

"Just a few weeks." She leads me to a table in a quiet corner. "I'll bring Zach over when he arrives."

"Thanks, Harper."

Sliding into the booth, I pull out my phone and see a text from Cole. ***Where r u?***

At Mac's. I'm meeting Zach.

K. Good luck lol

I shake my head and smile.

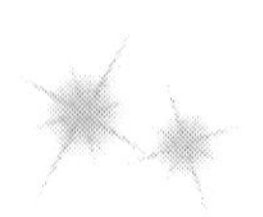

FORTY-FIVE MINUTES AND four texts later, it's clear that Zach stood me up. No calls. No reply to my texts. *I wonder if he did this as payback for blocking him?* If it is, then he's an even bigger dick than I thought.

"I take it he's not coming." I look up to see Harper standing beside the table.

"Guess not," I reply, leaning back in the booth and blowing out a breath. I can't decide if I'm pissed or hurt. "Are you off?" I ask.

"Yeah. May I?" She points to the empty booth across from me.

"Please do. I look pathetic sitting here by myself. Want to have dinner with me?"

"I could eat." For the next hour, Harper and I talk about nothing and everything while getting to know each other. I fill her in on my Zach drama and she listens intently, reserving judgement.

Harper is kind, but it's obvious she keeps people at arm's length. She's got her walls built up sky-high as if she's been through hell and back. I guess in a way she has. Her mom passed away just over four years ago and her sister died in a car accident a little over two years ago. Harper lives with her dad, but his job takes him out of the country for months at a time, so she pretty much lives alone and takes care of herself. I have so much respect for this girl and her strength. I might even hero-worship her a little bit.

My phone vibrates on the table and Zach's name pops up on the screen. I'm too pissed off to talk to him, so I send him to voicemail. A text immediately follows.

I'm sorry. Practice got out early and I fell asleep. Are you still at Mac's?

"Zach?" Harper asks.

I nod and hold up my phone. "He said he fell asleep." I snort. "Whatever." I roll my eyes.

"Do you think he's lying?"

"No... I don't know. I feel like I don't know him anymore."

"Well, you're here now, so maybe it's time to get to know him again. See if he's the same guy you fell in love with."

"Maybe." I sigh. "But he's not off to a very good start."

Zach

"ZACH," MY MOM whispers.

"Hmm?"

"Wake up," she says, a little louder this time with a hint of irritation in her voice.

"What?" I groan and reach for my cell on the nightstand, pulling it close to my face to check the time—8:15 p.m.

And four texts from Jay.

I'm here.

Where r u?

Hope ur ok.

U could at least text me back to let me know ur ok. Even if u stood me up on purpose.

Shit.

I try calling her first and, of course, my call goes straight to voicemail. So, I shoot her a text.

I'm sorry. Practice got out early and I fell asleep. Are you still at Mac's?

"You have company," my mom continues.

I roll to my back, swiping a hand over my face before looking over at her. "Who is it?"

"The slut." She curls her lip and flicks her wrist in a dismissive gesture.

I let out an irritated huff. "The slut" is Reagan, who is becoming a huge pain in my ass.

"Do you want me to tell her to leave?"

As much as I would love to let my mom go all bitch on Reagan, I need to put an end to this shit.

"No, I'll talk to her." Tossing the covers back, I roll out of bed.

"Zach—"

"It's fine, Mom," I toss over my shoulder as I head downstairs.

"Hey," Reagan says as I step out on the porch in a pair of basketball shorts and pull the door closed behind me. Her eyes move over my naked chest, up to my sleepy eyes and wild bedhead. "She could've told me you were sleeping."

"I'm up now," I reply through a yawn, running my fingers through my hair. Leaning with my backside against the wall near the door, I cross my feet at the ankles and my right arm over my chest to grip my left bicep. "What's up?"

"I was hoping to catch you after practice, but your Jeep was already gone when I got to the parking lot. You guys got out early today?"

I nod. "I'm not trying to be a dick, Reagan, but why are you here? What do you want?"

"To talk."

"If it's about Jay, I already told you at lunch that it's none of your business."

She rolls her eyes. "We never got things sorted out between us after we broke up."

"There's nothing to sort out. You cheated on me and I broke up with you. That was months ago, and since then you've been trying to hook up with my friends. So why are you here?"

"The truth is, I texted Evan by mistake. That text was meant for Cole."

"So, you admit you were trying to screw my best friend?"

"No. I was trying to get your attention. To make you jealous. It was stupid and I'm sorry. Cole went off on me at Brad's party and told me to stop texting him. I keep screwing up with you and I don't know how to make things right again. I made a mistake, Zach, and I'm sorry. Why can't you see that? I was stupid for listening to Chelsea and I know it's my fault. I messed everything up. Just.... Why can't things just go back to the way they were?" she cries.

I blow out a breath, deciding it's time to lay it all out for her so we can move on. If I plan on going after my future, I need to clean up my past. "Listen, I believe you're sorry and, no, you shouldn't have listened to Chelsea. I didn't go to California to 'chase after some girl who didn't want me'," I say, quoting her exact words. "But yes, I went there for Jay and her family. Honestly, I thought I was over her. I thought I was ready to move on. But then I saw her, and I realized I wasn't even close. And if given the choice, I would always choose her.

I'm not telling you this to hurt you. I should've ended things between us the second I came back from California. I liked what we had and I'm sorry if I made you feel used but it doesn't make it okay that you cheated on me." She winces.

"If you're so into her then why aren't you two together?" she asks swiping the tears from her cheeks.

I've been asking myself that for the past year. "I've known Jay for a long time. Things are complicated between us right now, but if there is a chance we can work through it and be together, then I'll do whatever it takes. You deserve to be with guy who wants to be with *you*. I'm just not that guy." I push away from the wall and pull her in for a hug. "I know plenty of guys who would love to go out with you. Just stay away from the ones with girlfriends." I chuckle and she smacks me playfully on the back. "Friends?" I ask.

"Friends."

TRACK 26:
A MILLION REASONS
Zach

"SUP," COLE SAYS, leaning against the locker beside mine.

"Not much," I reply as I reach out and tousle his hair. "Your hair looks pretty today."

"Asshole." He jerks his head back and does something with his fingers to make the strands stand up like a messy faux hawk.

He's such a fucking girl.

"Did you and Jay get your shit worked out last night?"

No, I made things worse. After Reagan left, I went back upstairs and tried calling her again and again, following up with several apology texts. She didn't reply. And we're right back to her ignoring my calls and texts. But on the bright side, she hasn't blocked me and I get to see her today. And every day.

"No, he stood me up," Jay answers, walking up to her locker, twisting the lock before flinging open the door, and blocking me from seeing her face.

Cole's eyebrows shoot to his hairline before he turns around to face her, putting his back to me.

"Jay," I begin just as Reagan walks up.

"Hey, Zach," she purrs. "I hope your parents were cool with me coming over last night." *Seriously?*

My eyes shift to Jay, but her face is hidden behind her locker door. Cole is saying something to her but I can't make it out. "What are you doing, Reagan?" I hiss.

"What do you mean?" She glances over her shoulder and then back at me. "I just wanted to tell you that I'm glad we talked and worked everything out."

I jerk my gaze to Cole, who's giving me a death glare over his shoulder. He shakes his head and mouths the word "dick" before turning back to Jay.

Jay slams her locker shut before they both walk away, neither of them glancing my way.

"Hello, Zach." Reagan snaps her fingers in front of my face.

"What?" I snap.

"What's your problem?" She cocks her hip with a smirk.

"You know exactly what my problem is. I thought we were cool. Why are you trying to ruin this for me?"

"I'm sorry."

"No, you're not. Stay away from her. And me." Slamming my locker shut, I storm off.

OF COURSE, THE universe hates me because when I walk into first period, there she sits. One row over and one seat up from mine. I could reach out and touch her, but I wouldn't dare. She'd probably rip my hand off and slap the shit out of me with it.

Instead of going straight to my desk, I make my way over to hers and drop to a knee so that we're eye level, even though she has her head down to avoid looking at me. "I didn't blow you off for her. She's—"

"Stop," she growls, holding her hand up and lifting her head, locking her angry eyes on mine. "I don't care what you do or who you do. Just leave me alone, Zach."

Mr. Baxter walks in carrying a briefcase and his usual Starbucks. "Good morning, everyone. Please take your seats."

"We'll talk later."

"Sure." She looks up at me with a fake smile. "Text me."

Oh, she's a smartass now.

TRACK 27:
BEG FOR IT
Jayla

"MMM. IT SMELLS good in here," I announce as I walk into Mimi's kitchen and find her pulling a pan of brownies from the oven. "Oooh, brownies!" I reach for one that's already cut and on a platter.

"No, don't eat those," Mimi snaps, making me flinch and toss the brownie back on the tray. "These are Mac Daddy's special brownies." She grins like the Cheshire cat and moves the tray to the other side of the counter. "You can have one of these." She points to the pan she just removed from the oven.

"What are special brownies?" I raise my brows. "Like pot brownies?" I'm only half joking because with Mimi, one can never be too sure.

"Damn!" She slaps a hand on the counter. "Why didn't I think of that?" She snickers. "Now that would be fun. But these are made with all the healthy stuff that Mac Daddy dislikes." She winks. "Got to keep my man healthy."

"He's a doctor. He should know better."

"He's also a man, sweetie." She gives me a look that says, "Enough said."

"A very lucky man," I agree with a wink.

"So, how is school going? I heard Alex is your teacher. That must be fun."

"School is good. The Project Mayhem class is my favorite one of the day."

"How are things going with Zach?"

"Not good," I admit before popping the last bite of brownie in my mouth. I haven't talked to him since our little exchange in class yesterday. "He asked me to meet him at Mac's for dinner Monday night and never showed up. The next day I found out he stood me up to hang out with his ex." I still can't believe he stood me up. Thank God Harper took pity on me and joined me for dinner. At least I got a new friend out of it.

"No," she gasps. "Zach? He's such a sweet boy."

I shrug. "He's not that sweet, Mimi. He's kind of a dick. He acts like he can barely stand to be around me and it's not because he's shy. I've seen him with three different girls since I got here." I shake my head. "I'm not into manwhores."

Mimi laughs. "Manwhore?"

I shrug again. "It's a—"

"Honey, I know what a manwhore is. His name is Liam Mackenzie."

I burst out laughing, nodding and pointing to her. "Liam would be so mortified if he heard you call him that." I make my way to the refrigerator for a bottled water. "I don't know, Mimi. Zach and Cole have this little clique of friends and I feel like an outsider. I don't know what I thought would happen, but I didn't expect Zach to hate me."

"Honey, Zach doesn't hate you. I'll tell you what I used to tell my kids. If you have something to say, then say it. If you want to know something, then ask. Don't make assumptions. Life is too short for 'would've, could've, should've.' If you want something to happen, don't wait for it. Make it happen."

"You sound like my father." I smirk.

"Marcus was a smart man." She winks.

Yes, he was.

"I appreciate the advice. I need to get going." Grabbing my purse, I pull it over my shoulder. "Thanks for listening, Mimi," I say, leaning over, kissing her on the cheek. "I wish I could hang out longer..." I look down at my watch. "...but my first pole-dancing class starts in twenty minutes." I snort and take off toward the front door as Mimi chases after me, whipping the hand towel at my butt.

Damn, she's fast.

"You better be joking," she calls to my back just as I yank open the door.

I smirk over my shoulder and answer her with a wink. Just as I pull the door closed, she calls out, "Smartass."

THE FIRST WEEK of school comes to an end, and Project Mayhem is off to a good start. It's only been a week, but things are going well, and Alex seems pleased. I know I am. Alex has split us up into two groups. In my group is Cherry, Olivia, Eric, and Jones. His name is Frankie Jones but he prefers to be called Jones. They're a talented bunch and they're eager to learn.

Cherry is a trip. She's beautiful with a head full of light brown spiral curls that bounce with each step, bright eyes, and a voice that sends chills up my spine. Olivia reminds me of a surfer girl with her white-blonde hair and cute little freckles across her nose. She comes off as shy... until you put a microphone in her hand. Eric is a fantastic singer, a boss on the guitar, and he's equally amazing on the keyboard. Jones has a great voice as well, although he just wants to play the drums.

We'll have to work on that.

Alex grades us by our performances. He issues a challenge and we perform. Today is the first pep rally of the school year to welcome everyone back to school and to kick off the first football game of the season against the Eagles. Our class has been practicing all week. Today we'll be performing alongside the marching band, dance team, and the cheerleaders.

Even though we have three classes together, I've pretty much kept my distance from Zach since our little exchange in class on Tuesday. I smile politely and I'm friendly in class when necessary, but I keep our interactions to a minimum. Even going as far as to eat lunch with my

Project Mayhem class in the performing arts building. Harper has been eating with me almost every day and sometimes even Lexi pops in for a while, which I'm sure probably drives Evan crazy. The guy can't be away from her for more than a minute.

Honestly, I think it's sweet.

Evan reminds me a lot of my dad and the way he was with my mom. I swear she couldn't be out of the room for more than five minutes before he was calling out for her.

Cole asks me almost every day to come eat with him at his table in the dining room. He's assured me that Zach didn't blow me off for Reagan, and though I'm still pissed Zach stood me up, I believe him. But still, Reagan's little stunt that day sticks in my mind, as if she'd done it on purpose to drive Zach and I further apart. As if she'd been doing it all along.

Either way, I'm not interested in getting tangled up with the mean-girl squad. In all honesty, smacking a bitch will only tarnish my sweetheart image, piss my mother off, and embarrass my father.

TRACK 28:
NOT WITHOUT YOU
Zach

JAY HAS BEEN keeping her distance from me all week, although she's not flat-out ignoring me. She says "hi" when we run into each other at our lockers or in class, but only if I say it first, and she doesn't make any other attempts to talk to me. When she comes into the dining room to get lunch, she'll stop at our table briefly, to talk with the guys and Lexi before she goes to the performing arts building to eat with her new friends. Sometimes Lexi eats with her. Pisses Evan off. I've given her space all week but after today, I'm done. We need to talk, or have it out. Whatever she chooses. But, either way, it's happening.

The first pep rally of the year usually starts out with Principal Avery making a few announcements before introducing the football players. Then the band performs, along with the dance team, while the cheerleaders get everyone pumped up for the upcoming game. It's been the same every year for a long as I can remember.

Apparently, the pep rally is taking place in the new building. The main area is set up like our old auditorium, but nicer. Much nicer.

"Well, this is different," Brad says, rocking back in the plush leather seat.

"Do you know what they have planned?" I ask, looking over at Cole.

Cole scowls. "How the hell should I know?" *Someone's bitchy today.*

"You gonna be able to play tonight, Mackenzie?" Brad asks.

Cole's brows pinch in confusion. "Yeah, why?"

"Because it sounds like you got your meriod."

"My what?"

"Your man-period," Brad explains. I grin as Cole flips him off.

Principal Avery walks out on stage holding a microphone. "Good afternoon, students and faculty of Heritage Bay Academy. On behalf of the Mayhem Foundation, welcome to our new performing arts building.

"This year, we're going to do things a little differently. As you know, we have a group of new and extremely talented individuals who have come to us through the Mayhem Foundation called Project Mayhem. These individuals have worked hard all week to perform for you, so I'm not going to stand up here and waste any more of their time. Please welcome the students of Project Mayhem, the Hurricanes cheer team, dance team, and marching band."

"Oh, I can't wait to see this." Brad chuckles.

Principal Avery walks off stage and that all too familiar chant from Queen's "We Will Rock You" begins. The curtain opens and the cheer team is on one side of the stage, the dance team is on the other, and Project Mayhem students are in the middle wearing jeans and school spirit T-shirts. *Stomp-stomp-clap… stomp-stomp-clap.* A skinny dude with spiky dark hair steps forward with a microphone in hand and starts singing the opening verse. Cherry moves to the front and sings along as the song rolls into Queen's "We Are The Champions."

"You know," Brad says, "I think Cherry might be my new favorite flavor."

Cole and I burst out laughing. "Dude, that was fuckin' awesome." Cole reaches over me and pounds his fist against Brad's.

As the song slows, the beat changes and Jay moves to the front of the stage, wearing a football jersey custom-made in her size with a number one on the front and "Mackenzie" across the back. She moves across the stage like a natural, bouncing around, commanding everyone's attention and singing about "crying to your mama" as the group behind her claps and sings along in the background. It's obvious she was born for this shit. I quickly glance over at Cole and see him watching her with a proud smile on his face.

From behind us I hear "Damn, that girl is fine. Those long legs wrapped around my head, those juicy lips wrapped around my—"

I turn in my seat, ready to rip the little shits a new one, but Cole beats me to it, pinning them with a death stare. "Say one more word about her and I'll put your asses on the permanently injured list before you can say the word varsity," he growls through gritted teeth. "You feel me?"

"Sorry," they all say at once. One of them continues, "Didn't know she was your girl."

"She's mine," someone growls and I freeze in my seat when I realize that someone is me. *What the hell?*

Turning back around, I direct my attention to the stage as Brad snickers beside me. Evan reaches over Brad and punches me in the thigh. Cole leans closer to my ear. "It's about time you got you manned-up," he says before leaning to look past me, pointing at Justin. "You owe me twenty bucks."

Assholes.

Jayla

THE LAST BELL of the day rings and I slip my notebook into my backpack. Alex tells us all we did a great job and to have a nice weekend. I flash a quick wave to Alex on my way out.

"You going to the game tonight?" Cherry asks, falling in step beside me.

"Yeah. Are you?"

She shrugs. "Maybe, if I can get a ride. My mom has to work tonight and she needs the car."

"I can give you ride."

"Or I can," Olivia offers. "I live closer to you and Carter invited me to his party after the game tonight."

"Thanks," she says with a smile. "I'll call you and let you know for sure."

"Okay. See you guys later," I say before heading toward the student parking lot.

As I cut across the courtyard, passing the guys' locker room, someone calls my name followed by a few wolf whistles. I laugh and wave to the half-dressed football players leaning against the wall outside the locker room. Tonight, the Hurricanes play their first football game of the season against the East Coast High Eagles.

"Jay," Zach says, falling in step beside me. "Hey."

"Hey," I reply, looking forward.

"You were pretty awesome up there today and the other night at Mac's, too. I had no idea you could sing like that."

"Thanks." I stop beside my driver's door and dig through my bag for my keys.

"Do you have any plans this weekend?"

"Just the game tonight. Why?"

"We still need to talk. You've been ignoring me all week, Jay. I'm sorry about Monday night. I know you don't believe me, but I didn't blow you off to hang out with Reagan. She's my ex for a reason."

"I believe you," I tell him and he grins.

"Maybe I can take you out tomorrow night," he suggests.

"Like on a date?" I ask, quirking a brow. "Do high school kids even go on dates?"

Zach shrugs. "Sure. Why not?"

"Okay."

"Really?" He rubs the back of his neck. It's Zach's tell when he's nervous or uncomfortable. He's been doing it for as long as I can remember.

"Yeah. But if you blow me off or pull that shit again, I'm done. I'm not getting in the middle of all your girl drama."

He chuckles and shakes his head. "I don't have girl drama. What are you doing after the game tonight?"

"I don't know. What does everyone normally do after the games?"

"We usually head over to Mac's for food, then go wherever the party is. There's always a party somewhere. Tonight, it's at Carter's house. Do you think your mom will let you go?"

I shrug. “I don’t see why not. Does he live on the island?”

“Yeah. He lives down the street from Cole.”

“Jay!” I look over to see Lexi running over to us. “Hey, Zach,” she says breathlessly before turning to me. “I’m so glad you’re still here. Can I catch a ride with you? I rode with Ashton this morning, but she has to stay for the game and Evan didn’t drive today.”

“I’ll see you girls later.” Zach kisses me on the cheek and jogs back over the locker room.

“Good luck tonight,” I call out. He turns around, jogging backwards, and winks.

“It’s about time,” Lexi murmurs as she makes her way to the passenger side.

“What are you babbling about over there?” I ask, tossing my bag in the backseat before hopping into the driver’s seat.

TRACK 29: BREAK THE SILENCE

Jayla

THE HURRICANES ANNIHILATED the Eagles 31-3. Seeing Zach in those tight-ass pants, doing his thing on the football field, does crazy things to my insides.

Evan sent a text to Lexi telling her to skip Mac's and go straight to Carter's house. Mom was surprisingly okay with me going to a high school party as long as I keep my phone on me and don't drink.

Cars are already lined down Carter's street when I pull the Range Rover up to the curb. Music and laughter drifts from the pool area as we make our way into Carter's backyard.

"There's Evan." Lexi points to a group of guys surrounding the keg.

Yeah, but where's Zach?

Lexi moves to Evan's side as Carter passes him a red Solo cup and I wave to Olivia. I don't see Cherry anywhere, so I guess she decided not to come.

Carter holds out a cup to me and I shake my head. "No, thanks. I'm driving."

Carter shrugs and throws his arm around Olivia. *Well, that was fast. But good for them.*

A few minutes later, there's some commotion before the crowd parts for the rest of the football team. I spot Brad, Cole, and Justin climbing on top of some patio chairs, pumping their fists in the air and chanting "Hur-ri-canes," and the crowd joins in. Hopping down from the chairs, the guys split up and go in different directions. Random people pat them on the back, raising a hand for high five or a fist bump as they shoulder their way through the crowd.

Zach works his way through the crowd, stopping to talk to a few people along the way, smiling and nodding politely and looking around. *I wonder if he's looking for me.* I wait beside Lexi and Evan for him to finish and make his way over to us.

But he doesn't.

A female voice calls his name and his head turns just as a blonde girl slams into his chest, making him stumble back a few steps.

I don't understand where this jealousy is coming from, but I really hate it. I've never been jealous of anyone before. I guess I never had a reason to be. *Until Zach.*

"Personally, I think green looks good on you," a male voice whispers in my ear. I look over my shoulder to see Grayson standing behind me, looking amused.

"What?"

Grayson jerks his chin, gesturing to Zach. "You're way hotter."

I don't have issues with my looks, but Grayson seems to think I need some reassurance. I snort and turn around to face him. "Thanks. What makes you think I'm jealous? Maybe I'm just curious. I've never seen her at school before." This is the third blonde I've seen Zach with. It makes me wonder if he just prefers blondes.

"Her name is Chelsea. She graduated with me last year. She and Zach are old friends." His gaze moves past me. I look over my shoulder to see that Zach has moved over to the outdoor sofa. Chelsea is squeezed between Justin and the arm of the sofa. Zach is perched on the arm while Chelsea chats animatedly with Justin.

But Zach's eyes are on me.

"What's the deal with you two?" Grayson asks.

I lift a shoulder. "Why?"

"Because he's looking at me like I stole his favorite toy. Just like he did at the party last week."

I breathe out a laugh. "While he was on a day date with *your* ex?"

Grayson smiles. "Yeah, that was awkward. So, is he trying to make you jealous or is he just being a dick?"

"Well, since he's the one who invited me, I'd say he's just being a dick." I pull out my phone and text my mom.

Heading home.

She replies, ***Come to Mac's and hang out with us. Alex and Dylan are playing tonight.***

It's still early, and I could go for a burger and fries. I text back, ***On my way. Will u order me a burger and fries? Pls.***

Got it.

"I think I'm gonna go," I say, shoving my phone in the back pocket of my denim shorts. I look around to see that Lexi and Evan have disappeared before moving through the crowd and heading for my car.

"You going home?" Grayson asks, following after me.

"Actually, I'm going to Mac's. There's a burger and fries waiting for me."

"Can I come?"

I pause and turn back around. "What about the party?"

"It's a high school party." He laughs, stepping forward and hooking his arm around my neck. "Besides, you seem like you're a lot more fun to hang out with."

"I'm not hooking up with you, Grayson."

Grayson smirks. "If I wanted to hook up with you, Jay, it would've happened already."

My eyebrows shoot up. "O-kay," I drawl before continuing toward my car.

Grayson laughs and tightens his arm, pulling me closer to his side. "It was meant as a compliment. I don't usually make friends with girls unless they come with benefits."

I scoff and push his arm away. "Your compliments suck, *friend*."

I find Lexi and Evan standing beside my car. "Hey, I was just grabbing my phone," Lexi says holding up her cell phone.

"I'm taking off," I tell her, pulling my key from my pocket.

"Are you okay?" she asks, her eyes flicking between me and Grayson.

"Yeah. We're going to Mac's. You guys wanna come?" I ask.

"Don't worry, Lexi," Grayson says, tossing his keys to Evan. "I'll take good care of her."

I roll my eyes as I open the door and slide behind the wheel.

"What about Zach?" Lexi calls.

"Zach's got his hands full with Chelsea," Grayson tells her.

I watch out the window as Lexi's face twists in confusion. "Bro, what are you doing? Zach's gonna lose his fucking mind," I hear Evan say. "This one is different."

This one? What is he talking about?

"I know, Evan, and it's not even like that. We're just going to get something to eat. And if he's so into her, then he should be the one leaving with her right now, not playing catch-up with Chelsea. Even I'm not that much of a dick."

Zach

I'M STILL FLYING high from our win as my teammates and I walk into Carter's backyard. Brad, Cole, and Justin hop up on the patio chairs and do their usual chant after a win. After they finish, I push through the crowd, looking for Jay. A few classmates stop me to congratulate me.

"Zach," a familiar voice calls out and I look up to see Chelsea just before she slams into me. If I wasn't so pissed off at her, I'd be happy to see her. I forgot how much I liked having the pain in the ass around.

"What are you doing here?"

"I came to watch my best friend play his first game of the season." She smiles. "Congratulations."

"Thanks."

"Chelsea." Justin pats the empty spot next to him on the sofa and waves us over.

Chelsea squeezes beside Justin and I perch on the arm. I'm not planning on sticking around for long, as Chelsea babbles on about college and the sorority she's pledging.

My gaze shifts to the covered pool deck where I find Jay standing near the keg, talking to Grayson. I stiffen. *What the hell?*

Jay looks at me over her shoulder. It's not jealousy I see, but disappointment. I can't ever seem to get my head out of my ass. I should go to her, but I know if I do, Chelsea will follow and most likely confront Jay. I don't trust her not to make a scene, especially after everything I told her about Jay.

Cole walks up. "You guys seen Jay?"

I look back across the patio, but both she and Grayson are gone.

"Jay?" Chelsea looks from Cole to me and back to Cole. "Your cousin?" Then she looks back at me. "She's here?"

I nod.

"She left," Lexi announces as she and Evan walk up.

"She left?" Cole pulls out his phone. "I can't believe she just left without telling me," he says, typing out a text. "Are you sure she left?"

"Zach, why didn't you tell me she was here?" Chelsea asks.

"Why, so you could act like a bitch to her?" Justin says, calling her out.

My thoughts exactly.

"Shut up, Justin."

"Yo, Mackenzie, if you're looking for Jayla, she just took off with Grayson," someone calls out in passing.

Evan smirks at me.

Dick.

Cole narrows his eyes at Evan. "Your brother better keep his fucking hands to himself."

Evan laughs. "Bro, it's not his hands you should be worried about."

"HEY," I SAY, standing up from the bench outside Mac's.

"Hi," Jay replies, stopping in front of me and crossing her arms over her chest. She looks over her shoulder and I follow her line of sight, expecting to see Grayson trailing behind her. Instead, I see a huge wall of a man at least two inches taller than me with a shaved head. *Bodyguard?* He narrows his eyes with a look that says "Give me a reason, motherfucker" as he moves to stand at her side. I'd say he's more like her guard dog by the way he looks ready to maul my face off.

"Bass, this is Zach. Zach, this is Bass."

Bass grins. "The quarterback." *Okay. Maybe his bark is worse than his bite.* He holds out his hand. "Good to meet you."

Taking his hand, I wince when he squeezes a little too hard and narrows his eyes again, silently asking me if I want to keep it.

Okay, maybe not.

"Be nice, B," Jay warns.

"Princess, I'm always nice." Jay rolls her eyes as Bass claps me on the back. "I'm just giving you a hard time, Romeo. You played a good game tonight. Impressive."

Romeo?

His compliment has me puffing out my chest a little bit. "Thanks. You played?"

"Defensive lineman. Good to meet you. I'll leave you to it." He nods at me and turns to Jay. "I'll be inside. Come and get me when you're ready to go."

"Okay."

As soon as Bass disappears through the doors she looks over at me and uncrosses her arms to tuck her hands into her back pockets. "What do you want, Zach?"

I shove my hands in my front pockets to keep from reaching for her. "I want to talk."

"Yeah," she scoffs. "You keep saying that, but it always ends up with you blowing me off for one of your blondes." She shakes her head. I open my mouth to defend myself, but she keeps going. "You're not the same boy I knew from summer vacations. You used to be shy and sweet. Now you're the popular football player with a harem of blondes and a cocky attitude. I don't know what kind of games you're playing, but I'm done."

"So, did you leave the party with Grayson because you were jealous, or were trying to get back at me for talking to Chelsea?" I smirk. "Who's the one playing games?"

"No, I left because I didn't feel like standing around watching a bunch of high school kids get drunk and act stupid." She takes a step forward and leans in. "I *kissed* Grayson to get back at you."

Oh, this little....

I take a step back, feeling as though I've been punched in the chest. "You kissed that fucker?"

"No." She lifts a shoulder nonchalantly. "But how did that feel? The next time you want to play head games and flaunt one of your blondes in my face, remember how it feels." She turns her head, clenching her jaw, nostrils flared.

"That's not what I was doing. Chelsea used to be my best friend..." Clasping my hands behind my neck, I tip my head back and sigh heavily. "It's a long story. I don't want to fight with you, Jay."

"Then what *do* you want, Zach?"

Suddenly, everything comes rushing to a head. Dropping my arms, my hands ball into fists. "I want to know why you broke my fuckin' heart!" I yell, leaning into her personal space. Jay's head snaps back as if I just slapped her. When she opens her mouth, I cut her off. It's my turn to talk now and I have plenty of shit to say.

A year's worth.

"The second you left St. Thomas, all I could think about was being with you, and that Labor Day couldn't get here soon enough. I told you I loved you and you just... I don't even know what happened. You just blew me off." I throw my hands up in the air. "No calls and no texts. Not even a 'fuck you, Zach'. Nothing. You blocked my number." I clasp my hands behind my neck. "Why?"

Something flashes in her eyes, but it's gone before I can determine whether it's anger or hurt. Could be either. Based on the slight flare of her nostrils and the way her eyes turn to slits as she pins me with a glare, I'm gonna say anger.

Jay crosses her arms and clenches her jaw.

Here it comes.

"Were you thinking about how much you loved me when you were hooking up with another girl that night? Were you thinking about me when you told her you didn't have a condom?"

"Wha—" My eyes go wide and my heart free falls into my stomach. *How?* "Jay... I..." I've got nothing. "It wasn't like that."

Shaking her head, she holds up her hand and pulls her phone from her back pocket. "That's exactly how it was. You pocket-dialed me and my voicemail recorded the whole thing." She holds out her phone to show me that she saved the message. "I thought it was some kind of joke, so I called you back and your girlfriend answered—"

"Girlfriend?"

She nods. "She called me a skank. She told me that you two broke up over the summer, but you were back together—"

"That's bullshit!" *Reagan Fucking Vaughn.* "She lied to you."

"I didn't want to believe her because my Zach would never do that to me."

"Because that's not what happened. Jesus Christ, I can't believe this whole time..." I shove my hands in my hair and let the words hang between us.

"But I had to let it go because my father was dying," she chokes out through a sob. "I had to let you go, Zach. Girlfriend or not, it never would've worked out between us being three thousand miles away. I'd always wonder what you were doing or who you were with. I'm sorry, but what did you want me to do? I needed to be there for my dad, not chase after someone who didn't give me a second thought before he moved on to the next girl."

"Come here." I reach out and pull her to my chest. "I'm sorry, Jay. God, I'm so sorry."

"Me, too." She sniffs into my shirt.

"I know it sounds cliché, but it's not what you think. Let me drive you home and I'll explain everything."

She nods against my chest. "Okay, but I need to let Bass know." She turns and hurries back inside while I wait.

"I CAN'T BELIEVE we lost a whole year because of that bitch," I say in disbelief.

"My mom always told me never to make assumptions, no matter what it looks like. That's why I called you. I wanted to give you a chance to explain."

"We kissed. That's all. The only reason I told her I didn't have a condom was —"

She reaches over and covers my mouth. "No. Don't tell me."

Grabbing her by the wrist, I pull her hand from my mouth and press a kiss to her palm. "Just listen. I told her I didn't have a condom because I didn't want to tell her about you and risk her telling Cole." I shake my head. "I already felt so guilty for even kissing her. I called you the next day to come clean about everything, but you never answered."

"It's bad enough I have to look at Reagan every day knowing you were with her. But knowing it was her who did this to us..." She shakes her head.

"Reagan was a mistake. I liked her in tenth grade, but she never gave me the time of day. Last year, after Labor Day weekend, we started hooking up." Jay winces and I give her hand a reassuring squeeze. "Sorry, but you need to know everything so she can't come between us anymore. She wanted to be my girlfriend, but I didn't trust her." I should've trusted my gut back then. "And three months after we officially became a couple, she cheated on me."

"Sounds like it still bothers you."

"*She* bothers me." I turn in my seat. "I don't believe in cheating. It's a coward's way out of a relationship. If anyone is guilty of head games, it's Reagan Vaughn. Do you want to know what her excuse was for cheating?"

"What?"

"Because I only wanted to be with her after the girl I was in love with dropped me. Those were her words. I'm gonna get her lying ass at school on Monday," I assure Jay.

"No, Zach. Don't say anything to her and stir up more drama. Just let it go for now. I'm pissed that she did this to us, but we can't change it. From now on, we just need to be honest with each other." She blows out a breath. "I'm gonna go ahead and put this out there so we're clear. I love you, Zach. I never stopped loving you. Even when I didn't want to love you anymore, I still loved you. Maybe I'm too young and inexperienced to know about love, but I know what I feel. And maybe it's crazy, but I know in my heart that you could be my forever. If that freaks you out, I'm sorry, but life is too short for regrets. My dad used to say, 'If you want it, then go after it.' So, this is me, going after what I want. I love you."

Fuck, I love this girl. "Don't move." Shoving the driver's door open, I hop out and jog over to the passenger side. Jay turns in her seat just as I jerk open the door. Reaching in, I grab the back of her neck, pulling her to me so that our foreheads are touching and my lips are hovering over hers. "The only thing that freaks me out is not being with you. I love you, Jay. You're still my girl."

Jay sighs against my lips and I'm done. My lips are on hers, claiming her with a deep, demanding kiss. She instantly moves her arms to wrap around my neck and when our tongues meet, her body melts against mine.

I slide my hand up her bare thigh and she parts her legs, allowing me to move closer. Her hands are everywhere, running up my back under my T-shirt before dipping into my back pockets, squeezing my ass. Breaking the kiss, I continue trailing small kisses across her jaw and down her neck to that spot behind her ear she loves so much, even though it tickles. She giggles and I groan. I want her so badly.

I place another soft kiss against her lips before I drop my forehead to hers. "I've missed you, Z," she whispers against my lips. *She called me Z.* My heart nearly bursts from my chest.

"I've missed the shit out of you too, Jay. Tell me we're okay and I'm still your guy."

"We're okay." She smiles. "I'm still your girl and you're still my guy."

I chuckle and press a kiss to her forehead before hesitantly pulling away. "I should head home. It's getting late and your mom and the big guy will probably be home any minute."

"You're not exactly small, Z." She laughs. "Don't worry about Bass. He's a giant teddy bear."

"More like a grizzly bear." I smack another kiss to her lips before helping her out of the Jeep and walking her to the side door leading to the garage. "The adrenaline from the game has worn off and I'm exhausted."

"Oh, yeah. *Duh.*" She crosses her eyes and wraps her arms around my waist. *Silly girl.* "Congratulations on your win tonight. I'm glad I was there."

I chuckle. "The team won, not just me."

"Oh, there's a team?" she teases. *She's cute.*

"Spend the day with me tomorrow. We can do whatever you want. Go to the beach, the mall, get pedicures. I don't care. I just want spend the day with you."

"Okay, but I'll let you pick since you asked."

"Yeah?" I grin. "Will the big guy let me take you out alone, or will I have to take the top off the Jeep to make room for him."

She laughs, smacking my chest.

"Will you be okay by yourself or do you want me to wait with you?"

"No, I'm fine. Grace is here."

"Who's Grace?"

"She's my...." Her mouth twists to the side as she mulls it over. "Grace was my dad's housekeeper for years before he met my mom. She's family. Mom refuses to let her clean up after us, but Grace takes care of us. She cooks and sometimes she does my laundry."

"I can't wait to meet her."

"Oh, believe me, she can't wait to meet you either."

I kiss her once more and wait for her to disappear inside before I get back in my Jeep and head home.

TRACK 30:
STARTING OVER
Zach

THE NEXT MORNING, I wake to a text from Chelsea. ***Where did you go last night?***

As happy as I was to see Chelsea last night, I hadn't forgotten about her running her mouth to Reagan. I still plan to confront her about it, but not today. And until we have that conversation, I'm not telling her about Jay.

Home.

What are you doing today? Maybe I can come by later.

Sorry. I have plans all day. Maybe tomorrow.

Ok. Sounds good. TTYL

Well, that was easy.

Too easy.

THE GATES AT the front of Jay's driveway are open, so I continue up the driveway and roll to a stop in front of the house. Wow. I hadn't taken in the size of her house last night because it was dark and I was solely focused on Jay, but I remember she called it her modern-day castle. And now I see why.

Jay's bodyguard, Bass, greets me at the door. "Hey, man, good to see you again," I hold out my hand and he shakes it with a firm grip before taking a step back and gesturing for me to come in.

"Princess said to tell you she'll be down in five minutes," he informs me as I step into the foyer.

"And to not embarrass her," a female voice says just before the infamous Emerson Mackenzie appears.

They say that if you want to know what your girl will look like in twenty years, all you have to do is look at her mother.

I'd say the future is looking pretty damn good.

Emerson Mackenzie King is a beautiful woman. Her black hair is in one of those messy buns and a pair of reading glasses are perched on top of her head, away from her vibrant green eyes.

She smiles and opens her arms. "Zach, it's so great to finally meet you." She pulls me in for a hug and I bend at the waist to meet her halfway. Pulling back, she looks up at me with another smile, slowly shaking her head. "I can't get over how much you look like your dad. I swear it was like déjà vu watching you out on the field last night. You played a good game."

"Thanks. I didn't know you were there," I say, rubbing the back of my neck.

"We were all there," Emerson says, smiling up at Bass before she turns her emerald gaze on me once more. "Back in the day, the Mackenzies never missed a football game."

Bass moves to stand beside Emerson with his arms crossed, pinning me with an intimidating stare. Emerson scoffs, backhanding him across the stomach. "Would you cut it out? You knew this day was coming." She turns to me and rolls her eyes. "Ignore him. He doesn't play well with others."

Bass lets out a deep chuckle. "I play just fine." He grins, raising a brow. "Just like a cat plays with a mouse before he devours it."

Emerson laughs.

"I heard that, B," Jay says as she skips down the stairs wearing a pair of cutoff jeans shorts that show off her long legs, a white T-shirt that says, "I have nothing to wear," and sandals. Her black hair is braided and draped over one shoulder. She playfully smacks Bass on the arm as she makes her way over to me and wraps her arms around my waist, stretching up on her toes and pecking me on the lips. "Hi, Z."

Bass pretends to clear his throat to hide the growl as Emerson giggles beside him.

"Hi." I smile. "I like your shirt."

"Thanks." She smiles and turns to Bass. "You told me last night that you approved, so be nice." She looks up at me and winks.

"Fine." Bass playfully rolls his eyes, throwing his arms out to his sides. The two of them exchange a look as if they're having a private conversation and I fight back a smile. Looks like Jay has the big guy wrapped around her finger.

"Grace, come meet Zach!" Jay calls out and an older Spanish woman comes walking in from the back of the house. "Zach, this our amazing Grace." She laughs. "Grace, this is my guy."

That statement sends my heart soaring.

Grace gives me a warm smile as she reaches up and hugs me.

Emerson laughs. "Sorry, Zach, we're a bunch of huggers. There's no such thing as personal space in this house."

"Speak for yourself, woman," Bass bristles.

"It's so good to finally meet you," Grace says to me before turning to Jay. "He's so handsome."

"I told you." Jay smiles. "Let's go, Z."

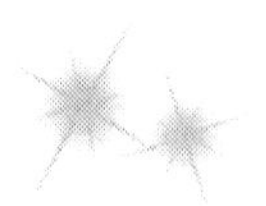

"SO, WHERE ARE you taking me?" Jay asks, fastening her seat belt as I pull out of her driveway and head over to Cam's.

He lives two streets over from Jay, on the beach side. His house is big but not even half the size of Jay's. "Cam's out of town this weekend," I tell her. "So, I figured we could go to his place and hang out on the beach."

"Awesome. I haven't been over to see his house yet."

"It's a typical bachelor pad." Cam bought the house in January when he left the Heat to play for the Tornadoes. He has all the basics to get by. There's a couch, a flat-screen, barstools, a pool table, and the bedrooms are furnished. The walls are bare, but the refrigerator always has beer, Gatorade, and water. And the liquor cabinet is now locked and off-limits since the Chelsea incident.

Jay rolls her eyes playfully. "Oh, believe me, I've seen Cam's *and* Liam's bachelor pads." She tells me about the house Cam and Liam shared in Malibu just down the beach from hers.

I roll to a stop at the gate and punch in the code. The gate opens and I pull up the driveway, pressing the remote for the garage door as I put the Jeep in Park.

We enter the house through the door from the garage and Buddy, my six-year-old Lab, greets us, wagging his tail. I dropped him off before I went over to pick up Jay. It's too hot outside to leave him in the car and I wasn't sure how long her mom and bodyguard were going to grill me before letting her leave with me.

"Aww, aren't you cute?" Jay squats down to give Buddy some attention, which he happily accepts. "I've never had a pet. Well, that's not exactly true. I had one of those beta fish once. But there wasn't time for a dog or a cat."

"Cats are pretty self-sufficient."

"I think my mom's allergic to cats. Or she just said that so she didn't have to get me one." She laughs. "What's his name?"

"Buddy." He was supposed to be Logan's dog, but he's the family dog and since Logan is away at college and I'm busy with school and football, he's become my dad's baby. Since my parents had errands to run today, I figured I'd bring him over to Cam's for some exercise on the beach.

Jay scrunches her nose. "Buddy? Really?"

I wrinkle my brows. "What's wrong with Buddy?"

"It's a lazy name." She rises from the floor and puts her hands on her hips. "Like you couldn't take the time to give him a cool name, so you just went with Buddy." She shakes her head, feigning disappointment. "That's just wrong."

"Logan named him," I inform her through a chuckle. "What would you name him?"

We both look down at Buddy, who is blissfully licking his nonexistent doggy balls.

Jay lifts her head and grins at me. "Sir Licks-his-dick-a-lot?"

I throw my head back and laugh. "Gangster. I like it." Grabbing her hand, I lead her through the back door and down to the beach, snagging a couple of beach towels on the way as Buddy follows.

Jayla

ZACH TOSSES A ball into the water before turning to wrap his arms around my waist. My arms instinctively circle his neck. "Tell me about this." He brushes his thumb over my tattoo and I flinch because it tickles.

"It was one of the last things my dad said to me before he died."

He nods and lifts my arm to rub his fingers over the "Conquer" tattoo on my inner bicep.

"And this one?"

"I'm a King." I flex my bicep. "King's don't cower. They conquer."

Zach's gaze moves from my tattoo back to my face. His blue eyes flicker as he stares into mine and he exhales forcefully. "I'm sorry."

I frown. "For what?"

"For everything. I'm sorry for hurting you. I'm sorry you lost your dad. I'm sorry your whole life has changed. But I'm not sorry you're here. I tried to let you go and move on, but I couldn't. I was miserable. And now I'm so fucking happy, it doesn't seem real."

"I know. Me, too. But we're still us, Z. We might not know everything about each other, but we're still the same two kids who grew up together over summer vacations. We're still Zachy and Sparkles." I burst out laughing and Zach shakes his head.

"Logan and his stupid nicknames." We sit down side by side on the shoreline, Zach continuing to toss the ball into the ocean so Buddy chases after it.

"How is Logan? I haven't seen him in years."

"Still the same annoying ass he always was, but he's doing well. We don't hear from him too much because he's busy with law school. He hasn't been home in nearly a year, but my dad went up there a few months ago to see him and to make sure he was doing okay."

"He's at Columbia?"

He pulls his legs up and drapes his arms over his bent knees. "Yeah."

"And what about you? Where are you going to college?"

"I'm still undecided."

"Cole has his heart set on South Carolina."

"I know. He's been talking about it since we were little. What about you? You're going on tour with Royal Mayhem?"

I nod. "Yeah. I think this tour will give me the closure I need to move on with my life." *Wow. This is the first time I've ever admitted that out loud.*

"What do you mean?"

I shrug. "*Jaybird* started as a side project; something fun for my dad and me. It wasn't supposed to turn into an album, much less a tour. But after we found out he was sick and wasn't going to get better, he wanted to make it a farewell album."

"That's sad, Jay."

"Now he's gone, and I feel like the pressure is on me now. I'm worried about how the fans will receive me. I'm not my dad. Royal Mayhem was his band. His baby. His life. Not mine."

God, it feels so good to finally let it out.

"So, you don't want to be a rock star?" he teases, bumping his shoulder against mine.

"I don't know what I want, but whatever it is, I want the choice to be mine. I spent a lot of my childhood on a tour bus. I don't think I want to spend my adult life living on one, too. The tour is something I need to do. I owe it to my dad, to the band, and I owe it to the fans. Maybe even myself, too. I worked hard on that album. But after the tour, I'm not sure what I want to do. I really like being involved with the Project Mayhem class." I shrug. "Maybe I'll continue to do that. Be a mentor, kind of like my dad was on *America's Voice*. Maybe I'll go to college and get a teaching degree."

I bump my arm against Zach's and look over to see him watching me. "God, I've missed you, Jay. This has been the longest year of my life."

"It's been the worst year of mine."

"I know."

Our eyes lock for a split second before he reaches out, grabs the back of my neck, and slams his mouth down on mine. I let out a soft moan as his tongue pushes past my lips and slides against mine. Without breaking the kiss, I fall back into the sand with my hands buried in Zach's hair as he moves over me. Sliding his hand up my thigh, he brings my leg up to wrap around his waist, rocking his hips, pressing his hardness against the spot that aches for him. I lift my hips to get more friction, earning a groan from Zach. He breaks away and I almost whimper in protest.

"Let's go inside," he murmurs.

"WHOSE ROOM IS this?" she asks.

"It's mine," I tell her. "No one uses this room but me."

"Uses it?" She curls her lip in disgust and takes a step back.

Jesus, Zach, you're an idiot. "I mean this is my room. I don't bring girls here, Jay." Only Chelsea's ever been here, but never in my bed. That's definitely a conversation I need to have with her. Sooner than later.

"Okay." She nods, smiling as she reaches behind her back and tugs the strings on her bikini top. The strings fall to the sides but the small triangles remain in place, covering part of her breasts. I'm on her in a flash, my hands sliding down the back of her bikini bottoms to grip her perfect little ass, guiding her backwards toward the bed. I lift her up, toss her on the bed, and she bounces forcing her breasts to pop out of her top, prompting both of us to burst out laughing.

I crawl on the bed beside her and tell her, "Jay, we don't have to do this. It's not why I brought you here."

"I know, but I want to. Just..." Her chest is heaving and she looks unsure.

"What?"

"Please don't hurt me again, Z," she pleads softly.

"Never. I'll never hurt you, Jay," I promise, pressing a kiss to her nose before scrambling from the bed in search of a condom. "I'll be right back." I know Cam keeps them in his nightstand.

"Hey, where are you going? Bring that fine ass back here."

Jayla

ZACH PRESSES A kiss to my nose and chuckles.

"Did I fall asleep?" I ask, stretching.

"Yeah, but only for like ten minutes. You okay?"

"Yeah." *And my lady J is a very happy girl.*

"Your what?"

Oh, shit. Did I say that out loud?

Zach throws his head back and laughs. "Yes, you did."

I snort, feeling the embarrassed flush creep up from chest to my cheeks.

"Are you blushing?" he teases.

"Well, I can't call it my Va-jay-jay because that's what Weenie calls me."

"Why do you call her Weenie?"

"Because I couldn't pronounce Evangeline. She was a little bitch when we were kids and wouldn't let me call her Eva, so now she's stuck with Weenie."

Zach shakes his head. "I can't wait to meet her. Are you hungry?"

"Kind of. I should probably check in with my mom."

"You do that and get dressed. We'll drop off Sir Licks-his-dick-a-lot at my house and go get some lunch." I smack his chest and burst out laughing.

"We can call him 'Sir' for short." I laugh again as I return one of Mom's three missed calls.

"What are you doing?" she asks in way of answering.

"We're at Cam's. Zach brought his dog over here and we were out on the beach."

"Cam's out of town." I know where she's going with this, so I steer the conversation another direction.

"I know, and you should see this house, Mom. It's worse than their bachelor pad in LA. I think Cam needs an interior intervention. This house is too nice to be this pathetic." She laughs and I know I've avoided an interrogation and a future uncomfortable conversation. "Anyway, we're leaving now to drop off Buddy at Zach's and then we're going to get some lunch. What are you doing?"

"Actually, I'm going out tonight. Some old friends are throwing me a 'welcome back' dinner at Oceanside Grill in Pelican Cove. I heard it's good."

"You heard that from me, goofball. Cole and I ate there last weekend."

"Oh." She laughs. "That's right. Anyway, Bass is going with me, so I'll need to know your plans before we leave."

"I should be back in plenty of time. We're just going to get lunch."

"Okay, I'll see you in a little bit. Love you."

"Love you. Mean it. Bye."

TRACK 31: NEVER AGAIN

Jayla

ZACH PULLS UP to a large two-story Mediterranean. It's not as big as Brad's, but it's not small. "This is your house?"

"Yeah." He smiles, pressing a button to open the garage before opening his door and climbing out.

"I always wondered what your house looked like."

"I'll give you a tour another time. I need food." He shuts the driver's door and opens the back. "Come on, Buddy." Zach lifts Buddy out of the backseat and sets him on the ground. "I'll be right back." He jogs into the garage and Buddy runs after him.

A second later, a white BMW rolls past the Jeep in the driveway and pulls in the garage. Obviously, they're Zach's parents. An older version of Zach gets out of the driver's side and eyes me curiously, as Zach's mother—the infamous Elizabeth Easton—a petite woman with long brown hair, climbs out of the passenger side and joins his father at the back of the car. Zach's father murmurs something to his mother before both look in my direction.

"Who are you?" his mother asks loudly. I can tell by her tone that she knows exactly who I am.

Okay, I'll play along.

Opening the passenger door, I step out and walk toward them.

This is awkward as hell for so many reasons. The main one being that they hate my mother. "I'm Jayla." I hold out my hand. "It's nice to meet you, Mrs. Easton."

Ignoring my hand, she looks me up and down, rolls her eyes before she turns and walks inside.

Okay, then.

Zach's dad shakes his head as he watches his wife walk away, then turns to me with a kind smile. Holding his hand out, he says, "I'm sorry about that. Apparently, she forgot to take her happy pills today." He chuckles awkwardly. "I'm joking. Kind of. I'm Michael Easton, but you can call me Mike."

"My mom wasn't kidding. Zach looks just like you."

He chuckles. "I could say the same to you. I feel like I'm looking at Emerson twenty years ago. It's nice to finally meet you. So, how do you like it here so far? You settling in okay at school?"

"So far, so good. I've made a few friends and I'm really happy to see Zach again."

Mike nods knowingly. "Yeah. He's pretty crazy about you."

Zach

THE DOOR LEADING into the house from the garage slams as I stand at the sink, filling up Buddy's water bowl. My mom storms into the kitchen with her face twisted in irritation.

I frown. "What?"

"That was fast," she says, slamming her purse down on the counter.

"What are you talking about?"

"I'm talking about the girl in my driveway."

If she wasn't my mom I'd tell her to fuck off and mind her own business, but she is my mom, so I say, "I'm sorry if it bothers you, but she's not Emerson." I move around her to set down Buddy's water bowl.

"Why her, Zach?" She throws her arms out. Now she's being

dramatic. "Out of all the girls in this city, why her?"

"Because I love her," I argue before heading for the door.

"You don't even know her!"

I turn to face her. "What are you taking about? I've known her since I was six fucking years old."

"Watch your mouth, Zach."

I take a deep calming breath. "I'm eighteen. You can't tell me who I can and can't love. You said you wanted me to be happy. Well, she makes me happy. And if you don't want to know her, then it's your loss. But I'm not going to stop being with her, so get over it. Now if you'll excuse me, I'm taking my girlfriend to lunch." I don't wait for a reply before I jerk open the door and walk out.

Jayla

"HEY, DAD," ZACH says, coming out of the garage looking a little irritated. He shoots his dad a look and I know it's because his mom must've said something about me.

"Hey, son," Mike says. "Jayla was just telling me you guys took Buddy to the beach."

Zach looks over at me and smirks. "Yeah. Did she tell you she changed his name?"

My eyes go as big as saucers. *Don't you frickin' dare, Zach.* "Zach—"

"Oh?" Mike looks down at me and I give him a polite smile.

"He's kidding," I say with an uncomfortable laugh.

Zach laughs. "Jay thinks the name Buddy is dull and boring—"

"Oh, my God, Zach, shut up." I swat at him, but he dodges my hand.

Mike plays along. "What's wrong with Buddy? Logan named him."

"Nothing. It's a cute name. Buddy is a sweet dog. It fits him perfectly," I rush out.

"So, she changed his name to Sir Licks-his-dick-a-lot."

I bury my face in my hands, mortified as Mike guffaws and Zach joins in.

"That's a mouthful," Mike says with a laugh. "I'll be sure to pass that on to Logan."

"Tell him Sparkles says hello," Zach adds and I backhand him in the stomach.

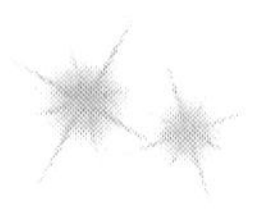

"YOUR MOM SEEMS... nice," I say before taking a bite of my sandwich. Zach and I are having lunch at this little bistro tucked between a clothing boutique and the Starbucks. Above them are loft apartments. I like this area. It's cozy.

Zach lowers his sandwich and his mouth forms a straight line. "What did she say to you?"

"Nothing. I think that *was* her being nice." I shrug. "I wasn't sure what I expected the first time I met your parents. I know they hate my mom."

"My dad doesn't," he offers. "I'm sorry if my mom was rude to you. She'll get over it."

I don't remember my mom ever saying she hated Elizabeth. "Did you ask your mom why she hates mine?"

He nods. "Yeah, but she wouldn't tell me. My dad said it's between them and to leave it alone. Honestly, Jay, I don't give a shit anymore. It's their problem."

"I agree. I'm not my mom, so if she doesn't want to know me and my awesomeness, it's her loss."

Zach grins. "You are pretty awesome."

After lunch, Zach drops me off at home and tells me he'll be back later to pick me up for our date.

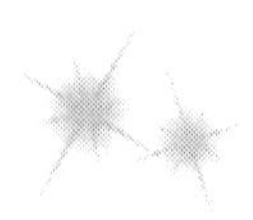

I FIND MOM inside her walk-in closet, digging through her clothes. Her closet is set up similar to mine, except for the two additional rooms I have for my shoes and bags. The other I use for storage and my luggage. I plop down on her gray tufted velvet sofa and prop my feet on the ottoman.

"Hey," she says. "How was your day with Zach?" I decide now isn't the time to tell her about my first face to face with Elizabeth Easton. Mom looks over at me and frowns. I stiffen.

Did he leave marks on me? "What?"

"Your face looks a little sunburned. Did you not wear sunscreen?"

I shrug. "I forgot."

"Jay, you have to wear sunscreen when you're out in the sun. I'm serious."

"Okay, calm down, woman. What are you wearing to your dinner tonight?"

She sighs, dropping her shoulders. "I have no idea." She's so cute. It's like she's going out on her first date or something. I shudder at the thought. *So not going there.*

I wave her off. "Pick out a few outfits and try them on. I'll tell you which one looks the best."

"Okay." She turns and disappears down one of the aisles. A moment later, I hear the hangers gliding across the rails.

I pull out my phone to check my messages while I wait for Mom to try on her outfit. There's a text from Evangeline. ***I miss you, Va-jay-jay.***

I snort and text her back. ***Miss you too, Weenie. When will u b back?***

Mom walks out wearing a pair of boyfriend jeans rolled up at the bottom with a cream-colored top that's open in the back and brown, open-toed ankle boots.

The top? Yes.

The boots? Yes.

The jeans? Fuck, no.

I shake my head and she looks down at her outfit. "What's wrong with it?"

"It's the jeans. I don't like those jeans on you. They're too baggy in the front." I know how boyfriend jeans are supposed to fit. I'm not the only one who lost weight after my dad passed.

"They're supposed to be baggy. They're boyfriend jeans."

"More like 'your boyfriend's jeans.' Are you smuggling a wiener in there, woman?" I snort. "They should be called 'boyfriend-repellant jeans.'"

My mom bends over, holding her side, and laughs her ass off.

I'm on a roll. "I think it's time to break up with the boyfriend jeans and find something that fits your body." She has a kick-ass body for a woman nearing forty.

"All right. Fine." She turns and disappears down the same aisle.

My phone vibrates on my lap and I lift it to see a reply from Evangeline. ***A few weeks.***

I can't wait to see you. I miss my Weenie. BTW, I spent the day with Zach.

What? And you're just now telling me, you bitch! Lol

Details later. With Mom right now.

Ur killing me. Okay. Fine. TTYL xoxo

Mom's phone starts ringing on the ottoman and I lean over to see who it is. "Cam's calling. Want me to answer it?"

"Yeah," she calls out from somewhere.

"Cameron," I sing into the phone.

Cam is silent for a beat before he says, "Jayla?"

"Hi, Cam. Mom's getting dressed for her party."

"What party?"

"Some dinner party some of her old friends are throwing for her at Oceanside Grill."

"Oh."

"Hey, I was at your house today with Zach. We went to the beach. And while I think your house is beautiful, it looks like a squatter has taken up residence."

Cam barks out a laugh. "It's not that bad. It has everything I need."

"Your godmother is a decorator. Why haven't you let her go to town in there? She did a fantastic job on our house." I wave my hand around even though he can't see me.

"I haven't had time to think about it."

Mom walks out wearing a pair of skinny jeans with the same top and ankle boots. I let out a whistle. "Damn, woman. If I weren't your daughter, or a female, and was into the whole cougar thing, I'd totally hit on you." I laugh, prompting Cam to laugh on the other end of the line.

She smiles. "So, this outfit is a yes?"

"It's a hell, yes." I give her a thumbs-up. "Talk to you later, Cam. Here's Mom." I hold out the phone to her. "I need to get in the shower and get ready. Zach will be here soon to pick me up."

TRACK 32: NO MORE GAMES

Zach

"Bowling?" Jay exclaims from the passenger seat, leaning forward to look out the windshield as the neon letters *B-O-W-L-I-N-G* light up one by one.

"Cyber bowling," I correct as I pull into the Pelican Cove parking garage. "Is that cool?" I could've taken her to a party, but I get the feeling she doesn't care for high school parties. Both times, she dipped out early.

She turns to me with excitement dancing in her eyes. "Heck, yeah!" she exclaims, reaching for the door handle. "I love bowling. You're going down, Easton," she throws over her shoulder, hopping out of the Jeep and closing the door. She moves to stand at the back of my Jeep, looking around cautiously while waiting for me to join her.

Jay is tense when I take her hand in mine. Gripping my hand firmly, she clings to my arm, scanning the brightly lit parking garage. I give her hand a gentle squeeze. "What's wrong?"

She grimaces and loosens her grip. "Sorry. Parking garages creep me out. Especially at night." She shudders.

I chuckle and look around. "Yeah, I guess they can be pretty creepy, but you're safe with me." I lift my arm and draw her to my side as we exit the garage and follow the walkway until we reach the doors of the bowling alley.

"Wow. This place is packed," she says, looking around and bobbing her head to the beat of Flo Rida's "My House."

"Good thing I called ahead and reserved a lane. We just have to check in and get shoes." Taking her hand in mine, we head toward the counter.

"Zach! Jay!" a female voice yells over the music. We both turn to see Lexi waving as she makes her way toward us. Surprise flashes across her face when she sees our joined hands. "Oh, my God! Are you guys on a date? That's so cute," she coos.

I chuckle and release Jay's hand. "I'm gonna go pay," I say, leaving the two of them to their girl chat.

The girl at the check-in counter looks up from her phone as I approach. She looks familiar, but I can't remember her name. She slips her phone in her back pocket and smiles. "Hi, Zach," she says, in a flirtatious tone, pushing out her chest.

"Hey—"

Jay walks up and wraps her arm around my waist, Lexi standing just behind her. "Z, Lexi says there's an open lane next to hers." She turns her attention to the girl behind the counter, who is openly glaring, but she either doesn't notice, doesn't care, or she's going for the 'kill 'em with kindness' act. "Hi," Jay says.

The girl sneers at Jay, then turns her attention back to me. "Sorry, we're full tonight. The wait is an hour."

I smirk. *So, it's like that.* "I have a reservation."

"Oh, uh... let me look it up."

Yeah, you just go ahead and do that.

She stares at the screen and taps a few keys on the keyboard, suddenly taking her job seriously. "So, have you talked to Lindsay lately?" she asks.

"Who?" I ask, confused.

"Why would he talk to Lindsay?" Lexi asks, as confused as I am.

The girl shrugs. "You guys were at Brad Manning's party together last weekend."

Oh, I get what she's doing. *Drama.*

"Oh, yeah," Jays jumps in and plays along. "How is Lindsay?" she asks in a sugary sweet tone.

"She's fine," the girl answers, keeping her eyes on the screen. "Your reservation is under Easton?"

"Yep."

"Kristen, can you put them at the lane beside Evan and me?" Lexi asks.

Kristen. That's right.

"What lane are you on, Lexi?"

"Eleven."

"Sure." She taps the keyboard again. "I put you two on lane ten."

Kristen asks for our shoe sizes then reaches below the counter to grab them while I swipe my debit card and enter my pin.

"Here you go." Kristen hands them over with a pair of socks, still new in the package.

"Thank you so much," Jay beams. "Tell Lindsay we say hello."

"I will." Kristen smiles. "Have fun."

I jerk my head with a stiff nod before heading to find our lane.

"Z, Lexi, and I are going to the snack bar. Want anything?" Jay asks.

"Surprise me. You sure you don't want me to come with you?"

"No. I'd rather not have anyone from your fan club handling my food or my drink." *So, she's a 'kill 'em with kindness' kind of girl. Good to know.* "You're gonna have to explain your relationship with Lindsay to me so that doesn't happen again."

"Lindsay's just a friend." I chuckle and lean over to kiss the spot just below her ear, making her giggle, then give her a gentle smack on the ass as she turns, hooks her arm around Lexi's, and walks off.

Jayla

"OKAY, I'M CONFUSED," Lexi starts as we make our way up to the snack bar. "You're here with Zach, but last night you left with Grayson. I'm not judging you and you can tell me to shut up and mind my own business, but Grayson is Evan's brother and Zach is Evan's best friend and—"

"Lexi, breathe." This girl. I love that she's protective of the people she cares about. I'm the same way with my friends and that makes me like her even more. "Grayson left with me, not the other way around. We went to Mac's and I had dinner with my mom. Grayson didn't even stick around to eat. He went upstairs to meet up with his friends."

"How did you end up with Zach?"

"He came to Mac's. We argued at first, but then he asked to drive me home and we talked." I fill her in about Reagan answering Zach's phone that night and telling me she was his girlfriend.

"God, I really hate that bitch. She needs a good ass-kicking."

"I agree. But it happened and there's nothing we can do to change it. All we can do is move on and show her that she can't come between Zach and me."

"So, are you guys dating now?"

"I'm not an expert on relationships, but dating sounds temporary. Zach's mine." I shrug. "Always has been. He's my guy. My forever."

"Aww," Lexi coos. "That's so sweet." She gives me a sideways hug. "I'm so happy for you. And you just don't know how freaking happy I am for Zach. Evan told me that Zach has been in love with you since you were kids."

I'll never tire of hearing that.

Zach

"HEY." EVAN NODS and pounds his fist against mine. "You here with Jayla?" he asks, looking over my shoulder.

"Yeah." I sit down in the empty plastic bucket seat beside him and drop the ugly-ass bowling shoes on the floor. "She's with Lexi at the snack bar," I tell him as I begin typing our names on the screen.

Evan slides further down in his seat, knees spread apart and arms crossed over his chest. "My woman better get me some nachos."

I chuckle as I toe off my shoes and slip my feet into the bowling shoes. Out of the corner of my eye, I see Evan staring at me. "What?"

"So, you got the girl?"

"No, I got *my* girl." I shoot him a teasing grin. "Don't worry. You'll get your money."

Evan raises his brows and a half smile tugs at his lips. "I forgot all about that. Keep it. Just be careful with that one."

I frown. "What do you mean? I've known Jay since we were kids."

"She ignored you for an entire year." He scowls. "And she left the party last night with my brother."

"She wasn't ignoring me. She thought she was doing the right thing." I fill him in on the details. "Jay had more important shit going on in her life than dealing with my stupid drama."

"Dude, that's some psycho shit," Evan says. "If Reagan's dad wasn't a judge, I'd let Lexi loose on her."

"Jay wants me to leave it alone for now," I tell him and he looks at me like I'm crazy. "She doesn't want any more drama."

"Z, I got you a bunch of fried stuff you probably shouldn't eat and a fruit punch," Jay says as she slides the tray on the empty table arranged between lanes ten and eleven. She passes me the fruit punch. "Hi, Evan." She passes him a drink. "Lexi is waiting on your nachos."

"Thanks," Evan says, then looks over at me and mouths "Z."

I flip him off and turn to Jay. "What did you get?"

"A cherry slushy." She pinches the straw and brings it to her plump lips, and I'm instantly hard. *It's the little things. What can I say?* "You wanna taste of my cherry?" She winks with a sly grin.

Damn tease.

"Oh, I *definitely* want to taste your cherry," I say, then add, "*Again.*"

Evan coughs beside me.

Jayla laughs, dropping into my lap and smacking her cold, cherry-flavored lips against mine before toeing off her sandals. "Hey, Evan, I hope I didn't give you the wrong impression last night. I like your brother. He's a nice guy and we made friends."

Evan snorts. "Grayson doesn't make friends with girls. He was trying to get in your pants. You made a much better choice with Zach because Grayson isn't the type of guy to stick around. I love my brother, but it's the truth."

Jay frowns. "There was never a choice between Zach and Grayson. It's always Zach."

I want to jump up and beat my fists to my chest. *She's mine.*

"I'm gonna be straight with you, Z," Jay begins as she laces up her shoes before she stands and takes a few steps backwards. "I totally suck at bowling." She smirks. "But I hate to lose, so I won't go down without a fight." She picks up a hot pink bowling ball from the ball return, turns, and in three long strides, she sends the ball gliding straight down the middle of the lane. Three quarters of the way down the lane, the ball veers off to the right and rolls into the gutter, yet somehow it jumps at the last minute, bounces up, and takes down one pin.

I chuckle, shaking my head as I make my way over to the ball return.

"What the hell was that?" Evan laughs from the other side.

Jay throws her arms in the air and spins around on the balls of her feet to face me, a grin spread across her face. "Did you see that?" Then she shrugs it off and skips over to Lexi.

"Get back over here," I call out. "You get another turn."

"Oh." She smiles and skips back over to me. "I told you I suck at this game."

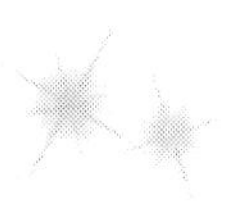

JAY WAS RIGHT.

She is the absolute worst bowler ever. I suggested she use the bumpers but she rolled her eyes with a "don't be ridiculous" look.

Now we're on the eighth frame and her score is forty-two. But at least she's having fun with Lexi, dancing to "Kiss" by Prince.

"Are you trying to distract me?"

Jay smiles at me over her shoulder. "Is it working?"

"Does it matter? Have you seen your score?"

She throws her head back and laughs, then dances over to me and snakes her arms around my neck. "I told you I sucked."

I laugh, resting my hands on her hips. "I'm pretty sure Willow bowls better than you."

She laughs as I slide my hands past her hips, slipping my fingers into the back pockets of her jeans. I love the way her ass fits in my palms. I give it a little squeeze before lowering my mouth to hers. Parting her lips, she teases my tongue with hers. Her mouth is cold and tastes like cherry.

Wolf whistles and clapping erupt around us, followed by Lexi and Evan shouting at us to get a room.

I pull back and narrow my eyes. "You fight dirty."

"Is there any other way to fight?" She jerks her eyebrows up and down.

I chuckle against her lips, reluctantly pulling my hands from her pockets, and smack her lightly on the ass. "Come on, dirty girl. Let's go."

We say our goodbyes to Evan and Lexi and head out.

Jayla

"WHERE'S YOUR MOM and Bass?" Zach asks as we walk into the quiet house.

"Out," I tell him. "But you just reminded me that I need to text her that I'm home." I pull out my phone. ***Home. Zach and I are going to raid the fridge and watch a movie.***

"Where's Grace?"

"She's probably in her apartment, either sleeping or watching the Hallmark Channel."

My phone dings with a reply from Mom. ***K. Have fun.***

No twenty questions or warnings about being alone with Zach? *Hmm. Someone's been drinking.*

The next text comes from Bass.

Romeo better keep his hands to himself.

Romeo? I laugh under my breath at Bass's new nickname for Zach. He must really like him.

Snickering, I type, ***Stop it, B. Zach is a perfect gentleman.***

Truthfully, Zach is a perfect gentleman. It's me who needs to get my lady J in check.

He better be. We'll be late tonight, Princess. Your mom is having a good time with her friends. Security is on the property, so you'll be safe.

I shake my head, picturing the Joes hiding in the bushes or in the trees watching me through the windows with binoculars. I text back, ***Have fun.***

Zach

As I SCROLL through the digital library looking for a movie, Jay walks into the media room wearing a T-shirt with the letters S-T-F-U across the front and a pair of tiny black shorts, heading into the mini-kitchen and bar area. "Did you find something to watch?"

"There's too much to choose from," I tell her. "What do you like?"

"Nothing scary. Suspense is fine, but I prefer comedies."

"You don't like scary movies?"

"Nope," she admits, setting down a tray of snacks and drinks on the ottoman. "I prefer to get my thrills in other ways rather than having the shit scared out of me." She laughs, grabbing the throw off the back of the sofa and straddling my lap.

"What are you doing?" I ask, smiling, movie forgotten.

"Watching a movie." She grabs the remote from my hand and presses a button. The whole room goes dark except for the light from the TV screen. Then she selects something with Kevin Hart—don't ask me the title because it doesn't matter—before tossing the remote to the side.

Watching a movie with Jay is now on my list of favorite activities.

TRACK 33: BEAUTIFUL LIAR

Zach

THE NEXT MORNING, I wake to a text from Chelsea. ***We need to talk. Breakfast at The Bistro?***

We sure as fuck do is what I want to say, but instead I reply with, ***Yeah. Give me 30 mins.***

Thirty minutes later, I walk into The Bristro and find Chelsea sitting in our usual booth.

"Thank you for meeting me," Chelsea says as I slide into the booth across from her and pick up the glass of orange juice. "I ordered your usual. I hope that's okay."

"Good, I'm starving." I tap my fingers on the table.

Chelsea laughs. "You're always starving."

"I'm a growing boy." I shrug. "So, what do you want to talk about?"

"I heard you were out with Jayla last night," she says. "Are you guys together now?"

"Yep." I smile. She plasters on that fake cheer smile that I hate. "Why are you smiling at me like that?"

"Like what?"

"Like you're uncomfortable or constipated."

"Shut up!" She laughs. "I do not."

"Yes, you do." I snort. "So, what do you really want to talk about?"

Chelsea slumps back in the booth and blows out a breath. "I just really miss my best friend. Everything got so messed up after..." She waves her hand between us and I nod.

The server arrives at our table and sets down our plates of food. I dig into my food as the door chimes in the background. "We're not best friends," I tell her calmly. "Best friends don't talk shit behind each other's backs."

"What?" she chokes out.

"You told Reagan about Jay."

"I—"

"Don't even try to deny it, Chelsea." I shake my head. "You told your mom about prom night. About Reagan. About us. About Jay. I trusted you."

Chelsea moves over to my side of the booth and slides in beside me. "I'm sorry, Zach. I am. I didn't do it to be spiteful to you. I was just trying to piss Reagan off. You know I can't stand her. And I didn't tell my mom those things to hurt you. I told her because she kept going on about how maybe one day you and I would be together. Blah-blah-blah." She rolls her eyes. "I just wanted to shut her up, so I laid it all out for her."

She lays her head on my shoulder and bats her eyelashes up at me. "Can we start over and work our way back to being friends again?"

I chuckle at her theatrics. "Fine." I throw my arm around her shoulders and pull her in for a side hug.

"I've missed you, Zach," she says, before lifting to smack a kiss on my lips.

I pull back and frown down at her. *What the hell was that?*

"Jayla, your order is ready!" The words ring out loud and clear, and I feel myself go pale.

Nooooooo.

I turn my head just in time to see Jay grab two coffees and a brown bag off the counter and storm out the door.

"Was that—"

"My girlfriend."

"Oh."

Jayla

STUPID.

That's what I am.

Fuck Zach.

Never again. I'm done.

I grab the two coffees from the cup holders, drop the bag of pastries into my purse, and walk into Mac's. It's early but the restaurant serves brunch on Sundays.

Harper greets me with a smile. "Hey, Jay. If you're looking for Dylan, he's in the kitchen and Alex is in his office."

"Where's that?"

"The hallway leading to the kitchen near the bathrooms. You can't miss it. You can cut through the bar. It's quicker."

"Thanks." I push through the heavy mahogany doors leading to the bar and make my way to Alex's office. Where I find him with his arms around a blonde woman who is *not* Evangeline.

Both heads turn toward the doorway at the sound of my gasp. I shoot Alex with a murderous glare. *I'm so telling Weenie about this.* Alex chuckles as he releases the beautiful woman who looks old enough to be his mother and gestures to me.

"Mom, this is Jayla. Jay, this is my mom, Sophia."

"Oh, Jayla." She moves over to me with her arms spread and pulls me in for an awkward hug. "It's so wonderful to finally meet you." She pulls back but grips my shoulders. "I've heard so much about you from Alex and Eva."

"It's nice to meet you," I say, holding out one of the coffees. "I brought an extra latte if either of you want it and there're pastries in my purse."

Alex takes the coffee and sets it on his desk. "What are you doing out and about so early?"

I hold up my coffee cup. "I figured I'd stop by and say hi, see what you were up to."

His brows pinch together. "What's wrong?"

"Nothing."

"You're lying." A smile pulls up on one side of his mouth.

"Nothing is wrong, Mr. Alex." I smirk back. Alex has spent enough time with me over the years to know when I'm full of shit. *Dammit.*

"I'm gonna head out," Sophia says. "I've got some errands to run. Love you, baby boy." She rises onto the balls of her feet and kisses Alex on the cheek before turning to me. "It was so nice to meet you, Jayla."

"You too, Sophia." As soon as Sophia walks out of the office, I turn to Alex. "Baby boy?" I tease.

Alex shrugs. "How was your date with Zach?"

I huff out a laugh. "Your girlfriend is a gossip." I set down my purse and coffee cup on his desk before plopping down in one of the empty chairs in front of his desk.

"Who else does she have to tell?" Alex chuckles. "It's either me or you."

"I know." I let out a heavy sigh. "Our date was perfect, but I don't think it's going to work out."

He perches on the edge of his desk with one foot on the floor. "What happened?"

"Nothing. Forget I said anything." I wave him off and look away. "I'm just being a girl."

He chuckles again. "You are a girl. Tell me."

I lift my head to see the concern in his eyes. "I just saw him at The Bistro with that Chelsea girl."

Alex nods. "I know Chelsea."

"Did they date?"

He shrugs. "Not that I know of, but I'm not as good at keeping up with the gossip like Eva."

I snort. *True.*

"I saw them kiss." Alex stays silent, so I continue. "Mom always told me not to make assumptions because it isn't always what it looks like. Doesn't mean it didn't hurt." My eyes well up with hurt and jealousy. "See, I told you I was getting all girly." I laugh. "I've loved Zach for a long time. I want to be with him, but I don't know how this relationship stuff works. I just want to be happy and be me. I don't know how to be anything else."

"You're perfect just the way you are. And if Zach doesn't see it, then he doesn't deserve you. You're beautiful down to your soul and that's what makes you stand out from the others. Zach is genuinely a nice guy. I never pegged him as an idiot. I'm surprised you didn't dump your coffee on his head."

"I know." I laugh and stand from the chair. That's definitely something I would've done if I was more pissed and less hurt. I just wanted to get the hell out of there. "Thanks for listening." I wrap my arms around Alex. "Weenie is a lucky girl."

"I know." He boasts.

"Hey, I actually did come by for another reason. What do you think about the Project Mayhem class performing here one night a month as part of their grade or extra credit? If they're serious about being in the music business, they need to get a feel for performing for an audience other than their peers. Maybe send out an e-mail to the parents and see how they feel about it. Invite them along."

"I think that's a great idea. Your involvement in this class is impressive. I hope you're serious about getting more involved with the foundation. After graduation... and the tour, of course."

"I am." I shrug. "I just don't want to let anyone down. Especially my dad."

"That's not possible."

Zach

STANDING IN THE doorway of Alex's office, I see him typing away on his laptop, looking deep in thought. I knock twice on the open door and Alex raises his head. "Hey, man," he says, leaning back in his chair and clasping his hands behind his head. "What's up?"

I don't know Alex all that well, but he's always seemed like a pretty cool guy and until recently, I had no idea that he and Jay were so close.

"I'm looking for Jay. Has she been by here?"

A smirk appears. "Yeah, she stopped by earlier." He looks down at his watch. "She left about fifteen minutes ago. Why?"

"I'm sure you know why," I say, rubbing the back of my neck.

Alex raises his eyebrows and straightens in his chair. His expression turns serious as he gestures to one of the chairs in front of his desk. "Have a seat, Zach. Let's talk."

Dropping down in the chair, I lean forward, propping my forearms on my thigh. He leans forward with his elbows propped on the desk. "I know we don't know each other all that well, considering how much we have in common, but I've heard only good things about you." He narrows his eyes at me. "I'm also aware of your history with Jay. More than I care to know, but I guess that goes without saying when my girlfriend is her best friend."

"Jay mentioned that." I nod, hoping to move on from this uncomfortable conversation. "Good for you, man. Evangeline is a beautiful woman."

"She is." He smiles proudly. "So, what's your endgame here, Zach?"

My eyebrows twist in confusion. "What?"

"Are you just trying to get laid? Screw the rock star's kid?"

I jerk up from the chair. "Are you serious right now?"

"Take it easy, Zach." He chuckles. "I had to ask. Consider yourself lucky I'm the one asking and not Eva or Bass. I'm sure you've met him by now."

"Yeah."

"Eva loves Jay like a sister. They grew up together and Eva is very protective of her. Trust me, you do not want to be on the receiving end when the claws come out. I've seen her in action and it's not pretty." He drums his fingers on the desk seeming to ponder over his next words. "I'm sure you're aware that the past year has been rough for Jay and her family. Especially Jay." He shakes his head. "Marcus was a great guy, practically a saint. Kind, genuine, and a very smart man. I respected the hell out of him. But he was also an overprotective father and he kept his little girl on a very short leash. Jay's kind-heartedness comes from her core. She's humble and forgiving. But she's also clueless which puts her in a vulnerable position and makes her a target for people who have less than genuine intentions. I made a promise to Marcus, and to Eva, that I'd watch out for Jay and that's exactly what I'm going to do." He points a finger at me. "Your intentions better be genuine."

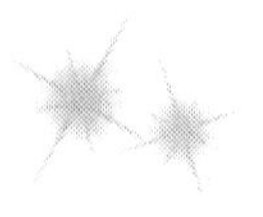

I PULL UP to the intercom at the end of Jay's driveway and press the Call button.

"Helloooo. May I help you?" Bass's deep voice drawls.

"Uh... hey, it's Zach. Is Jayla home?"

"I'm sorry, I don't know anyone by that name. This is where the princess lives."

I snort. *This guy.* "Can I speak to her?"

"You tell me. Can you?"

I let out a frustrated sigh and let my head fall back against the headrest. I'm being schooled through an intercom speaker. Taking a deep breath, I try again. "May I speak to her?"

"Enter at your own risk." His laughter is interrupted by a buzz and the gate slowly swings open.

Shaking my head, I steer my Jeep through the gate and navigate up the driveway, parking in the courtyard in front of the house.

As I make my way up the steps, the front door swings open and Bass's massive form fills the doorway, wearing a shit-eating grin. "To what do we owe the pleasure, Romeo?" he asks.

Apparently, he's sticking with Romeo.

"Quit messing with him, Bass," Emerson calls out before she appears at his side. "She's in a mood today. Don't make it worse."

Jerking her head to the side, Emerson says, "Come on in, Zach." Stepping inside, I follow her down the hall to a set of double doors. "She's in here." Twisting the knob, she pushes open one of the two doors and steps inside. "This is her office."

Jay's office is a mixture of blues and grays with silver accents. It's feminine and sleek. But it's the painting over the sofa that catches my attention. The painting is all black and white. It's a set of eyes, fringed in long, thick, black eyelashes. The only color is the blue-green irises. *Jayla's eyes.*

"Marcus painted that," Emerson tells me. "Every painting or picture in this house is sentimental."

"Is that rug made from real zebra skin?"

Emerson laughs. "God, no. Jay would flip out."

The sound of a piano drifts from the adjoining room. Emerson smiles and gestures to thc hallway. "That's her music room."

As I make my way down the short hallway, I skim over the framed photographs lining the walls. One picture in particular grabs my attention, and I pause to get a closer look. Marcus King has his arms around the shoulders of two little kids. One is Jay, with her long skinny legs, knobby knees, and electric blue streaks in her black hair. The other is a skinny kid with shaggy blond hair. Lucas Wild. Skimming over the other photos, they're mostly of Marcus with his band, other musicians, or celebrities.

I stop at a framed sheet of paper with black squiggly lines scribbled across the page in what looks like crayon. Emerson moves to my side and lightly brushes her fingers across a little gold plate inscribed with "Jaybird's First Song."

"She was barely six years old when she wrote this," she says, smiling like a proud mom. "You should ask her about it sometime. It's a cute story." She winks.

Hmm.

The adjoining music room is much larger than the office but keeping with the same color scheme. The walls are lined with framed gold and platinum records, more photos, and albums. On the right is a door with silver letters across the top, spelling out the word Studio. There's a light above the door and a long two-way mirror strategically placed to the right.

To the left is Jay, sitting in front of a large, shiny, white grand piano, centered in front of the floor-to-ceiling windows.

Her eyes remain closed as her fingers glide over the keys, losing herself in the melody. I like music as much as anyone, but it's just always been background noise to me. I've never paid attention to the lyrics of a song unless it's a song by one of my favorite bands, but for some reason her words draw my attention. Something about how nobody knows her heart, how she cries when she's pretending to sleep. It's beautiful yet sad, and it makes my chest ache.

"She's amazing, isn't she," Emerson says, reminding me that she's still here. "I'm sure you've been warned, but now *I'm* warning you. She puts on a hell of a front, which is what she's been taught to do by me. But she's fragile. She's my baby girl and she's all I have left. She cares for you. She always has. I'm asking you nicely to be careful with her heart, Zach."

"I will," I promise.

"Thank you." She lightly pats my arm. "Treat my daughter with respect and make her happy and you'll always have my support and protection from that big motherfucker out there waiting for you to screw up." She laughs as she turns around and heads back down the hall. "Good luck," she calls out from the other end of the hallway.

Shaking my head, I push off the wall and make my way over to Jay. Without looking up or breaking her stride, she slides over to one side of the piano bench, making room for me. It's an invitation I happily accept by lifting my leg and straddling the bench so I'm facing her. I watch in amazement as her fingers float effortlessly over the piano keys.

The love I felt for her before dulls in comparison to the love I feel for her now that she's mine again. I still can't believe she's here.

I never thought it was possible for me to be this happy.

Yet somehow, I keep screwing things up.

Jay stops playing and drops her hands into her lap, then twists to face me.

"Journey?" I ask.

She nods. "'Faithfully' was the first song I learned to play on the piano. Journey is one of my mom's all-time favorite bands." She looks away and smiles as if she's remembering.

"My mom is a big Journey fan too. I'm pretty sure I knew the words to every one of their songs when I was little. What about the other song? The one you were playing before. Was that one of yours?"

She snorts. "No, that was Pink. It's called 'Nobody Knows.'"

"I liked it."

She looks away and takes a deep breath before turning back to me. "Thanks," she says, forcing a smile. It appears I've got my work cut out for me. "It's been a while since I've played."

"Doesn't sound like it. I can't believe I've known you all these years and never knew you were so talented."

"Back then you would've thought I was being a show-off. I just wanted to have fun like the rest of you." She shrugs. "So, what are you doing here? Isn't there a blonde somewhere waiting to suck your face off?"

Again with the sassy mouth.

I drag my hands over my face. "Either I have the worst luck or you have the worst timing." I shake my head and sigh. "Ever since you got here, it's been one 'It's not what it looks like' situation after another and I feel like I have to keep explaining myself to you."

She arches an eyebrow with an "are you kidding me?" look. "I never asked you to explain anything."

"I didn't mean it like that, and, of course, I want to explain. We agreed to be honest with each other from now on. Remember?"

"Then tell me about Chelsea."

So, I do. I tell her how Chelsea and I have known each other our whole lives. I tell her how I confided in Chelsea about St. Thomas and my feelings for Jay. I tell her about how Reagan cheated on me prom night with Grayson, who was dating Lindsay at the time, and that I made a huge mistake by hooking up with Chelsea, which made things awkward and eventually ruined our friendship.

"That's pretty messed up, Zach."

Great, I'm back to being Zach again.

"I know, Jay. I tried to make things right, but she wouldn't let me. Friday night was the first time I've seen or talked to her since she left for college. She texted me yesterday and wanted to meet up, but I told her I had plans. Then she texted me this morning and asked me to meet her for breakfast. I figured it was the perfect opportunity for us to hash our shit out, so I could move on with you, and not have that guilt hanging over my head."

"If she's just a friend, then why didn't you introduce me to her Friday?"

"Because all she knows is that you hurt me. She's not the nicest person." I laugh lightly. "I was afraid she'd confront you and make a scene."

"I can take care of myself, Zach."

"I know you can, but I didn't want her airing out our business in front of everyone," I explain. "This is between you and me, Jay."

Jay looks down at her hands for a second, then back up at me. "So, if you're just friends, why did she kiss you?"

"I have no idea. She's never done that before." I shrug. "It's never been like that with us except for the one time I fucked up. She's always been like family to me."

She nods. "Like me and Lucas."

"Yeah," I agree, even though I know very little about her relationship with Lucas Wild but there's no way he could look at this girl every day and not feel some sort of attraction toward her.

"But I would never have sex with Lucas," she tells me and shudders at the thought.

I sigh. "Don't make me feel worse than I already do, Jay. I know I messed up, but it wasn't just me. It was Chelsea, too. I'm only telling you this because I don't want any more drama to come between us."

"Well, I don't like her, and she'd be wise to keep her hands and her lips off my man."

I smile, standing from the bench and holding out my hand. "Come on. Let me take you to lunch."

TRACK 34:
GIVE IT YOUR BEST SHOT
Jayla

HERE'S A FUN FACT about high school cheerleaders and football players that I did not know. Each cheerleader is assigned a football player—or two—and is responsible for decorating his locker and or making posters displaying the player's number.

One guess who Zach's cheerleader is.

Yep. *Reagan.*

But that's about to change.

"Jayla, this is Kali," Lexi says. "She'll be Zach's cheerleader from now on." I know Kali. She sits beside me in first period. Kali is cute. Her auburn hair is in an adorable pixie cut, her face is petite with a small spattering of freckles, and her eyes are golden brown.

"Thank you." I wrap my arms around Kali and pull her in for a hug. "How'd you pull that off?" I ask Lexi. "Do you have to scrub your wicked stepsister's toilet for a week?"

Lexi laughs. "Hell, no. Your cousin took care of it."

"Took care of what?" Zach asks, walking up to his locker.

"Kali is your cheerleader from now on," I tell him and he smirks. "Unless you'd rather have Reagan." I raise a questioning brow.

Zach looks down at Kali and grins. "Thanks. You just saved me a whole lot of drama."

Kali laughs. "No worries."

ZACH DID THE sweetest thing tonight at the beginning of the game. He found me in the stands, pointed to me, kissed the index and middle fingers of his right hand, and tapped them over his heart. Then he threw up both hands with the universal rocker sign as he jogged backwards onto the field. I swear I felt everyone's eyes on me. But I didn't care. I stood up, wearing my new custom designed jersey with Zach's number "6" on the front and "EASTON" across the back, and blew him a kiss.

After the game, we decided to forego any of the parties and spend a quiet night stuffing our faces with junk food and watching movies.

Wink wink.

LABOR DAY WEEKEND, I invite all my new friends over for my first barbecue get-together and to meet my best friend. "Everyone, this is my best friend, Evangeline and you guys already know Alex. Weenie, this is Brad, Cherry, Lexi, Evan, Olivia, Carter, Harper, Kali, Justin, you know Cole—"

"Unfortunately," Evangeline teases. Cole responds with a cocky smirk, flipping her off.

I curl my arm around Zach's waist. "And this is Zach. Zach, this is my sister for life."

Evangeline looks him up and down, then nods. "I approve."

Zach laughs and I roll my eyes. "Ignore her. She's a bitch, but once you get to know her, she's still a bitch." Everyone laughs.

"It's nice to finally meet you, Evangeline," Zach says.

"You, too." She smiles as my friends all stare open-mouthed at her.

"How did you two meet?" Olivia asks.

"Our moms went to college together," I lie.

"Oh," she says. "That makes sense how you know Alex."

I shake my head but Evangeline cuts in.

"Actually, I met Alex through Jay's cousin, Dylan."

Zach

I'M HAPPIER THAN I've ever been in my entire life and it's all because of my girl. Being in a relationship with Jay is easy because she's so laid-back about everything, which isn't something I'm used to. She's extremely affectionate, but, at the same time, she isn't clingy. She splits her time between lunch with our friends in the dining room and eating in the performing arts building with her Project Mayhem classmates. She's liked by everyone, except for the bitch squad—Hannah, Ashton, and Reagan. Jealousy being the main factor with all three of them.

Jay doesn't seem to care one way or the other. She and Lexi have become extremely close, which is not only good for Jay, but for Lexi, too. The two of them have formed their own social circle with Harper, Cherry, Olivia, and Kali. Jay is a good judge of character and seems to surround herself with people she trusts while keeping everyone else at arm's length, but still approachable. She laughs at Brad's goofy jokes, which I think is good for his ego. And she set him up with Cherry. I hadn't realized how deeply Brad had been hurt by Hannah because he's good at hiding his feelings behind his sense of humor.

"I DIDN'T KNOW the Pussycat Dolls reunited," Hannah says and Ashton laughs out loud, prompting all of us to turn our heads to see Jay, Harper, Lexi, Kali, Cherry, and Olivia walking toward our table.

I laugh under my breath because they do look like the Pussycat Dolls, but way hotter. However, Hannah's jab wasn't meant to be funny; she's being a bitch as usual.

"Hey, Z," Jay says as she and the girls squeeze in at our table.

"Last time I checked, this table is for the athletes, not a bunch of music nerds," Hannah barks out, curling her lip.

"Wow," Jay says, arching a brow.

"Shut up, Hannah," Brad says, then turns his gaze on Cherry and wiggles his eyebrows suggestively. "Music nerds are hot."

"I've got a better idea," Cole says standing from the table with his tray in his hand.

"Where are you going?" Ashton whines.

Ignoring Ashton, Cole takes his tray and moves to a different table. The rest of us follow, leaving Ashton, Hannah, and Piper at the table with the rest of the athletes.

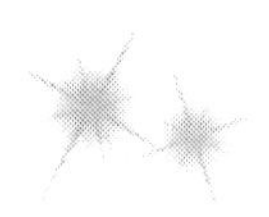

"WHAT ARE YOU reading?" I ask, shoving my textbook into my backpack. Every day, except Wednesdays and Fridays, after football practice, I come over to Jay's. She reads or writes while I do homework or study. It's the easiest way to spend time with my girl and keep my grades up, or as Jay puts it, "a win-win."

"It's a story about a teenage girl who loses her mom and her aunt to breast cancer, and she's convinced that she has it too," Jay answers with her eyes still glued to her iPad.

"That's awful. Why are you reading that? Do you think that's gonna happen to you?"

She sighs and looks over at me. "I hadn't thought about it. Thanks a lot, Z." She rolls her eyes playfully before returning her attention to the book.

Suddenly, the thought of losing her makes my heart twist painfully in my chest and I shudder. Feeling my stare, Jay turns to face me and arches a brow. "What?"

"I love you." The words just leap from my chest.

She stares at me, letting those three little words linger between us. It's not like we haven't said them a hundred times already, but for some reason they feel different. Stronger. Deeper.

Sensing my inner meltdown, she slowly closes the cover on her iPad and sets it on the table before rolling over on her side to face me. Raking her hand through my hair, she captures me with those blue-green eyes like she's staring into my soul. "I love you too, Z." She pauses. Her eyes flick back and forth over my face. "I knew it from day one. At the time, I didn't understand what I was feeling. I just knew I liked you." She smiles. "The first time you held my hand, I felt it in my heart. The first time you kissed me, I felt it in my gut. And the first time we" —she blushes— "you know, I felt it in my soul. I love you so much that it scares me."

"Why?" I ask, resting my hand on her hip, my thumb caressing the skin exposed between the hem of her T-shirt and the waist of her yoga pants.

"Because I never want to lose this feeling. I don't think I'll survive another heartbreak."

"I would never hurt you, Jay. Not on purpose, anyway. I can promise you that much."

Her brows pinch in confusion. "What do you mean 'not on purpose'?"

"I'm a guy." I shrug as though that should be reason enough. "We do dumb shit. I'm sure I'll do something to piss you off at some point in our relationship, but I'll never disrespect you by lying or cheating. I know what it feels like to not be with you and I don't want to ever feel like that again. My heart has always belonged to you, Jay. You'll always be my girl. You'll always be *the* girl."

What else is there to say?

Her hand slides from my hair to the back of my neck. She pulls my lips to hers and I roll on top of her, claiming her. A soft sigh escapes her as she parts her lips, brushing her tongue against mine. We've tried to slow down on the physical stuff, but it's impossible to keep our hands off each other in moments like this.

TRACK 35:
BELIEVE ME
Zach

WEDNESDAY AFTER PRACTICE, I pull into my driveway and my phone rings. *Evan*. "Yo!"

"Your girlfriend is beginning to piss me off," Evan grits out instead of hello.

I chuckle. "What'd she do *now*?"

"I'll show you. Meet me at the square."

"Are you serious?" I ask through a laugh, but he doesn't reply. "Hello?"

He hung up.

Shaking my head, I back out of the driveway and head over to the square, where Juliette's Dance Studio is located.

Then it hits me.

It's Wednesday.

Jay has dance class on Wednesdays and I'll bet Lexi is with her.

A few minutes later, I'm pulling up next to Evan's Ford F-250. I climb out of my Jeep to find Evan leaning against the wall outside Juliette's with his arms crossed and a scowl on his face.

"Evan." I laugh out loud. "You can't be serious. It's a dance class."

His eyebrows shoot upward. "Have you seen this class?"

"No. This is Jay's thing."

"Oh?" He huffs out a laugh and swings his hand toward to the door. "Well, come check it out."

Shaking my head, I open the door and Evan follows me inside.

"Zach?" I look over to see Trina, my next-door neighbor, sitting behind the counter.

"Hey, Miss Trina. I came to watch my girlfriend," I tell her.

She arches an inquisitive brow. "Oh? Who is your girlfriend?"

"Jay."

"Oh, Jayla." She clasps her hands together and brings them to her chest. "Good for you." She winks.

Evan leads the way down a short hallway to a waiting room with two long, leather sofas facing a one-way mirror and his cousin Levi lounging on the one of them.

"Dude, what the fuck are you doing here?" Evan barks out. "How did you even get in here? I was standing out front the whole time."

"I'm working, dickhead," Levi snaps. "I came in the back door. What are you doing here?"

Evan sweeps his hand toward the one-way mirror. "Lexi is in there." He jerks a thumb at me. "Jay's his girl, but you already know that."

Levi looks up at me and smirks. "Sorry, man. I'm just doing my job." Levi Martinez is a former Marine in his late twenties. He works security for Evan's father, Jason Martinez, who owns one of the most prestigious security companies in the country and oversees all the security on the island. And, apparently, he's Jay's new bodyguard. "For what it's worth, you got yourself a good girl. She's a fuckin' trip." He chuckles.

"Does Jay know you're here?" I ask.

He shrugs. "She knows, but she pretends she doesn't. She makes my job a hell of a lot easier than most."

Dropping down on the sofa beside Evan, I scan the group of girls huddled at the back of the room until my gaze lands on Jay as she breaks from the group and moves to stand behind Juliette, facing the mirror. Jay's wearing a pair of short-as-fuck shorts and a sports bra, which is the same shit she wears when she runs. But the knee socks are new.

Seriously, what's with the knee socks?

"So why are you here instead of the big guy?" I ask Levi.

Levi smirks. "You'll see."

Some song called "Give It To Me" blares through the speakers and the girls start moving. My eyes stay glued on Jay as she rolls her hips and spins around, giving us all a view of her barely covered ass, bends her knees, and begins twerking.

I bite down on my lip holding back a laugh, imagining the look on Bass's face if he were here right now. I love Jay's ass. It's a great ass. It's proportionate with her lean frame. It's cute and round and looks good in a pair of jeans. It also fits perfectly in the palms of my hands. But there isn't a whole lot of junk in her trunk. She can dance, though. I'll give her that.

I'm aware there are other girls in the room, but my eyes are permanently locked on Jay as she rocks her hips and wiggles her adorable ass in time with the music. Dropping to her knees, she spins around from one to the other—*guess that explains the knee socks*—before bending over and lifting her half-naked ass in the air and thrusting her hips.

Well.

Shit.

"Man, I really love my job sometimes," Levi says, prompting Evan and me to whip our heads in his direction. He waves us off. "Relax. There *are* actually *women* in this class." He jerks his chin to the mirror. "Juliette is hot."

Juliette *is* hot. She's also one of Cam's *special* friends.

The class repeats the same routine two more times and I decide it's time for me to get out of here before I embarrass myself. Shifting to hide my hard-on, I tell Evan, "I need to go."

Evan's whole body shakes with silent laughter beside me. "I told you."

Jayla

After dance class, Lexi and I change out of our hoochie mama dancewear and head to Mac's, with Levi trailing behind us. Wednesdays have sort of become our girls' night out ever since Lexi started taking the class with me. I don't really need a bodyguard, but Bass insists that I have one when I'm out at night.

As Lexi and I come walking out of the parking garage, I spot a familiar redhead standing outside of Mac's, having a conversation with a woman. The woman looks pissed or upset. It's dark, so I can't tell for sure.

Before I can decide, the crazy woman cocks her hand back and slaps Harper across the face.

"Oh, hell, no," Lexi and I shout at the same time before rushing toward them. "Hey, lady!" Lexi yells. "What the hell is wrong with you?"

Levi rushes past us and steps between them, facing down the woman. "Ma'am, you need to leave before I arrest you for assault."

"I'm leaving." She reaches around Levi and points at Harper. "Stay the hell away from my husband." Then she storms off.

Say what now?

"Are you okay, Harper?" I ask.

"Yep," she answers, but her shaky voice says otherwise.

"What can we do?" Lexi asks.

"Nothing. I'm fine."

"Harper, whatever is going on, you can tell us," I prompt. "If you don't want to talk about it, that's okay, too, but don't lie to us. You're not fine. We're not judging you. It's your life and your business, but if you want to talk or if you need anything, we're here for you. No questions asked and no strings attached."

"Do you really mean that?" She turns her head to look at me.

"Of course, we do," Lexi adds.

She blows out a breath. "Good, because I need a place to stay until I can get things figured out."

"What about your dad?" Harper told me she lived with her dad, but he travels a lot for work.

"You said no questions asked."

"You have to give me something, Harper, or Emerson Mackenzie will be all up in your business."

Harper winces.

“I’d offer to let you stay with me, but I live under the same roof with Satan herself,” Lexi admits, prompting all three of us to laugh.

We all turn to Levi who looks uncomfortable with the entire conversation. “I’ll be over there,” he says, pointing toward the entrance to Mac’s.

Once Levi’s out of earshot, Harper takes a deep breath. “This conversation stays between us and I’m giving you the short version because I have a lot of baggage that I’m not ready to share.” Lexi and I both nod. “After my sister died, I met Josh. He’s older and apparently, he’s married—but I didn’t know that. I don’t live with my dad. In fact, I’ve never met him. I live with Josh. And now I need to move.”

My eyes nearly bug out of my head. “Shit,” I drawl and look over at Lexi who is stunned silent. I turn back to Harper. “Yeah, no, that won’t fly with Emerson. What else you got?”

TRACK 36: MAKE YOUR MOVE

Zach

Jay is in the passenger seat, searching for a station on the radio when she finds "Closer" by The Chainsmokers. "Oh, I love this song." She sings along, bopping her head. She's even got that whole snap combination down like a boss. And just when she's really getting into it, the song gets cut off by an incoming call from Cole. Rolling her eyes, she tsks, mumbling a curse under her breath and I laugh to myself as she leans forward and stabs the phone button on the dash.

"What!"

"JJ, come see me," Willow's sweet voice echoes through the car.

Jay looks over at me and smiles as she responds to Willow. "Boo, you want me to come see you?"

"Uh-huh."

"Where are you?"

"At my's house." She giggles, prompting Jay and me to laugh.

"Where's Cole?"

"He right here."

"Yo!" Cole's voice booms through the speakers.

"What's going on?" Jay asks.

"Willow wants you to come see her."

"Because," Jay urges.

"Fine." He sighs. "Mom and Dad are out. Dylan is working. I have a date and I'm not leaving her here alone with Aiden."

"He's thirteen. He's old enough to watch her."

"Back up," I cut in. "You have a date?"

Cole ignores my question and continues his plea. "He doesn't watch her. He's too busy playing his Xbox."

"Since when does Cole Mackenzie go on dates?" I tease. "With who?" I already know who, but I want to hear him admit it. Harper has been living with Jay for the last few weeks because her dad took a job overseas and Harper didn't want to leave school in her senior year.

"Harper, and not a word, asshole." And Willow cute little voice echoes "asshole" in the background. "Why do you always choose to repeat the bad words, Willow? Stop it," Cole admonishes.

"You stop, Co," Willow sasses back.

"All right," Jays says with a laugh. "We'll be there in a few minutes."

"Thanks, Jay."

Cole hangs up and I glance over at Jay with my bottom lip pushed out.

"Don't worry, Z," she says. "We can watch a movie later."

She knows me so well.

"OKAY, WILLOW IS down," Jay announces as she sashays into the living room and drops down on the sofa beside me. "What are you guys playing?" she asks, stretching her legs across my lap.

"Call of Duty," Aiden answers. He's stretched out on the opposite end of the sofa still wearing his baseball uniform from practice.

"So, baseball is your sport, huh?" I ask Aiden.

"Huh?" He gives me a sideways glance not wanting to take his eyes off the game.

"Baseball. You wanna be a professional ball player like your Uncle Liam?" Liam Mackenzie is a badass on the field and one of the best shortstops in the MLB.

"Yeah." He smiles and turns his attention back to the TV. "And I want a supermodel girlfriend like Evangeline," he adds.

Jay snorts. "Aiden, play ball because you love it. Because you're passionate about it. Not because you want a supermodel girlfriend."

"Do you love singing?" he asks her.

"Yeah. Why?"

Aiden shrugs. "You just don't seem all that into it."

"I like singing, for fun. But I love writing music and mentoring others."

"So, your passion is teaching and helping others become successful," I add.

Jay smiles. "Yeah, I guess it is."

And that right there is just another reason why I love this girl so much.

"HAVE YOU GIVEN any more thought about college?" Jay asks, running her fingers through my hair. I love when she does this.

My eyes roll to the back of my head. "No, but my dad got a call from Coach Morgan, who got a call from the coach at Gulf Coast University. They want me to play for their team. Their football team is still fairly new and he guaranteed I'd get plenty of playing time."

Her hand stills in my hair. "Are you considering it?"

"I don't know. Maybe."

"What do your parents think?"

I shrug. "The decision is mine and they'll support me no matter what." I peek open one eye. "What do you think?"

"I agree with your parents. Trust your gut, Z, and do what feels right."

"What about you? Have you thought more about what you want to do after the tour?"

"I love my Project Mayhem class. I like performing and I'll continue to write music, but I don't want to be a rock star. I was thinking about what you said before, about teaching others, and I'm going to talk to Principal Avery about becoming a volunteer in future Project Mayhem classes."

"You're amazing." I reach up, cupping the back of her head, and bring her lips to mine. "I love you."

"I love you, too, but I'll love you even more if you get me some water."

I smile against her lips. "How can I say no to that?"

Pressing one more kiss to her lips, I roll out of bed, pull on my boxer briefs, and head to the kitchen. Cam's house is quiet and dark, but the moonlight shining through the wall of windows gives off plenty of light for me to see my way to the kitchen.

"Oompf."

"What the—"

"Shhh!" Cam shushes me while cupping a hand over Emerson's mouth. "What are you doing?" he whisper-yells.

"Getting a water," I whisper-yell back and take in Emerson's appearance. Messy hair and legs bare. And wearing one of Cam's T-shirts. "What are *you* doing?"

"Ow!" Cam yanks his hand away from Emerson's mouth and shakes it. "Why'd you bite me?"

"Is Jayla here?" Now she's whisper-yelling.

"Yeah."

Her eyes nearly pop out of her head when she sees that I'm in my underwear. "Are you…? Did you…?" She slaps a palm against her forehead and groans. Cam attempts to cover Emerson's mouth again, but she slaps his hand away.

"Zach!" Jay calls out from the bedroom. "Did you get lost? Where's my water?"

Emerson pinches her lips together and points at me. "Not a word. And if you hurt my daughter or get her pregnant, I will see to it personally that Bass breaks your pretty little face and your throwing arm. Got it?"

"I didn't see anything." I hold my hands up in surrender. "This is so fucking weird," I grit out, sidestepping Emerson to get to the fridge.

"Zach! Seriously, I'm dying of thirst in here. What are you doing?"

"I'm coming!"

TRACK 37:
TRY
Zach

AFTER FOOTBALL PRACTICE, I notice Jay's Range Rover is still in the student parking lot. Lately, she's been staying after school at least once a week to rehearse with Alex. Quickly, I change and head over to the performing arts building auditorium, taking a seat in the back row, so not to disturb them. Jay and Alex are both on stage. Alex is perched on a stool strumming his guitar. Jay is standing with her hands cupped around the mic, eyes closed, belting out the lyrics to one of her songs. She's changed out of her uniform and is now wearing a tight half t-shirt with the word *Princess* written in hot pink across the front. It reminds me of the t-shirt she wore to Disney the first time we met. Who knows? It could be the same shirt. It's that small. Her leggings have music notes printed down the sides of the legs and *Jesus* she's wearing combat boots. *Just when I thought she couldn't be any sexier.*

"What's up with them?" Cole says, dropping down in the seat beside me, pulling me out of my daydream.

I realize the music has stopped. Jay has her back to us and by the jerky movements of her head, I'd say she and Alex are arguing.

I shake my head. "I have no idea."

"Screw you, Alex!" Jay yells as she kicks Alex's stool before she storms off the stage. Alex shakes his head and he hops off the stool to follow after her. Cole and I both leap from our seats and jog over to the adjoining classroom.

"You're not taking this seriously," Alex accuses.

"What are you talking about? I performed that song the same way I always have," Jay argues. "I think I know how to perform the music I wrote, Alex, or I wouldn't be going on tour. Remember, I'm the one who chose you to be a part of it."

"Marcus chose me."

Oh, shit.

I leap forward and curl my arm around Jay's waist just as she lunges for Alex.

"I chose you!" she yells again. "It was my decision. Had I known you were gonna be an asshole, I would've picked someone else."

"How am I being an asshole? All I said was that you need to stop daydreaming about your boyfriend for five minutes and focus on what's important."

"Maybe he's what's important. Maybe I'm sick of having my life dictated for me. Maybe I don't want to do this shit anymore." She jerks out of my hold, snatches up her bag, and turns back to Alex. "You're not my father, Alex," she snaps out before she storms out of the room.

Cole and I look over at Alex.

Alex shakes his head before he rounds his desk, drops down in his chair, and blows out a breath. "Go after her Zach." He waves me off. "I don't want her driving home when she's upset."

I look over at Cole. "Follow me so you can bring me back to get my Jeep."

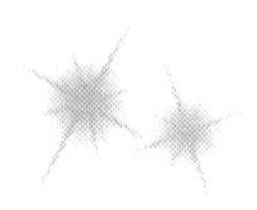

"HOW DARE HE say that me!" she yells from the passenger seat. "I've been singing and writing songs for a lot longer than he has. I could sing every song on *Jaybird* backwards and forwards. I wrote that fucking album." She turns in her seat to face me and stabs her finger into her chest. "I'm the one who chose him."

"Why did he say Marcus did?" I ask and cringe, expecting a fist to the temple. Because she's that mad. In all the years I've known Jay, I never knew she had a temper.

Not gonna lie… it's hot.

"Because he *was* my dad's choice, but my dad left the decision to me." She huffs out a humorless laugh. "Funny, considering I don't have say in anything else."

"Like what?"

"Like all of it." She throws her hands up. "Why can't everyone just back the fuck off and let me have a normal life?"

"Jay, if you don't want to do it, then don't."

She turns her head to look out the passenger window and in a low voice she says, "I have to."

BEFORE I CAN put the Range Rover in Park, Jay is out of the car and stomping through the front door. Grabbing her bag from the back seat, I slowly make my way to the front door where Bass is waiting.

Bass quirks an eyebrow.

"It wasn't me," I say holding up my free hand in surrender, handing over her bag.

"It was Alex," Cole says coming up behind me. "They got into an argument and Uncle Marcus's name came up." He shakes his head.

"She's pretty pissed," I add.

"I kinda picked up on that when she came storming through here." He chuckles. "What's the matter, Romeo? You didn't know Princess had a temper?" He throws his head back and laughs. "Oh, this is gonna be fun." He turns on his heels and heads down the hall with Jay's bag thrown over his shoulder.

I look over at Cole and he smirks. "Don't look at me. She's your girlfriend."

"HEY." I PAUSE, my fingers hovering over the piano keys, and look up to see Alex slowly moving toward me. His hands are shoved in his front pockets, shoulders slumped.

"Hey," I reply, softly.

"I'm sorry, Jay. I shouldn't have said what I did. I'm honored that you chose me and that I was your only choice. And I'm not trying to take your dad's place. I know he was tough on you at times and that wasn't my intention. It's just lately, you just don't seem as devoted to your music and that concerns me. Especially with the tour next year."

I shrug. "That's not true. It's just that for the first time in my life... I actually *have* a life. I get to be a normal teenager. I have a boyfriend and friends. And I'm happy."

"And I want that for you. But I also don't want to see you let your talent go to waste. You have a gift many people would kill for. Don't take it for granted."

"I know. I'm sorry, too. I overreacted. And just for the record, I wasn't daydreaming about my boyfriend. I was actually thinking about what it's going to be like with the two of us up on stage next year." I smirk.

"Oh? Well, that's more like it." He leans forward, resting his arms on top of the piano. "Why didn't you just say that?"

"Because you pissed me off."

A smile pulls up one side of his mouth. "You've got quite the temper."

"Only when you piss me off."

"I think you scared Zach."

"Maybe he'll think twice before pissing me off," I snicker.

TRACK 38:
FAKING IT
Jayla

JAYBIRD,

Your mother tells me Homecoming is an important dance. Not as formal as prom but just as important. I don't understand the difference, but you have my vote for Homecoming Queen. I wish I could be there to see my baby girl all dressed up for her first dance, but I know you'll look beautiful as always. Have fun tonight but not too much fun, and remember to make lots of memories.

I love you always.

Love,

Daddy

P.S. Tell your date to keep his hands to himself.

"YOU OKAY?" HARPER asks from my doorway.

I nod. "Yeah," I say, swiping away the tears before carefully sliding the note back into the envelope and tossing it inside the top drawer of my nightstand. Harper has been staying with me now for nearly a month. She still won't talk about her 'baggage' and I'm keeping my promise. Even though I'm dying to know, I respect her privacy.

On a side note, she knows about my dad and I'm hoping maybe when she realizes I trust her with my shit, she'll trust me with hers.

Standing from the bed, I sniffle but smile, grabbing my purse and moving toward the door. "I have an appointment with Xavier. What time is yours?" Harper is going to Homecoming with Cole.

Ashton is pissed.

"Not until one. Do you want me to go with you?"

"Nah. I need to clear my head." I reach out and hug her. "Thanks."

"Of course, Jay. I know what you're going through. It's been over four years since my mom died, but I still miss her so much. But losing my sister and my niece is something I'm not sure I'll ever get over." This is the first time she's mentioned a niece and I wonder if she realizes she just let that bit of info slip. I'm tempted to ask her about it, but I'm sticking to my promise of no questions asked.

Nodding, I say, "I'm sorry. I guess sometimes I get so lost in my own misery that I forget I'm not the only one who's going through this."

"It's okay. It's called grief. You lost a parent. It's only been eight months. Your heart is still healing. If you ever need to cry, I've got two shoulders. If you need a hug, I've got two arms. If you need someone to just listen, I've got two ears. And if you ever just need space... well, I've got two feet that can carry me to the next room." We both laugh. "Sometimes life just sucks and we wonder 'why me?' But trust me, the day will come when you wake up and it doesn't hurt so much."

CAM IS SITTING at the breakfast bar, sipping coffee, and reading on his iPad when I walk into the kitchen.

"Hey," I say, heading straight for the refrigerator and pulling out the orange juice. I'm not a coffee drinker unless it's one of those sweet girly drinks Jay gets for me. Which, by the way, taste nothing like coffee.

"Hey, I was just about to wake you."

"Why?" I ask, glancing over my shoulder as I pull a glass from the cabinet.

"I just got off the phone with Em. She said Jay was pretty upset this morning when she left for her appointment."

"Why? Did Emerson finally admit to Jay that she has a secret boyfriend?" I smirk.

"No," he says, eyeing me over the rim of his coffee mug before taking a sip and setting it down. "Jay gets a little sad when she reads one of Marcus's notes. Em thought it would be nice if you took her out to lunch or something, after her appointment."

I shake my head irritated. "Of course, those notes are going to upset her. I get that Emerson is protective, but maybe she should back off a little and give Jay some space to work it out. It's okay for her to be sad."

Cam huffs out a laugh. "Believe me, I agree. But then again, I don't have any children, so I don't get an opinion. Em's right to worry, though. Jay took Marcus's death pretty hard."

"I've heard."

"Really?" He raises his brows. "She told you about the hospital?"

"Hospital?" I frown. *What the hell is he talking about?*

Cam closes his eyes and exhales slowly through his nose. "What have you heard?"

"Just what I said. What happened at the hospital?"

Cam curses under his breath. "Nothing happened *at* the hospital. A couple of weeks after Marcus died, Jay was hospitalized for severe depression and dehydration. She was practically starving herself."

"What?" I breathe out. "On purpose? She would never—" The words are stuck in my throat.

"She claimed she wasn't trying to hurt herself on purpose. She was sad and hadn't realized what she was doing."

"Does Emerson believe her?"

"She does, mostly. At least she wants to, but that's why she's so far up her ass." He shrugs. "Jay's all Em has left of Marcus."

"I believe her. Jay would never hurt herself intentionally. She cares about way too many people to hurt them, let alone leave them."

"How long have you two been sneaking over here to have sex?" I smirk at his not so subtle change in subject. With only a ten-year age difference, Cam has always been more like an older brother to me than my uncle. We've exchanged our fair share of stories about our hookups in the past. Mostly his. But now that I'm with Jay and he's apparently banging her mom, there will be no more sharing from now on—or *ever*.

"Are you asking as my awesome Uncle Cam or Emerson's boyfriend?"

"Neither." He pauses to run a hand down his face, "I'm asking as Cam, who's known Jayla since she was a kid. I love and adore that girl. Liam loves and adores that girl. And he'll kick your ass if you hurt her. Hell, I'll kick your ass if you hurt her."

"I love her. I'm not gonna hurt her or get her pregnant. We're both covered. What do you think Liam will do when he finds out his best friend is banging his sister?" I ask, quirking a curious brow.

"He's not going to find out until we're ready to tell him. Unfortunately, Em and I put you in a difficult position last night but you absolutely cannot tell Jay. I mean it, Zach."

"What are you doing, Cam?" I cross my arms over my chest. "Do you have any idea how many people are going to get dragged into this if things don't work out?"

Cam presses his index finger to his lips, then leans his head back to look down the hall toward the guest rooms before looking at me. "Logan is here," he says quietly. "All I need is for word to get back to your mom or mine."

"He wouldn't say anything to Mom. But he'd definitely call you out for being a cougar-fucker."

"She's not a cougar," he defends. "She's not even forty. And she's sexy as fuck."

Okay, I'll give him that. Emerson is hot... for a mom. But still, it's weird. And when Jay finds out—because she will—shit is gonna hit the fan.

"When did Logan get here?"

"Early this morning. He'll probably sleep most of the day."

Honestly, I can't remember the last time I talked to my brother. We've texted a few times, but he's been busy with law school and I've been busy with football and Jay. Logan doesn't even know that we're together. Unless my parents told him. Which is likely.

"So, what exactly is going on with you and Emerson? Are you guys just fucking or are you in love?" I tease.

His expression is blank as he rubs his hand over the short scruff on his jaw. "I'm in love with her."

My eyebrows skyrocket up to my hairline. "Seriously? Does Emerson know how you feel?"

He nods slowly. "She does."

"Does she feel the same?"

He blows out a breath. "It's complicated."

"Well, at least now you can update your Facebook status," I say with a laugh.

Cam chuckles. "Asshole. I know she loves me, but she's afraid it's too soon after losing Marcus to admit it. I think she's worried what people will think of her—what Jay will think of her. That she didn't love Marcus enough if she's able to move on so quickly. Right now, I'm just giving her the space she needs."

"I hope you guys figure it out before Jay does."

"Emerson and I are friends. Jay is used to seeing us together. When Em is ready to be with me permanently, then we'll talk to Jay."

"What do you mean permanently? Like married?"

He shrugs. "I'd marry Em in a heartbeat. I know you think it's weird, but I love her, Zach. I have for longer than I care to admit. She's an incredible woman. An incredibly stubborn woman, but that's one of the things I love about her. You see her as Jayla's mom, but I see her for the beautiful, strong woman she is. Everyone thinks Jayla gets her caring heart from Marcus, but she gets it from Emerson, too. They're a lot more alike than you think."

"I can see that. I'm not judging you, Cam. I'm happy for you. I'm just worried. I know you think it's about you and Em, but there are a lot of people who will be affected if things don't work out. What about Mom?"

"What about her? It's none of her business."

"I agree. But if things progress between you and Emerson, maybe you should try to get her and Mom in a room together to talk things out. I still don't understand how those went from being best friends for eighteen years to suddenly hating each other."

"I have no idea. I asked Em about it once and she shut me down."

I move over to the sink and rinse out my glass before putting it in the dishwasher. "I'm gonna hop in the shower. Will you drop me off at the salon?"

"Sure."

Jayla

AN HOUR AND a half later, I'm feeling very relaxed. Probably from the two mimosas Xavier fed me. Xavier is brushing on the last coat of polish on my nails when there's a soft knock on the door.

"Come in," Xavier calls out. The door swings open and the hottest guy I've ever laid eyes on walks in. "Damn," Xavier mumbles under his breath.

I smile. "Hi, Z. Whatcha doing here?" I ask, eyeing him up and down. He looks fine as hell with his jeans sitting low on his narrow waist and a light blue T-shirt stretched across his broad, muscled chest. But it's the backwards baseball cap that does it for me. *He's so damn hot and he's all mine.*

"I came to see if you wanted to have lunch," he replies, standing in the doorway with his hands shoved in his front pockets, looking uncomfortable under the heat of Xavier's stare.

"Sure, I'd love that." I shoot him a flirty wink. "I'll be done in ten."

"Okay. I'll wait for you up front," he says, before quickly closing the door.

"Damn, girl, that man is fine. Does he by any chance have a gay twin brother."

"He is, isn't he?" I snort. "He has an older brother, but he's straight."

He huffs. "Figures."

"You're hot. Why hasn't some gorgeous man snatched you up

yet?"

"Because I'm a picky bitch." He smiles and suddenly the gorgeous face of Brice Manning pops in my head, but I'll have to play matchmaker another day. I have a lunch date with my hot boyfriend. "Okay. You're all set." Xavier stands up and moves over to the door. "Have fun tonight and send me lots of pics." He opens the door and kisses me on the cheek.

I snake my arms around his waist and give him a squeeze. "Thank you for taking care of me today." I press a kiss to his cheek.

"My pleasure, girl." He smiles as he edges me out the door. "Now go get that fine-ass man of yours out of here before one of these cougars sinks her claws in him."

TRACK 39: I GET IT

Zach

"I'M READY, Z," Jay says, holding out her hands. Tossing the magazine on the coffee table, I reach for her hands and she pulls me from the sofa and out the door. "Where did you park?" she asks once we're outside.

"Cam dropped me off. Give me your keys. I'll drive."

Letting go of my hand because she needs both of hers to dig through her large purse, she pulls out her keys.

Surprisingly, the weather has cooled down, so we sit outside on the patio under one of the umbrella-covered tables. "You okay?" I ask cautiously.

She furrows her brows. "Yeah, why?"

Shrugging, I lean back in my chair. "You seem a little sad."

"I got a note from my dad this morning. His notes always make me a little sad, but not like before."

"Before what?" I realize my mistake and so does Jay.

She narrows her eyes and studies me for a moment. "Who told you?"

"Does it matter?" I pause. "Why didn't *you* tell me? I thought there weren't supposed to be any secrets between us."

"Tell you what? That I got so sad that I made myself sick and ended up in the hospital? That my family probably thinks I did it on purpose?"

"No one thinks that." Reaching across the table, I take her hand, urging her to stand and guiding her around the table until she's sitting in my lap. I curl my arms around her waist and press a kiss below her ear. "Hey." I take her chin between my fingers and turn her face to me. "I know my girl would never intentionally hurt herself. I get it. You were sad. I can't imagine what you went through."

"It hurt so much, Z," she says with a shaky breath. "I couldn't get out of bed. All I wanted to do was sleep away the pain until it didn't hurt anymore. Some days I'd try reading a book to escape reality for a few hours. Those were my good days. Grace would bring me food and water, but I guess I wasn't eating or drinking enough. I felt weak and just so tired. My mom blames herself for not paying attention, but it wasn't her fault. It wasn't anyone's fault. We were all sad. Sometimes we just get so caught up in our own pain, we forget about everything and everyone else. We lose the ability to care. That's what happened. I stopped caring."

Our waitress brings our food and sets it on the table before scurrying off. Jay stands from my lap and moves back to her seat.

We pick at our food in comfortable silence and after a few minutes I ask, "What did the note from your dad say?"

She smiles. "That he wishes he could be here to see me dressed up for my first high school dance. And that my date better keep his hands to himself." She snorts. "I swear, every time I read one of his notes, it's like he's right there reading it over my shoulder and I imagine the sound of his voice as I read it. I look forward to his notes because it feels like I'm getting more time with him. Does that make sense?"

"Of course, it does. I'm sure your dad's intentions weren't to upset you, but to remind you he's here with you for all the special moments in your life."

"What scares me the most is what happens when there are no more notes? I'm not sure if his notes are helping me or hurting me. Am I only getting by because of his notes, or am I healing because of them? Either way, I don't want them to stop. I guess that's something I need to talk to Dr. Ramos about."

"Who is Dr. Ramos?"

"She's my therapist. And I'm pretty sure Liam is fucking her."

I cough out a laugh. "Wow. Okay." I glance at the time on my phone. "What time do you need to start getting ready?"

She smiles knowingly. "Dinner is at five, so I need to start getting ready around three thirty." She looks down at her watch. "It's one thirty," she says, scooting back from the table. "That gives us a couple of hours of play time."

Yes!

I jerk to my feet. "Cam took off with my grandparents for the day, so we have the house to ourselves." Pulling some cash from my wallet, I toss it on the table and take her by the hand. "Let's go."

"GET NAKED," I command, toeing off my shoes and pulling my shirt over my head, tossing it next to hers on the floor.

"You are so freaking hot!" Jay purrs from the middle of my bed where she lies naked as a... well, a Jaybird. Her hair is fanned out over the pillow and her arms are stretched over her head.

I shove my jeans to the floor and kick them to the side before crawling onto the bed. I pause, hovering over her. "You're beautiful," I say, rolling to my back, bringing her with me so she's straddling my hips. She leans forward, placing one hand on my chest, the other guiding me to her entrance. Her mouth parts slightly with a small gasp as she stares down at me with a mixture of love and lust swirling in her blue-green eyes.

I'm still amazed that this beautiful girl loves me. And she's mine.

A flash of movement in my peripheral vision has me turning my head slightly in the direction of the bathroom where I see Logan standing in the doorway, wide-eyed and mouth open in the form of an "O". Damn. I forgot about Logan.

There's nothing I can say or do because the tingling sensation at the base of my spine renders me speechless. I'm past the point of no return. Closing my eyes, I bury my face between Jay's breasts and let go with a growl.

TRACK 40:
KICKING ASS & TAKING NAMES
Zach

STANDING IN THE driveway, I wave as Jay backs out and drives off before I storm inside to kick Logan's ass. If Jay knew he was there, she didn't say anything.

Shoving open his door, I find Logan lying in bed with his hands tucked behind his head and a shit-eating grin on his face. "What the fuck, Logan!"

He whistles through his teeth. "Holy shit, little bro." He laughs. "That was one hot piece of ass."

"Don't talk about her like that!" I pause, taking a deep breath to rein in my temper. "You're lucky she didn't see you."

"She didn't." He waves me off. "Nice sex face, by the way. Of course, I'll have to block that part out when I'm replaying the image her getting off in my head." He throws his head back and lets out a high-pitched moan like a girl.

"You know you could've just shut the door. Not stand there and watch like some creeper." I move to punch him in the thigh.

He laughs and holds up his hands in surrender. "I'm sorry. I just woke up and I was taking a piss. The door was unlocked. I didn't know you had company. Who was that? I thought you were bangin' that little blonde. Melanie or something?"

"Reagan." I shake my head. "We broke up in May. Good to know you were paying attention during our little chats, big bro," I retort.

"I do listen. I just forgot for a hot minute. Reagan is the judge's daughter, right? She cheated on you with Grayson Martinez at prom." I nod. "See, I listen," he declares. "So, tell me... Who's the babe?"

I hold back my laugh and tell him, "Jayla."

Logan's eyes go wide and his mouth pops open. "Sparkles?" he chokes out. "Shit, Zach. Dad mentioned you were spending time with her. I completely forgot." He smirks. "I told you she'd grow up to be hot. So, you finally made your move."

"Actually, I made my move last summer. Several times." I waggle my eyebrows.

"How do the Mackenzie boys feel about you bangin' their little cousin?"

"She's my girlfriend." I correct him. "And they're cool with our relationship."

"You know her dad was Marcus King, right?"

"Yeah. How'd you know?"

"Dylan." Logan smiles like a proud big brother. "Good for you, Zachy." I punch him in the thigh. "Ow! Dude, lay off the steroids. When the hell did you get so fuckin' strong?"

"Football, dickhead. You should pull your nose out of those law books and hit the gym once in a while."

"Fuck off!" He punches me in the arm. It doesn't hurt. "I try to go to the gym when I can. I'm just busy."

"I know." I drop down on the edge of the bed. "You look good, asshole. Tired, but good. What are you doing home, anyway?"

"I have some legal stuff I need Dad's help with. I'm flying back tomorrow night. What are you up to for the rest of the day? You wanna do something?"

"I wish I could, but our Homecoming dance is tonight and I have to be at Jay's house for dinner at five." I stand up from the end of the bed and stretch my arms over my head. "I need to go home and get ready. You should come with me to the house and then over to Jay's for dinner. Meet her mom, Emerson."

"Ah. The enemy," Logan jokes, rubbing his hands together.

"Emerson's pretty chill," I tell him as I head for the door. "Cam will be there and so will our grandparents."

Logan rolls from the bed and slips on his shoes. "So, how long has Cam been sleeping with the enemy?"

His question has me jerking to a stop in the doorway and turning around. Logan laughs and holds up his hands in defense. "Don't worry, I'm not gonna say anything. Everything echoes in this house. Cam should really consider putting some furniture in here."

LOGAN MAKES HIS way into the kitchen and my mom squeals in excitement as I jog up the stairs to my room for a shower. Homecoming isn't as formal as prom; we're only required to wear a suit and tie. After my shower, I put on my black Calvin Klein suit and hang the silver tie Jay bought for me to match her dress loosely around my neck. Grabbing my keys, wallet, and phone off my bed, I hurry downstairs to find my mother so she can help me with my tie.

Logan's raised voice carries from my dad's office. "Did you at least see if Zoe was okay before you slammed the door in her face?" he asks.

"Zoe wasn't with her," my mom replies.

"Logan, this isn't her fault," my dad demands. "We'll find Zoe, I promise."

"What if we don't?" Logan asks, his voice sounding worried.

"We will," my dad promises.

I use the break in conversation to step inside the office. "Mom, can you tie this for me, please."

"Oh, my God, Zach." She brings her hand to her forehead. "I completely forgot about Homecoming. I'm the worst mother ever."

"No, you're not." I chuckle.

"I didn't even get to congratulate you on your win last night. Why are you leaving so early?" she asks.

"Because I'm having dinner at Jay's."

"Oh?"

"Don't act surprised, Liz," my dad says. "We were invited."

"You were?" I ask.

My dad nods. "Actually, your grandparents invited us at

Emerson's request, but your mom didn't think it was a good idea. I'm sorry, but we won't be able to make it."

I shrug. "It's fine. You guys are the ones missing out on my senior year."

"Hey," my mom says. "That's not fair. You're never home anymore."

I shrug again. "It's true. You don't like Emerson and since you aren't interested in getting to know my girlfriend, I spend my time over there or at Cam's. Tonight is Jay's first school dance, you know? Emerson spent the entire day putting together this big dinner party for Jay's friends and their families."

Regret flashes in her eyes and now I feel bad, but she's so damn stubborn.

"He's right," Logan adds with a smirk. "I've seen them together and I know she makes Zach *very* happy."

He's such an asshole.

My mom finishes off my tie, then stands on her tippy-toes to kiss me on the cheek. "Have fun tonight, sweetheart." She pats my chest and heads upstairs.

I look over at my dad with a frown. He shakes his head. "She'll get over it." He pats me on the back before pulling me in for a hug. "Have a good time tonight."

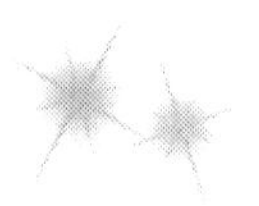

"JESUS," LOGAN SAYS, ducking his head to look out the windshield at Jay's massive castle as I steer up the driveway. "I thought the Manning's house was big, but this is ridiculous. It looks like a hotel."

I laugh. "I know. We're taking Jay's Range Rover to the dance, so you can use my Jeep tonight if you want."

"Are you guys coming back to Cam's after?"

"It's up to Jay, so I'm gonna say that's highly likely since she's not a fan of high school parties."

Logan laughs. "For some reason that doesn't surprise me. She grew up around adults."

The front door opens and my beautiful girl appears in the doorway wearing a formfitting silver dress that stops just above her knees. Logan hops out of the Jeep and runs over to Jay, scooping her up in a hug and spinning her around. "Look at you, Sparkles, all grown up."

"Shut up, Logan," Jay warns through a laugh. "This time I won't be aiming for your shins."

"How did you know I was here?" I ask.

She holds up her phone. "Whenever you use your code at the gate, it notifies me."

"Is Cam here yet?" Logan asks.

"Everyone's here. They're in the back," she tells us as she closes the front door.

"Sweet." Logan kisses her on the cheek and jogs toward the back of the house.

"You look gorgeous, Z," she says, slipping her hands underneath my jacket and pressing a soft kiss on my lips.

"Jayla, does my grandson know you're going around kissing handsome young men?" I turn and smile at Grandma Kate. "Well, hello, handsome. You look just like my grandson."

I hug my grandma and kiss the top of her head. "Hi, Grandma. I'm sorry I haven't been around much. I've been busy with school and football."

"And me," Jay adds.

"Grandma, Logan's here," I tell her. "He just went out back."

"Oh, Logan," she says in surprise, pressing a hand to her chest. "I feel like I haven't seen him in years." Her voices carries as she hurries off in the same direction.

TRACK 41:
NOT WHAT IT SEEMS
Jayla

HOMECOMING IS BASICALLY a high school party with pretty dresses and no alcohol. It's not like in those movies where someone spikes the punch. Instead, everyone parties beforehand. It's called pre-gaming. Maybe I'm boring, but getting wasted before a school dance isn't my thing. Maybe it's because it was my first dance and I wanted to remember it. Or maybe it's just how I was taught to act in public. Honestly, I wasn't all that impressed with Homecoming. I had more fun at dinner with my friends and family. But at least I can check Homecoming dance off my bucket list of things to do as a normal teenager. And I can say that I went to said dance with my guy.

The highlight of my night was performing with the Project Mayhem class. But, of course, what's a school function without some drama? First, Ashton threw a bitch fit because Cole brought Harper as his date. Even a blind person could see that one coming. Cole quickly shut Ashton down with a few gruff words and basically told her to get over it. I kind of felt bad for Ashton because there were tears and clearly her feelings for Cole are unrequited. But she had to know she was taking a risk getting involved with him in the first place. I love Cole because he's my family, but he's not exactly Mr. Romantic and he's never claimed to be. I know he has a good heart, which he keeps guarded for some reason, despite what others might think. I've never known him to be serious with any girl. Harper is the first and I worry she might get hurt. But she's assured me that she's got it under control.

We'll see.

The second temper tantrum was from Hannah when Brad brought Cherry as his date. Hannah even stooped to spewing hateful words about Cherry's mixed race. But Cherry, being the tough girl she is, didn't even flinch at Hannah's ugly words. Instead, she took the high road, smiled, and curled her arm around Brad's waist, keeping her dignity intact. However, Brad did not. He literally lost his shit. Honestly, I didn't think Brad had it in him.

Hannah is a complete psycho. And I don't mean she's a psycho because she's an ex-girlfriend. The girl is cray-cray. You can see it in her eyes.

Reagan, surprisingly, kept her distance, staying beside her date, a guy from the baseball team. But I caught her watching Zach and I, more than a handful of times.

The second highlight of the night was when Lexi was crowned Homecoming Queen and Cole was crowned Homecoming King. However, this prompted the grand finale of all temper tantrums. I don't think I could've rolled my eyes any harder at Ashton, not feeling the least bit sorry for her that time. Sometimes I find it hard to believe that she's a senior in high school; she throws more temper tantrums than Willow.

Instead of the king and queen sharing a slow dance, the DJ switched it up with a booty dance, making things less awkward for Evan and Harper watching from the side.

Let me tell you, Cole can get down with the best of them. He had the whole room cheering him on. Then we all joined him and Lexi on the dance floor. Zach surprised me, too. I had no idea he could move like that.

But the one thing that stuck with me the entire night was my conversation with Piper. It was a rare moment where we found ourselves sitting at a table alone. Piper has never gone out of her way to rude to me like Ashton, Hannah, and Reagan. She's the friendliest of the cheerleaders, aside from Kali.

"Why don't you have a date, Piper?" I asked.

Piper shrugged. "Because they always expect something by the end of the night. No thanks."

I frowned. "Like what? Sex?"

She nodded. "I'm not claiming to be an angel or anything, but give a blow job or two and you're labeled a slut for the rest of your high school days, even though I'm still a virgin."

"You're kidding?" I'd heard rumors about Piper, remembering the first time I met her. It was right after she came out of the bathroom with Zach. Sure, I could make assumptions and buy into the rumors. But high school rumors are no different than tabloid rumors as far as I'm concerned. Things aren't always what they seem. So, I reserve judgment for those who've earned it. Like Reagan. Piper has always been nice to me and her reputation is none of my business.

"Nope. Every guy I've ever gone out with has tried to get in my pants because he thinks I'm easy. Now I don't even bother with them. Not with high school guys, anyway."

"That's awful. I'm sorry."

She shrugged again. "It is what it is. Soon high school will be over and I won't have to put up with this shit anymore."

"You shouldn't have to put up with it now." People are gonna think what they want so why worry about it. "Who cares what people think? Don't let them ruin the most memorable year of high school."

"I agree, but what can I do?"

"You can start by surrounding yourself with better people. My dad used to say, 'You are the company that you keep.'"

"I like that."

"Me, too."

TRACK 42: IT'S YOU

Jayla

"HEY, DO YOU guys have any plans next weekend?" I ask, setting down my tray and pulling up a chair next to Zach.

"No. Why?" Brad asks.

"Because it's my eighteenth birthday and I want to do something different and fun with my friends."

"You're not having a party?" Zach asks.

I give him a look, reminding him how I feel about parties. "No, I was thinking of a weekend in Orlando at Universal Studios Halloween Horror Nights. Emerson booked the whole top floor of the Hard Rock."

"I'm down," Brad says.

"I'll do whatever you want, babe," Zach says, kissing my temple.

"Yay!" Lexi claps.

"Tickets, hotel, and food are covered. Just bring a change of clothes. We'll leave Friday after school since you guys don't have a game that night. And get this, my mom's chartering a bus. It'll pick everyone up in the Heritage Bay Beach Club parking lot."

"Is Cherry coming?" Brad asks.

"Of course, I am," Cherry says, taking a seat beside Brad. "Don't you want me to come?"

Brad wiggles his eyebrows. "Always."

"Stop," Cole gripes. "I'm eating, assholes."

"You're eating assholes?" Brad laughs. "That's just gross, Mackenzie. Now I've lost my appetite." He pushes away his tray, pretending to be disgusted and we all laugh.

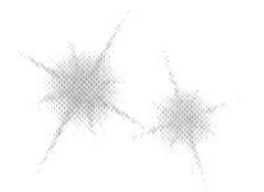

"WHAT THE HELL was I thinking?" I say, digging my fingernails into Zach's arm as we walk out of the haunted house. I feel his arm flex under my grip. "I think I peed my pants, Z."

Zach laughs, prying my hand off his arm and wrapping it around me, tucking me into his side. "I'll protect you, babe."

"I think I'm gonna throw up," Olivia groans beside Zach and me, holding her stomach, just before she turns to the bushes and pukes.

"Oh, come on!" A guy with a fake bush on his head jumps up and I let out an ear-piercing scream. "Okay, I definitely peed."

"Oh, my God, that's gross!" Cole backs away, covering his mouth.

"Shut up, Cole! Like you've never thrown up."

"Yeah, but it's still gross."

"Then walk away," Zach says, annoyed.

"We need to get her back to the room," Evangeline says from behind me.

Pfffffffffffffft.

Lexi and I look at each other with wide eyes.

"Well, that's my cue to walk away," Evangeline says with a laugh.

Zach's eyes go wide. "Did she just—"

"Z!" I shake my head in warning. Zach brings his fist to his mouth to stifle a laugh and Olivia groans in embarrassment.

"Oh, man," Evan says, screwing up his face.

"Shut up, Evan!" Lexi snaps.

"Sorry," he chokes out through a laugh.

I shoot Evan a death glare.

"What? She's the one who farted," he whispers and shudders in disgust.

"Newsflash, Evan. Girls fart, too," Lexi argues. "It happens. See." Lexi proceeds to stick out her ass and fart loud enough for the whole group to hear.

Oh, my God. I freaking love this girl. I fall against Zach and wrap my arms around his waist as I laugh my ass off.

"Lex!" Evan chastises. "Don't ever do that again."

I bite down on my lip and look up at Zach. "Don't even think about it," he warns, shaking his head.

Lexi stands up and points to herself. "That's right, everyone. You heard it. The Homecoming Queen just farted. Whatch'all gotta say about that?"

"Word," Evangeline shouts.

I raise my hand. "And I peed my pants."

"Everything okay over here?" a security guard asks, walking up and shining his flashlight over us.

"Yes, sir," I answer. "My friend just got a little grossed out from the last haunted house."

"Yeah." He nods and lowers his flashlight. "It happens. You guys have a good night." He walks off.

Carter jogs over carrying a bottled water and squats down to rub Olivia's back. Thank God, he wasn't around hear it. For anyone other than Lexi, that's just downright mortifying.

"Careful, man," Evan warns.

"Evan." I shake my head, silently telling him to shut up.

Carter looks up at Evan, confused.

"Evan, say one more word and I'm not talking to you for the rest of the night," Lexi threatens. That shuts Evan right up.

"You okay, Livi?" Carter asks.

I think it's so cute that he calls her *Livi*.

Olivia nods but keeps her face buried in her hands. Poor girl. "I'll take her back to the hotel and get her something for her stomach," Carter says.

"We'll go with you," I offer before turning to Zach. "I need food and a change of panties."

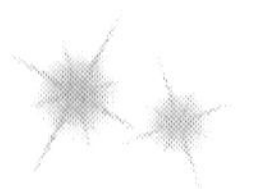

"WHERE'S THE BIRTHDAY girl?" a familiar voice calls out through the sound system.

I jerk my head up to the stage and see Lucas smiling down at me. It takes a second to register that it's Lucas, and he's really here. Cupping my hand over my mouth, I stand up from the table.

"Is that—" Zach starts to say, but Lexi shrieks over him.

"Oh, my God, that's Lucas Wild."

"He's so hot," someone says.

"So is Ace Matthews," someone else adds as Ace walks onto the stage and takes a seat behind the drums.

"Oh, my God, Wesley Brooks." Wesley walks out, pulling his guitar over his head.

Lucas hops off the stage and walks toward me. In one swoop, he's got me in his arms, hugging me tight. His hug tells me he's missed me as much as I've missed him. Lucas and I have never been apart for this long.

Evangeline, Lucas, and I are growing up and our lives are pulling us in different directions.

It's a painful realization.

"Hey, everyone! I'm Lucas," he says into the microphone and then gestures to the guys on the stage. "That's Ace." Ace winks and taps out a drum roll. "And Wes." Wes strikes a chord on his guitar and shoots me a wink. I wave. "We're here to wish Jay a happy birthday."

Zach

I HAVE NEVER seen Jay so happy. She's beaming, lit up from the inside with a permanent smile on her face. It makes me smile. There's a strong bond between Jay and Lucas; it's clear as day the love they have for each other.

Someone sits in Jay's empty seat and I don't have to look over to know that it's Bass. He's kind of hard to miss.

"I haven't seen her this happy in a really long time," he says.

"I was just thinking I've *never* seen her this happy," I reply, keeping my eyes on Jay as she and Lucas sing Pepper's "Fuck Around." Lucas claimed it was one of Jay's favorite songs a few years ago and she played it all the time.

Tapping the tambourine against her thigh, she glances over her shoulder at the drummer, Ace, who shoots her a wink, prompting Jay to curl her lip and roll her eyes.

Bass chuckles. "That one's a flirt. Marcus told him if he ever touched his baby girl, he'd have to learn to play the drums with his feet." He breaks into a full-on belly laugh, shaking his head.

JAY PULLS ME aside. "Zach, this is Lucas. Lucas, this is my boyfriend, Zach. And before you go all big brother and embarrass me, remember it's my birthday and I *will* punch you in the throat."

Lucas laughs and holds out his hand. "It's good to meet you, dude. I hope you're taking good care of my girl." *She's* my *girl.* "This is my dad, Andrew." He gestures to the older version of himself.

Jay told me that her dad and Andrew grew up together in foster care and started Royal Mayhem while they were still in high school. For some reason, I feel like it's Andrew Wild who needs to give me his seal of approval to assure all is right in Jayla King's world. "I hope you're treating my goddaughter right."

I nod. "Of course."

"Uncle Drew, you're making him nervous." She smacks him playfully on the arm.

I let out a soft chuckle and wrap my arm around her. "It's fine, Jay." I kiss her on the temple.

Andrew smiles. "As long as you keep my little girl happy, then I'm happy."

"I'm eighteen, Uncle Drew."

"Sweetheart, you'll always be my little girl and Lucas will always be my little boy." He winks.

Lucas introduces me to the guys from his band, Ace and Wes. They're all chill and they adore Jay. The rest of the dinner is filled with music and laughter from the embarrassing stories between Evangeline, Lucas, and Jay.

Whether Jay accepts it or not, hanging out with rock stars?

This *is* her normal.

TRACK 43:
SPECIAL
Jayla

Jaybird,

Happy 18th birthday to my baby girl. I love you so much. I was hanging on to this for a special occasion. Today is the perfect occasion. Enjoy.

I love you always.

Daddy

Inside the envelope is a little pink flash drive with "Jaybird" written in small print on the outside.

"What is that?" Zach asks.

"I don't know, but if I had to guess I'd say it's a home video. We have a ton of these."

"Go plug it into the TV," Mom suggests.

I get it set up in the great room while Zach, Mom, Bass, and Grace settle on the sofa. Bass picks up the remote and switches on the TV.

The video is being shot from my bedroom doorway. It starts with me looking baller in a black Royal Mayhem T-shirt, leopard leggings with a hot pink tutu around my waist, a matching hot pink boa around my neck, lime green heart-shaped plastic sunglasses, and hot pink plastic heels. I'm holding a sparkly microphone and singing my heart out for Bass, who is sitting on my pink couch pretending to be my audience.

"Are you getting this, Em?" my dad asks. Then he appears in the shot as he walks into my bedroom. "Baby girl, what are you singing?" he asks, scooping me up from the floor before settling me in his lap and peppering kisses all over my face.

My eyes well up with tears.

"It's my song, Daddy. I wrote it." I wiggle off his lap, skip over to my little white desk, and pick up a piece of paper.

"She did," Bass confirms. "Princess is a genius."

I look over at Bass and see him nodding. That makes me smile.

"See, Daddy?" I push the paper into his hands and bounce on the balls of my feet. Clearly, I'm excited. "Want me to sing it again?"

"Yes." He smiles. "But wait for Mommy." He turns to look at the camera with a huge grin spread across his face. "Em, come here."

I turn my face to the camera. "Mommy!" I hop up and wave her in. "Come here."

She moves into the room.

"Jaybird wrote her first song today and she wants to sing it for us."

"You did?" she says. "I can't wait to hear it." The camera stills and she says, "Okay, baby. Let's hear it."

I sing my six-year-old heart out. The song is about sunshine and the sky. It makes no sense, but I was freaking cute. When the song ends, my dad stands up, grabs me in his arms, and spins me around.

"That was beautiful. What's the name of your song?" Mom asks.

"Zach!"

Em and Bass burst out laughing and I feel myself blush with embarrassment. Grace just smiles and shoots me a wink.

"You wrote your first song about me?" Zach asks.

"I was six." I roll my eyes playfully and snort. "Don't let it go to your head."

"Too late." He hugs me to his side and kisses my temple.

TRACK 44: YOU'RE GOING DOWN

Jayla

"JAY! ZACH," HARPER calls as she hurries down the hallway toward Zach and me, carrying a stack of books with a bunch of papers stuffed between them.

"Do you need some help?" I ask, but I'm already moving in her direction with my arms extended. Suddenly, she stumbles forward, trips and falls on her face. Books and papers are scatter all over the floor.

Laughter erupts from a few of the students as they pass by, stepping over the mess.

How is this funny? What the hell is wrong with people?

Zach runs over and helps Harper to her feet as blood surfaces from a small cut below her chin. A few students stop to ask if she's okay and try to help me gather her books and papers before they get stepped on. The hallway traffic is busy.

I've got all the books and most of the papers neatly stacked at her feet. As I reach for one of the last pieces, I see a flash of black and a pain like I've never felt before shoots through my hand, up my arm, and down to my toes, taking my breath away. I see spots. "Ow, fuck!" I scream and jerk my hand to my chest, covering it protectively with my other hand as my eyes fill with tears. I squeeze my eyes closed and try to breathe through the pain.

"What happened?" I open my eyes to see Zach squatting down to look at me with furrowed brows and concerned eyes.

I can't answer him because the pain has rendered me speechless. All I can do is breathe through my nose and fight the urge to pass out. Familiar female laughter drifts from behind me and I look over my shoulder to see Hannah and Ashton with her little minions beside her. Hannah shrugs and mouths "Oops" before she turns away and continues down the hall.

Oops?

Oh, hell, no.

Zach

"OW, FUCK!" JAY screams and it's so loud that people stop in the middle of the hall to look. The busy hallway chatter lowers to a light buzz as everyone stares at her cradling her hand to her chest, eyes squeezed closed.

"What happened?" I reach for her just as she opens her tear-filled eyes, a pained expression on her pale face. Ashton's annoying laugh echoes over the hallway buzz, prompting Jay to glance over her shoulder. I follow her line of sight and see Hannah shrug and mouth "Oops" before she walks off.

Oops?

What the fuck?

"Babe, did sh—" I turn to Jay, but she's already running down the hall. *This can't be good.*

"What happened?" Cole asks, dipping his head to get a look at Harper.

Suddenly, female screams drift from down the hall. "Shit." I sprint down the hall, pushing my way through the crowd. "Get the fuck out of the way," I yell, knocking people into each other because, apparently, they don't know what *'get the fuck out of the way'* means.

Pushing my way through, I find Jay straddling Hannah with her injured hand tangled in Hannah's hair, repeatedly punching her with the other.

Now, none of this is funny.

My girl is hurt.

But if the situation were different, I'd be laughing my ass off right now because Jay's skirt is bunched up around her waist and "Property of Easton" is printed across the ass of her spanks. I want to puff out my chest like a fucking peacock right now.

"I see you took my advice," Brad says beside me, pointing to Jay's ass. Reminding me of the night I came back from St. Thomas and told him about Jay. He said, *"You should've locked that shit down. Marked your territory. Stamped 'Property of Zach Easton' on her ass. Something. We don't grow girls like that around here."*

Ashton reaches over and grabs Jay by the hair, spurring Lexi to appear out of nowhere, tossing her backpack to the floor before taking Ashton to the floor. The two fall to the ground, pulling hair and calling each other a bitch. Skirts are up and asses are out. Evan would literally pass out if he were to see this shit. Honestly, this fight between Lexi and Ashton has been a long time coming.

"This is better than porn," Brad adds with a chuckle. "Dude, you need to get your girl."

Just as I step in and reach for Jay, Reagan leans in and punches Jay on the side of the head.

My knee-jerk reaction is to punch Reagan in her head, but common sense comes to the forefront of my brain and reminds me that I can't hit a girl.

But Jay doesn't miss a beat. She untangles her hand from Hannah's hair, hops to her feet, turns to Reagan, and clocks her right in the face. Twice.

I wait for Jay get her punches in—because no one gets away with sucker punching my girl—before I grab her in a bear hug from behind and pull her away.

The scream of a whistle causes everyone to freeze in place and go silent. Everyone except my sassy, smart-mouth girlfriend. "Hey, Hannah!" Hannah looks at Jay as Ashton helps her up off the floor. "*Ooooops!*" she drawls out angrily with sarcasm. Hannah sneers and Reagan curls her lip. "Wipe that look off your face, Reagan." Jay

Huffs. "You had it coming. The first one was for that weak ass sucker punch and the second was for lying to me last summer." Reagan averts her eyes. "You didn't think I'd figure it out, did you? Lying bitch."

"Zach, Jayla, Hannah, Ashton, Lexi, and Reagan, in my office, *now*!" Principal Avery hollers. "The rest of you get to class or you're suspended."

Everyone scatters.

I lean into Jay's ear. "Baby, take a deep breath and calm down. Okay?"

She nods, lowering her head, and blowing out a breath.

"Come on." I wrap my arm around her waist and guide her to Avery's office. Leaning in once more, I whisper, "Nice spanks, by the way."

She snorts, bringing her injured left hand to her chest and covering it with her right.

My gaze drops to her swollen hand. "You okay?"

"I think my hand is broken, Z," she breathes out, almost whimpering in pain.

Principal Avery holds the office door open. Once the six of us pile in, he slams the door and moves to sit behind his desk. "None of you are to speak unless I ask you to. Zach. What happened?"

"Harper tripped and fell. Her books and papers scattered all over the hallway. Jay was picking up her stuff then she screamed. I bent down to see what happened and she was holding her hand to her chest."

"What happened, Jayla?"

"Either Hannah or Ashton stomped on my hand. I think my hand and at least one of my fingers is broken."

Avery pales. "Hold on." He leans over and presses the intercom button on his phone.

"Patty speaking."

"Patty, could you see if Miss Sarah is in the clinic."

"She just stepped out."

"All right. Will you send her in as soon as she gets back?"

"Will do."

"Thank you." He leans back in his chair and gestures to Jay.

"Then what happened?"

"I heard someone laughing down the hall and when I looked back, Hannah mouthed 'Oops.'"

Avery's head swivels to Hannah. "Did you step on her hand on purpose?"

"It was an accident," Hannah whines.

Someone knocks on his office door. "Come in," Avery calls out. I'm expecting to see Sarah the nurse, but instead it's Alex.

And he looks pissed.

Avery waves him in and Alex walks in, followed by Cole and Harper, holding a paper towel to her chin.

"What happened to your chin, Harper?"

"Someone tripped me in the hall," she explains with a pointed glare at Ashton.

"I have never in all my years as an educator seen such despicable behavior. This is the second time there's been an incident involving the two of you." He waves his finger between Ashton and Hannah. "There is a strict no tolerance policy on bullying in my school." He reaches over and presses the intercom button.

"Patty speaking."

"Patty, please contact the parents of Reagan Vaughn, Ashton Grant, and Hannah Scott, and let them know I am requesting a conference right away."

"Yes, sir."

"Thank you." He turns to Lexi. "I never expected this from you, Lexi."

"Sorry, Principal Avery." Lexi shrugs. "Jayla is my friend. Ashton and her friends were ganging up on her. I couldn't just stand there."

Cole is glaring holes into Ashton's head. He looks seconds away from leaping across the room and strangling her.

Ashton's mouth falls open. "We weren't ganging up on her. I was trying to get her off Hannah."

"By pulling my hair," Jay snaps.

"What about you, Reagan?"

"I was just trying to get her off Hannah."

I have to bite my tongue to keep from saying something along the lines of "And how'd that work out for ya?"

"By sucker punching me in the head?" Jay sneers.

"You girls make yourselves comfortable. Cole and Zach, you're excused for the afternoon. I'll let Coach know you might not make it to practice. Go with them over to the medical center so Jayla can get an X-ray on her hand. Harper probably needs stitches." He pauses and looks at Harper. "Do you need me to call anyone?"

"No, my dad's out of the country. I'm staying with Jay."

Avery nods. "I'll call Emerson."

"I'll call her, Principal Avery," Jay offers, standing up from her seat. "Trust me. Your eardrums will thank me later."

The corners of Avery's mouth curve upwards as he shakes his head.

"Principal Avery," Hannah says. "Why are we in trouble and Jayla's not? Look at my face."

"You purposely stepped on her fingers!" He slams his hand down on his desk.

"It was an accident!" she yells in defense.

"People don't say 'Oops' when it's an accident. They apologize. Clearly, she was hurt. You could've stopped to see if she was okay. Now be quiet or I'll expel you for assaulting another student. Which is still an option."

ONCE WE STEP out of Principal Avery's office, Alex turns to me. "Let me see your hand."

I hold my hand out and he carefully looks it over. "Don't breathe a word of this to Weenie, Alex. She'll freak out."

"I won't," he mumbles. "Yeah, it looks like your ring finger might be broken. Do you want me to call Emerson, or do you want to call her?"

"I'll call her. I just need to get my stuff from my locker."

"Yeah, I shut your locker on the way to the office. Your phone and everything was in there," Harper says.

"Are you okay, Harper?" I ask.

"Fuck, no. My chin hurts. I know it was Ashton who tripped me."

"I'll deal with Ashton," Cole says.

"No, you won't," Harper argues.

I turn to Zach and breathe out a laugh. "I can't believe Reagan sucker punched me in the head."

"I made sure you got in yours before I stepped in."

"Thanks for having my back, Z." I grin.

"Always, babe." He kisses the side of my head where Reagan punched me.

"Where's Lexi?" Evan jogs up to us in a panic.

"She's in the office," Cole tells him.

"What the hell happened?" He dips his head to look at Harper's chin before moving his gaze to my hand.

I laugh. "Girl fight."

Evan huffs out a quick laugh. "Is she in trouble?"

"No. I don't think so."

Lexi walks out and Evan reaches for her. "Did you get into a fight, crazy girl?" He laughs.

"Yep." She nods. "I got two days in-school suspension." She shoots me a wink. "It was totally worth it."

"WHAT'S WRONG?" EMERSON says when she answers.

"Why do you think something's wrong?"

"Because you're calling from your cellphone when you should be in class. Are you okay?"

"Um... it's a long story, but right now I need you to meet me at the medical center for an X-ray."

"*What!*" she exclaims, the sound echoing through the speakers. "I'm on my way."

Click.

I lean back against the headrest and take a deep breath.

"Your mom is nuts," Cole says with a laugh from the backseat.

My thoughts exactly. I dial Bass's number.

"We're on our way, Princess. Are you okay?"

"B, my crazy mother hung up before I could tell her I'm okay, but I definitely broke a finger or two."

"How did you manage to do that?"

"Some crazy bitch stomped on my hand. And I think Harper needs stitches."

Silence.

"B?"

"I'm here. We'll discuss it when I get there. Is Romeo with you?"

"Yes," Zach says into the Bluetooth.

"Me, too," Cole adds.

"See you in a few minutes," he says before he hangs up.

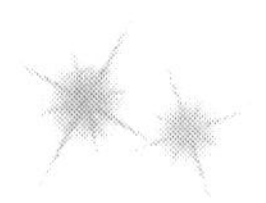

"THIS ONE IS definitely broken," Mac Daddy says, pointing to my ring finger on the X-ray film. "See this here? This is a hairline fracture. You'll need to wear a soft cast for a couple of weeks so your hand can heal."

"Great," I say, rolling my eyes. "I guess it's a good thing I beat her ass first."

"Jayla," my mom admonishes. "You better be kidding."

"She's not," Zach informs her, ignoring my death glare. "You'll probably be getting phone calls from some angry parents."

"Not if I call them first." Mom narrows her eyes at me.

"What? She purposely stomped on my hand. And while I was on the floor screaming in pain and trying not to pass out, she laughed about it, and mouthed 'Oops'. She might as well have just said, 'Fuck you.'"

"Jayla!" Mom's eyes dart to my grandfather.

"Sorry, Mac Daddy."

"It's okay, sweetheart." He laughs. "I live with your Mimi. I hear that word at least once a day."

"They ganged up on me. Ashton Grant pulled my hair and then..."

I gesture to Zach. "...his ex-girlfriend, Reagan, punched me in the head." I snort.

Mom doesn't find any of this funny.

"Are you having trouble with these girls?" Mac Daddy asks.

"Not really. I don't think it was me they were targeting."

"They?" Bass prompts.

I nod. "Hannah Scott and Ashton Grant."

"Hannah is Harold Scott's daughter," Mom tells Mac Daddy.

Who the hell is Harold Scott and how the hell does she—You know what? I don't know why I even bother asking. Mom probably has a file on every student at Heritage Academy.

"Which one is Ashton?" Mom asks.

"She's a cheerleader, and she acts like she's the queen of the school because she used to mess around with Cole."

Mac Daddy laughs. "Ah, I see. What happened to the redhead?"

"That's Harper," I explain.

"I thought Cole was sweet on her?"

"He is." I use my good hand to point to my broken finger. "Hence the broken finger."

"Ah." Mac Daddy nods. "I get it now. They targeted her, but you stepped in to help and they hurt you instead."

"Yep." I nod.

"Got it. I'll be right back to get started on your cast."

Mac Daddy leaves the room. I look over at Mom and Bass. "Are you mad?"

"I'm not mad at you, Jay, but no more fighting. Stooping to their level makes you just as much of a bully as the rest of them." She moves to the door. "I need to make a call and check on Harper. I'll be right back."

OH YEAH, YOU better believe Emerson Mackenzie marched her ass right into Principal Avery's office and threw her weight around. Home girl does not mess around when it comes to her only child.

Hannah was suspended for five days because she deliberately

stepped on my hand, which goes against Principal Avery's strict anti-bullying rules and was threatened to be expelled if she ever put her hands on another student again. I'm sure my mom gave Hannah's parents an earful, as well.

Ashton and Reagan got three days in-school suspension. Lexi got two days and I got one day. I didn't even argue; I'm guilty, too, so I took my lumps like the rest. I'm just thankful it's my left hand.

TRACK 45:
NEVER FAR APART
Jayla

JAYBIRD,

This is our first official Thanksgiving apart and I'm sorry for that. I'm so thankful for my girls and our time together. I'm also thankful for my wonderful friends and family who are looking out for my girls. I love you, baby girl.

Happy Thanksgiving.

Love always,

Daddy

My heart is heavy.

Today is going to be an emotional day for my entire family. Not only is my dad not here, but my extended family is scattered all over the country. Evangeline's parents are flying in early this afternoon. Lucas and Andrew are still on tour. Tommy and Chaz, the remaining band members of Royal Mayhem, stayed in California to be with their families.

Everything just feels off.

I pull my phone from the nightstand and look over my text messages.

Harper: I know I'm in the next room but Happy Thanksgiving. xoxo

She's such a dork.

Lexi: Happy Thanksgiving, bitch. Love you <3

Cherry: Happy Thanksgiving. Today I'm thankful for you and Brad.

Awwwww.

Dude LAW: Happy Thanksgiving from me and the guys. Miss U. Luv U.

Lucas is probably thankful that he's on tour. He likes to deal with the emotional stuff in private. I know today is just as hard for him and Andrew.

Drew: Happy Thanksgiving, baby girl. Today's going to be a tough day for all of us. Love you.

Kali: Happy Thanksgiving, Jay. I'm in Colorado with Lucas. Eek!

Aw. That makes me smile. Lucas and Kali met at my birthday party and hung out the rest of the night together. I've never seen him show this much interest in a girl. He must really like Kali if he flew her out to Colorado.

Brad: Happy Thanksgiving, Holly!

I snort. He's been calling me Holly ever since the fight.

Xavier: Today I'm thankful for you. Thank you for introducing me to this gorgeous man! Happy Thanksgiving. Xoxo

Attached is a photo of Xavier and Brice blowing a kiss at the camera. Yes, I played matchmaker and they're both very happy.

Brice: What he said, lol! Happy Thanksgiving! Xoxo

Piper: Happy Thanksgiving, Jay.

Piper and I haven't talked much since Homecoming, but I did invite her to my birthday weekend. She came with Brooklyn. She also sent me a text while I was getting my cast put on my hand, asking if I was okay.

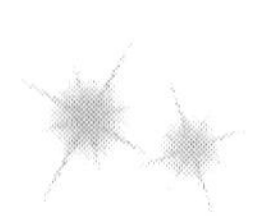

"HAPPY THANKSGIVING," UNCLE Liam says from my doorway with a smile that brightens my dark mood. I've been so caught up in Zach, I forgot how much I've missed hanging out with Liam. And Cam, too. The three of us used to hang out all the time back in the day when Liam and Cam lived down the beach from me. Back in the day when they weren't traveling for baseball games. Back when Cam still played for the LA Heat.

"Hey, stranger," I reply, patting the empty side of my bed and Uncle Liam happily climbs in next to me. Turning on my side, I prop my head up on my good hand. "I feel like I haven't seen you in forever."

"I saw you a couple of months ago." His eyes fall to my cast. "I heard you got into some trouble. Everything good?"

"It is now."

He smiles. "I heard all about it from Mimi and Em. Don't tell your mom, but I'm proud of you for fighting back. When do you get that thing off?"

"A week or so. What's new with you?"

His lips stretch into a devilish grin. "Same shit, different chick."

"You're such a manwhore." I playfully smack him in the arm. "I thought you were dating Dr. Ramos."

Liam shakes his head. "Jasmine and I are just friends. I don't date." Changing the subject, he asks, "How are you today?" His green eyes reflect his concern.

I let my head drop to my pillow and roll to my back. "I'm sad, but I expect everyone is feeling the same." I sigh.

Harper squeals from inside her bedroom, "Cole!" Then a loud laugh mixed with Willow's giggle, echoes from the hallway outside my door.

"Looks like Cole caught himself a girlfriend."

"Surprisingly, yes," I agree. "Harper is amazing. Life has dealt her a shitty hand. And if that isn't enough, she's in a relationship with Cole Mackenzie, of all people." I say the last part a little louder because I'm aware that he's standing in my doorway.

"I heard that," Cole says, walking in the room carrying Willow piggyback.

Liam and I laugh. "I know."

"JJ, me have torekey and pumfin pie," Willow announces proudly, making us all laugh.

I can't even with this kid. So freaking cute.

It's Willow's adorable face and her excitement for "torekey" and "pumfin pie" that has me rolling out of bed and heading downstairs to greet the rest of my family.

"What's up, badass? I heard you fucked shit up at school." Aiden laughs, holding up his hand for a high five.

"Aiden, watch your mouth." I smack his hand away. "There are tiny ears running around here." I wink and lean in to whisper, "It's Miss Badass, and I totally fucked shit up." I hold up my casted hand. "With one hand."

Zach

CAM, LOGAN, AND I walk through Jay's front door, into chaos, and "24K Magic" by Bruno Mars playing over the sound system. Hysterical laughter and cheers drift from the back of the house, but it's Jay's laugh that pulls me in the direction of the great room.

Jay and Harper are dancing with Mimi. Willow is beside them giggling and rocking from side to side. Everyone is laughing and Emerson has her phone out recording the whole thing.

"Ella, what in the hell are you doing?" Mac exclaims, startling everyone.

"I'm twerkin' with my granddaughter, Mac. What does it look like?" she explains as she bends her knees, arches her back, and begins thrusting her hips.

I've never laughed so hard in my life.

"That's your godmother," I say to Cam who shaking his head and laughing. I'll admit, as hilarious as it is, it's also kind of disturbing.

"It looks like you're having a goddamn seizure," Mac continues. "I thought I was gonna have to call for an ambulance," he teases, turning to Emerson, who has her phone aimed at him. "She's finally done it,

Emi bear. Your mother has lost her mind." He shakes his head in mock disappointment and heads out the back door with a giant turkey in his hands. As he passes by, I hear him mumble under his breath something about a "crazy broad."

And to finish things off, Cole and Aiden jump in and start twerking beside Mimi.

Jay finally notices me standing here and squeals as she runs over to me, jumps in my arms, and wraps her legs around my waist. "What are you doing here?"

"I can't stay long, but I came to see my girl," I tell her, then lower my voice so only she can hear. "And give her something to be thankful for."

She snorts. "You're such a horndog. I can't with all these people here. Would you settle for a heavy make-out session on the third floor?"

"I'll take it."

Jayla

"LET'S GO TO Pelican Cove," I suggest. Dinner is over and everyone has gone home for the night. And Bass left with Lisa. The two have been spending a lot of time together, ever since the night of my mom's welcome back dinner. Mom introduced them and I'm really happy Bass is finally getting a life. Now it's down to Mom, Liam, Cole, Harper, and me. I haven't heard from Zach since he left earlier, but he promised he'd be back over later.

"Everything is closed, Jay," my mom says.

"The stores are open for early black Friday shopping," I remind her.

"I'm too full to go shopping and deal with the crowds," my mom replies.

"Then let's go to the movies," I propose.

"I'm down," Liam says. "Let's go walk off some of this food."

Cole looks over at Harper. "Let's go," Harper says with a wink.

We all pile into my Range Rover and head to Pelican Cove. I shoot a text to Zach instead of calling since my phone is linked to Bluetooth and I don't want everyone in the car to hear my conversation.

"We should get a big tub of popcorn to share," I suggest.

"You can't possibly eat popcorn after all that food we just ate," Mom says.

"You can't go to a movie and not get popcorn," Liam says.

"I'm not sharing popcorn," Cole states. "That's just as bad as double dipping. Think about it. You stick your fingers in the popcorn, then stick them in your mouth, and then stick them back in the popcorn. Then there's the finger licking." He shudders. "It's gross."

I laugh. "Wow, you've really put some thought into that, huh?"

"I never realized you were such a germophobe," Harper says with a laugh.

"Ha-ha. Laugh all you want, you two, but if I licked my fingers and stuck them in your popcorn, would you eat it?"

I scrunch up my nose as Harper and I say at the same time, "No."

We stand in front of the movie kiosk, debating over which movie to see. "How about *Bad Santa*?"

"Zach!" a female squeals from somewhere in the sea of people coming out of the theater. I know there's more than one Zach in this city, but out of habit I turn my head and spot *my* Zach skipping through the crowd with Chelsea on his back, his parents, and another couple, I assume Chelsea's parents, walking behind them.

As if he could feel the heat of my stare, Zach turns his head in our direction and jerks to a stop. He mumbles something to Chelsea and she immediately slides off his back, dropping to the ground, before they both make their way over to us.

Well, this is gonna be awkward.

"Don't jump to conclusions, Jay," Mom says at the same time Cole leans into my ear and reassures me that "They're just friends."

"I thought you were dating Zach?" Liam asks, confused. "Did something happen between the two of you, or is this as bad as it looks?"

Always so protective.

"Ohmigod, will you guys relax. It's fine." There's something about Zach and Chelsea's friendship that makes me uncomfortable, but I can't pinpoint it. Maybe it's because they had sex. Zach swears they're just friends and I believe him. Zach isn't the cheating type. But there's something else that just doesn't feel right.

I push my jealousy aside because technically Zach isn't doing anything wrong. It could easily have been Lucas and me doing the same thing.

"Liam, be nice," Mom warns. "Zach's very good to her."

Zach reaches for me, careful of my cast, and pulls me to his chest. "Hey, babe." He kisses me on the forehead.

"Hey, man." Liam jerks his chin to Chelsea. "You steppin' out on my niece?"

Zach frowns.

"Liam," Mom chastises. "What did I just say?"

"You told me to be nice. I'm just asking a question."

"This is my friend Chelsea." He gestures to her. "Chelsea, this is Jay, her mom, Emerson, and her Uncle Liam. You know Cole, and this is Harper."

Chelsea nods at everyone before her eyes come back to me. An expression quickly crosses her face before I can read it, but it wasn't a friendly one. *She hates me.* A fake smile spreads across her face like a Cheshire cat as she says, "It's nice to finally meet you, Jay. I've heard so much about you." Her last words are more of a warning than a compliment.

But she doesn't scare me. "Good to meet you, Chelsea," I sneer, not bothering with my perfected fake smile.

Cam walks up with his arm around my dance instructor, Juliette. *Cam and Juliette? Random.* "Hey, man," Cam says, reaching out to give Liam the one-arm pat on the back. As if he hadn't just seen him earlier today. "You remember Juliette?"

"Of course, I do." Liam smiles and leans over to hug her.

"She's also my dance instructor," I add, waving to Juliette.

"Ah." Liam smirks. "So, you're the one responsible for all that 'twerking' my mother shamelessly demonstrated for the family today."

We all laugh.

Liam pulls out his phone, taps out a text before shoving it back in his front pocket and says, "Well, if we're not gonna see a movie, then I've got somewhere to be."

Mom waves him off. "Go. I'm too tired to sit through a movie." She reaches inside her purse, digging for her keys, and I wonder how long it'll take before she realizes that we rode together in my car.

"We're gonna take off," Cam says. "Zach, you coming?"

"Nah. I'm staying with Jay."

Liam leans over and drops a kiss on Mom's head and then mine. "I'm gonna catch a ride with Cam. I'll see you guys tomorrow."

"I better get back to my parents. It was nice meeting you, Jay. I'll see you around," Chelsea says, but what she means is "I hate your fucking guts, Jay, so watch your back."

"Looking forward to it," I reply, but what I mean is "Bring it on, bitch."

"Baby, you're so freaking cute when you're jealous," Zach singsongs and my mom laughs. "You know you have nothing to worry about, right?"

"I trust you, Z. It's her I don't trust. You guys looked like you were on a date, all of you coupled up."

He chuckles. "I came with Cam and Juliette. We ran into Chelsea, her parents and mine on the way out. I called you earlier to see if you wanted to come with us, but your phone kept going straight to voicemail. I thought about stopping by, but I didn't want to interrupt your time with your family."

"Sorry." I pull out my phone. "Willow was playing with my phone earlier."

"So, you've changed your mind about seeing a movie, then? *Bad Santa* was pretty funny."

"Nah. I'll pass. Besides, Cole won't share his popcorn with me."

Harper laughs and Cole rolls his eyes.

"I didn't know Cam was dating Juliette," I say to Zach.

"He's not."

"I'm ready to go home, throw on some comfy pants, and read a book," Mom says as we head back in the direction of the parking garage. She's still searching for her keys.

"Em." Harper laughs. "You can stop looking for your keys now. We came in Jay's car."

TRACK 46:
UP TO NO GOOD
Zach

"GOOD AFTERNOON, GENTLEMEN," two young sales assistants, dressed in all black, greet us at the front of the store. "What brings you in today?"

"I'm looking for the workout stuff," I speak up first. I'd already bought Jay a Fitbit, but she could always use more yoga pants. And the sports bras are just an added bonus for me.

"Our sportswear is in the far left corner. If you need anything, my name is Cassandra." She smiles and turns to Cole, Evan, and Brad. "Now what can I help you gentlemen with?"

"I'm going with him," Evan says, following me. "I think Lexi would prefer yoga pants over a sexy nightie."

"Really?"

"I said Lexi, not me."

I chuckle as a female voice says from behind us, "Can I help you guys find something?" I look over my shoulder to decline her offer and see her checking out my ass. I clear my throat and her eyes slowly move up to my face as she bites down on her bottom lip. *The fuck?* I look over at Evan and, by the expression on his face, he noticed.

"I think we're okay," I reply.

"You're Zach, right? From Heritage Bay Academy. You know my

friend Lindsay Miller."

Lindsay has a lot of friends. "Oh, yeah. Tell her I said hi." I lift a pair of yoga pants from the rack and hold them out to inspect them.

"Those look too big for her," Evan says. "They look too big for Lexi and she's got an ass."

"Shut up." I laugh. "Jay's ass is perfect."

"For you." He chuckles.

"Those run bigger," she states, reaching around me to grab another pair that are almost identical. "These are true to size." She lifts her shirt and turns to show us her ass. "I'm a small and these are a small." She turns back around to face Evan and me with a knowing smile. "What size do you need?"

"Extra-extra small," Evan quips, and I jab him in the arm.

"Are you shopping for your little sister?" She does that flirty pose, twirling her hair around her finger.

"Girlfriend," a familiar voice says and I turn to see Eva and Alex. "And since she's my best friend, I'll help him pick something. Thanks."

The poor girl just stands there in a mixture of shock and awe, unsure of whether she should ask for an autograph or walk away. She chooses the latter. And I agree; it's a wise choice. Eva is, without a doubt, a bitch. Luckily, she likes me.

Alex stands back holding a shopping bag in one hand, the other hand shoved in his pocket, laughing under his breath and shaking his head. "Babe, you didn't have to be so rude. She was just doing her job."

"She was showing them her ass." She gestures to Evan and me. "Who does that?"

"No, she wasn't," I argue. She *was* showing off her ass, but I prefer to play ignorant because there is only one ass I'm interested in.

"She was flirting with you," Evan admits.

"I know, right?" Eva exclaims. "I was watching her."

"Why aren't you at the salon with the girls getting ready for the Winter Ball?"

Eva points to the bags in Alex's hand. "We had some shopping to do."

"Well, since you're here, can you help me pick out some stuff for

Jay?"

"Me, too," Evan adds. Thank God, because he's as clueless as I am in the gift department. All I've ever seen Evan buy for Lexi in the past few years is a Kindle and Amazon gift cards. Sure, he buys her the things she likes, but sometimes our girls like it when we get creative.

"Alex, go over there and pick out something lacy and skimpy for later." She winks.

See?

Alex grins and jerks his eyebrows up and down before heading to the lingerie section, calling over his shoulder, "You don't have to threaten me with a good time."

"It's not a threat, baby. It's a promise," she calls out to his retreating back.

It's a good thing Eva is here because there is entirely too much stuff to choose from. I don't even know Jay's bra size—unless "more than enough" is considered a size. Evan follows my lead, only Lexi is about two inches shorter and a little curvier in the hips. And as far as her rack goes, I'm not touching that. I settle on two pairs of yoga pants, two pairs of running shorts, two T-shirts, and three sports bras.

"Thanks for helping, Eva." I pull her in for a side hug.

"ALEX SAID THE sales girl was hitting on you," Cole says from the driver's seat.

"No, she wasn't."

"She was checking out his ass," Evan adds from the backseat.

"She was a friend of Lindsay's."

"What'd she look like?" Brad asks.

"Short with reddish-blonde hair."

"Heidi." Cole nods knowingly.

We all stare at him.

"And, no, I never tapped that," he says, keeping his eyes on the road. "I recognized her in the store. She *is* a flirt, and believe me, Eva will tell Jay."

Right on cue my cell starts ringing, Jay's beautiful face gracing my screen. I hold up my phone to show the guys. "She knows. Be quiet and I'll put it on speaker." I set the phone in my lap as I answer on speakerphone. "Hey, babe."

"Zach, did some girl really show you her ass to try to sell you yoga pants, or is Weenie fucking with me?"

Brad snickers and brings his fist to his mouth. I put my finger to my lips, gesturing them to be quiet.

I chuckle. "Babe, she was just showing us how they fit."

"I'm calling bullshit. Weenie said she was checking out your ass and flirting with you. That bitch is lucky I just got my nails done or I would go in there and kick her ass. Who the hell does that? That's what the fucking mannequins are for."

"Chill out, babe. You just got your cast off. No more fighting."

"I hope you didn't buy anything from her."

"Nope. I didn't buy anything from *her*."

Lowering her voice, she growls into the phone. "That ass is mine, Z." Cole makes a gagging noise and Jay laughs. "Hi, Cole."

"I'll see you later. I love you."

"I love you, too. Bye."

"She took it better than I expected," Cole says.

Evan's phone buzzes next and Cole glances in his rearview mirror. "You know you're not getting off as easy as he did, right?"

Evan rolls his eyes. "Thanks a lot, Zach."

TRACK 47: CLOSURE

Jayla

THE HERITAGE BAY Annual Winter Wonderland Ball is at the Oceanside Aquarium. It's black tie and my guy looks hot in a tux. My dress is another design by Anna Sizemore. A light blue satin gown with a beaded bodice and a slit up the side, allowing me to move freely.

Harper is wearing an emerald-green silk gown to match her eyes, an early Christmas gift from me. And, of course, Cole, as always, looks amazing in his tux.

However, Zach and Cole are all about the food. If they have to dress up in a monkey suit, there better be food—Cole's words.

Soon after we sit down, the rest of our friends arrive and we spend the next thirty minutes talking over each other until our food arrives.

After dinner, we move to the next room for the festivities. The entire room is set up with carnival games. Every toy won and every ticket earned gets donated to Toys for Tots.

The ceiling is draped in red and white fabric, giving us the illusion that we're under a circus tent. Booths line three of the four walls, with every game from throwing the dart into the balloon to a dunk tank, and a merry-go-round sits in the middle of the room. Zach and I stop and watch as Cam attempts to knock down the stacked milk bottles.

You'd think it'd be easy, what with him being a pitcher and all. It's not.

Bass goes for the "Bell Ringer" with the big sledgehammer and Cole goes straight for the dunk tank.

I've discovered I'm much better at skee ball than I am at bowling. "Let's go over to the fortune teller, Z."

"I'd rather not."

"Why? It'll be fun."

"Because they give me the creeps." He laughs.

"Oh, come on." I drag him over to the old lady in the booth and slide a twenty-dollar bill across the counter. She pulls out her tarot cards and flips them over face up.

"You recently lost someone, yes?"

I nod. "My father."

She flips over another card and flinches.

"Okay, babe." Zach takes my hand and gives it a gentle tug. "You've had your fun. Let's go ride the merry-go-round."

I tug back and turn to the fortune teller with a frown. "What do you see? Is it death, again?"

She shakes her head. "No." She gestures to her cards. "It's not... death."

Zach clears his throat and she immediately flips over another card. "You're going to travel. I see love, maybe marriage." Zach snorts. "I see children. Lots of children." That makes me laugh as I pull out another twenty and slide it over to her.

"Thank you." Once we're out of her sight, Zach and I burst into laughter. "I'm gonna go to the restroom."

"I'll wait out here."

Just as I reach the door, I hear yelling coming from inside the bathroom.

Pushing the door open, I catch sight of Harper backed up against the vanity in the far side of the bathroom. Ashton and Hannah are screaming in her face while Chelsea leans against the sink looking bored. Chelsea and I haven't seen each other since our silent showdown on Thanksgiving.

"What the hell do you think you're doing?" I move forward, taking in Harper's disheveled dress.

Hannah looks down at my hand. "Looks like your hand healed up nicely," she sneers.

"I wish I could say the same about your face." I notice a small tear in Harper's dress and I see red. "Did you tear my dress?" I realize my mistake and wince. I meant to say hers because it *is* hers. It's *my* design and I had it custom-made just *for* her.

"*Your* dress?" Ashton laughs and turns to face Harper. "Figures this piece of trash can't even afford to buy her own dress."

"Oh, and you can?" I ask, incredulous. "Or does your mommy buy you dresses with the money your dad sends so he doesn't have to deal with you."

"Fuck you!" Ashton shouts. "You don't know shit about me."

"And you don't know shit about Harper except that Cole wants her and not you." I turn my attention to Chelsea. "What's up, Chelsea? The college girls won't put up with your shit so you have to come here and pick on high school girls?" I shake my head. "Pathetic."

Chelsea laughs, pushing off the sink, standing up straight and crossing her arms over her chest. "What's pathetic is you think this thing with you and Zach is real." She pauses, blinking, and I can tell by her expression, she's wondering if she's gone too far. But then she goes on. "He's using you. Don't get too attached. Once he gets what he wants, he'll toss you aside."

"And what is it that he wants?" It's my turn to laugh. "Sex? Because he gets plenty of it. You sound like a bitter ex-girlfriend who got used and tossed aside."

"I did."

I scoff. "No, you didn't. You're supposed to be his friend but what you are is a shitty person, Chelsea, and an even shittier friend. Honestly, I don't know why Zach is still friends with you. You do realize in making me your enemy, you're pushing him away. If you really care about Zach, you'd get your head out of your jealous ass and be a true friend. Not that it matters one way or the other once he realizes his bestie is a fake and a liar."

She sneers down at me, says, "Let's go," and moves to step around me. At the last second, she attempts to shoulder-check me, but I'm ready for it. I dig my heels into the marble floor, causing her to stumble to the side. Chelsea bumps her hip against the vanity before she loses her balance and clips the corner of the metal paper towel holder. *Ouch!*

That's definitely gonna leave a mark.

"Ow! You bitch," she cries out, grabbing hold of her arm.

"I didn't even touch you." I laugh. "It's not my fault you don't know how to walk in heels."

She huffs, turning and storming out of the bathroom with Ashton and Hannah on her heels.

Once the bathroom door closes, I let out the breath and turn to Harper. We burst out laughing. "What was that all about?"

"Cole," she replies, shaking her head. "Ashton wanted me to know he still calls her and that he's only with me because she's not ready for sex." Harper shrugs. "Her loss."

"Ewww!" I laugh and head for the door. "Come on, girl. Let's go round up the guys and head home."

I step out of the bathroom to see Zach leaning against the wall looking pissed. "I heard what she said."

I wave him off. "Who cares?"

Cole walks out of the bathroom and stops in his tracks.

"Are you guys ready to go?" I ask.

"Yeeees! Thank you," Cole says, wrapping his arm around Harper's waist and leading the way to the exit.

Zach leans in to my ear. "Did you hit her or something? I heard her yell 'ow' and 'bitch'."

"Hell, no, I didn't hit her. Do you think I'm an idiot? She tried to shove past me with her shoulder and her plan failed." I snort a laugh. "Clumsy bitch." I laugh a little louder. "Just let it go, Z. She's a shit friend who acts like a broken-hearted ex-girlfriend."

Zach

IF I HADN'T heard it myself, I'd never believe Chelsea could say those things behind my back.

Over the Thanksgiving break, she was my best friend again. Fun and funny. To my face, she acts as if everything is great, but behind my back, she's talking shit to my girlfriend.

I realize now this is exactly what Chelsea did with Reagan. Unfortunately for Reagan, she didn't have the advantage of knowing the truth the way Jay does. Reagan's knee-jerk reaction was to hurt me by cheating on me. But her plan backfired because she didn't hurt me, she pissed me off. Jay's knee-jerk reaction was to defend me and put Chelsea in her place. Those are the actions of someone who loves you.

Standing outside waiting for the valet to bring up Jay's Range Rover, Chelsea walks up with my mom at her side.

Chelsea has tears streaming down her face and I fight back an eye roll.

"What's the matter, Chels?" I ask, feigning concern.

"Ask your girlfriend," my mom says, glaring at Jay. My mother thinks the sun rises and sets with Chelsea and it pisses me off. She's been looking for a reason to go off on Jay and Chelsea just gave it to her.

I keep my mouth shut because I want to see how this plays out. I want Chelsea to show me what a liar she really is.

"Ask me what?" Jays says. "What's wrong with Chelsea?" She shrugs. "I don't think we have that kind of time." She smirks and I hear Cole snicker under his breath. I have to look away to hide my smile. I love this girl and her sassy mouth. "You're full of all kinds of drama, Chelsea," Jay continues. "Funny how you weren't crying ten minutes ago when you and your friends had Harper cornered in the bathroom."

"What?" Cole growls and turns to look at Harper. "Who was it, Harper?"

Harper waves him off. "I'll tell you later."

"Apparently, that Ashton girl was arguing with Harper in the bathroom," my mom says. "Chelsea was there, but she wasn't involved."

"Mom, Chelsea can speak for herself. Stop babying her. It's annoying as fuck."

"Zach, don't talk to me like that."

"Jay pushed me into the sink counter. I lost my balance and

scraped my arm on the metal paper towel dispenser on the wall."

I look over at Harper. "Did she corner you?"

"She was there, but she wasn't the one who cornered me. It was Ashton and Hannah."

Jay looks over at me. "I swear I never laid a hand on her, Z."

"I know, Jay."

"She didn't," Harper adds.

"She's the one who tried to shove me. It's not my fault she doesn't know how to follow through." Jay laughs.

"Oh, you think you're funny, smartass?" my mom seethes.

And then... I watch in horror as my mom reaches out and shoves Jay.

I love my mother. I do.

And up to this point, she's held her tongue, minded her business, and allowed me do what makes me happy.

Up to this point, she's acted like an adult.

Until she shoved my girl.

"Mom!" I yell at the same time my dad yells, "Liz!"

Jay stumbles back, wide-eyed and shocked, into Bass's chest before she fires back, lunging at my mom. I should've expected it because Jay doesn't take anyone's shit. And my mother is no exception.

Someone gasps and I look over to see Eva and Alex standing on the other side of Harper. Alex with his arms locked around Eva's waist and Eva struggling to break free.

I reach for Jay, but luckily, Bass's reflexes are quicker than mine. He wraps her up in a bear hug from behind, lifts her from the ground, and carries her away just as Emerson comes barreling through the crowd toward my mother.

"Kick her ass, Em," Eva shouts.

"Elizabeth!" Emerson rushes past me and reaches for my mom, but Troy, one of Jay's bodyguards, grabs hold of her. "Who the *hell* do you think you are?" she exclaims, her fists balled up at her sides and her whole body shaking with anger.

"*Someone* needs to teach that daughter of yours some respect, Emerson," my mom argues. "She attacked my goddaughter."

"Still overdramatic as always, Elizabeth." Emerson rolls her eyes.

"Respect isn't taught—it's given because it's earned. My daughter is not a wild animal. She doesn't attack people. You had no right to put your hands on her."

"Well, that explains a lot," my mom argues back. "Your lack of parenting reflects in that little bitch."

At this point, I'm tempted to reach out and slap my mother. *What in the hell is wrong with her?*

"Liz, shut the hell up!" Cam hollers, shoving his way past me to face off with my mom before he turns to my dad. "Take her embarrassing ass home."

My mom is wrong. And Chelsea....

I'm fucking done with her.

"You're one to talk," I add, glaring at my mother. "If anyone needs to learn some respect, it's you." I point.

"Zach," my dad warns lightly. I turn to look at him, silently asking him "What the hell?"

With a slight shake of his head, he's saying to let them have it out.

"What's going on?" I turn to see Rebecca and Chris, Chelsea's parents, taking in the scene.

"Oh, nothing much. Just typical Chelsea drama, as usual," I say, gesturing to the queen of drama, herself.

"It figures the troublemaker belongs to you two," Emerson sneers and I can't help but laugh.

"Let's go, Liz," my dad says, taking her by the arm and guiding her toward the car.

I look around and notice Jay, Cole, and Harper are gone. "Cam, can I get a ride with you?"

"Zach," Chelsea cries out, but I ignore her as I follow Cam to his car. "Zach," Chelsea says again. I turn as I open the passenger side door of Cam's truck and see she's followed me to the parking lot. "Why are you mad at me?" she asks, like she can't believe I would be mad at her. If she only knew.

"Because you're a liar, Chelsea, and I'm done with you," I say before climbing into Cam's truck and slamming the door. "Can we stop by the house so I can grab some clothes? If you don't mind, I'll crash at your place until we leave for New York."

"You have a room there for a reason, Zach. You don't have to ask."

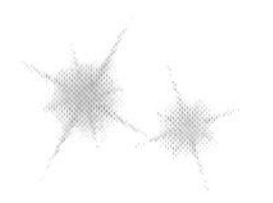

"HEY," I SAY when I walk through the front door and see my dad sitting on the couch with his elbows on his knees and his face in his hands. My mom is nowhere in sight. Probably locked herself in the bedroom. Perching on the arm of the chair opposite my dad, I ask, "What is wrong with her?"

"She's angry, Zach."

I scoff. "No shit. I can't believe she put her hands on Jay. Why does she hate Emerson so much, Dad? Tell me the truth. Did you screw Emerson behind Mom's back or something?"

"No," he insists. "But she thinks I did."

"Don't lie, Dad. Did you?"

"No, Zach. Your mom, Emerson, Chris, and I were best friends. I probably shouldn't be telling you this, but Emerson and Chris dated all through high school. He wanted to marry her." I raise my eyebrows. "I have always been in love with your mom. Emerson is the one who set us up because I was too chicken shit to ask her out myself." My dad rakes his hand through his hair and leans back against the couch.

"Then why does Mom think that?"

He shakes his head. "I don't know." *He does know.* "I can't believe all of that just happened."

"Chelsea was lying, you know? She didn't know I was standing outside the bathroom when all of that went down. I heard everything she said. Jay never laid a hand on her."

"I believe it," he admits. "That girl has always been a pain in the ass. She's trouble just like her mother."

"What are we gonna do about Mom? She can't keep acting like this. Those were some pretty harsh words she threw at Emerson. Jay is the center of Emerson's world. She lost her husband and Jay is all she has left. Mom needs to think about how her actions and her words are affecting us all. She needs to put herself in Emerson's shoes for a minute and think about how she would feel if the roles were reversed.

You need to set her straight, Dad."

I look him straight in the eyes so that he knows I mean it when I say, "I've already cut Chelsea out of my life. Mom's next."

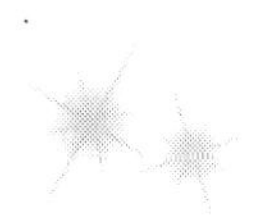

OPENING THE BACK door, I toss my suitcase in the backseat while Cam is still on the phone trying to calm Emerson down. I hate to say it, but I think Em could take my mom. A car pulls into the driveway beside me and a sobbing Chelsea gets out of the back.

"What are you doing here?"

"Zach, please, I'm so sorry," she cries. "Jayla was right. I've been a shitty friend."

"Why?"

"I don't even know anymore. At first, it was because I was jealous of her." She sniffs. "I knew she'd take you away from me."

"I wasn't yours to take, Chelsea."

"You were my best friend." She wipes at her tear-soaked face. "Last summer, while you were in St. Thomas, Reagan started asking about you. I never liked her—you know that—so, I told her you were on vacation with your family and your girlfriend. When you came back from St. Thomas, you were different. Happy, but different. And when you admitted that you loved her and I got so jealous, I couldn't see straight. In a way, I was happy she hurt you because then she couldn't take you away from me. But all it did was push you toward Reagan. When you went to California, I told Reagan you went to see Jayla. Everything spiraled out of control from there. She cheated. Things got awkward between us. And by the time I left for school, you and I were barely speaking. And just my luck..." She throws her hands out to her sides. "...I leave for college and she shows up. Ashton was going on about how Cole's cousin Jayla was all anyone could talk about and how you got up in the middle of lunch and went chasing after her. It pissed me off that you would do that after what she did to you. I knew she was at Carter's party that night after your first game. I saw her before you did and when I saw you looking for her, I ran up to you. I wanted to piss her off. I saw you watching her and Grayson."

"Jesus, Chelsea," I say.

"I know and I'm sorry." She takes a deep breath. "That morning when we met for breakfast, I saw her come in. I knew she'd see us, so—"

"That's why you kissed me?" I ask, cutting her off.

"Yes. Thanksgiving night at the movies, I saw her first, so I jumped on your back and screamed out your name to get her attention. And I did. Everything I've done was to hurt her."

"You don't even know her."

"I didn't need to know her to not like her. She hurt you and I wanted to hurt her back."

"Chelsea—"

"—and tonight, in the bathroom, I told her that you use people. That you used me."

"I heard you."

"You did?"

I nod. "Do you want to know why she hurt me? Because of you and Reagan." I point. "You told Reagan about her. The night I came back from St. Thomas, Jay called me while I was asleep and Reagan answered. Reagan told Jay she was my girlfriend. For a whole year, I'd been wondering what I did wrong. And because of your and Reagan's lie, I lost her for an entire year."

"I'm sorry. I didn't know. And I didn't expect things to go as far as they did tonight. I know your mom doesn't like her, but I didn't realize she was just waiting for a reason to go after Jayla or push her. I certainly didn't expect Jayla to fight back. And, holy shit, I thought *your* mom was intimidating, but her mom is downright scary. Zach, I'm really sorry for everything."

"You owe everyone an apology, including my mom for lying to her."

"I know. I'm going inside to apologize to your parents and I promise I'll apologize to Jayla, too. But, Zach, you should probably tell her the truth about prom night before she finds out from someone else."

"She already knows, Chelsea. She knows everything."

TRACK 48:
UNEXPECTED
Zach

Today is the last day of school before winter break and I have an important midterm exam second period. I've been staying with Cam for the last week after what happened with my mom, but since my parents are out of town, I've been staying at the house with Buddy.

Grabbing what I need for my exams, I rush downstairs, yank open the front door, and almost run smack into a woman standing on the front porch. Her hand is raised in a fist as if she were just about to knock. She startles and takes a step back. "Oh, you scared me."

My eyebrows go up. "Sorry, I didn't expect anyone to be standing on my porch at..." I look down at my watch. "...seven fifteen in the morning.

"Hi," a little voice says, and I look down into the face of an angel who looks about the same age as Willow. Shoulder-length, curly dark blonde hair, big blue eyes, long eyelashes, and the sweetest smile.

"Her name is Zoe." *Zoe? Why does that sound familiar?*

"Did you at least see if Zoe was okay before you slammed the door in her face?" Isn't that what Logan said to Mom the night of the Homecoming dance?

Shiiiiiit!

Logan has a kid.

And he didn't tell me. What a dick!

I pull my gaze from the little cherub back to the woman. "I'm Tina. I'm a friend of Zoe's mom, Whitney. I've seen pictures of Logan before, so you must be Zach."

"Yeah," I breathe out.

"I'm sorry for showing up like this, but Logan ain't returning my calls. Whitney got arrested last night for drug possession and petty theft. Thank goodness Zoe was with me when Whitney got popped. Whitney wants me to bail her out, but I can't do it no more. I tried to get in touch with Whitney's parents, but they ain't takin' my calls neither. They think I'm a bad influence on her." She snorts. "Funny, since I'm not the one on drugs. Never touched drugs or alcohol in my entire life except for some champagne once on my wedding night. Whitney and I go way back. Best friends since middle school. She went off to college and I got married to my high school sweetheart."

She rakes her hand through her greasy blonde hair. This woman has seen better days. Tina strikes me as one of those women who goes without to help care for others. And judging by her lack of hygiene, ratty sweatshirt, and oversized sweatpants, she's been going without for a long time. It's heart-wrenching. "I tried to help Whitney, but you can't help someone who don't wanna be helped. Listen, Zoe's a sweet kid, but I can't take care of her and, truthfully, she deserves better. My husband Danny died over in Afghanistan two years ago. I'm raising four kids of my own, plus I'm helping out my little sister with her two."

And there you have it. Heart wrenching.

As if I'd ever turn away Logan's little girl. My niece. "Does she have any bags or clothes? Does she have a car seat?" I have no clue what a toddler needs.

She sighs in relief. "Yeah, I'll grab her stuff from the car." She squats down, curls her bony arm around Zoe, and points up at me. "Zoe, this is your Uncle Zach."

I squat down so that I'm close to eye level with Zoe. "Hey, Zoe." I smile and hold out my hand like she's a wild animal that might attack me.

"Hi," she says with a toothy smile and that little dimple in her chubby cheek appears. She's the cutest little thing I've ever seen.

Tina comes back carrying a car seat that's almost as big as she is and a little pink suitcase. "Okay. Here's her car seat and her bag. I put a list of her favorite foods in there. She doesn't have any allergies that I'm aware of and I've been taking care of her for months. She really is a good kid, Zach. She never cries. I can only imagine what's going on in that innocent little brain of hers."

"Thank you for taking care of my niece and for making sure she's with her family. Can I get your number in case Logan has any questions?"

"He's got my number. I left it on his voicemail all ten times I called."

"He's in New York," I tell her. "He had exams today."

She winces. "Sorry, I didn't know."

"It's okay. You were just trying to do the right thing. You *did* do the right thing. My family appreciates it." Reaching in my back pocket, I grab my wallet and pull out two hundred-dollar bills.

Tina holds up her hands and backs away. "No. I don't want your money, Zach."

I hold out the money. "It's Christmas and you've got six little ones. Buy them a few extra gifts for under the tree."

She smiles sadly as she takes the money. "Actually, now I can get a tree," she says in a shaky breath and that cuts me deep. I pull another two hundred dollars out of my wallet and hold it out. I don't normally walk around with this much cash, but it's easier to pay for things with cash at Christmastime.

"Get some decorations, too."

She clears the emotion from her throat and reaches for the money. "Thank you."

"No, thank you, Tina."

"Up tack." *Huh?* Zoe lifts her arms and bounces on the balls of her feet. "Up. Up tack."

"She's saying 'up, Zach,'" Tina informs me with a laugh. "I speak fluent toddler."

I lift her into my arms and ask, "Do you want to go for a ride, Zoe?"

She points to Tina's faded red... I'm not even sure what it is.

"No, we're going in my car." I point to my Jeep then turn to Tina.

"Hey, before you leave, do you think you can help me with the car seat?" I ask. "I have somewhere to be."

Tina smiles. "Sure."

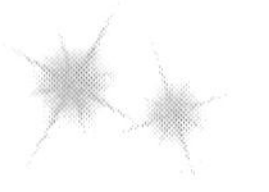

"LOGAN, CALL ME as soon as you get this message. I have Zoe." I punch in my personal code on the call box and the gate swings open. When I pull up in front of the house, I see Emerson standing in the doorway looking concerned.

Turning in my seat, I say to Zoe, "I'm gonna get out and come around to get you."

Zoe responds with another toothy grin and kicks her legs in excitement.

"Zach, why aren't you at school?" Emerson starts toward me.

"I have a sort of an emergency," I tell her, pointing to the back door.

"What's wrong?" Her concern shifts to panic as she moves quickly toward my Jeep.

I pull open the back door and gesture to the toddler in my backseat. "This is Zoe." Emerson's eyes nearly pop out of her head. "She's Logan's," I tell her as she pushes past me and takes Zoe from her car seat.

"Hi, Zoe," Emerson coos, hugging her close to her chest.

"Tack!" Zoe points her tiny index finger and reaches for me. I take her in my arms and she cuddles into my chest with her head on my shoulder.

"Someone is a sleepy girl," Emerson says in that sweet mom voice, caressing her back.

"Her bag is on my front seat. Would you mind grabbing it?"

Emerson grabs Zoc's little suitcase and leads the way inside.

"Is she hungry?" she asks.

"I have no idea. Her mom's friend Tina just dropped her off at my house less than twenty minutes ago. She said there's a list of her favorite foods in her bag."

"Where's her mom?" Emerson asks, opening Zoe's bag and pulling out an envelope.

"Jail."

Em's head jerks up with wide eyes, mouth agape. "For what?" she whispers.

Bass comes into the kitchen from the garage, stopping short when he sees me sitting at the counter with Zoe in my arms.

"Something you need to tell me, Romeo?"

"She's Logan's," Emerson tells him with a laugh. "Her mom is in j-a-i-l." She spells out the word as if Zoe knows what it means.

"Did her friend say why?" Emerson asks.

"Drug possession and petty theft," I tell them and Bass's eyebrows shoot up.

"Have you talked to Logan?"

"He's not answering his phone. It's midterms. I have them today too, crap!"

"I can watch her if you think she'll be okay staying with me. I don't want to confuse her."

"She's cute," Bass says, then narrows his eyes. "Don't get any ideas."

I chuckle. "That's not happening for at least ten years."

Bass grins. "I knew there was a reason I liked you."

The garage door slams and Jay storms into the kitchen. "What the hell, Z? I've been freaking out. You haven't been answering your ph—" She comes to a halt when she notices the toddler in my arms. An expression I can't quite pinpoint crosses her features, but it's gone just as quickly. She quirks a brow and says, "Is this where you tell me that you knocked up some—"

"Dial down the crazy, babe. She's Logan's."

"Oh, thank God." She exhales in relief and slaps a hand over her heart. "I'm way too young to be a stepmom."

That has us all laughing.

She's so fucking funny.

Zoe lifts her head from my shoulder and looks curiously over at Jay. "Zoe, can you say hi to Jay?" I whisper to her.

"Hi, day."

"Hi, pretty girl," Jay coos and holds out her hands. "Can I hold you?" Zoe leans toward Jay with no hesitation. Jay pulls Zoe to her chest, hugging her tight, before settling her on her hip. "Are you hungry? You want some fruit?" She carries her over to the refrigerator and pulls out a giant bowl of fruit. *This girl and her fruit.* "Auntie JJ loves fruit."

Grace walks into the kitchen and does a double take. "Oh, a baby." She smiles.

"She's Logan's," Jay tells her.

"Hold on before you give her any of that," Em says. "We need to make sure she doesn't have any food allergies."

"Tina said she doesn't have any allergies," I tell her.

"Who's Tina?" Jay asks.

"The woman who's been taking care of Zoe. I felt so bad for her, Jay. She couldn't have been more than twenty-two. Her husband died in Afghanistan and left her with four kids, plus she's taking care of her sister's two kids. She was driving some piece of sh—crap. I gave her some money. She wouldn't take it at first, but I reminded her that it's Christmas, told her to take it and put some extra gifts under the tree. She said she didn't even have a tree, which means she probably doesn't have any gifts for her kids."

"Aww. That's so sad."

I nod. "I gave her four hundred dollars. I would've given her more, but that's all I had in my wallet."

Bass smacks me on the back. "You did a nice thing."

I snort. "Did you get her information or her number? Maybe we can do something nice for her," Jay offers, setting Zoe on the counter and positioning herself in front of her. "You want a strawberry?" Jay asks, pulling off the lid. "Auntie JJ always has fruit." She plucks a strawberry from the bowl and holds it out for Zoe.

"Have you talked to Logan?" Jay asks, popping a piece of melon in her mouth and my eyes zero in on her perfect, plump lips. She stops mid-chew and grins at me. *The little tease.*

"I left him a message to call me and I sent him a text."

"Where are your parents?" Emerson asks.

"Out of town. I stayed at home last night. It's a good thing I did or I'm not sure where Zoe would be now."

"I'll make her some breakfast," Grace says, pulling some eggs from the refrigerator. My stomach rumbles. I want some breakfast, too, but.... I lift my wrist to look at my watch. "If I don't get to school in the next fifteen minutes, I'll lose my perfect attendance."

"Oh, my God, you're such a nerd." Jay rolls her eyes. "Go to school. We'll take care of Zoe. Right, B?"

"What about you? Won't Alex be pissed?"

She shrugs. "All I have to do is mention cramps. It works every time." She waves me off. "Go. I'll keep trying to get in touch with Logan."

"Or you can both go to school and I'll take care of her," Em offers.

Jay pushes out her bottom lip. "But I want to stay here and play with Zoe."

Em rolls her eyes.

"Let me get her car seat in case you need to go anywhere." I start for the door.

"No, just take my car," Jay offers.

"Zach, do you want me to call the school?" Em asks. "I'll tell David you had a family emergency. He'll understand."

"Yes, please."

"Bye, Zoe." I kiss her on the nose.

"Bye, tack."

I chuckle. *She's so sweet.* I smack a kiss on Jay's lips and then I'm out the door.

Jayla

"HEY, B, I NEED a favor."

"Princess, your favors scare me."

"I promise this is an easy favor." I give him an innocent smile and he gestures for me to keep going.

"I ordered a few things online for Zoe. The order was pulled and it's ready to be picked up. All you have to do is go to the customer service desk and show them this receipt." I hold out the printed confirmation. "I put the order under your name, so there shouldn't be any problems."

He smiles, taking the receipt and shoving it into his pocket. "I'll take care of it."

"You're probably gonna have to fold down your seats." I smirk.

"I'll be back." Bass chuckles, grabbing his keys off the counter and leaving through the garage door.

Mom and I spend the next hour entertaining Zoe with cartoons while we wait for Bass to return.

"She looks like Zach," Mom says.

"I know, right?" I agree. "I wonder what our kids will look like."

"Slow your roll, sister. There's plenty of time for marriage and babies. You haven't even graduated from high school yet."

My phone rings and Logan's name pops up on the screen. Suddenly, I'm a bundle of nerves.

"Hi, Logan."

"I just got my brother's message," he rushes out. "You have Zoe?"

"Yes. Oh, my God, Logan. She's so adorable."

"She is, isn't she? Is she awake?"

"Yeah. She's sitting right here, watching cartoons with Mom and me. Call me on FaceTime so she can see you."

"Okay." After a moment, Logan's face pops up on the screen.

Zoe's eyes go wide with excitement and she points to the phone. "Daddy."

My eyes instantly fill with tears, as do Logan's. He puts his fist to his mouth and clears his throat. "Hi, baby girl. Daddy's coming to see you."

Zoe gasps, looks up at me with wide eyes, and in a hushed voice full of hope, she says, "Daddy comin'?"

Mom laughs.

"Thanks for watching her, Jay. I'm trying to get a flight out of here, but with it being so close to Christmas, it's crazy."

"I have a plane, Logan," I say.

"I already took care of it," Mom says, looking down at her watch. "George should be there within the hour. We'll text him the information."

Logan blows out a breath. "Thank you. I really appreciate it."

"Don't worry, Logan. We're taking good care of her. Just get packed and come home to your little girl," I tell him.

"Thank you so much, Jay. Zoe, Daddy will see you soon."

Zoe points to the phone. "Daddy," she says, then she does the cutest thing I've ever seen. She kisses the phone. And I melt into the sofa.

Mom sniffs beside me. I turn to look at her and see her messing with her phone. "Did you just record that?"

"Yeah. Logan deserves to have this beautiful moment captured on video."

I smile. "You're beautiful. I'm so lucky to have you as my mom."

"Ugh, Jay. You're killing me." She wipes her eyes. "I love you, my little miracle child." *She's such a dork.*

"I love you, too. Now go and wash your face." I tug Zoe closer to my side. "You're scaring, Zoe." I snort as she tosses a pillow at my head.

Zach

MY JEEP IS exactly where I left it this morning. I park Jay's Range Rover in the garage and enter through the garage door. Stepping into the kitchen, I'm met with excited laughter and giggles.

I tiptoe through the kitchen and look around the corner to see them all in the foyer. Zoe is tucked inside a mini white Range Rover.

She didn't.

There's clapping and cheering as Zoe grips the steering wheel and squeals with laughter while the car goes in circles.

Jay turns and sees me peeking out from the kitchen. "Z!" She skips over to me and throws her arms around my neck. "How freaking cute is that? She's has a Range Rover like her Auntie JJ. It's remote controlled." She points to Bass.

"When did you buy that?"

"Today after you left," she says, leaning back to gauge my mood. "Are you mad? All she had in her bag was a freaking teddy bear and she kept asking for her daddy. I had to do something to keep her entertained."

"I'm not mad, babe." I kiss her on the forehead. "It's more than I would've done. I would've put on ESPN and called it a day."

"You're such a guy. Do you think Logan will be mad? You know... maybe he wanted to be the one to buy her this stuff."

Stuff?

I look over to the great room. It looks like Toys R' Us threw up all over the entire room.

"I'll wrap some of it up for Christmas. I just didn't want Logan to have to worry about anything. Maybe we can give some of it to that Tina lady."

"Logan told me you sent your jet." I cup her face in my hands and kiss her on the mouth gently, sweetly. "You're the most thoughtful, selfless person I've ever known. Thank you."

"Actually, I offered, but Mom beat me to it." Her eyes glisten and she smiles. "I got some pretty cool stuff. Wanna see?"

"Yes, I do."

It's entirely too much shit for a two-year-old, but I keep my opinion to myself because she's proud of herself. I think Jay is more excited than Zoe. Who am I to burst her bubble? Besides, she also bought the necessary stuff, like a highchair, a stroller, and an extra car seat. Things Logan would never think of. Not until he needs it.

"She went a little overboard," Emerson admits, "but she means well. She didn't have this growing up. Well, she had the stuff, but she never got to share it with anyone." She leans in and says, "Except Bass," then snorts.

"Z, Logan's here," Jay whispers, as if it's Logan's surprise party. She looks ready to jump out of her skin. "What should we do?"

"What do you mean? Open the door and let him in." *Who is this crazy person right now?* She nods, biting down on her thumbnail. *Why is she so nervous?*

"I'll go get him." I walk outside and wait for Logan to climb out of the car.

"Hey."

"Hey," he says, his voice full of emotion as he reaches for me. We do our usual brotherly hug pat on the back, but this time he doesn't pull away. Instead, he tightens his hold as his body shakes. I squeeze back, comforting him, and giving him what he needs. He pulls away and lifts his shirt by the hem, using it to wipe his face. "Did Jayla tell you about our FaceTime call today?"

She didn't. "No. And just so you know, she's nervous."

He frowns. "Why?"

"She was trying to be helpful and she went a little overboard. She thinks you're gonna be mad."

Logan chuckles and shakes his head. "She sent her plane to New York to bring me home to my daughter. I don't care if she bought her the goddamn Eiffel Tower."

I snort. "Close enough." Logan starts to move past me, but I grab his arm. "Hey, did you ever call Tina back?"

He exhales through his nose. "Yeah. She filled me in. I'll talk to Dad about it tomorrow."

"Have you ever met her?"

"No. Why?"

"That poor woman is struggling, Logan. I couldn't stop thinking about her trying to take care of six kids at Christmastime."

Logan's eyes go wide. "Six?"

Nodding, I tell him, "I gave her some money. She didn't want to take it, but I insisted. You need to do something nice for her."

"Okay. I'll figure something out, but right now I want to go inside and see my daughter." I cock my arm back and slug Logan hard in the shoulder. "Ow! What the hell was that for?"

"That's for not telling me you had a kid. Seriously, what the fuck, Logan? I'm your brother, asshole. You don't keep shit like that from me. Ever."

"I'm sorry, Zach. I'll explain everything later. Right now, I just want to see my daughter."

Logan steps into the foyer and his eyes instantly fall on the mini Range Rover. "Really?"

"It's not the Eiffel Tower." I laugh as we make our way into the kitchen and find everyone standing around the island piling their plates with spaghetti, salad, and garlic bread.

"Daddy!" Zoe squeals from her highchair, her face smeared with spaghetti sauce and pieces of noodles. She waves her hands in the air and kicks her feet with excitement.

Laughing, I look over at Logan, but he's already pulling his spaghetti-covered daughter from her highchair and squeezing her to his chest. Zoe squeals again, puts her little hands on Logan's cheeks and says in more of a whisper, "Hi, Daddy." Her big blue eyes are wide and the expression on her face is so serious.

It's like she can't believe he's here.

My heart fills with pride for my brother and my eyes well up with tears as this scene plays out in front of us. I look around the room and notice Jay has her head lowered, wiping her eyes. Bass seems to be interested in something on the floor and Grace is busying herself at the stove. Emerson has her phone out recording the whole thing.

These people are amazing.

Over the next hour, we eat dinner while Zoe babbles as if she's telling Logan her life story. She's still covered in spaghetti, and Logan has two spaghetti handprints on his cheeks. I laugh and pull out my phone to snap a picture.

"Logan, she looks sleepy and she's covered in spaghetti. You can use my bathroom to give her a bath." The look Logan gives Jay is priceless and she laughs. "Do you want me to give her a bath?"

"Would you mind?" he asks, grimacing.

She waves her hand dismissively. "Don't be ridiculous." She reaches for Zoe. "Come on, sweet girl. Auntie JJ is going to give you a bath." She looks over at Emerson. "Mom, can you grab some of that stuff and bring it upstairs?"

Just then, we hear the door coming from the garage shut. Jay turns to me and mouths, "Harper."

"Hey, guys! What's up? Well, hello there, spaghetti girl. Aren't you cute," she coos. "Who belongs to this cutie?"

Logan raises his hand. "That's me."

"Nice job, Daddy. She's beautiful."

"Zoe, say hi to Harper," Jay urges.

"Hi, ahpa," Zoe says in her sweet soft voice. Jay giggles and parrots her words. "Hi, ahpa. I'm Zoe from Boston." Everyone laughs.

"Need help?" Harper asks.

Jay nods toward a pile of stuff on the couch. "Can you grab the bathroom stuff, pull-ups, and a pair of pajamas?"

"I'll help," Emerson says.

"I'm taking her into the guest room next to Harper's room," Jay calls over her shoulder as she heads for the stairs. Emerson and Harper pile as much stuff in their arms as they can fit and trail after her.

"How you doing, Logan?" Bass asks with genuine concern.

"I'm great now that I have Zoe back. I've spent the last six months trying to track down her mother."

"Drugs will do that. Some people just don't appreciate the beautiful gifts they're given. Zoe is lucky to have a father who cares. If you need anything, we're here for you."

"Thank you."

Bass nods and disappears through the kitchen, leaving Logan and me alone in the great room. Logan is silent while he looks around at all the stuff for Zoe. He snorts and shakes his head.

"So?"

Logan sighs and runs a hand over his hair. "Whitney and I dated briefly in college."

"I remember Whitney. You brought her home that one year for Thanksgiving."

"Yeah. We broke up right before Christmas, and then she left school. I never heard a peep from her again until she showed up with Zoe, claiming she was mine. I didn't need a DNA test to know she was mine. She looks just like you and Dad. Which is weird." He shakes his head. "Of course, the first thing I did was call Dad and got a DNA test for legal reasons. The tests proved Zoe was mine. Whitney moved in with me and stayed home to take care of Zoe while I went to school. Everything was good, until I came home from school one day and she was gone and her phone was off. I've been looking for her for ever since. Dad contacted her parents, but they'd disowned her after she stole money from them. That's why I came home that weekend in October. The private investigator we hired said she was in Heritage. She stopped by the house but Mom slammed the door in her face. That was probably when she was staying with her friend Tina."

"Tina said Zoe is a good girl and she never cries."

He nods. "She's mellow like her Uncle Zach. She's a sweet girl."

"Yeah, she is. So, what are you going to do? Take her back to New York?"

He shakes his head. "No. I'll have to transfer and finish out law school here. It's not like I won't have a job when I'm done. But, truthfully, that's the least of my worries. The first thing I need to do is find out how much trouble Whitney is in and get sole custody of Zoe before she comes back for her."

"My creeper senses are on high alert with this one. Be careful, Logan. Drugs make people do some fucked up shit."

"She's not getting her back."

"Hey, Logan," Harper says softly. "Jay asked me to come down and get you. Zoe's tired and wants her daddy." She snorts a laugh.

"What's so funny?" Logan asks, amused.

"You have little spaghetti handprints on your face. It's cute." She giggles.

TRACK 49: EVERYTHING'S GONNA BE ALL RIGHT

Jayla

Merry Christmas, Jaybird,

You didn't think I'd break tradition, did you? Try to stay on your feet this time. (wink wink)

Enjoy.

Love always,

Daddy

Every year, as a tradition, my dad buys me a new pair of ice skates for ice-skating in Central Park. Our whole family flies into New York after Christmas and stays through New Year. The ice skates are sort of an inside joke between my dad and me because I totally suck at it, but that never stops me from trying every year. And I'll try again this year.

"Jayla, it's Miles Townsend. How's it going? Did you have a good Christmas?" I haven't spoken to Miles since he interviewed me for the *Jaybird* article.

"It was nice, considering..." I let the words hang in the air. Miles gets it. "How about you?"

"Great. The kids were very pleased with Santa this year." He laughs. "The reason I'm calling is because I've finished the tribute article for the February issue. I want you to read it before it goes to print."

I can't believe it's been almost a year since my dad passed. "Send it over. I can read it on the plane ride to New York."

"Will do. Enjoy your trip. And Happy New Year if I don't hear from you before then."

"You too, Miles. Talk to you soon."

Zach

I WAKE TO the sound of Jay whimpering beside me. Rolling over, I hook my arm around her waist and press my lips to her neck. Her body is on fire and she's shivering. I lift my head to look at her face. "Babe, are you okay?"

"No," she croaks without opening her eyes. "I think I'm dying, Z. Oh, my God, I've never felt so sick in my life."

Rolling out of bed, I tuck the covers around her. "I'll be right back."

Emerson, Bass, his girlfriend Lisa, Grace, Cam, Liam, Jay, and I flew into New York a few days earlier than the rest of her family, who are due to arrive tomorrow. Jay's apartment is two stories, overlooking the city and spacious enough to easily accommodate her big-ass family. Marcus must've had the Mackenzie's in mind when he bought this place.

We've been going nonstop since the day we arrived. Shopping during the day and dinner out every night. Did I mention shopping?

We visited a few museums and then went ice-skating in Central Park, which Jay says is a tradition, even though she falls on her ass every time. And she did, while I watched from the bench with my hot chocolate. The last thing I need is to fall and break my damn arm. *Goodbye, scholarship.*

Passing through the living room, I head toward Emerson's room and knock lightly on the bedroom door. A few seconds later, Emerson opens the door half-asleep and confused. "Em, I'm sorry to wake you, but Jay is sick."

"What's wrong with her?" she asks, blinking awake, pulling her robe tighter and darting across the apartment toward Jay's room.

"I don't know but she's burning up."

"Fuuuuuck!" she whisper-growls under her breath and steps into Jay's room. "Jayla, baby, what's wrong?"

"Everything. Help me, Mom. I feel like shit."

"Zach, you go run the bath," she instructs. "But not too hot. I'll get her undressed."

I go into the bathroom and run her a bath on the cooler side before going back to the room.

"She's too big for me, so you're gonna have to carry her to the bathtub," she says with an apologetic tone.

My mouth curls up slightly. "I've seen her naked before, Em."

She narrows her eyes. "I'm going to pretend you didn't say that."

Scooping Jay up in my arms, I carry her into the bathroom and set her down in the lukewarm bathwater.

"Don't leave me. I feel like I'm dying."

"You have the flu, baby," Em says, squatting beside the tub and cupping her face. "I'll be back in a few minutes. Okay? I'm going to get you some medicine to help you feel better. Zach will be right here." Em stands and leaves the bathroom.

Jay rolls her head toward me but keeps her eyes closed. "This sucks, Z," she whines.

"I know, babe."

SHE WASN'T LYING.

This does suck.

Now I'm dying and I want my mommy.

I hear the toilet flush followed by the sound of the running water. A moment later, the bed dips and Jay curls behind me. "Babe, you're shivering," she whispers. "Do you want me to run you a bath?"

Yeah, but who the hell is gonna carry me?

"No. I can't move."

She presses herself closer to my back and curls her arm around my waist.

The bedroom door opens and Eva pokes her head in with her hand over her nose and mouth. "How are you feeling, Jay?"

"Like shit," Jay croaks. "Tell my mom that Zach has it now, too."

"Oh, my God," Lexi says, peeking her head inside. "You guys are sick?"

"You're sick, too, bro?" Cole asks and I grunt in response. "Blah. Close the door, Eva."

"Ugh!" Eva quickly shuts the door.

"I see JJ," Willow's demand echoes from the other side of the door.

A few minutes later, Emerson walks in wearing a medical mask over her nose and mouth, setting down a mug of something on the nightstand.

Dramatic much?

"I'm not being dramatic, Jay." *Huh?* I could almost laugh if I didn't feel like I was dying. I love that my girl and I think alike. "Who's gonna take care of you if I get sick?" Emerson points to the mug on the nightstand. "Drink this, Zach. It'll help with the fever and body aches."

Grace walks in behind Emerson, also wearing a medical mask, a tray in hand, and sets down two Gatorades, two orange juices, and two plates of scrambled eggs and toast. "I love you both and I'm sorry you're sick," Emerson says. "It sucks, but it is what it is. You're officially being quarantined. There are too many people here who can't afford to get sick. If you need anything, text me."

And that's how Jay and I spent the rest of our vacation in New York. Cuddled up in bed, watching movies with my girl, while Grace kept us fed and hydrated. Can't really complain.

Jayla

HAPPY NEW YEAR, JAYBIRD.

I figure right now you're in New York ringing in the New Year the right way with family and friends. Hope you're breaking in your new skates in Central Park. Try to stay on your feet this year.

Just kidding.

Love always,

Daddy

Not only did I fall on my ass but I also got knocked on my ass by the flu. The upside to all of it was that I got to spend a week in bed snuggling up to my guy watching holiday movies. Even with the flu, it didn't suck to be me.

"HAPPY NEW YEAR," Chandler greets on the other end of the line. "How's our little Jaybird feeling?"

"Much better, thank you."

"Good to hear. Well, I have some news. You and the guys have been invited to present the award for Best New Artist at the Grammys this year."

I gasp. "You're kidding me."

"No kidding. I've already cleared my schedule. You'll be here from February eleventh through the thirteenth. Unfortunately, you'll need to leave your entourage at home because your trip will be short and we have a lot of business to discuss."

I blow out a breath. "Okay. I understand."

"I just got off the phone with Miles Townsend. Alex is scheduled to meet with him for his interview as the new lead vocalist for Royal Mayhem. Miles is probably going to want to ask you a few questions too. This is it, sweetie. Are you ready?"

I take a deep breath and nod even though he can't see me. "I'm ready."

TRACK 50:
FALLING APART
Jayla

THE LIMO ROLLS to a stop at the curb. Levi steps out first, then Bass follows.

"Listen up," Mom says as we're all still tucked inside the limo. "Evangeline, I know this isn't your first rodeo and, Jayla, we've been over this a million times, but I'm gonna say it anyway. Smile pretty for the cameras and move on. Don't answer any personal questions. Stick to who you're wearing and the award you're presenting tonight. That's it."

I nod. "Got it."

Mom turns to look out the window and smiles fondly when she sees my dad's bandmates, Andrew, Tommy, and Chaz. Beside them are Lucas, Ace, and Wes.

"Stay with Lucas and we'll be right behind you."

"I see my parents," Evangeline says, looking out the window, then turns to me and winks. "Come on, Va-jay-jay, let's make this red carpet our bitch."

Mom shakes her head before tapping on the window. The back door opens and Bass helps her out first. Alex gets out next and offers his hand to Evangeline. The crowd roars when she emerges from the limo.

This is it.

The first time I will officially walk the red carpet as Jaybird.

God, I wish Zach was here.

The sound of the screaming fans is muted by the pounding of my own heart. Bass holds out his hand and as I set one foot outside the limo, he leans down into my ear and says, “Princess, listen closely. Keep your eyes on me and don’t look directly into the cameras. Then turn to the stands and wave to the fans.”

The moment I’m out of the limo, camera flashes come at me from all angles. Lucas appears at my side and places his hand on my back. “You ready?” he asks, giving me a side squeeze before releasing me and taking my hand in his.

I smile and nod once. “Let’s go.”

He tugs my hand and leads me over to the bleachers where people are screaming. I look over my shoulder and see that Ace and Wes are right behind us, waving to the crowd.

“Jaybird, Jaybird, Jaybird,” the crowd chants over and over. A rush of adrenaline pumps through my veins and a cocktail of emotions cause tears to prick the corners of my eyes. People are leaning over the barrier with their cell phones; little girls are crying and waving posters. I catch a glimpse of one of the posters held up by a young girl that reads “I love you, Jaybird” and a girl beside her holding another that says, “The Royal’s Princess.” I point to the girls, then blow them a kiss and wave. Lucas grabs a phone from one of the fans and turns it around so that we can take a selfie with them in the background. We pose for more pictures, sign autographs, and high-five a few hands hanging over the wall before Bass and Levi walk over and steer us back to the line.

Mom stands there shaking her head, but she’s smiling. Lucas and I continue to make our way down the red carpet, stopping for photos. I pose with the band, pulling Alex into a few more and confusing the hell out of the photographers. We haven’t made any formal announcement about Alex being the new lead singer for Royal Mayhem. We plan to do that tonight.

Yesterday, Alex and I met with Miles Townsend at *Rhythm & Riffs* for our interviews and photoshoot. The Marcus King Tribute issue came out at the beginning of this month with a young Marcus

King on the cover. The story was told by people close to my dad, including Miles himself, and my mom. I wasn't lying when I said Alex could pass for a young Marcus King and the fans will see for themselves in the May issue, right before the release of *Jaybird*.

Zach

"WELCOME BACK TO the Grammys Red Carpet Special coming to you live. I'm Julia Rappaport. Let's check in with Ross Sterling."

"Julia, I'm here with the lovely Jayla King and Lucas Wild."

"Hello, Miss King. It's a pleasure to finally meet you. We were beginning to think you were a mythical creature."

Jay smiles. *"It's a pleasure to meet you too, Ross."*

"She looks so hot," I say out loud to no one in particular. Logan bristles beside me.

"Look at you. I'll bet you have all the boys falling at your feet. Do you see this gorgeous girl, Julia?"

"She's stunning."

"That she is. Who are you wearing?"

"Thank you. This is a piece from the Project Mayhem T-shirt line designed by Anna Sizemore and myself."

"That's amazing. You modeled for Miss Sizemore, correct?"

"Yes."

"And you're still in high school, correct?"

"Yes, I've made a lot of friends at my new school. Hi, guys." She blows a kiss to the camera. *"I miss you!"*

"Boyfriend?"

"I'm dating, but nothing serious."

My eyebrows shoot straight to the sky. *Ouch! What the fuck?*

"Don't get all salty over it," Cole says. "She's sticking to the script."

"He's right," Logan adds. "If she'd said yes, we'd have reporters hiding in our bushes by the end of the week. Then you'd find out real quick who your true friends are."

"That's a little extreme," I say.

"It's not. She's 'Jaybird.'" Cole throws up his hands. "Do you have any idea how long people have been waiting for this? The media is probably going apeshit trying to dig up dirt on her."

"Congratulations on Jaybird. *And 'Piece of Me' is already in the top ten on the charts right now."*

"Really?" She smiles. *"I didn't know that."* Jay smiles over at someone off camera, probably Emerson, and gives a thumbs-up.

"We're joined by Andrew Wild, Tommy Stone, and Chaz Vargas of Royal Mayhem. Hi, guys. Come on up. And who is this?" He gestures to Alex.

"Ross, this is Alex," Andrew says. *"He's our new lead vocalist."*

"Well, hot damn." Ross fans himself. *"Pleasure to meet you."*

Alex smiles uncomfortably. *"Thank you. It's good to meet you, Ross."*

Ross presses his hand over his heart. *"Has anyone ever told you that you could totally pass for a young Marcus King?"*

"He does resemble Marcus a little," I admit.

"It's the Latin features," Cole says. "Dark hair and light eyes."

"Have you seen his mom?" I ask. "Jay said she's a blonde."

"Never met her."

Alex laughs. *"I've heard that, yes. I actually knew Marcus for a few years before he passed and he used to joke about it too."*

"Alex is an incredible performer," Andrew adds. *"He's worked with Marcus in the past. Marcus would be pleased that Alex was our choice for lead vocalist."*

"Well, you've got some pretty big shoes to fill, my friend."

"Don't I know it." Alex smiles.

"You guys are presenting the award for Best New Artist, yes?"

"We are."

"And LAW is a nominee." He turns to Lucas, Ace, and Wes.

Lucas nods. *"We are. It's surreal to be grouped in with so many incredibly talented artists."*

"Well, good luck to all of you."

"Thank you, Ross."

Jay smiles and waves to the camera once more before latching onto Alex and continuing down the red carpet. Ross watches them walk away, then turns back to the camera and mouths "Wow."

Julia's face pops up on one side of the screen. *"Wow is right. She's gorgeous."*

Ross nods in agreement. *"For sure. And that Alex? Now that's a nice-looking man."* They both laugh.

My phone vibrates with a text from Lexi. ***I saw Jay on TV. You know she loves you and that's all that matters.***

I know.

My phone buzzes again. This time it's from Jay. ***I love you, Z, but I'm not ready to share you with the rest of the world just yet.***

I chuckle and text her back, ***I understand. I love u too.***

I miss you so much. I hate being away from you. How am I gonna survive months away from you when I'm on tour when I'm already going crazy after two days?

We'll figure it out.

It's me and you, Z. We're a team. Always and forever. Xoxo

Always and forever.

Losing her isn't an option.

We'll make it work.

"HEY, ZACH," REAGAN leans against the locker.

"What?" I shove my books into my locker and check my phone. It's against school policy to carry our phones during school hours because of something to do with invasion of privacy.

"Have you talked to your girlfriend today?"

"No, why?"

"Maybe next time you talk to her you should ask her to explain this." She thrusts her phone in my face. Grabbing her phone, I take a closer look at the screen and my heart sinks in my chest, when I see a picture of Jay kissing some guy. He looks familiar.

"Where'd you get this?" I ask, pushing her phone back into her hand.

"It's all over *Celebrity Wall*. That's Ace Matthews from LAW. According to the *Wall,* Jayla and Ace dated until he hooked up with Nikki Fox at a party. Do you think this was taken at the Grammy's after-party last night?"

"She didn't go to the after-party," I happily inform her, shutting my locker and walking away. I was on the phone with Jay for half the night before I fell asleep.

Walking into the dining room, I feel everyone staring as I make my way over to our new table, where Cole is sitting with Harper, Brad, Cherry, Evan, and Lexi.

Pulling out a chair, I spin it around to straddle the seat and prop my arms on the back. "I saw it," Cole tells me before I can say anything. "You know they're friends. You met the guy at her birthday party. That picture was taken last year at the Mayhem Foundation charity dinner. I was there. Of course, there's no picture of what happened afterwards, when she pushed him away and called him a dick." He chuckles, shaking his head. "Gotta love the media."

TRACK 51:
CIRCUS OF LIFE
Jayla

BEING BACK IN California feels weird, like I've been away for years. Even the house I grew up in on Malibu Beach no longer feels like home, but a distant memory. Zach is my home and I miss him like crazy.

Besides the Grammys, this trip has been all business between meetings and interviews.

My first and only meeting today is with my lawyer, Jack Reynolds. On my way out, I see Tyge Reynolds, Jack's son, in the waiting area, talking with Bass and Levi. I've known Tyge since I was a kid, so I guess you could say he's a family friend. He's also the pitcher for the LA Heat and my Uncle Liam's teammate. "Hey, stranger." I smile as Tyge pulls me in for a hug. "What are you doing here?"

Tyge jerks his head to the side, gesturing to one of the girls behind the desk. "Dropping something off." I shake my head. This guy is too much. "You guys heading out?" he asks. "I'll walk with you."

"Yeah." I look down at my watch. "I've got a plane to catch." The elevator pings and we step inside.

"You legal yet?" he jokes, smirking as he shoves his hands in the front pockets of his jeans.

Bass and Levi laugh quietly.

I snort and playfully backhand him in the stomach. "I have a boyfriend."

The elevator opens at the bottom floor and Bass and Levi step out first. Tyge jerks his head, gesturing for me to step out before he follows. We make our way through the lobby and push through the doors out onto the sidewalk.

"It was good to see you again, Jay." He throws his arm over my shoulder. "Say hello to your mom for me."

And that's when I hear it.

Click. Click. Click.

Zach

"WHAT'S WRONG WITH you?" I ask when Cole comes walking into Brad's house.

"Harper and I got into it and, no, I don't wanna talk about it," he says, falling to the couch and dragging his hands down his face.

"What time is Jay supposed to back?" Brad asks, changing the subject.

"She should be home by seven."

My phone chimes with a Google alert notification. I set the alert this afternoon after Reagan showed me that picture of Jay and Ace Matthews.

"Hello, from your local bird watcher. Looks like there's been a Jaybird sighting today in downtown LA. Jayla King, who we also know as Jaybird, was spotted leaving Finnegan's Bistro with LA Heat's Tyge Reynolds. Click here for photos. There's no denying the heat, pun intended, between these two. Whoa! Seriously hot. An inside source claims that the two dated on and off for a while, but King broke things off and moved on to LAW bad-boy drummer, Ace Matthews. A reliable source told us that the two broke up just after a month when Matthews cheated on her with America's Voice *winner, Nikki Fox. Things are getting interesting. Check back for updates."*

Because my curiosity outweighs my common sense, I click on the link and picture after picture pops up. More pictures of Jay and Ace and a dozen pictures of Jay and Tyge stepping out of the restaurant with Tyge's arm around Jay. My heart sinks and my blood boils all at once. I think I might actually be sick.

"What's wrong?" Cole asks, and I pass my phone to him.

His brows furrow and a frown tugs at the corners of his mouth. "Where do they get this crap?" He passes my phone back to me. "Ignore it."

"What's wrong, Zach?" Lexi asks. I hold up my phone with the picture of Jay walking out of a building with Tyge Reynolds's arm around her. Lexi grabs my phone and glances down at the screen while Evan looks over her shoulder.

Evan raises his brows and exhales a whistle through his teeth. Lexi passes my phone back to me. "You don't believe any of that, do you?"

"Not really. I mean, I know the media is full of shit, but what's she doing with him?"

"She knows him," Cole explains. "He's Liam's teammate and his dad is her lawyer."

Lexi plops down on the couch beside me and picks up the remote. "Have you tried calling her?"

"No," I reply, checking the time on my phone. "She's probably on her way to the airport."

"What are you worried about, Zach?" Cole asks.

"That she's not the perfect little princess he thought she was," Reagan adds with a Cheshire cat grin.

"Shut up, Reagan," Cole snaps. "Why are you even here?"

"She's here with me," Ashton pipes up.

"And why are *you* here?"

"Because I invited them," Brooklyn says.

"This isn't a party, Brook," Brad tells her. "Mom and Dad will be home after their business dinner."

"You have friends over. Why can't I?"

Brad rolls his eyes before he looks over at me and says, "She'll be home in a few hours, so just hold off on jumping to conclusions."

"I think we both need a drink," Cole says and I couldn't agree more.

Jayla

BASS STEERS THE car up the driveway of the Malibu beach house and I'm out the door before he can even put the car in Park. "Princess, wait!" he calls out, but I don't. I blow through the front door and up the stairs. My mom isn't answering her phone and I need her to do some damage control. Now.

"Em," I call out as I reach the top of the stairs and head into the master suite. The shower is going, which explains why she wasn't picking up. "Mom!"

Reaching the bathroom door, I hear it.

A moan—female.

A groan—male.

What the hell?

I pause outside the door with my hand on the knob.

Moan.

Groan.

Turning the knob, I slowly push open the door, step inside and freeze.

"I love you, Em," Cam says.

Oh. My. God.

Zach

I WALK DOWN to the beach for some privacy and to call Jay, but she beats me to it.

"Jay?"

"Oh, my God, Zach!" she cries into the phone. "I'm so sorry."

"What's wrong?" My heart twists in my chest.

"The cameras were everywhere and..." She's hysterical. I can't understand what she's saying. "...I promise I'll fix this. I love you,

Zach. I have to go," she rushes out the last part before the line goes silent.

"Jay?" She hung up. I redial her number and it goes straight to voicemail. *What the hell just happened?*

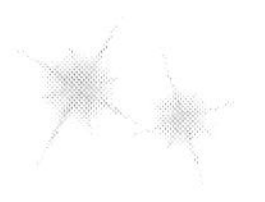

TWO HOURS AND too many drinks to count later...

"Tonight on Celebrity Dirt*...."* It cuts to a clip of Jay walking through the airport behind Bass with Levi at her side, sunglasses shielding her eyes. Alex and Eva are trailing behind them. *"Look who flew into town. It's Jaybird."* The camera cuts back to a group of reporters standing around in a newsroom. The reporter, Kyle, says, *"Jayla King was spotted at LAX."*

"Jaybird," Harold, the boss, clarifies.

"Yes. It's rare to see Miss King out and about, but today she was spotted twice." A video clip of Jay and Tyge Reynolds coming out of a building starts playing.

"So, what? Celebrities eat. Big deal. Why is that newsworthy?" a female reporter says, rolling her eyes.

"Hello, that's Tyge Reynolds," another female reporter chimes in. *"The man is hot."*

It's my turn to roll my eyes.

"It gets better." Kyle grins.

"You plan on taking up the entire show with this story?" Harold asks, cutting in with a laugh.

"Trust me. This will be our best segment yet," Kyle says with a chuckle. *"So, it started with King and Reynolds leaving Finnegan's Bistro."* They cut to the video of Jay and Tyge coming out of the restaurant again. *"They seem pretty cozy,"* Kyle adds. *"Throw in those sexy photos of King and Ace Matthews and I smell a love triangle."*

The TV cuts to a commercial and everyone's eyes turn to me. I lean my head back on the couch and close my eyes.

"That's bullshit," Cole yells at the TV. "Poor Jay."

Jay's words replay in my head. *"The cameras were everywhere and... I have to go. I love you, Zach."*

She called me Zach.

I'm frustrated, confused and, if I'm being honest, slightly humiliated. I know it's not Jay's fault, but it doesn't help that sinking feeling in my gut.

"I agree," Lexi says.

"Me, too," Brad adds.

The commercial ends and *Celebrity Dirt* comes back on. *"Freelance reporter Kelly Cunninger is getting a lot of recognition for her* Operation Bird Watch *blog posts,"* Kyle says.

"That's just creepy," Cole says.

"Now here is where things get interesting. Apparently, Ms. Cunninger caught up with King, Evangeline, and Alex Reyes, the new lead singer for Royal Mayhem, at LAX..."

"They have a new lead singer?" Harold asks.

Kyle shakes his head. *"Dude, where have you been? They introduced him at the Grammys last night. Watch this."*

The show cuts to the same video clip of Jay walking through LAX with Bass and Levi in front of her and Eva and Alex behind her. Reporters are shouting questions as quickly as they flash their cameras.

"Miss King..."

"What's your relationship with Tyge Reynolds?"

"We're friends," she responds.

"What about Ace Matthews?"

"What about him?" she scoffs and I imagine she's rolling her eyes behind her dark sunglasses.

"Is Reynolds angry with you over those photos of you and Ace?"

Jay looks straight at the cameras. *"You guys have a wild imagination."*

Bass's deep voice booms over the chaos. *"You guys need to back up!"*

"Are you happy with your father's replacement?"

Jay stops to face the cameras.

"Oh, shit!" someone says from behind me.

"She looks pissed," I say.

Yep. She's pissed.

Flash. Flash. Flash.

"No, Jay," I hear someone say. I think it's Alex.

"My father wasn't and will never be replaced. Royal Mayhem was his band. I've known Alex for several years now and he's the perfect fit. The band is happy with the decision to bring Alex in and I believe the fans will be, too."

"Excellent. Can't wait to hear him live this summer," a male reporter says.

Jay smiles and her head turns slightly, most likely looking at Alex.

"Miss King, can you tell us about your relationship with Tyge Reynolds?"

"I just told you, we're friends."

"I have a trusted source who claims the two of you were, in fact, involved up until last. Care to comment?"

"I'm sorry, what was your name again?"

"Kelly Cunninger, from Daily Gossip.*"*

"Ms. Cunninger, you're the one with the blog Operation Bird Watch*, correct?"*

"Yes."

"And you're stalking me why?"

"I'm just doing my job."

"Okay, then let me make your job easier. I have never dated Tyge Reynolds or Ace Matthews. If there are pictures floating around, then they're old and have most likely been taken out of context, as usual. Dig all you want. No matter how many times or different ways you ask, the answer is the same. Tyge is a friend. Ace is a friend. That's it."

"What about Liam Mackenzie or Cameron Parker? It seems you have a thing for ballplayers. I hear third baseman, Steven Stratton, is back on the market."

"What the fuck is her problem?" I bark out as this Kelly lady drills Jay with the same questions like she's some kind of criminal.

Cole snorts. "That lady just stepped in a big ole pile of fuck you. Here it comes in 3, 2, 1...."

"Seriously, lady?" Jay throws her head back and laughs. *"My name is Jayla Mackenzie King. Liam Mackenzie is my uncle. You obviously haven't been doing your research, you ignorant orange—" Bleeeeep.*

There's my girl.

"Oooh." Cole brings his fist to his mouth, rocking back against the sofa and slapping his knee. Everyone is laughing.

"Although I appreciate your concern for my love life, I don't appreciate you painting me as some cleat-chasing tramp sexing my way through the MLB. I suggest you find a new source and do your research. Until then, you need to get out of my face."

A chorus of "Day-ums" rings out around the room.

"So, you're single, then?" Kelly keeps going.

"Why?" Eva steps in front of Jay. *"Are you asking her out?"* She laughs. It's not the kind of laugh when something is funny. I've been around Eva enough to know it's her "I'm about to fuck shit up" laugh.

"Oh, shit. She just poked the bitch." Cole slides to the edge of his seat, resting his elbows on his thighs, which are bouncing with nervous excitement. He smiles, keeping his eyes glued to the TV.

"Miss Cuntinger—" Eva sneers.

"It's Cunninger."

"My mistake," Eva says with a shit-eating grin. The sneer on her face contradicts the sugary sweetness laced in her tone. *"Your interest in my friend's love life sounds more like an obsession. I'm aware of your little blog, too, and I think you're behaving like an overzealous fangirl."* She smirks. *"Or a stalker."*

"I'm gonna go with stalker," Carter speaks up for the first time.

The camera turns to the stunned reporter holding the microphone. She isn't at all what I expect her to look like. She's short with bleached blonde hair shaped around her face like some sort of hair helmet. Her eyes are big and blue and covered in about five inches of makeup, and, holy shit, her skin *is* orange. I burst out laughing.

"Is it the TV or is she orange?" someone asks. It sounds like Reagan.

"It's her shitty spray tan," Lexi answers.

"Miss King, is it true that you were admitted to a mental health facility just three weeks after your father passed?"

Oh, no.

Jay pales, but Evangeline once again comes to her defense. *"Are you kidding me?"*

"I'm just doing my job, Evangeline."

"No, you're not just doing your job. You're harassing her. It's because of people like you that have kept her from the public eye. People like you who ruin it for other reporters..." She waves her hand around. *"...who really are just doing their jobs. Here's a little piece of advice, Ms. Cuntinger. Stop. She answered all of your ridiculous questions, and if you don't like what you hear, that's your problem. If you really want to do your job, then round up your little camera crew and get back to the chocolate factory before Willy Wonka realizes he's missing an Oompa Loompa."*

"Told you," Kyle, the reporter says with a laugh and, with that, the show is over.

Oh. My. God.

That was priceless.

The whole room bursts into laughter as the camera cuts back to the reporters in the newsroom doing the same. Harold is bent over at the waist and the two women are wiping their eyes.

"I knew it!" Cole barks out a laugh and stands up, waving his arm and high-fiving everyone in the room. "I love that bitch."

"Oh, my God!" Lexi laughs out loud. "That was hilarious! I wish we would've recorded that."

"I'm sure that shit's all over social media and I'll bet Emerson is pissed." Cole laughs and turns to me. "That stupid lady just got her ass handed to her in front of the whole damn country. Zach, stop stressin'. It's written all over your face."

Doubt settles in the pit of my stomach like poison. This is what her life is gonna be like for God knows how long.

We keep saying we'll figure it out, but I think it's just our way of avoiding the inevitable. The honeymoon phase is coming to an end and, eventually, we'll both have to leave our little bubble and venture out into the real world. She'll go on tour and I'll go off to college. That scares the hell out of me. "I need another drink."

Cole slaps me on the shoulder. "Come on, let's go out back."

I stand up and follow him down to the bonfire on the beach.

TRACK 52:
BAD DAY
Jayla

SO, MY DAY sucked ass. First, the paparazzi blindsided me and nearly blinded me at the same time.

The whole world thinks I'm a crazy slut.

Oh, yeah, and then I walked in on my mom and Cam screwing in the shower. The shower she used to share with my dad.

Good times.

She wanted to talk about it on the plane ride home, but I didn't. So, I stuck my headphones in my ears and ignored everyone the entire plane ride home.

Truthfully, I don't know how I feel about seeing her with someone who isn't my dad. It's weird. I mean, I get it. She deserves to be happy, too, and I want her to be happy. Clearly, Cam makes her happy.

Right now, my focus is on Zach and fixing this clusterfuck of a day. His phone keeps going to voicemail and mine is messed up because I threw it against the wall. I might have been aiming for Cam's head. I'll never tell.

We pull up to the house and, of course, Zach isn't here. *Goddammit.* For some reason, I knew in my gut he wouldn't be here.

Climbing out of the car, I pull my keys from my purse and head straight for my Range Rover. "Jay, where are you going?" Mom calls out.

"To see Zach."

ZACH'S JEEP IS in the driveway when I pull up and I sigh in relief. I press my hand against my stomach to calm the nervous butterflies as I ring the doorbell and silently pray Zach or Logan answers. My prayer falls on deaf ears as the bitch appears in the doorway. Elizabeth Easton tilts her head up at me with a look of disdain. In my high-heeled knee boots, I tower over her like a giant and I'm tempted to bonk her on the head.

"What do you want?" she sneers.

"Is Zach home? He's not answering my calls or texts."

"Why would he?" She takes a step back and goes to close the door.

I slap my hand on the door before she can slam it in my face. "Is he here or not?"

"No." She tries to shut it again, but I stick my foot in the doorway, pushing against it.

"Grow up, Liz. I know you hate my mom. Blah, blah, blah." I roll my eyes, so over her bullshit. "Get over yourself. I'm not her. I've been nothing but respectful to you, even after you shoved me and continued to treat me like shit. You're never going to accept me and I'm okay with that. I'm done playing nice. Think what you want, but you don't know me or what's in my heart. I love Zach and that's never going to change, so I couldn't give a flying fuck what you think of me."

"There she is," she coos sarcastically. "I knew you were a little spitfire just like your mother. It's not just because you're Emerson's daughter that I don't like you. It's because when I look at you, all I see is that backstabbing whore who was supposed to be my best friend." I frown and she nods. "And from what I've seen all over the Internet, the apple doesn't fall far from the tree."

I suck in sharp breath and take a step back, dropping my hand from the door. "Did you just call me a whore?"

"Elizabeth!" Mike yells from somewhere inside the house and she looks over her shoulder.

"What is wrong with you?" I whisper. A look passes over her features, regret, and something else. Before I can work it out, she disappears into the house and Logan takes her place at the door.

"Hey. You okay?" I blink away the shock of Elizabeth's harsh words and shake my head.

"Jayla?" Mike walks up behind Logan with a frown on his face.

Shaking my head, I turn around and head back to my car.

"Jay!" Logan calls out. I turn around as he jogs up to me. "I heard what you said to my mom." He chuckles. "She had no right talking to you like that. I'm glad you put her in her place." He pulls me in for a hug. "Are you okay?"

I shake my head. "Not really," I breathe out.

"Come on." He motions to my car. "Zach is over at Brad's. I'll ride with you."

MY PHONE RINGS through the speakers and the Bluetooth lady tells me it's Lexi calling. I press the button and skip my normal greeting. "Where have you been? I've been trying to get in touch with you for hours."

"Working. Jeffrey called and asked me to cover his shift for a couple of hours. I was at Brad's long enough to see *Celebrity Dirt*." She laughs. "Evangeline is hilarious."

"Yeah, she is," Logan agrees from the passenger seat.

"Are you okay, though? That was pretty brutal. Who's that in the car with you?"

"I'm fine. I'm with Logan and we're on our way to Brad's."

"Cool. I'm just pulling in now. Hey, have you talked to Cole or Harper?"

"No. Why?"

"I'm not sure what happened, but I overheard Cole telling Zach that he and Harper got into a fight. Cole and Zach were pretty drunk when I left."

Great.

"Okay, we're almost there. I'll see you soon." The call disconnects and my phone immediately starts ringing again. *Mom.*

Inhaling a deep breath through my nose, I answer. "Hey."

"What's going on, Jay?"

"Nothing. I just got to Brad's. Can I call you back?"

"Yes, but for the love of God, don't do anything to make matters worse. I've got enough to deal with, okay?"

I roll my eyes. "Whatever. I have to go." I hang up before she can say anything else. I'm not in the mood.

CARS LINE BRAD'S U-shaped driveway. I recognize most of them from our usual crowd.

"Hey." Logan grabs my hand as we follow the pathway down the side of the house leading to the backyard. "Just remember we guys do some pretty dumb shit when we're pissed off."

"Like what?"

"I'm just saying if he's drunk and pissed off, he'll act like a baby and say a bunch of shit he doesn't mean. I know my brother."

"Too bad." I push forward and hurry my steps. "He could've at least shown up and waited for me. I've had a really bad day, Logan." It's not like I've ever given Zach a reason not to trust me.

Lexi and Evan are alone by the pool when Logan and I round the corner. Evan pulls away and opens his arms out to his sides. "The 'Hollywood Harlot' has returned," he says with a laugh.

I know he's joking, but seriously, what's with everyone calling me a whore tonight?

"Evan!" Lexi screeches and smacks him in the chest. "Hey!" She throws her arms around me and I return the hug. "God, I've missed your face. Hey, Logan!" She smiles up at him, then returns her gaze to me. "Girl, just a heads-up. They're all pretty drunk. Even Cole, Mister I-never-drink-at-parties."

"Sorry, Jay. It was a joke. Bad day?" Evan smirks.

"You could say that. Where's Zach? He hasn't answered any of my calls or texts. And neither have my so-called *friends*." I huff out a harsh laugh. "Funny how every call went straight to voicemail and not one person replied to a single text. Coincidence? I seriously doubt it." Evan gives me a sympathetic look, but I wave it off. "It's whatever. Bros before hoes and all that."

"No one wants to get in the middle of it, Jay," Evan explains. Collective sounds of easy chatter and laughter drift from the beach. "Everyone is down on the beach."

I scan the faces of the small crowd gathered around the bonfire until my eyes land on Zach. He's leaning back in an Adirondack chair, arms crossed over his chest, staring into the orange-red flames of the bonfire like he's deep in thought. A beanie covers his wavy dark blonde hair and a few stray curls peek out around the edge. A dark gray thermal Henley covers his wide chest and muscular arms. His jean-clad legs are stretched out in front of him and crossed at the ankles.

He's so beautiful and yet I have the urge to punch him.

I've had the day from hell and he's here having the time of his life.

Fuck that.

Evan throws his arm over my shoulder. "His phone is dead. That's probably why you haven't been able to get in touch with him. And everyone else has their phones on silent because they don't want to get involved. As much as the guys love and respect Zach, they care about you, too."

"How fucking sweet." I roll my eyes.

Evan chuckles. "And you didn't call everyone."

"That's because usually when I call Lexi, you two are joined at the hip. I didn't realize she'd gone in to cover for Jeffrey. My bad." I shrug. "You're off the hook."

"Don't worry, I've been keeping my eye on him. He's drunk as fuck right now, but he'll be fine after he sleeps it off. He and Cole are just feeling sorry for themselves."

I turn my angry gaze on Evan. "Are you kidding me right now? I've been accused of screwing half the MLB, including my uncle, and for being crazy. And then...." Jesus, I almost throw all my shit out there for the world to hear. I shake my head. "He was supposed to meet me at my house. I called him earlier, upset after what happened. You'd think he'd care enough to come check on me. But nooooo! He's over there having the time of his life with that bitch." Evan winces.

"Exactly."

Reagan sneers in my direction as she walks over and hands Zach a beer before perching on the arm of his chair. *Is this bitch for real?* And then my heart cracks in half when Zach looks up at her, smiles affectionately, and thanks her. *Is this seriously happening right now?* I can't decide if I want to throw up or slap the goddamn smile off his face. I choose the latter.

My body trembles with hurt and rage.

I storm down to the beach as someone calls out, "Yo, Zach!"

He lifts his head, then swivels it in my direction.

"Busted!" someone else shouts, followed by bunch of "Oh, shits," and "Uh-ohs."

"She looks pissed," someone says.

"Dude, you're so fucked right now." Cole laughs.

It's not easy to stomp through beach sand in high-heeled boots, but I'm so determined to knock some sense into him, I could probably walk on water right now. I cross my arms over my chest and glare down at Zach. A glare that could easily burn a hole through his head. He's aware that I'm standing right in front of him, but he looks everywhere else except for at me.

Cole reaches over and smacks me on the thigh with the back of his hand as he drops down in the chair between Zach and Carter. "What's up, Va-jay-jay?" Cole drawls, drumming on the arms of the chair. "Saw you on TV. Evangeline tore that Kelly lady a new one."

"That lady is a psycho," I say, rolling my eyes. "Mom's trying to figure out where the hell those pictures came from."

"Could've been anyone at that dinner."

"Problem is, everyone at that dinner is affiliated with King Records."

"Well, look who's here. It's Jaybird," Ashton says, feigning excitement as she walks over and sits down on Cole's lap. "Can I have your autograph? Not," she sneers.

My eyebrows go up to my hairline. Now that the truth is out, I have to keep my temper in check. So, smacking the shit out of Ashton isn't an option. I wouldn't put it past these bitches to sell me out.

"Did you and Harper break up?" I ask Cole.

Keeping his eyes on me, he hooks his arm around Ashton's waist and tugs her closer to his chest. "Yep," he answers, popping the *p*, then turns to Ashton and winks. *Gross.*

I can't get into it with Cole right now; I have my own relationship to deal with.

Logan walks up beside me, looking down at Zach. "You about ready to head home, little bro?" he asks.

"Nah, man," Zach replies, looking at me briefly before turning his attention to Reagan. "I'll probably just stay here tonight."

Reagan smiles triumphantly, bumping her arm against Zach's.

"What are you—" Logan starts, but I quickly cut him off.

"Reagan, if you touch him again, I swear to God I'll pick up where I left off and make it worth the trouble."

Zach scoffs. "But it's okay for other guys to touch *my* girlfriend?" He hooks his arm around Reagan's waist and she shoots me a look that says, "Take that, bitch." My knees buckle and it takes everything I have not to crumble right here in the sand.

"What are you doing right now, Z?"

Ignoring me, Zach twists the cap off his beer and takes a swig. "I'm drinking with my friends."

I gesture to Reagan. "So, she's your friend now?"

Zach shrugs and holds out his beer. "She used to be a good friend." He winks and I want to throw up. I can't decide if I should stay and fight or walk away. My gut tells me that neither is going to end well.

"Zach!" Logan admonishes. "What are you doing?"

"Fuck off, Logan," Zach slurs, then shifts his angry scowl to me. "You, too, Jay."

My head jerks back as his words slam into me, forcing the air from my lungs.

"No, *you* fuck off, Zach," I yell and point my index finger.

I turn to face Cole with the unspoken question of "Are you just going to sit there and let him talk to me like that?"

Cole holds out his hands in defense. "Don't look at me. I tried to tell him."

"What is going on with you?" My eyes flick to Ashton.

"Nothing." He scowls. He's lying. I can see the hurt in his eyes.

"What are you doing with her, anyway? After all the shit she's done to Harper. You're being a dick right now. You both are."

"Not everything is about you, *Princess*," he clips out. "This isn't a fairy tale, Jay. It's real life. You of all people should know there's no such thing as happily ever after."

I suck in a sharp breath.

Wow.

Just... wow.

"Jesus, Mackenzie!" Carter snaps out, slugging Cole in the arm. "What the fuck is wrong with you?"

Regret flashes in Cole's eyes before he looks away, cursing under his breath. My gaze shifts to Carter who is shaking his head and silently asking me if I'm okay.

I'm not.

"Holy shit!" Ashton barks out with a laugh. "Her royal highness just got dumped on her ass."

"Shut up, Ashton!" Cole snaps out, shoving her off his lap and into the sand.

"Ah—Cole! What the hell?" she shrieks and gets up to brush the sand from the back of her jeans.

"Looks like you just got dumped on *your* ass, Ashton," Lexi says with a laugh.

"I'm over your bullshit, Cole," Ashton says before storming off.

I turn to Zach and blink back the tears. My heart has shattered for the last time. "You promised," I say softly. I need to get out of here before I lose it. Before I even realize it, I'm already walking through the gate. I'm aware of my phone vibrating in my back pocket, but I can't bring myself to answer.

Rounding the corner, I see Grayson and Justin climbing out of Grayson's truck. "Look at you, girl, all famous and shit." Grayson laughs as he rounds the front of his truck, but his laughter quickly fades when he sees my expression. "What's wrong?" He cups my face and frowns down at me with concern.

I feel like the wind has been knocked out of me.

I can't breathe.

I can't speak.

"What happened?" Justin moves closer.

"Jay," Cole calls out, the sound of his footsteps pounding against the concrete grows closer. "Hey—"

Pulling away from Grayson, I spin around and point a finger at Cole. "Get away from me!"

Cole's eyes go wide. I've never yelled at him before. I've never even been mad at him before. Not like this. He takes a step back and shoves his hands into his hair. "Shit, Jay! I'm sorry. I didn't mean to take my shit out on you. It's not even about you—"

"Just shut up!" I shout, cutting him off. I press my hand over my heart and take a deep breath through my nose, slowly exhaling through my mouth.

"Jesus Christ! What the hell did you do to her?" Justin asks accusingly, stepping between Cole and me as Grayson pulls me back against his chest.

Lexi rushes past Cole and slams into me, wrapping her arms around me tight before looking over her shoulder at Cole. "I seriously hate your right now, Cole Mackenzie! I hope you get a STD and your dick falls off."

I love her.

"Do you want me to take you home, Jay," Grayson offers.

Levi walks up the driveway. "I got her, Gray."

"No. I can drive myself." I pull away and walk over to my car. As I reach for the door, a body presses against me from behind. "I'm sorry, Jay," Zach pleads, burying his face in my hair.

"Sorry for what? For getting drunk and acting like an asshole? For humiliating me in front of our friends—who I pray didn't have their phones out—as if I haven't been humiliated enough today. For telling me in front of everyone that you're gonna screw Reagan tonight? Or for basically telling me that she was a good screw? Which is it?"

Zach's body leaves mine and suddenly he's got me turned around, his forehead pressed against mine. "I'm sorry. That was a really stupid, fucked-up thing to do. I'm pissed, but I would never cheat on you. You know that, right?"

I lift my head. "Isn't that what you wanted me to think?" I swing my hand toward the group gathered just a few feet away from my car. "You promised you'd never hurt me on purpose," I say in a low voice.

"You hurt me!" he hisses, slamming his hands against my car, caging me in. "I'm the one who's fucking humiliated."

"Oh, was it your face being splashed all over the TV and social media? All over the world?"

"No, but you're my girlfriend. It affects me, too."

"You have no idea what I've been through today." Grabbing the handle, I shove him back and open the driver's door. "I'm leaving. Do you want a ride home or would you rather stay here and finish your night with a bang?"

"Fuck," Zach growls under his breath, rubbing his temples. He sighs. "I'm coming with you."

"SEE YOU LATER, Jay," Logan says, climbing out of the backseat.

"Bye, Logan. Give Zoe a kiss for me."

"Will do." He closes the back door before jogging up to the front door and disappearing inside.

"This is where you get out, Zach," I say, staring straight ahead.

Zach sighs and turns to me. "I love you, Jay. I'm sorry I hurt you."

"I love you, too. We have a lot to talk about when you're sober."

"I know. I'm just confused right now."

"No, you're drunk. You want to break up with me, but you're afraid you'll regret it tomorrow—"

"No." He shakes his head.

"Just tell me you're not dumping me for Reagan."

"What? No, Jay. I'm not—"

"I get it. You don't want to be the asshole who dumped Jayla King—"

"Would you be quiet for a second and let me talk. I don't want to break up with you. I don't give a shit about Reagan. I love you. I just need to work some stuff out in my head."

"Like what?"

"Like how to deal with the media shitstorm every time my girlfriend is out of my sight."

"You deal with it by trusting me."

"I do trust you, Jay, but seeing all of that play out on TV tonight, and knowing that it's just the beginning, really freaks me the fuck out. That wasn't high school drama on TV tonight. That was a whole new level of drama. I'm a little out of my league here."

My stomach twists in knots. I want to burst into tears and beg him to change his mind, but I get it. "Okay."

He leans over to kiss me, but I turn away and give him my cheek. "You're not even gonna let me kiss you. You've been gone for three days."

"Work your shit out first, Zach."

"Fine. What the fuck ever." He shoves his shoulder against the passenger door and climbs out, slamming it behind him and storming inside the house.

On the drive home, I realize Zach has a point. If being away from him is going to drive a wedge between us every time, is it even worth it?

Is love enough?

Is trusting each other even enough, anymore?

It's not like I can wake up tomorrow and change who I am.

It's another painful realization.

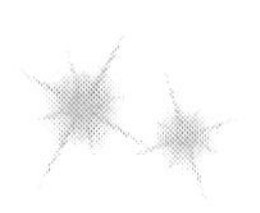

AFTER A LONG hot bath, I pull on a pair of leggings and a baseball tee, then slip on a pair of thick fuzzy socks. Grabbing my phone off the charger and a soft throw from the back of my sofa, I make my way out to my favorite spot.

I want to talk to Harper but she hasn't come home from work yet. Mom's in her room pouting because I don't want to talk to her about my feelings. Between the media "shitstorm"—as Zach called it, Mom and Cam's... relationship, Elizabeth basically calling me a whore, Cole's hurtful words, and Zach's "freak out," I'm emotionally drained.

I light a fire in the small fireplace and curl up on my daybed, tucking my blanket under my chin. The air is damp and smells of rain. The dark gloomy sky is the perfect backdrop for my mood and the dozens of emotions swirling through my mind.

The patio door opens and a moment later Grace appears with a tray of coffee, tea, and a couple slices of her homemade banana nut bread, placing it on the little side table, before taking a seat on the edge of the daybed.

"I brought coffee, but I think tea would be better for you after the day you've had."

"Thank you, Grace. Just what I need to get this pity party started," I say sarcastically.

"Thanks for inviting me," Grace retorts. "And you know I never show up to a party empty handed." A snort bursts out of me. Grace giggles and then I lose it. I don't know if I'm laughing, or crying, or crying because I'm laughing. Tears roll down the side of my face and into my hair.

"Are you okay?"

"God, no. I'm so *not* okay."

"You need to talk to her," Grace says, meaning my mom.

"I will. I'm not mad at her, Grace. I'm just... not ready to deal with her newfound relationship with Cam when my own relationship is falling apart."

"I understand." She nods and looks over my shoulder. I lift my head and follow her gaze to see Bass standing in the doorway.

"Princess, you look terrible."

I snort again. "I feel terrible." My voice is hoarse from all the ugly crying I did in the shower. "Welcome to my pity party." I gesture to the coffee and banana bread. "There's coffee, tea, and banana nut bread."

"Then let's get this party started," Bass says, pushing himself off the door, snatching a piece of banana bread before perching on the edge of the daybed. Grace moves to the adjacent chair. "Tell me what happened with Romeo."

"He's freaked out, B. He tried to hurt me by acting like a dick in front of our friends, but when he realized I wasn't gonna stick around and take his shit, he came after me and apologized. What can I do? He's not used to this. Honestly, I wasn't prepared either and I've been around it for most of my life. But no matter what kind of crap is being said on the Internet or the TV, Zach has to trust me."

"That's right," Grace says.

"Come here, Princess," Bass says softly, patting his lap and extending his arms. "Let me hold you." A cuddle from B is exactly what I need. I crawl into his lap and he wraps his arms around me. "Marcus didn't want this for you." He rests his chin on the top of my head.

"No," Grace agrees. "Marcus and Emmi had a hard time in the beginning, just like you and your Zach. Your mother had to put up with a lot of drama when she married Marcus. Women claimed they were having an affair with your father. Some even said they were pregnant with his child. The magazines even said he was having an affair with his nanny."

"I didn't have a nanny."

"Exactly." She winks.

"In our minds, we're always playing out the what-if scenarios and how we'd react but when it actually happens, it never plays out the same way," Bass says. "We act on instinct. I can only imagine Zach felt hurt and most likely insecure. Even though he trusts you, it doesn't mean he wasn't hurt or embarrassed. And it probably wasn't good for his ego either. He's the captain of the football team, the star quarterback with a promising football career and the most beautiful girlfriend in the world—"

I roll my eyes. "You're laying it on a little too thick, B."

"This is my story, Princess, so let me finish. Zach is the envy of all the guys, so imagine how he felt when that mess played out on TV in front of his friends, teammates, and peers. This is where your lives are different. I'm not saying it's a bad thing, but this is what your life is like. Either he accepts it and learns to ignore the rest of the bullshit, or you have to let each other go. You're both still so young and—"

"I love him, B," I cry.

"I know you do, Princess."

"But you're right. This is my life. I can't change it and I'm not going to let anyone make me feel guilty for being who I am." I sniff. "I just wanted some normalcy. To be in high school with kids my own age. And to do things normal teenagers do. But you know what I realized? I'm not a normal teenager no matter what I do. Friends are overrated. High school isn't something you experience—it's something you survive. Forget this normal shit. I want a do-over. I want to go back in time to when my father was alive and healthy and no one knew who I was. I want my daddy back."

TRACK 53:
MY BIGGEST MISTAKE
Zach

Boom. Boom. Boom. Boom.

The hell?

I peel my eyes open and wince at the light beaming through the windows. "Are you fucking kidding me right now, Logan?" He's standing over me banging on one of Zoe's toy drums. "You're the worst brother ever." Groaning, I roll to my back and pull a pillow over my head. "I feel like shit."

Logan drops down on the edge of the bed and yanks the pillow off my head. He points to the mug on my nightstand. "I thought you might need that."

"Thanks," I say before reaching for the mug.

He gives me a sympathetic look. "I need to tell you something."

"What?" I bring the mug to my lips and wince at the taste of coffee. *Blah.*

"Yesterday Jay came by looking for you. She and Mom got into it at the front door and Mom pretty much called her a whore—"

"Jesus Christ! Is she ever gonna stop?" I set the mug down and drag my hands down my face. "What time is it?"

"Almost seven."

"Shit. I'm gonna be late for school." I toss back the covers and head for the shower. The doorbell rings, followed by heavy pounding on the door.

I frown at Logan and he shrugs. "Go shower. I'll go see who it is."

Stepping out of the bathroom, after my shower, I find Bass standing in the open doorway of my bedroom and nearly drop my towel.

His phone is pressed to his ear. "Yep. I'm here now." He sighs and rubs his temple. "She's not ready, Em. Give the girl some space. How would you feel? Okay, then... I'll see you later... Okay... *Okaaay...* Jeezus, woman, I said okay. Will you let me get off the phone so I can wrap this up? It is Valentine's Day, you know? I got romantic shit to do... Bye."

Without taking his eyes off me, Bass shoves his phone into the front pocket of his jeans and crosses his arms over his chest. "You wanna tell me what went down last night, Romeo?"

"I fucked up, B."

"You did," he agrees as he pushes off the doorway and steps further into my room. He sits on the end of the bed with his forearms resting on his thighs and his hands clasped together.

"How is she?"

He huffs out a humorless laugh. "How do you think she is?"

There isn't much I can say to that. "Why aren't you pounding my face in right now?"

He shakes his head. "I don't believe in kicking a man when he's down."

He pats the side of the bed for me to sit next to him.

"Em and me, we go way back, since freshman year of college. She's my best friend and a huge pain in my ass, but I'd do anything for her. Marcus... he loved that girl hard. He was a good husband. Loyal. But sometimes love wasn't always enough. Em struggled with the media and the tabloid gossip. Women claiming they'd had affairs with Marcus or pregnant with his child. They fought about it. A lot. But then Em finally realized she either had to grow a thicker skin or walk away. She loved Marcus too much to walk away. So, she got a degree in PR and learned how to play the game. She's good at it, too. Then my princess came along and our lives changed. Marcus..." He shakes his head. "...I've never seen that man happier than the day she was born. He said, 'Bass, promise me that if anything ever happens to me you'll protect my little Jaybird.' It was like he knew. I love my princess with every breath in my body. She stole my heart the first time she wrapped her tiny hand around my index finger, and now she's got me wrapped around her finger. I was there when she said her first words, took her first steps, wrote and sang her first song, and played her first instrument. I was the first person she informed when she shaved her legs for the first time and when she got her period for the first time." He shudders. "I was also the first person she told about a boy named Zach, and that one day she was gonna marry him." Bass chuckles. "She's a beautiful girl, there's no denying that, but she's even more beautiful on the inside because she carries so much love in her heart.

"I didn't come here to kill you, Romeo. Princess loves you, but for the first time, you made her feel ashamed of who she is. That cut her deep. She's hurt and she's mad. To be fair, she's mad at a lot of people right now."

"I don't want to lose her. It's just..." I can't think of a single word to describe what I'm feeling right now. I shake my head.

"You'll figure it out."

I chuckle. "How do I fix this?"

"It's Valentine's Day. Start there. I can't promise you it will be easy because—and this may come as a shock—she's stubborn and she has a little bit of a temper." He holds up his thumb and index finger and I breathe out a laugh.

"No shit."

"But if you're serious about her like I know you are, then you have to fight for her. If she pushes, push back. And if you ever tell her I said that, I *will* kill you." He smiles. "Just kidding."

He's not kidding.

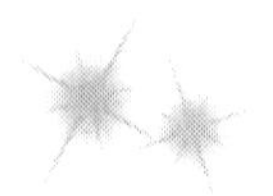

MIKE EASTON IS a big guy. He can be intimidating at times, but mostly, he's pretty laid-back. He doesn't get mad often, but when he does, he can be downright scary. Like right now, standing at the bottom of the stairs, he looks pissed. "In my office, Zach. Now."

My dad's not a physical punishment kind of guy. He prefers to throw out verbal lashes that have us walking away with our tails between our legs. Probably why he's a good lawyer.

Bypassing the leather club chairs, I toss my backpack on the floor and drop down on the sofa, leaning my head back. My dad takes a seat behind his desk.

"What time did you get home last night?" he asks.

"I don't know."

"Were you drunk?"

I shrug. "I wasn't driving. What's with the interrogation?"

"Watch your mouth and look at me when I'm talking to you," he yells. I lift my head from the cushion and scowl at him. "Why were you drinking on a school night in the first place? And what were you doing with the Vaughn girl?"

"I wasn't—"

"Michael!" My mom interrupts. "Why are you yelling?"

"Because I'm disgusted with my son's behavior," he replies in a raised voice, keeping his eyes trained on me. "Now tell me what the fuck you were doing with the Vaughn girl last night."

"What are you talking about?"

"What am I talking about? Let's see if I can get this straight." He drags his hands down his face. "This all started because of a few pictures posted on the Internet."

I shrug.

"So, what? You run to the ex-girlfriend for a little revenge screw?"

"It wasn't even like that, Dad," I defend with a scowl. "Where did you get your information?"

"From Brick Manning. Were you not at his house last night?"

"Yes, but I wasn't doing anything with Reagan."

"That's not what Brick just told me. He said Brooklyn told him you wrapped your arm around the Vaughn girl in front of your *girlfriend*, and I quote, said 'fuck you.'"

"It was fuck off," Logan adds from the doorway.

"Logan, be quiet," my mom snaps. "Michael, that's enough!"

"I say when it's enough, Elizabeth." He slams his fist down on his desk. "You don't get a say in this, so you can either sit down and be quiet or get out of my office."

She does neither. Instead, she crosses her arms over her chest and stews in silence.

My dad leans back in his chair and clasps his hands behind his head. “What do you think your life will be like when you’re a big shot in the NFL?”

“I don’t know. That’s a long time from now.”

Zoe waddles into my dad’s office and rounds his desk. My dad smiles as he lifts her into his lap and kisses her on the head. He softens his tone. “Humor me. Hypothetically speaking, if you signed with the NFL tomorrow and became a star player, what do you think would happen? Do you think you could walk through the mall without someone asking for a picture or an autograph? Do you think you could just walk into Mac’s and shoot pool with your buddies and not have someone approach you? Do you think there will never be pictures of you on the Internet? Most athletes just want to play the game and not get caught up in the media spotlight. I’m sure it’s the same for actors, actresses, and musicians, too. They just want to do their job. Unfortunately, their lives on are display for the whole world to watch and judge. Do you think that’s fair?”

“No.”

“So, how is it fair to Jayla? To you, to us, and to everyone in this town, she’s Jay Mackenzie. An eighteen-year-old high school student with a pretty face, bright personality, and a golden voice. To the world, she’s *Jaybird*.” He turns his attention to my mom. “She shouldn’t be punished for who her parents are or for things that aren’t her fault.” He turns back to me. “This is the life she was born into, Zach. Marcus King was her dad, but to the rest of the world he was a rock star and a reality TV star. He was famous, and whether or not she asked for it, she is, too. It is what it is. Deal with it or move on.” He covers Zoe’s ears and I chuckle. “I’m done with this bullshit. Elizabeth, you will apologize to Jayla and you pull that stick out of your ass and work your shit out with Emerson.”

I scoff. “Mom will be lucky if she even gets a ‘fuck you’ from Jay after the way she treated her last night.”

“Watch your mouth,” Logan says. “Her ears aren’t covered.”

My mom turns to me. “I’m sorry, Zach.”

“You should be. We’ve been together for seven months and you never once gave her a chance. Whether you like her or not, you should've have made an effort for me because I'm your son and she's the girl I love. The girl who makes me happy. How would you feel if Emerson treated me the way you've treated Jay?"

"I wouldn't like it."

"Of course, you wouldn't. But you don't have to worry about that because Emerson doesn't carry around a twenty-year-old grudge. You know why? Because she's got better things to do with her time, like taking care of her daughter. Before you hated Emerson, she was your best friend for eighteen years. Think about it." I stand up, grabbing my backpack off the floor, and walk to the door. "I'm going to school and afterward I'm going to buy some flowers for my girl and pray she forgives me." I turn my attention to my mom. "Dad's right. You need to work your shit out."

"Watch your mouth."

Jayla

RIHANNA'S "LOVE ON The Brain" is playing when I walk into the kitchen and spot a giant bouquet of ranunculus in various shades of light pink and ivory with a card in the middle addressed to *Jaybird.* I pluck the card from the bouquet and open it.

> ***Jaybird,***
> ***Happy Valentine's Day.***
> ***I love you always.***
> ***Love,***
> ***Daddy***

"Happy Valentine's Day, Miss Jayla," Grace singsongs, setting down a plate of heart-shaped pancakes in front of me.

I smile at her. "Thank you, my amazing Grace. Have you seen Harper?"

"She left early for a meeting," she replies.

Mom walks into the kitchen and leans over the counter to face me. "Are you gonna talk to me today, or do you still hate me?"

"Jesus, Mom." I throw my hands up. "I don't hate you. I could never hate you. You're my ride or die. Just give me some time to process, okay? The past twenty-four hours have been pretty frickin' shitty."

"I don't know what 'ride or die' means, but I'll take it." She smiles, reaching into the pocket of her robe and setting a rectangular jewelry box on the counter with the word "Cartier" embossed on the top. "Happy Valentine's Day. This is from your dad and me."

My eyes burn as they well up with tears. I reach for the box and lift the lid. It's a white gold necklace with a heart-shaped diamond pendant. "Oh, my God. It's beautiful. Thank you." I stand up from my stool as she makes her way around the counter to me, throw my arms around her and we burst into tears.

"Jayla, I know you don't want to talk about what happened last night and I'll respect that. On one hand, I want to send Bass over to kick Zach's ass for hurting my little girl, but on the other, I get it. I've been in his shoes. I've felt what he's feeling. It's overwhelming. You don't have to take my advice, but before either of you does something you'll later regret, you should give each other some space. Just for a few days."

I nod, wiping the tears from my face. "Thanks, Mom."

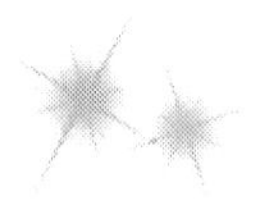

I PASS THROUGH the common area with my shoulders back and my chin held high. I won't apologize for who I am. My peers are watching me, judging me. Some of them wave and congratulate me.

"Hey, girl."

I slow and turn to see Cherry's smiling face fast approaching. She throws her arm over my shoulders, falling in step beside me as we head inside to my locker.

"First, let me say congratulations on your number one song," she squeals. "I saw you on TV. Your friend Evangeline is a trip." She laughs. "Are you okay though? That lady was an asshole."

"I'm fine." I wave her off. "You guys aren't mad at me?"

"Not at all. Honestly, I had a feeling. I mean, come on, your birthday party was insane. LAW? People don't hire rock bands to play at their parties much less grow up with them, unless they're mega-rich or famous." She pauses. "We respect you, Jay. You've been nothing but supportive in our class. You're still you. Why does anything have to change?"

I blow out a breath, relieved. "I'm glad to hear that. I don't want you guys to change your opinion of me just because of who my dad was."

"It's because of your dad that we're even here." She gives my shoulder a squeeze as she leans in and murmurs, "Brad told me about you and the QB."

"Yeah." I laugh once in disbelief, remembering Zach with his arm around Reagan and my stomach turns. "He was humiliated. So, instead of being a mature boyfriend, he got drunk and cozy with Reagan and made a point to rub their past relationship in my face." I roll my eyes and stop in front of my locker.

"What?" Cherry gasps. "Brad didn't tell me *that*."

"Hey, Jay," Justin says, leaning against the locker next to mine. "You okay?"

"Yeah," I lie. "Thanks for asking."

Justin nods. "Are you coming to my party on Friday?"

"Yeah, I'll be there. But now that the cat's out of bag, I'll probably have to bring Levi with me."

"Better him than that Bass dude." He laughs. "I'll see you guys later." He walks off.

The locker beside me opens with a click and I freeze. I'm not ready to deal with Zach. Cherry catches my eye and says, "Hey, Harper." I let out a sigh of relief. "I'll see you at lunch, Jay." Cherry gives me a quick hug before she walks off.

"Hey," I say. "Grace told me you had to leave early for a yearbook committee meeting this morning. How'd it go?"

"Boring." She rolls her eyes. "Sometimes I forget what a total nerd I am."

"A hot nerd." I jerk my eyebrows up and down.

"Yeah, right," she frowns.

"I heard you and Cole broke up yesterday. I tried to wait up for you so we could talk, but I think Grace spiked my tea and knocked me out. Yesterday was a pretty bad day."

"I saw bits and pieces of it on TV at work. You okay?"

"No," I huff. "I'll fill you in on everything after school. Are *you* okay?"

"Not really. Cole and I got into a fight yesterday because Josh showed up at Mac's."

"Oh, shit." My eyes bulge out before I lean in and whisper, "The married guy?"

"Yeah," she says. "I thought it was just a fight and after he calmed down we'd talk about it, but, apparently, he had other ideas."

"I'm sorry, Harper."

"For what? You didn't do anything wrong. You're the only person who ever tries to do the right thing. You're a good friend, Jay."

"Cole is an asshole, but I know he loves you."

Her eyes fill with tears. "It took me months to finally trust him and one night to lose that trust. One bad fight and he runs straight to the one girl who's made my senior year a fucking nightmare. Because of him."

"That's not true, Harper."

We both turn our heads at the same time to face Cole while Zach opens his locker and switches out his books. "I didn't," Cole pleads. "She sat in my lap for all of two minutes. That's all. You can ask Jay." He gestures to me. "She was standing right there."

Harper ignores him and smiles sadly at me. "We'll talk later." She squeezes my arm before disappearing into the sea of students crowding the hallway, leaving me to face off the two fucktards alone.

I turn back to my locker, keeping my face hidden behind the open door. Cole pulls the door back and steps into my personal space. "I'm sorry for what I said last night. You'd been through hell and you didn't deserve that. I was drunk and pissed off because of my own insecurities. I fucked up, but I didn't do anything with Ashton. You know me, Jay. Help me out here."

If he didn't look like a wounded animal, I'd tell him to kiss my ass and that he doesn't deserve Harper. And maybe mess up his hair or something. I'm not ready to accept his apology for the things he said last night but if he wants my advice... I tilt my head back and take a deep calming breath before turning to him. "Listen closely, Cole..." I slam my locker shut and pull my backpack over my shoulder. "...because you are riding on my last nerve. Stay away from Ashton, and, most importantly, stop being an asshole. It's Valentine's Day, for fuck's sake!"

"Happy Valentine's Day, babe." Zach leans in to kiss me.

I palm his face and push him away. "Save it for Reagan." With that, I walk away and right out the door.

I don't feel like being here today.

Fuck Cole.

Fuck Zach.

Fuck Valentine's Day.

I BLOW OFF school for the rest of the day for some time with me, myself, and I. And because Xavier—my stylist, angel from heaven, and half of my favorite gay duo—loves me, he worked me in for a pedicure and a much-needed massage. However, with the way he's sanding down my feet, I'm not feeling the love. "What's going on with you?"

"Nothing," he clips out without looking at me. "Why?"

"You're lying. I'm sensing a 'tude."

He scoffs and rolls his eyes. "I do not have a '*tude*."

Oh, he definitely has a 'tude. And if that's not a dead giveaway, the snap of his head on the last word sure is.

"Oh, okay. Mr.—" I push out my lips and jerk my head side to side, imitating him. "What did my feet ever do to you? If you scrub them any harder, I'm not gonna have any skin left. Now put down the scrubby thingy and tell me what's got your thong in a twist."

Xavier's mouth pulls to the side as he tries not to laugh. "Scrubby thingy?"

I cross my arms and raise my brows. "Quit stalling and talk to me."

He lets out a dramatic huff and drops his shoulders. "Brice and I ran into his ex at the club last night."

"So?"

"So? He's freaking gorgeous."

"Of course, he is."

Xavier clicks his tongue and gives me the stank face. "Thanks a lot."

"Don't look at me like that. Brice is hot and I doubt he's ever dated an ugly guy. Have you seen you?" I wave my hand up and down. "I rest my case. How did Brice react to seeing his ex?"

"Like they were old friends and it was no big deal." He waves his hand around, dismissively.

"His ex probably took one look at you, went home, downed a bottle of wine, and cried in the bathtub for hours. Brice is very happy with you. Don't push him away with your insecurities and bitchy attitude. It's Valentine's Day. Do something special to show him how happy he makes you."

Xavier's lips pull to the side. "Girl, what am I gonna do with you?"

"Well, you can start off by apologizing to my feet. I happen to know they like massages and if you massage them for like ten minutes, they'll accept your apology. They're very forgiving like that."

Xavier laughs. "I'm not the only one with a 'tude. What's got *your* thong in a twist?"

"Zach and I are taking a time out." Zach just doesn't know it yet.

Xavier pauses mid-rub and gasps. "Shut up." He blinks in shock. "You two are so perfect together. Tell me you're kidding."

I tell him everything about California—leaving the part out about my mom and Cam—and coming home to find Zach drunk.

"I saw *Celebrity Gossip*. Evangeline is my hero." He laughs. "Sweetie, that boy loves you so much. I'm sure this is hard on him, too. You're both so young and under so much pressure. You're kind of a big deal these days."

"I know. But right now we just need to take a step back from each other and breathe."

My phone pings with a text notification from an unknown number. ***Jayla, this is Liz Easton. I would like to apologize to you in person. Would you be willing to meet me for coffee?***

"You've got to be kidding me." I roll my eyes and hold up my phone for Xavier.

His eyes bulge out of his face. “What are you gonna say?”

LIZ IS ALREADY seated in a corner booth when I step through the doors. Her hands are wrapped around her coffee cup as she stares out the window. Turning, she notices me and lifts her hand. I wave back and make my way to the counter, to order my usual from my favorite barista, Jeffrey. He waves me off to let me know he’ll bring me my order.

Liz Easton is a bitch, but she’s a beautiful bitch. I’d always imagined she was beautiful just by the looks of her sons and her brother, Cam. We’ve established that Zach takes after his father and Logan definitely looks like his mother. She and my mom have a lot of the same mannerisms. I can almost picture them as teenagers with their smart mouths, raising hell.

“Nice shirt.” Liz nods toward my shirt that says, “Abracadabra... Nope, you’re still a bitch.”

Seemed fitting for the occasion.

“Have a seat.” She gestures to the empty seat across from her. “I don’t bite.”

“I beg to differ,” I say, sliding into the booth. “I wasn’t sure if you were here yet since I didn’t see your broom parked out front.”

Liz smiles over the rim of her coffee, keeping her eyes on me.

I raise my brows in a challenge.

“Here you go, Jayla girl,” Jeffrey says, setting my coffee on the table in front of me. He runs the show at Starbucks. I’m his favorite customer because one, he loves me and, two, I tip well.

“Thank you, Jeffrey.” I reach in my purse and pull out a twenty.

“Hm-mm.” Jeffery rests his hand on my shoulder and shakes his head. His expression is sympathetic. He’s either seen the news or talked to Lexi. “Not today, girl. It’s on me.” He winks. “Let me know if you need anything else.”

I thank him again before he sashays back behind the counter.

“Thank you for meeting me. I wasn’t sure you’d show after the way I treated you yesterday." She gives me a sad smile. "I'm truly sorry for the things I said, and for the way I've treated you. I hurt you and, by hurting you, I hurt my son." She turns her head to stare out the window for a moment before looking back to me. "Believe it or not, I'm a nice person when you get to know me."

"I believe it. You just never gave me the chance." She winces. "But I do believe it. I can tell just by being around Logan and Zach that they come from amazing parents. I think Logan takes after you. He's outspoken and protective, but he's also caring and considerate. Zach is more like his dad—laid-back, easygoing, but if you push him too hard, he'll push back and things might get ugly."

She laughs. "You definitely know my boys."

"You should be proud. They're good guys."

"Do you have a best friend, Jayla?"

"I have several."

"But do you have one friend in particular who you sometimes swear you need to breathe?"

"Yes. Lucas and Weenie."

"Who?"

"Sorry." I laugh. "Lucas and Evangeline. I call her Weenie." I wave my hand. "Long story."

"Evangeline is the model, right?"

I nod. "Yes. Lucas, Evangeline, and I grew up together. I couldn't imagine not ever having them in my life."

Liz gives me another sad smile. "That's exactly how I felt about Emerson." A tear slips down her cheek and she quickly wipes it away. "You already know that our mothers are best friends. Mimi is my godmother and I was named after her. The same goes with Emerson and my mother. We were inseparable from the time we were babies until a few weeks after we graduated from high school. Nothing and no one could ever come between us."

Another tear rolls down her cheek that she quickly wipes away.

"I don't hate Emerson."

"Yes, you do. It's a little late to try to spare my feelings now. The question you need to ask yourself is if you can ever forgive her?"

She laughs once. "I hadn't thought of it that way."

"You need to decide..." I wave my hand around. "...because it's affecting your families."

"I know." She sighs, running her finger across the edge the table. "Mike isn't too happy with Zach, or me, at the moment. And Zach isn't speaking to me."

I lift my eyebrows. "Is that why you called me here? You're apologizing so Zach won't be mad at you."

She shakes her head. "No, I'm apologizing for the way I treated you because it's the right thing to do. You didn't deserve it. I won't make excuses for Zach's behavior last night, but he loves you and he's terrified of losing you."

"I don't want to lose him either, but this is my life. I didn't ask for this, nor do I want the attention, but this is who I am and I won't apologize for it. I can't control what the media says about me. I don't want to constantly worry about Zach's reaction to every photo that gets posted online. I'm going on tour in less than five months. This is only the beginning."

"Jayla," she says in a low voice, reaching across the table to rest her hand on my arm. "I know I have no right to ask you for anything, but, please, give Zach a chance to make things right. He knows he messed up and, just in case he forgets, Logan has been doing a fabulous job of reminding him." She laughs. "I hope maybe one day you'll forgive me too."

"I already have and I hope one day you can forgive Emerson."

"I'm working on it."

I FIND GRACE in the kitchen when I walk in from the garage. "Miss Jayla, Mr. Z was here looking for you," she tells me. I laugh to myself. I love when she calls him "Mr. Z." It makes him sound like a superhero.

"What did he want?"

She points to another flower arrangement—ranunculus. "There's a card too."

I move over to the island and pick up the card, carefully opening the envelope and pulling out a folded piece of paper. It's a handwritten note.

Jay,

I love you. I love you with my whole heart and I always will. I'm sorry for hurting you and I promise I will never let anyone or anything come between me and my girl, ever again.

Happy Valentine's Day.

Love,

Z

TRACK 54: OUT OF CONTROL

Jayla

"HEY, YOU MADE it," Justin greets us in the foyer with another guy who looks like an older version of himself. Tonight is the Phillips' annual "CEOs and High-class Hoes" party. Justin lets out an appreciative whistle. "You two are killin' it tonight. This is my brother, Owen." He gestures to Harper and me. "Owen, this is Jay and this is Harper."

"You're Zach's girl, right?"

"Just Jay." I smirk.

It's been a rough few days, putting space between Zach and me, but right now, it's what we both need.

Absence makes the heart grow fonder, right?

Owen's eyebrows shoot upward. "Really?" His eyes rake over my dress and back up to meet mine. "I thought he was the smart one."

"I heard that, dickhead," a familiar voice says behind me. I look over my shoulder and smile at Logan.

"I didn't know you'd be here," I tell him.

"I couldn't miss my best friend's party." Logan gestures to Owen. "Your cousin Dylan is around here too, you know."

"Shit, I forgot she's a Mackenzie," Owen says.

"Yep." Logan hooks an arm around Harper's neck. "This one here has Cole wrapped around her finger."

Harper snorts and shakes her head unconvinced. She's hasn't quite forgiven Cole just yet. Not for Cole's lack of begging.

"Oh, yeah?" Owen laughs. "That's impressive. Well, I gotta get back to the party. It was nice meeting you both." He turns to Logan. "I'll catch up with you later. Come on, Justin."

"I'll see you two later," Justin says before he disappears into the crowd.

"My brother would shit if he saw this outfit," Logan says. "It figures you'd be the one to make slutty look classy." He laughs.

"The invitation said High-class Hoes." While I was in LA, Evangeline and I stopped at this boutique that specialized in nightlife lingerie. I bought several pieces, but the one I chose to wear tonight is a short light blue shimmery lace dress made of silk that fits snug to my body. The top has a scoop neck, long sleeves, and an open back with a tightly knitted, perfectly placed pattern, designed to conceal the private areas but to also leave enough to the imagination. I bought one for Lexi in a deep blue color and one for Harper in an emerald green. I love that color on her. I also bought myself one in black and red. I switched out the thong that came with the dress for a pair of cheeky panties.

Harper is wearing an oversized men's business shirt with a loose tie around the collar, a black lacy bra and matching cheeky lace panties underneath, garters, and high heels. Cole would seriously shit twice and die if he saw her right now. She looks hella hot.

One of the many things I love about Harper, is that even though she's quiet and keeps to herself most of the time, she's comfortable in her own skin. She's confident and, though she doesn't flirt or flaunt her body, she's aware of her beauty, which, in turn, makes her sexy. I can totally see the appeal that once attracted an older, married man and why Cole is so in love with her.

"Jay—"

"I don't want to talk about it, Logan."

"He's devastated, Jay. You've been ignoring him all week. Talk to him."

"He's the one who's confused."

"Give him a break. It's a lot to handle for anyone. Including you. Don't make him out to be a bad guy for trying to do the right thing."

"Oh, and feeling up Reagan in front of me was the right thing?"

"He knows he screwed up." His eyes move over to Harper. "They both do," he says before he turns and disappears into the crowd.

Zach

I'VE GOT A hot date tonight with Zoe and a Disney movie marathon. I can't tell you which movies she picked, only that there's a prince and a princess. Speaking of princess, Jay has completely cut me off. Again. She ignores me in class, she eats lunch in the performing arts building, she won't answer my calls, and she barely answers my text messages. I made a mistake. Using Reagan to hurt Jay was a shitty thing to do. I have no excuse for it, other than I'm an asshole.

I grab my ringing phone from the coffee table and see Logan's name on the screen. "It's only been an hour and you're interrupting our Disney marathon," I say by way of answering. "She's fine. I promise."

Logan laughs and I can hear the party going on in the background. "You're off duty."

"Off duty?"

"Yeah. Mom and Dad are on their way home from dinner to watch Zoe. Get dressed and get your butt over to Owen's."

"No, Logan. I'm not in the mood for a party."

"Jay's here with Harper."

"Wh—she's there?" I hiss. Of course, she's there, because she hates me. "What is she wearing?"

"More than most. So, I'll see you soon?" No doubt, Logan is loving this. He's been giving me shit all week.

My reply is to hang up on the asshole and call Cole.

"Yo!"

"Come pick me up. We're going to the Phillips's party."

"No way. I'm already on Harper's shit list."

"Jay and Harper are at the party."

"You're shitting me? I thought Harper was working tonight. Give me thirty minutes."

Thirty minutes later, Cole pulls into the driveway and lays on the horn. "I'll see you guys later," I call out to my parents as I head for the door.

"Hold on, Zach," my dad says, meeting me at the door. "What's your plan?"

"I'm going to the Phillips's party. Don't worry, I'm not drinking."

"Please don't let tonight turn into a repeat of Monday night."

"It won't. I promise."

I'm going to get *my* girl.

Jayla

HARPER AND I make our way over to the bar and order a couple of lemon drop shots from a guy named Chad, our bartender for the evening.

"Jayla." I look over my shoulder to see Chelsea coming our way, dressed in a short black satin nightgown with a matching robe hanging open and black furry heels.

I'm so not in the mood for her shit tonight. A few days after the Winter Ball incident, Chelsea sent me an apology text. I never responded.

I roll my eyes and turn back to Harper, clinking my shot glass with hers before tossing it back.

Chelsea stops in front of where Harper and I are facing each other. "I saw what went down with that reporter lady," she snickers. "Justin told me what Zach did to you. That was a dick move."

The sincerity in her voice catches me off guard. I raise my brows and wait for her to laugh in my face, but she doesn't. Instead, she says, "Zach doesn't handle being humiliated very well." She winces. "I'm sorry." Her apology seems genuine, but I'm still skeptical.

She must see it on my face. "Look, I know you don't trust me, and I don't blame you. I was a total bitch to you because you hurt Zach and I wanted to hurt you. I've known Zach my whole life and I care about him. He told me what Reagan did to you. I hate that bitch and

I'm sorry for whatever part I played in that. I wish I could take it all back. Especially now that I know what you were going through. I'm sorry about your dad."

"Thanks."

"I truly believe that you and Zach were always meant to be. Maybe when things settle down, we can all get together and you and I can get to know each other for real."

"I'd like that." It's true. I'd take an ally over an enemy any day.

Justin appears at Chelsea's side, grabbing her hand. "Come on, Chels, let's go dance."

Chelsea shoots me a wink as Justin pulls her toward the dance floor.

Logan moves to stand beside me, leaning against the bar with a drink in his hand. There's a twinkle in his eye and I realize it's the first time I've seen him with a drink since Zoe came along.

"What'd Chelsea say to you?" he asks.

"She apologized."

"Hmm." He nods before taking a sip of his drink. I've been so far up Zach's ass lately, I never appreciated just how beautiful Logan is, too. Somewhere out there is a woman who is going snag Logan Easton and that woman is one lucky bitch.

Brad and Cherry squeeze through the crowd and appear in front of us. "Hey, Cherry." I reach over and hug her. "You look so pretty." She's in a pink strapless dress with a red skinny belt and red patent leather peep-toed heels. Her wild curls have been straightened making her silky light brown hair fall to the center of her back. She's so sweet and perfect for Brad.

"Thank you," Cherry says, giving me a once-over. "You look hot."

"Smokin' hot," Brad says, wiggling his eyebrows.

"Bow-chica-wow-wow!" I sing as I rock my hips from side to side. "Is Brooklyn here?"

"Hell, no," Brad scowls. "Brooklyn isn't allowed anywhere near this party."

"Jay!" Lexi calls out, weaving through the crowd tugging Evan behind her.

"How did you get out of the house dressed like that?" Evan asks, gesturing to my dress.

"My mom was out." I wink. "Besides, I'm overdressed compared to most. Have you seen what these girls are wearing? The invitation said 'High-class Hoes,' not strippers and porn stars."

Harper playfully jabs me with her elbow and laughs.

I hook my arm around Harper's neck. "Harper's my CEO."

"Harper, I would pay money to see the look on Cole's face right now," Brad says with a laugh.

Harper rolls her eyes.

"Better get out your money, bro," Evan says, jerking his chin. "Because they're here and heading this way."

I look over at Logan. "You told him I was here, didn't you?"

"He's my brother." He shrugs.

I smack him in the arm. "You're lucky I love Zoe, you jerk."

Grabbing my shot from the bar, I toss it back and lean over to Harper. "Let's go dance." We push off the bar. "Cherry," I call over my shoulder and point to the dance floor. "Come on, Lexi." I hook my arm through Lexi's and the four of us make our way to the middle of the crowded dance floor.

"Oh, *hell*, no!" I hear Cole's big mouth yell just as Maroon 5's "Animal" starts playing.

I yell out, "Oh, snap! This is my jam, bitches."

Zach

BY THE TIME Cole and I arrive at Justin's house, the place is packed with half-naked girls in lingerie and guys dressed in disheveled business shirts and ties hanging loosely from their necks.

Cole takes the lead and shoves his way through the sea of bodies and I follow closely behind. "Zach, your girl is here," a chick I've never met before yells over the music.

Some random guy steps in our path and slaps Cole on the back. "Dude, Harper is sexy as fuck. You still hittin' that?" Even with the music blaring, I can hear the growl rip from Cole's throat as he cocks his head to the side, peering over the guy's shoulder. The guy backs away with his hands raised in surrender. "Sorry, man, just sayin'. You're a lucky guy."

"Oh, *hell*, no!" Cole charges forward, shouldering past the random guy. "Did you see what Jay was wearing?" he asks me over his shoulder.

"No. Where is she?" Logan, Brad, Evan, and Levi, Evan's cousin and Jay's security, are standing near the bar laughing.

"What's so funny?" Cole asks with a scowl.

"What's up, Harry Potter?" Brad laughs again, causing the rest of them to laugh harder. Me included.

"Shut up, dickhead," Cole snaps. "I wasn't planning on coming and I'd already taken out my contacts," he explains as she scans the makeshift dance floor before turning his gaze on Levi. "You let Jay leave the house wearing that outfit?"

Levi's lip curls up before he shoots back, "I'm her security, not her fuckin' stylist, asshole."

"They're out there dancing and having a good time," Logan says. "Don't do anything stupid or you'll screw up any chance you have of fixing this. You hear me?" He points at Cole. "Especially you, Mackenzie."

"I know, I know. Believe me. I've been getting my ass chewed out all week and Willow thinks I'm a meany-face."

"Damn. Willow doesn't pull any punches." I chuckle.

"Jay and Harper have been tossing back shots like water. I counted four before they went out on the dance floor."

"Harper doesn't drink," Cole says. "And Jay knows better."

"She does now," Brad says with laugh. "And I don't think Jay gives a shit."

I turn to my brother and ask, "What's Jay wearing?"

"Nothing like that." He jerks his head in a nod, gesturing to a blonde dressed in a leather corset with matching leather boy shorts and high-heeled boots. The blonde throws Logan a flirty smile over her shoulder and he groans. "I need to get laid."

Cherry walks up breathless and giggling, and leans in to Brad. "Jay is a trip."

"What are they doing?" Cole asks.

"They're dancing," Cherry replies in a clipped tone, then shifts her gaze to me. "They're having fun." *Translation: leave her alone.* Cherry has become another Evangeline. She's very protective of Jay. I'm pretty sure she kind of hates me right now.

Lexi emerges from the dance floor and makes her way over to Evan. "Oh, my God! I can't keep up with those long-legged bitches," she pants, fanning herself.

"Save some of that energy for me." Evan wiggles his eyebrows.

I shift my gaze over to the dance floor when the music switches to a slow song and see a flash of red hair next to a familiar head of black hair pulled up into a high ponytail.

"What the fuck is she wearing?" I growl and jerk forward, ready to throw Jay over my shoulder and get her out of here. Jay's see-through dress is not meant to be worn outside the bedroom. Light blue lace, and though you can't see her nipples, it's obvious she's not wearing a bra. And her panties... *Fuck!*

Harper is wearing a men's dress shirt open in the front with a black lace bra and panties underneath and a loose tie around her neck. Jesus, she's wearing garters. Clearly, she's trying to give Cole a heart attack. As the two weave through the crowd, heads turn and eyes drop to their asses.

Cole follows my gaze and his eyes nearly pop out of his head. "Harper is so getting her ass spanked for this," he growls and I raise my brows.

Okay. Wow.

Logan puts his hand on my chest to stop me from going all "caveman," as Jay would say. "She's been drinking. Do you *really* want to go another round?" He smirks and I blow out a breath in an effort to calm down. "Didn't think so."

Harper brushes past Cole without a word or even a glance in his direction and makes her way up to the bar. Jay does the same.

Cole, being the stubborn ass that he is, shoves his way past Logan and positions himself behind them.

"Jay, I can see your tits and ass through that dress," he says with a clenched jaw. "I'm *pretty* sure neither Emerson nor Bass would approve of this outfit or..." He gestures to her dress. "...piece of fabric."

Jay spins around. "Last I checked, I'm an adult and you're not my father." She pauses to take in Cole's getup and bursts out laughing, pointing to his glasses. "You look like fucking Clark Kent." She doubles over, one hand on her side and the other holding on to the bar. "Look Harper, it's Cole-ark Kent." She laughs even harder at her own joke. Harper eyes him over her shoulder and snorts.

Not gonna lie, it's kind of hard to take Cole seriously in those glasses.

"I'll take that as a compliment," Cole quips, pressing up against Harper, with his hands on the bar, caging her in. "I'm the man of steel." He thrusts his hips forward. "Isn't that right, Harper?"

"Ugh, you're an idiot," Jay says, rolling her eyes.

"What the fuck are you wearing, Harper?" Cole hisses.

"She's wearing her 'fuck off, Cole' outfit," Jay quips. "It's couture from the line of 'guys are assholes.' It was made especially for Harper." *My girl is on fire tonight.*

"Mind your biz, Jay," Cole warns.

"It is my biz, Cole. She looks hot. Get over it. Maybe you should try complimenting her instead of acting like a jealous control freak. What do you care, anyway? This isn't a fairy tale, Cole. Trust me. I, of all people, know there's no such thing as a happily ever after."

With every word she spews, her eyes get darker and her face gets redder. A clear sign that her temper is hot and she's about to lose her shit.

"I told you I was sorry. I didn't mean it."

She scoffs. "Yes, you did. You just don't like hearing your own words thrown back in your face."

"Babe, you're drunk," I cut in.

"Well, shit." She holds up her hands, gesturing to Cole and me. "We've got Superman *and* Captain Obvious!" she says sarcastically.

Anyone within earshot is laughing. I'll admit I have to look away and tuck my lips between my teeth to keep myself from joining in. She's funny as hell when she's sober, but her sass is on point when she's had a few drinks.

And to make matters worse, a gazelle wanders—more like, sashays—right into the lion's den. "Hey, Cole," a tiny blonde says as she squeezes between me and Cole. She's wearing one of those little baby doll nighties that parts in the middle, the biggest tits I've ever seen up close, on display, and tiny lace—see-through—panties, leaving nothing to the imagination. It's completely inappropriate no matter what the invitation says.

But we're guys.

If there's a pair of giant tits on display for all to see, we're gonna look. It can't be helped.

Cole's gaze drops down to the giant boobs, constrained by the thin, lacy material. A smart guy, whose girlfriend is standing less than a foot away, would quickly look away. But this clueless asshole continues to stare down at the set of tits, now pressed against his arm. *What a dumbass.* I shake my head at him and turn my attention to Jay, who is staring holes into both Cole and the blonde.

I've seen that look before. Nothing good comes from that look.

This girl has no idea what she just walked into.

I glance over at Harper who looks like Cole just screwed this chick right in front of her. "Do I know you?" Cole asks with furrowed brows. His question would've been much more convincing if he didn't still have his eyes zeroed in on her chest.

Logan lets out a disbelieving chuckle as Brad mumbles, "Mackenzie is an idiot," at the same time Lexi asks, "Is she serious right now?" Evan shushes her. He's enjoying the show. I love how he went from hating on my girl to hanging on every word that comes out of her mouth. *The dick.*

I turn my attention back to Jay, who looks like she's seconds away from punching this chick in her tits.

"Stacey," the blonde purrs as she wraps her arm around Cole's. "Remember we, uh...." She looks around and lowers her voice. "We hung out at that lake party last summer."

What lake party? I smell drama.

A shot glass slams down on the bar with a loud smack and all our heads turn toward Harper. Cole closes his eyes, looking a mixture of guilt and pain, and exhales through his nose as he pulls his arm free from Stacey.

"Excuse me, Lacey?" Jay purrs, mocking Stacey, crossing her arms over her chest. She's preparing for a battle.

And here we go.

Logan, the fucker, whoops from behind me and says, "Let's get ready to rumble!"

"It's Stacey," she shoots back with a sneer.

Stacey clearly has no sense of danger, but in fairness to her, Jay looks harmless. In my head, I'm yelling, "*Run as fast and as far away as you can.*" But since I'm already on Jay's shit list, I'm just gonna stand here and watch as the gazelle hands herself over on a silver platter to the lioness.

My lioness.

"Who cares," Jay says with a dismissive flick of her wrist. "Did you not see we were in the middle of a conversation—one of us being his girlfriend?" She jerks her thumb to Harper and pauses for dramatic effect, then smacks her palm against her head. "Oh, my bad. You probably couldn't see over those enormous tits. Seriously, you should put those things away before someone gets hurt. And FYI, that outfit you're wearing screams desperation."

"Jealous?"

"Of what? Future backaches? A place to hide small children?" She cups her breasts. "Does it look like I have anything to be jealous of?"

"Jay," I warn gently, fighting back a smile. Harper is now hunched over the bar, slapping her palm against the wood as her whole body shakes with silent laughter.

Stacey frowns up at Cole, but his head is turned away; he's also laughing his ass off. "Cole Mackenzie doesn't do relationships. Everyone knows that."

My eyebrows shoot upward. *What the hell is she talking about?* There's no doubt someone put her up to this. *Ashton.* "Someone didn't get the memo," I murmur.

With a flirty smile, Stacey turns her big chest away from Cole and aims it my way. She arches her back, pushing her tits further in my direction. I'm not exaggerating when I say that if she arches her back any further, she might tip over.

"You're Zach, right? Didn't we hook up at Devin Milner's party last summer?"

Bullshit. I jerk my gaze from her to Jay in a panic, and then back to her. "Uh... no. I don't.... I think I would—"

"Finish that sentence Zach, and I will punch you in the dick." Jay's angry glare remains on Stacey as her hands move to her hips.

She's in full battle mode. "Excuse me, Lacey... tits for brains." She snaps her fingers in front of Stacey's face. "He's private property and you're trespassing. Walk away or..." She reaches behind her and grabs a toothpick off the bar. "...I'll use this to pop those water balloons." She waves her hand, shooing her away. "Now go away before I smack you."

"I'd like to see you try."

Jay's eyebrows shoot up to her hairline and her lips curl up on one side, smiling devilishly.

You know that part in the movies, that "uh-oh" moment where someone says or does something stupid, followed by the sound of a record scratch and the whole room goes silent?

This would be that moment.

I move to wrap my arms around Jay and whisper in her ear, "Something's up. She's goading you on purpose. It's okay to show your teeth, but don't bite. There are too many people here with cell phones."

"Are you crazy, girl," Cole speaks up, finally. "I'm not trying to be a dick, but you should probably walk away, Lacey, before she tears you apart."

"It's Stacey," she whines.

"I don't care what your name is," Cole replies, sounding annoyed.

"Lacey—Stacey, lower your tits so we can see your *face-y*," Jay sings and then snorts, once again laughing at herself. I drop my forehead to her shoulder and burst out laughing and so does everyone else. Even Levi is laughing. I can't believe Lacey—Stacey is still standing here.

Lacey—Stacey curls her lip like she just smelled something foul. "Excuse me?"

"For?"

"Huh?"

"Ho say what."

Oh, yeah, she's done.

"What?" Lacey—Stacey's eyebrows pull inward, confusion marring her face and Jay doubles over in laughter. "Ugh! Whatever, bitch," she mutters and storms off.

Finally.

“I’ll be back,” Logan says. “Lacey looks like she could use some comforting.”

Everyone bursts into another round of laughs.

“That was fun,” Jay says, winking at Harper. “Did you see the girl on those boobs?”

Cherry laughs. “You mean boobs on that girl?”

“Oh.” Jay snorts.

“And she’s back.” Cole laughs.

“And you’re still an asshole,” Jay shoots back.

Cole runs his fingers through his hair. “I’m sorry, Harper.”

Harper whirls around angrily. “You’re always sorry,” she snaps out. “You have no problem running your mouth and putting people in their place...” She gestures to Jay. “...but some skank presses her big nasty tits up against you and all of a sudden you forget how to speak. You have no respect for me or my feelings and I’m sick of it. Fuck the hell off, Cole. I’m done.”

“Don’t say that, Harper,” he pleads.

She picks up another shot, tosses her head back, and then slams the empty shot glass on the bar before turning around, shoving past Cole, and heading for the dance floor.

Cole gives me a pleading look.

“What are you doing?” I ask, shooing him away. “Go after her.” I shake my head as Cole hurries off. “Sometimes I can’t believe he’s my best friend.”

“I can’t believe I’m related to him.”

“Go easy on him, Jay. He feels bad for what he said to you and he really does love Harper.”

“I know, but he seriously needs to stop being an ass.”

Lexi and Evan move to the spot Harper just vacated. Logan has disappeared and the rest of our friends head for to the dance floor. Probably to watch Cole beg.

“Girl, that was so funny,” Lexi says, running her fingers below her eyes, wiping away her smeared mascara. “I think you could give Evangeline a run for her money.”

Jay smirks. “I learned from the best.”

“You confused the shit out of that girl.” Evan guffaws.

“I confused myself,” Jay admits with a laugh as she pulls from my arms and turns to the bar. "Anyone want to do a shot with me?" She looks over at me. "Except you. I think you should stay away from alcohol for a while."

"I will," Lexi volunteers.

"I wasn't planning on it," I admit. "Besides, I'm driving you home tonight."

"I'm not going home with you, Zach." She signals for Chad, Owen's friend, who's working the bar tonight.

"Hey, Chad." I jerk my chin in a nod. "I'll take a Coke, please." I turn to Jay. "I said I was driving you home. You drove here and you're drinking. How did you think you were getting home?"

"Levi. *Duh.*" She rolls her eyes.

Chad catches my eye as he sets my Coke down on the bar. He waits for Jay to turn away before he swipes a hand past his throat, gesturing that she's cut off before sliding a bottle of sparkling water across the bar.

I mouth, "Thanks," and turn to put my back to the bar.

The lights dim and "I Don't Wanna Live Forever" starts playing.

"Aww, I love this song," Jay coos.

"Dance with me." I hold out my hand.

"It's too hot out there."

"I'm good right here."

"Fine," she says before snaking her arms around my waist and resting her head against my chest. "This doesn't change anything."

"I know," I say, burying my face in her neck. "I miss you, Jay."

"I miss you, too." She sighs. "Zach?"

"Hmm?"

"Did you hook up with Lacey?"

I chuckle into her neck. "No and neither did Cole. I think that whole scene was a setup to cause drama."

"Damn, I should have used that toothpick."

I chuckle again. "I love you, Jay."

"I love you too, Z."

TRACK 55:
FINALLY
Jayla

"UGH," I GROAN and peel my tongue from the roof of my mouth. "Who the hell let me drink all that tequila?" *And why does my lady J feel like I dry-humped a piece of sandpaper?*

A deep chuckle comes from behind me. "Because you were bouncing up and down on my dick like a goddamn pogo stick all night," Zach answers in that sleepy voice that makes him sound even sexier. *God, I've missed him.*

I feel the flush creeping up my neck and across my cheeks when I realize I said that out loud.

"I did not." *I totally did.*

He shifts behind me, pressing against my back. Curling his arm around my waist, he says in that deep, sleepy voice close to my ear, "I had no idea you were such a little freak when you're drunk." He rolls me onto my back and moves to straddle my hips. "You were all like..." He thrusts his hips and in a breathy voice, no doubt, imitating me, sings about "fucking like an animal" and I realize he's singing the lyrics to "Closer" by Nine Inch Nails.

I throw my head back and laugh. "You're so full of shit." I grab the pillow beside me and smack him in the head.

He falls beside me on the mattress, props his head on his hand

and continues to sing.

I laugh so hard my bladder nearly bursts, making me scramble out of bed and run to the bathroom.

"Where are you going?"

"To pee," I tell him. I barely make it to the bathroom in time, sitting down on the toilet and crossing my eyes in relief.

Finishing up, I walk back into my bedroom to find Zach lying on my bed with his hands clasped behind his head. "Shame on you for taking advantage of me last night." I push out my bottom lip, pretending to pout as I straddle his lap.

"That was all you." He smiles, resting his hand on my hip. "You're a horny little thing when you're drunk."

I grin. "More than usual?"

He nods slowly before rolling on top of me, settling between my thighs, and bracing his arms on either side of my head. I push my fingers through his hair and stare into his blue eyes. "As much as I enjoyed the angry, make-up sex, I never want to fight like that again. It shredded me to be apart from you these last few days." He presses a gentle kiss to my lips. "I love you. Tell me you love me and that we're okay."

"I love you, Z, but you need to ask yourself that question. You wanted me to love you and I do. With everything I have. You have to decide if you can handle this. I'm still mad at you for shoving your relationship with Reagan in my face."

"I'm sorry. Reagan was the stupidest thing I've ever done. Shoving it in your face is a close second to hooking up with Chelsea. Can we move past it?"

"Fine. But if you ever pull that shit again, I'm done. I was content with pretending it's only been me."

"When it comes to my heart, it's only *ever* been you. None of that other stuff matters. Will you tell me what you were doing with Tyge Reynolds?"

"I wasn't with him. His father is my lawyer and his office is in that building. Tyge was there to see his... flavor of the week. I've known Tyge for a long time, but we're not close and we weren't having lunch. We were leaving at the same time."

"I'm sorry for acting like a jealous asshole. I do trust you, Jay.

Just give me some time to adjust to all of this, okay?"

"You don't really have a choice, Z. Not if you want this relationship to work. Now move, I need coffee and food."

A teasing smile tugs at his lips as he circles his hips, grinding against me. "You worked up quite an appetite last night, freaky girl."

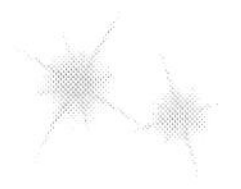

THE WHOLE GANG is here and seated around the table stuffing their faces. Grace is standing at the counter making a pot of coffee. "Good morning, Miss Jayla and Mister Z." She smiles over her shoulder.

"Good morning, Grace," I say, hugging her from behind and kissing her on the cheek. "Thank you for feeding my friends."

I move to the island where the food is set up buffet-style. Zach kisses Grace on the cheek and follows my lead. We both pile our plates with pancakes, bacon and eggs and make our way over to the table, where everyone immediately goes silent. I look around to see them smiling.

"How are you feeling?" Evan snickers.

"I feel fine." I reach for my coffee and bring it to my lips.

Brad coughs. "So, Jay, I really liked your version of that Nine Inch Nails song. Cherry and I decided to add it to our playlist." He wiggles his eyebrows.

I pull the cup away from my lips and turn my head to laugh.

"Seriously." Cherry snickers before taking a sip of her orange juice. "After that performance, I'm pretty sure every cat in the neighborhood is pregnant."

Zach laughs and leans over to kiss my shoulder.

"What are you laughing at, Zach?" Evan slumps down in his chair and throws his head back. "Oh, shit, Jay. Just like that. Oh. Yeah. Oh, *fuuuuck!*"

"Come on, man." Cole groans and covers his ears. "I don't need to hear that shit."

I snort. "Hey, don't talk like that in front of Grace." I look over my shoulder to see her busying herself in the kitchen, but I know she can hear every word. *Poor Grace.*

"Jay." Lexi laughs. "You had me laughing so hard last night."

"Oh, God." I roll my eyes. "What did I do?"

"You don't remember?" Zach asks.

I frown, furrowing my brows. I don't remember doing anything out of the ordinary. Shots, dancing, and sex. Apparently, I rode Zach like Seabiscuit last night and then passed out.

"The blonde," Evan presses.

"Oh, my God, yes! The girl with the giant boobs?" I shake my head. "Snarky little bitch. She's lucky I was in a good mood."

"I don't think I've ever laughed so hard in my life," Lexi continues.

"She was disgusting," Cherry adds. "I could see her slit through her panties."

"She wasn't that bad," Cole insists, jerking his eyebrows up and down as he sips his coffee. A poor attempt at a bad joke.

I drop my fork. "You did not just say that."

"What?" He grins and looks over at Harper. "I'm kidding."

Harper pushes away from the table abruptly and storms off, but not before slapping the back of Cole's head on her way out.

"Ow! What the fuck, Harper? It was joke."

"Well, it wasn't funny," I say. "Have you not been listening to her? Are you being a dick on purpose so she'll dump you for good?"

Cole struggles to rein in his temper, his nostrils flaring as he stands from the table. He rocks his head side to side, stretching his arms over his head, bouncing on the balls of his feet, and throwing a couple of jabs in the air before trailing after Harper.

"What are you doing?"

"Preparing for a fight," he calls over his shoulder as he rounds the banister and jogs up the stairs.

A moment later, my mom and Cam walk into the kitchen from the garage. *Guess they're not keeping their relationship a secret anymore.* My mom slides her phone across the table. "Well, that didn't take long."

I pick up her phone to see the headline: *Jaybird's Mystery Guy* and below it is a picture of Zach and me slow dancing at Justin's party last night. His head is buried in my neck and my face is partially covered by his bicep. It's a sweet picture. I shrug and pass her phone back to her. "There's nothing wrong with this picture."

"No, but I heard you were drinking. You know the rules, Jayla."

"I know. I'm sorry." I flick my gaze to Cam. "And I'm sorry for throwing my phone at your head."

Cam chuckles. "I've had worse thrown at me."

"What happens now?" Zach asks.

"It means no scratching your balls in public," Cam replies with a chuckle.

"When you're out in public, act as if there's always a camera on you," Emerson adds. "Because most likely there will be."

Our conversation is interrupted by the sound of Cole shouting, drawing everyone's attention to the stairs. A few seconds later he jogs down the stairs and right out the front door, slamming it behind him.

Zach pushes back from the table and follows after Cole.

"What the hell is going on?" My mom asks.

I shrug. I have no clue.

AFTER EVERYONE LEAVES, Zach and I head back up to my room. I poke my head inside Harper's doorway and see her sitting on the edge of the bed with her face buried in her hands, crying. "Harper? Are you okay?"

She shakes her head.

"Do you want to talk about it?"

"No," she says into her hands. "I just need to be alone right now. I'm sorry, Jay."

"It's okay. If you need me, I'll be on my balcony."

"Thank you," she says as I reach for the door and pull it closed.

"I should probably call him," Zach says as we go into my bedroom.

I grab a couple of blankets while Zach tries to reach Cole. When Zach went after him earlier, Cole was already halfway down the driveway by the time Zach got out the door. Of course, he's not answering. I didn't expect he would. He needs time to calm down.

Zach follows me out to the balcony and we curl up on the daybed facing each other.

"Did you know about my mom and Cam?"

Zach's eyes widen in surprise and he smiles sheepishly. "I was wondering what that was about earlier. Yes, I knew, but I wish I didn't. I hated keeping it from you, but Cam made me promise to keep my mouth shut and leave it up to your mom to tell you. She finally told you?"

I snort. "No. I caught them in the shower together while we were in California."

"Damn. And you threw your phone at Cam?" He laughs. "I'm sorry, babe. Are you okay?"

I shake my head. "I don't know. Maybe I'm acting like a spoiled brat, but don't you think it's too soon?"

Zach shrugs. "I think your feelings are valid. I'm sure it's hard to see your mom with another man. But I think the only person who gets to decide when it's time for your mom to move on is your mom. Do you want her to be alone for the rest of her life? I don't think your dad would want that. He'd want her to be happy. If being with Cam makes her happy, who are you to tell her she can't be?"

"She should've talked to me about it. That's not an image I can easily erase from my brain."

"You're right. But maybe she was afraid you wouldn't approve or would think less of her."

"I don't think less of her. She's still my mom. It's her life and of course, I want her to be happy. Clearly, Cam makes her happy."

"What's gonna happen now with that picture of us floating around?"

"I don't know. That's Emerson's department. Trust me. She'll handle it."

TRACK 56:
FAMILY AFFAIRS
Zach

"ZACH, YOU NEED to get home. Emerson, Cam, Chris, and Rebecca are all here. There's a lot of yelling going on, listen." Logan pauses and I can hear people shouting in the background.

"We're on our way."

"What's going on?" Jay asks.

"I don't know. Your mom and Cam are at my house and so are Chelsea's parents. Logan said everyone is shouting at each other."

"Let's go."

Chelsea is waiting outside on the porch when Jay whips her Range Rover into the driveway, throws it in Park, and shoves open the driver's side door before I can even unclench my ass cheeks, pry my hand from the "oh, shit" bar, and climb out of the passenger side.

"What are you doing out here?" Jay asks.

"My parents told me to wait out here. It's bad in there." She wraps her arms around her waist and looks down at the ground.

The front door flies open and I can hear my mom shouting as Rebecca storms out with Chris right behind her. "Let's go, Chelsea," Chris says, calmly heading for the car.

"I don't know what's going on with our parents, but I hope it doesn't affect our friendship," Chelsea says.

"It already has," Jay says, "but not because of us. Because of them. I say the three of us start over and build a friendship between us. Leave our parents' baggage out of it."

"I agree," I say.

"Me, too," Chelsea adds, looking over her shoulder at her parents and sighing. "I better go. I'll call you later, Zach." She hugs me, then turns and hugs Jay. "Give me a call sometime."

"I will," Jay says as Chelsea turns and heads to the car.

The screaming has stopped and the front door opens again. This time it's Emerson who storms out and looks like she's been crying. "Let's go, Jayla," she calls over her shoulder as she heads straight for the passenger side of Jay's car.

Cam comes out and calls after her. "Em, wait!"

"Fuck you, Cam," she yells over her shoulder. Jay and I watch with raised brows as Cam runs over to the Range Rover. He places his hands on the roof, and leans into the passenger side.

"I'm not sure what to do here," Jay says, watching her mom and Cam go at it. "I never saw my parents fight. The only time I've ever seen my mom this mad was the day Hannah stepped on my hand and when your mom pushed me."

Em shoves Cam out of the way before reaching for the door and slamming it shut.

Jay turns to me with a sad smile. "You should go inside and check on your parents. I'm gonna take my mom home. Tell Logan to call if he needs me to watch Zoe." She gives me a kiss goodbye and heads to her Range Rover where Emerson waits in the passenger seat.

Cam stands off to the side with his hands on his hips and his head down. I stand on the porch as Jay backs out of the driveway and drives off. *What the hell is going on?*

I FIND MY mom stretched out on one of the loungers beside the pool with a big glass of wine in her hand. Her eyes are red and swollen and her face is wet with tears.

"Hey," I say, dropping down on the edge of the lounger. "You okay?"

"No. But I will be," she says with barely a whisper as another tear rolls down her cheek. She doesn't even bother to wipe it away. She pauses as if she's pondering something, then bursts out laughing.

She's losing it.

"What's so funny?" I ask.

She waves me off. "Nothing and everything."

Yep. She's lost her mind.

"Mom?"

She smiles sadly. "I'm so sorry, Zach. I've been a shitty mom and an even shittier person. God." She sighs. "The way I treated Jayla.... I have a lot of mending to do with my family and the Mackenzie's."

"It's okay. I love you, Mom." I lean over and hug her.

"I love you, too, my baby boy. Is everything okay with you and Jayla?"

"We're working on it, but I think we'll be fine. I'll be in my room if you need me."

"Thank you, Zach."

Walking into the house, past my dad's office, I catch the tail end of an argument between my dad and Cam.

"You don't think I tried to tell her?" my dad yells.

"Obviously, you didn't try hard enough. For twenty years, you let my sister believe that bitch was her best friend."

"She threatened to divorce me and take my kids if I ever brought it up. I tried to tell her, but she wouldn't listen. I didn't want to risk losing my family. What choice did I have? What about you? Have you told your parents about your dirty little secret?"

"She's not my dirty little secret!" Cam defends. I assume he's talking about his relationship with Emerson.

I leave my dad and Cam to their argument and continue to up to my room, remembering something Brad said once. *"Secrets never stay secrets for long, my friend. Remember that."* True.

TRACK 57:
IT'S BEEN SO LONG
Jayla

YESTERDAY WAS THE one-year anniversary of my dad's death. Mom and I spent the day in our pajamas bawling our eyes out while watching home movies and looking at old photos.

Family and friends called throughout the day but knew we needed our space. Bass spent the day with Lisa and Grace stayed in her room. Dr. Ramos called on FaceTime to check up on both of us. We had a nice talk and I realized how much I miss talking to her.

Zach called and we talked on the phone a little. He understood it was a bad day, deciding to stay home and spend some time with his mom.

My mom wouldn't talk about her fight with Cam, but after a long talk, I gave her the okay to move on. Not that she needed it, but I knew she needed to hear it.

I pull into my usual parking space beside Zach's Jeep and see Reagan sitting in the passenger seat with her back to the window. *What in the ever-loving fuck!*

My emotions are too raw from yesterday to even bother putting up a fight. Grabbing my bag from the front seat, I climb out of my car and hurry through the common area heading straight for my locker.

"Hey." Cole leans against the locker beside mine. He looks

terrible.

"Hey," I say. "Are you okay? I haven't heard from you since you stormed out of my house Saturday."

"No," he breathes. "This shit with Harper...." He shakes his head.

"What happened?"

"She lied. That's what happened."

My stomach flips. "Lied about what?"

"Everything." He shakes his head again. "I don't want to talk about it right now. It's a long story, but I promise to tell you later."

"Okay. I'm sorry, Cole. Is there anything I can do?"

He shakes his head. "I'm sorry I didn't call you yesterday. How are you? How's Em?"

"We're fine. We spent the day together, just the two of us, in our pjs, watching home videos, looking at old pictures and missing my dad."

An arm comes around my waist and pulls me against a solid chest. "Hey, babe. I missed you," Zach says, kissing me on the neck.

I pull away and shut my locker. "It didn't look like you were missing me a few minutes ago," I snap. "You just can't stay away from her, can you?" I walk off and head to my first class.

"What are you talking about?" Zach calls out to my retreating back. I lift my middle finger in the air and keep walking.

Zach

"WHAT WAS THAT about?" Cole asks.

"As always, your cousin has the worst goddamn timing. Reagan climbed into my Jeep this morning before I could even put it in Park. Jay must've seen her sitting in the passenger seat."

"What'd she want?"

I shrug. "Don't know. Don't care. I told her to get out."

Cole shakes his head.

"It's my fault for dragging Reagan into my shit in the first place. I never should've used her to hurt Jay." I look over at Cole, taking in his appearance. "Dude, you look like shit."

"Fuck! I know." He rakes his fingers through his hair and walks off as I step into my class.

I head straight for Jay's desk as she busies herself pulling her book from her backpack, pretending she doesn't see me coming. Leaning over so that we're eye to eye, with one hand pressed flat on her desk and the other gripping the back of her chair, I growl into her ear, "I don't care what you *think* you saw. It wasn't like that and you know it."

"I think you're still *confused*," she drawls.

"What happened to not making assumptions?"

"We're way past that, Zach."

I let out a low growl under my breath. "We *will* talk about this after class."

"Talk? Don't you mean you'll *explain*? Again?" She rolls her eyes. "Oh, my God, Zach. I'm so sick of lies, excuses, explanations, misunderstandings, and all the other 'he said, she said' bullshit. I'm done. Let's just call it quits and move on."

I'm going to let that comment slide because she's obviously still emotional from yesterday. However, she's so full of shit and I want so badly to call her on it, but Mr. Baxter walks in with his usual Starbucks in hand. "Break it up, lovebirds."

"Ease up on the crazy, Jay. You're being ridiculous. We're not calling it quits." I press my lips to the spot under her ear. "I love you." I stand, pinning her with a hard stare. She stares back, unfazed with a raised brow.

Mr. Baxter continues, "Okay, class, open your books to page one fifty-eight. You have twenty minutes to review the material and then there will be a test. Get started."

Dropping down in my seat, I pull my backpack into my lap and dig out my book and a pencil before dropping it on the floor beside my desk.

"Psst...Jay," Dex whisper-yells. Jay glances at him over her shoulder. "Girl, that dress you was wearing Friday night was sexy as *fuuuuck*," he sings. "I need to get one for my girl. Where'd you get it? Victoria's Secret? Frederick's? Hoes R' Us?" He laughs. "Come on, tell me."

Rolling her eyes, she flips him off and turns back around in her seat.

"She did look sexy in that dress," I add in a whisper, "but you know what looks even better on her?"

"Huh?"

"Me." I wink.

A few people in the surrounding desks snicker.

Her leg stops mid-bounce as she whips her head around and pins me with a glare. After a pause, she gives me that sarcastic smile she smears on right before she tells someone to eat shit or to fuck off.

"You can't just play with me when it suits you, Zach. I'm not wired that way."

I chuckle. "You like when I play with you."

"Yeah, well maybe it's time for someone else to play with me." She smirks and high-fives Kali, before she turns back around in her seat. A chorus of "oh, shits" and "day-ums" circulates around the classroom.

Derek the douche raises his hand and snickers. "I volunteer."

I shoot Derek a murderous glare before turning to Jay. "Don't start, Jay," I hiss. "I was joking."

"Someone is pissy today." Dex chuckles. "We just messin' witchu, Jay. You know Dex ain't got nothin' but love for ya, baby girl."

She smiles. "Thanks, Dex."

Just as we turn in our tests, the bell rings and the little sneak slips out the door before I can even get to my feet.

"Damn, Easton." Dex laughs, gripping my shoulder. "What'd you do this time?"

I don't have time to explain Jay's impeccable timing to Dex, so I just shake my head and hurry after her. I see her weaving through the busy hallway, moving as fast as her long legs can carry her, heading to our next class. Too bad for her that my legs are longer and I'm faster. Dodging and weaving is what I'm good at.

Hooking an arm around her waist, I pull her to my chest and turn my back to the nosey fuckers walking by. To them we look like the typical affectionate couple they see every day.

"Stop fighting me," I growl in her ear, tightening my hold on her. "Reagan jumped in my car before I'd even parked. If I had to guess, that psycho bitch saw you pull into the parking lot and timed her little move perfectly just to piss you off. She said she wanted to talk. I told her to get the fuck out. She got out. I got out. That's it. End of story. No more fighting, Jay. Not in front of our friends, classmates, at school, or in public—period. After everything that's happened in the last week, people are more curious than ever. I was an idiot for doubting us and it won't happen again. I love you and you love me. Let's stick with that. No more drama. Okay?"

She nods and her body relaxes against mine. "Fine. Okay."

"Now give me those delicious lips." She tilts her head back with her lips puckered for a kiss. *That's my girl.* I press my lips to hers and slide my tongue across the seam, teasingly. She moans affectionately. I pull away with a smirk. "I haven't forgotten about that smartass comment in class, but you're gonna make it up to me after school."

"Oh, yeah?" She arches an eyebrow. "I thought you loved my smart ass. And what about your douchey comment?"

"I do love your smart ass. And your smart mouth." I smack another kiss on her lips. "I'm sorry for what I said. It *was* douchey, but I'll make it up to you after school." I grin.

She huffs out a laugh. "You're such a horndog."

"I love you."

"I love you, too."

"Good." Unhooking my arm from her waist, I step back and hold out my hand. "Now hold my hand like a loving girlfriend and let's get to class. We're late." Taking her hand in mine, our fingers entwined, we make our way to our next class.

TRACK 58: CAN'T HOLD ME DOWN

Jayla

THE LAST FEW weeks have been rough between the fights, the secrets, and the revelations. Cole broke up with Harper. Believe it or not, Ashton doesn't seem to care; she's moved on to the varsity baseball team's superstar. Kali broke things off with Lucas. And my mom still isn't speaking to Cam.

But on a high note, Zach and I are good.

Chelsea has texted me a few times. She and Justin are going strong. Reagan has kept her distance, which means she's probably off somewhere trying to ruin someone else's relationship.

Today, Zach is out on the boat with his dad and Logan. Things have been tense at Zach's house after the big blowout, and the truth came out that Mike cheated on Liz with Chelsea's mom, Rebecca. It happened over twenty years ago, they were kids, but the whole time, Liz thought it was my mom who'd betrayed her. This time Mimi and Zach's grandma Kate have stepped in to help mend our families, as well as my mom and Liz's friendship.

Zach has lost a lot of respect for his dad. Unfortunately, he can't disassociate himself from his own father. Mike made a mistake and Liz made the choice to forgive him. Zach needs to accept it. Mike has been a good husband to Liz and a good father to his sons. That's what

Zach needs to focus on.

So, with all that drama behind us, the girls and I hit the mall for a little retail therapy. I even brought my two favorite girls along for a trip to Build-A-Bear.

After a little shopping, lunch, and two hours in Build-A-Bear with Willow and Zoe, who are clearly overdue for a nap, I'm ready for a nap myself, and some alone time with my guy.

"Let me call my mom and tell her to meet us at the car." Lexi and Kali rode with her, since I had two car seats in my backseat. Mom and Mimi left us at Build-A-Bear while they went to pick up some shoes Mom had on hold at Nordstrom. The plan was for us to meet up at the exit leading to the second level of the parking garage so we could all leave together, since my mom gave our bodyguards the day off. *No signal.* "The call won't go through."

"You guys go ahead. I'll go down to the shoe department and let her know we're ready," Lexi offers.

"Okay. Thanks," I say, then turn to Harper. "You stay here with the girls and Kali and I will go get the car." In my excitement of picking up the babies for a trip to the mall, I forgot to bring a stroller, so I had to rent one.

Kali and I leave Harper in the vestibule with Zoe and Willow and head to the car with our bags. I pass my bags over to Kali so I can dig out my keys.

Parking garages have always given me the creeps. Like someone is gonna jump out and grab me. So, when the overwhelming feeling of unease settles in the pit of my stomach and my instincts are telling me to turn around and go back inside the mall, I should do just that.

But—

"Kalista!" an unfamiliar male voice calls out and Kali jerks to a stop.

"Oh fuck!" she whispers, her voice laced with panic.

Pulling my keys from my purse, I look over at Kali to see her pale and frightened face. Turning my head, I follow her line of sight and see two guys leaning against the trunk of my mom's Maserati.

"Is he talking to you?" I ask.

One is tall with dark brown hair and the other is blond, a few inches shorter but stockier. They're both clean-cut, preppy, and look like they're in their early twenties.

"I can't believe he found me." She looks over at me with sad eyes. "I'm so sorry, Jay."

"What are you talking about, Kali?" I whisper. "Who are they?"

Before Kali can say another word, the dark-haired guy is standing in front of her, hands in his pockets and a triumphant gleam in his eyes. "I've missed you, *Kalista,*" he says sweetly, contradicting the anger pouring off him.

"Why?" Kali snips. "Couldn't find another punching bag?"

In a flash, he moves, grabbing a fistful of Kali's short hair, yanking her head back so she's looking up at him. "Watch your mouth, Kalista," he says through gritted teeth before he slams his mouth down on hers. Kali struggles and, when he pulls away, she turns her face to suck in a breath. "I've missed this mouth." He grabs her face in a vice-like grip and jerks her head to face his. "This little hide-n-seek game is over. It's time to come home. We have a wedding to plan and you need to do something about this fucking hair. You look like a boy."

I gasp, prompting him to turn his leering eyes on me. "Who's your pretty friend?"

"I'm Jay. Who are you?" I shoot back.

"I'm Austin. Kalista's fiancé." He nods toward his blond friend. "This is Tripp."

Tripp winks and crosses his arms over his chest. "You look familiar," Tripp says, tilting his head and narrowing his eyes, scanning my face for recognition. "I know you from somewhere. You a model or something?"

I scoff nervously. *Fuck.* "No." The key fob digs into the palm of my clenched fist, and then I remember. *The panic button.* Unclenching my fist, I slide my thumb over the key fob until I feel the oddly shaped panic button, press down, and hold. *Three seconds.*

Three seconds doesn't seem like a long time, but when every second counts, it feels like a lifetime. I can only hope that it's been three seconds when Tripp reaches out, grabs me by the ponytail, and spins me around so my back is pressed against his chest. He pins my arms to my side and presses his forearm against my windpipe, making me drop my purse and keys.

I struggle to break free from his hold and suddenly everything I learned about self-defense escapes me. The more I struggle, the tighter his grip becomes. The scruff along his jaw feels like sandpaper against my cheek. He drags his lips over my jaw, up to my ear, before he bites down on my earlobe hard enough to make me flinch. "Keep fighting and wiggling that sexy ass, pretty girl," he hisses, thrusting his hips forward. "Mmm. You smell good." He trails his lips down my neck, nipping at the skin where my neck and shoulder meet.

"Leave her alone, Tripp," Kali pleads, then turns to Austin. "Let her go and I'll go home with you. Please, just leave her out of this."

Austin's expression is blank, as he seems to be considering her plea, but the anger is still there in his eyes. He's not gonna let me go.

Suddenly, he reaches out and snatches Kali by her hair again, slams his fist into her face repeatedly before he shoves her to the ground and proceeds to kick her in the side. "You don't get to call the shots, Kalista."

A small cry escapes me seeing my tiny friend curled up on the ground, not moving.

Austin shakes out his hand and runs it through his hair before he turns to me. My body trembles as tears stream down my face. Rage surges through my veins. I want so badly to rip this motherfucker's head off.

Austin reaches out and grabs my face the same way he did Kali's and slams his mouth down on mine. He presses his fingers deeper into my cheeks, forcing my lips apart, and pushing his tongue into my mouth. His other hand travels roughly up to my breasts and down over the front of my jeans. I flinch when he pulls away and drags his teeth over my bottom lip. I jerk my head to the side, out of his grip, and gasp for air. Tripp continues to press down on my windpipe. "She tastes good," Austin says to him, keeping his eyes on me, slowly allowing them to travel lower. "I'll bet she feels even better."

"Mmm," Tripp hums close to my ear as he grinds his hips into me from behind. "She's got a nice little ass."

Austin reaches out and squeezes my breast through my shirt. "Nice set of tits too. A little skinny, but I could have fun with this one."

I try to convince myself that they're just trying to scare me, but my gut tells me they're serious. Closing my eyes, I inhale through my nose, forcing myself to remain calm as I pray someone shows up to help. *How is there no one around in broad daylight?*

Someone gasps and then I hear a familiar sweet voice. "JJ?"

Willow.

Then Zoe starts to cry.

Sucking in a breath, I can't turn my head, but I can see Harper out of the corner of my eye, standing there shocked and wide-eyed with two confused toddlers at her side. Her eyes fall to Kali curled up on the pavement and slowly she begins to back away.

"Where do you think you're going, red?" Austin says with a smile. He looks over at Tripp. "All these pretty girls. My day just keeps getting better."

You're a fighter, Princess.

My protective instincts kick in and, with everything I have, I lift my leg and kick Austin in the balls hard enough to drop him to his knees. I've never been more grateful for my long-ass legs than I am right now. "Run, Harper!" I choke out before bringing the pointy heel of my boot down on the top of Tripp's foot.

Tripp howls in pain, his hold on me loosening just enough for me to throw my head back and connect with his face. He stumbles back and cups his hand over his nose. "Fuck! She broke my nose." His cry is all muffled and nasally. *Obviously, these guys aren't used to girls fighting back.* And I'm not done. I throw my elbow back and connect with his jaw, dropping his ass to the ground.

B would be proud.

Then I run.

"Get that bitch!"

Harper screams for help as she runs back to the mall entrance, dragging Zoe and Willow by the arms. A pair of arms wrap around my thighs from behind, bringing me to the ground. I put my hands out to brace myself, but it only softens the blow as my head slams against the pavement with a smack and a sharp pain shoots through my head, down to my toes.

I'm disoriented as I'm rolled over on my back and dragged before Austin straddles my chest and wraps his hand around my throat.

They say that right before you die your whole life flashes before your eyes. Like photographs on shutter speed. But as I drift in and out of consciousness, it's not my life that flashes before my eyes; it's the faces of the people I love, and the fear of leaving them behind.

And regret for everything I've taken for granted.

I buck my hips and kick my legs, trying to knock Austin off me, but he's too heavy and I'm fading fast. My lungs burn, begging for air as I switch between clawing at the hand around my throat and blocking the blows to my head, face, and ribs.

My limbs grow heavy.

I'm so tired.

Austin's rage-filled face blurs and fades to black.

"No! No! Jayla! Nooo!" *Mom.*

"Motherfucker!"

Oomph!

TRACK 59:
DEEP IN MY SOUL
Zach

LOGAN LEAPS FROM the front of the boat onto the dock to help Dad guide the boat onto the lift while Cole and I gather the trash from inside the boat.

All I want is a shower and my girl. I missed her today. I always miss her when she's not around, but today just felt... off. I can't explain it. But the sooner I get off this boat, the sooner I can get to her.

"Zach!" Logan looks over his shoulder and I stare past him to see Brad running toward us with a panicked expression on his face. Hopping from the boat to the dock, I start toward him. "Jesus, we've been calling you," he rushes out breathless.

I pull out my phone and see a shit-ton of missed calls from Brad, Evan, Justin, my mom. There's more, but I don't bother looking because my heart is racing, my stomach is in knots and everything around me starts to spin.

"What's wrong?" Logan asks from behind me.

"It's Jay and Kali. They were attacked at the mall today," Brad explains, running his hands through his hair. "It's bad."

"What?" I breathe out.

"Where's Zoe?" Logan asks in a panic.

"Your mom has her."

I turn to Bass. "Yo, B!"

Laughing, he turns to me and holds up his index finger. "Hold up, Romeo," he says, pulling his phone from his pocket. Looking down at the screen, he frowns before answering, "Levi?" With the phone to his ear, he leaps from the boat onto the dock. My heart nearly beats out of my chest as Bass's steps falter, every muscle in his body tenses, shoulders rising, and his knuckles are nearly white from the grip he has on his cell phone.

Then his hand falls to his side as he lowers his head. Taking a deep breath, he turns to face us and says in a tone I've never heard from him, "We gotta go. Now!" Bass doesn't wait for a response before he turns and sprints toward his truck. I stare after him in shock.

"Zach, did you hear me?" my dad asks, gripping my shoulders. I blink several times before shifting my gaze to him.

"What?"

"Son, we need to get to the hospital."

My chest heaves as tears pool in my eyes. "Jay?" I choke out.

He nods once. "Yes. She's at the medical center. She has a pulse and she's breathing. That's all I know." I look around and notice that everyone is gone.

"Where is everyone?"

"They left. Come on, we need to go."

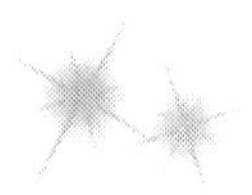

NEWS VANS FROM every station in town are lined up along the curb outside Heritage Bay Medical Center. Police are blocking the entrance and reporters are set up on the sidewalk, speaking into cameras.

"What the hell?"

Dad shrugs. "I assume it's to protect Jay from the media. This is private property," he says, pulling into an empty parking spot. The medical center isn't a hospital, but it's owned by Dr. Mackenzie, and it's on private property. It makes sense why they would bring her here.

A black town car is idling in front of the entrance. The driver pulls a suitcase from the trunk and wheels it over to the walkway under the awning. The back door swings open and Evangeline steps out, wearing sunglasses and pulling a large bag over her shoulder. She thanks the driver, grabs the handle of her suitcase, and heads toward the sliding doors.

"Need some help?" I call out as I jog toward her.

Eva spins around, ready to tell me to fuck off, but she realizes it's me. "Oh, my God, Zach," she cries, dropping her bags before slamming into my chest. "What happened?"

"I don't know," I say, hugging her close.

Dad retrieves Evangeline's bag and suitcase and leads the way into the atrium. Security is guarding all the entrances and elevators. Levi sees us and leans over to speak to a man with a blond buzz cut wearing a dark blue T-shirt, gun holster on his side, and a badge clipped to the front of his jeans.

The man looks at us and then says something to Levi before he makes his way over. "You can let them through," he says to one of the guards. "Hello, I'm Special Agent Avery." He extends his hand and I raise my eyebrows. *Avery?*

"Wow, it's been a long time, Patrick," my dad says as they shake hands.

He nods and offers my dad a tight smile. "It has, Mike, and I'm sorry that we're reuniting under these unfortunate circumstances."

"This is my son Zach. Zach, this is Patrick Avery. Your principal's son."

I hold out my hand. "Good to meet you. What's with all of the security?" I ask.

"It's necessary," he replies.

"Where's JJ?" Evangeline asks.

"She's with the doctors." He points to a set of doors. "There's a private waiting room upstairs on the fourth floor." He reaches into his pocket and pulls out a business card. "Things are a little chaotic at the moment, but if you have any questions you can reach me on my cell."

"Sure." Dad takes his card and shoves it in his pocket.

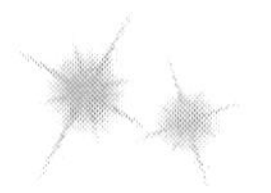

BRAD, CHERRY, JUSTIN, Carter, Olivia, and everyone from Jay's Project Mayhem class are in the waiting room with their eyes glued to the flat-screen television suspended from the ceiling in the far corner. The ticker moves across the bottom of the screen, says, "Austin Boyd, son of Congressman Boyd, arrested in beating of two young women."

"Kalista Rosewood, heiress to the Rosewood Winery, and Jayla King, daughter of the late Marcus King, were rushed to Heritage Bay Medical Center this afternoon after being attacked and beaten. Sources say Austin Boyd, son of Congress Boyd, and Tripp Daniels were arrested and taken into custody and may be looking at charges of assault and battery and attempted murder."

"Hey." Brad stands and pulls me in for a hug before reaching for Eva. The rest of us exchange hugs and handshakes.

"Does anyone know what happened?" I gesture to the television.

"I don't know, dude," Brad says. "I was in the parking lot when Max pulled up with Emerson and Mimi. Emerson was so hysterical she was puking. I heard her say..." He shakes his head as a tear rolls down his cheek and he quickly wipes it away.

"What?" Eva presses.

"She said, 'He was killing my baby and I couldn't save her,'" Justin finishes.

Eva whimpers beside me and exhales a shaky breath. "I need to find Alex and make some calls," she chokes out as she leaves the waiting room.

"Dude, it was awful. I feel so bad for her." Brad hangs his head.

"Zach," Cole calls from the doorway, jerking his head to the side for me to follow.

"I'll be back," I tell them before turning to leave the room.

The hallway is flooded with security as nurses flutter in and out of the rooms. Two large men stand side by side outside a closed door while the others work to secure the rest of the rooms.

"Hey," Cole whispers, leaning against the wall outside another closed door. He gestures to the door. "Zoe and Willow are in there sleeping. My dad and Dylan are in there with your dad and Logan."

"Were the girls hurt?"

He drags his hands down his face and exhales. "Emotionally, yes. A few cuts and scrapes on their legs and knees. Zoe was really upset. Willow is confused. She said a man was hugging JJ and then Harper screamed and hurt her arm. Then she made her fall and hurt her knee." He huffs out a hollow laugh, shaking his head. "She doesn't understand what happened. She's more upset over dropping her doll on the ground and getting it all dirty." He rolls his eyes and I smile. "I've already called Build-A-Bear and talked to the manager. After I explained the situation, she offered to drop off two new dolls on her way home."

"Where's Harper?"

"With the detectives." His expression turns to anger.

"Kali is in there." He points to the door blocked by two bodyguards. "I have no idea what that's all about." He gestures to the bodyguards.

"According to the news, Kali's real name is Kalista Rosewood. Supposedly, she's an heiress or something. One of the guys they arrested was the son of a congressman."

Cole's eyebrows shoot upward. "What the hell? This is some *Lifetime* movie shit."

"What did your dad say?"

"Just that Mac called and said that there was an emergency and to get over to the mall. Dad said when he got there, the paramedics were putting Kali in an ambulance. Em was too hysterical to ride in the ambulance with Jay, so Alex rode with her. My dad drove Em and Mimi here. And Evan and Lexi brought the girls in Jay's car."

"What was Evan doing there?"

"I don't know."

"He said Kali was beat up pretty bad, but Jay got the worst of it." He takes a deep breath. "She has a serious head injury."

I drag my hands down my face. I'm going to be sick.

The door across the hall opens and Mimi walks out arm in arm with my grandma Kate. Cole pushes off the wall and moves to wrap her in a hug as I do the same with Grandma Kate.

"Mimi, are you okay?" Cole asks.

Mimi pulls away and my grandmother hands her a handkerchief. "No, baby, I'm not okay." She dabs the handkerchief at the corner of her eyes. "I'm heartbroken, my daughter is heartbroken, and my granddaughter is just... broken," she cries. "We almost lost her today and if it weren't for those friends of yours, we might have."

I turn to Cole with raised brows and a silent question. *What friends?* Cole shakes his head in response, telling me he has no idea.

"What friends, Mimi?" he asks.

"Those Martinez boys." She sniffs. "They saved her life."

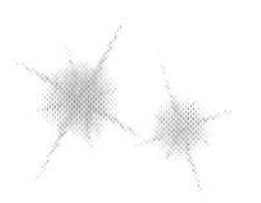

"ZACH." I LOOK over to see my dad standing in the doorway. "Come on, son."

Standing up, I look around the room at the curious eyes of our friends pleading with me not to leave them hanging. With a nod, I silently tell them all that I'll let them know something as soon as I can.

Eva and Alex are standing in the hallway outside Jay's room. Eva throws her arms around me. "She looks really bad, Zach," she cries into my shoulder. "You know I'm not one to sugarcoat and I'm not going to start now. You need to prepare yourself. Whatever you're expecting—it's worse."

"Babe," Alex gently admonishes.

"What, Alex? He needs to be prepared."

Alex sighs, running a hand over his face. "She doesn't look good, Zach, but Mac said most of her injuries are superficial."

I nod and follow my dad into Jay's room. Bass is sitting in a chair beside her bed with his head in his hands, his entire body shaking as his girlfriend Lisa tries to comfort him by running her hand over his back.

It won't work.

His whole world revolves around his princess.

Cole's mom, Grace, my grandma, and Mimi are sitting on one of the sofas lined along the wall. Emerson and Cam are in the bed beside

Jay's. Emerson is asleep against Cam's chest and my mom is perched on the edge of the bed stroking her hair, like the last twenty years never happened. *Women are so weird.*

I make my way over to Jay's bedside and all the air leaves my lungs. I don't recognize the girl laying in this bed, broken. *How could someone do this to her?*

A strong hand clamps down on my shoulder and delicate arms wrap around my waist as my parents stand at my side. "She's gonna be okay, Zach," my mom assures me, tightening her hold.

The door opens and Mac walks in holding a clipboard under his arm, followed by my grandfather, Cole, Alex, and Eva. His gaze immediately falls on Emerson with a concerned expression on his face as he makes his way over to Mimi. "How you holding up, Ella, sweetheart?" he asks, bending down to place a kiss on her forehead.

"I'll be fine, Mac, as long as my family is safe," she replies in a shaky voice.

My parents and I make room for Mac as he perches on the edge of the bed. Leaning over, he brushes the back of his hand across Jay's bruised and swollen cheek.

"Our granddaughter is a fighter, Ella."

"That's because she's a Mackenzie, Mac."

These people are killing me.

Mac looks over at Cam. "She needs to be awake for this."

Cam leans down and whispers in Emerson's ear. A moment later, Emerson stirs and lifts her head. Her gaze immediately shifts to Jay and she bursts into tears.

Mac moves over to her bedside and pulls her into a hug. Emerson sobs into his chest as he shushes her. "She's going to be okay, Emi bear. I know she looks bad, but she's a Mackenzie. She's tough. She's a fighter." He pulls back and pushes Emerson's hair away from her face. "Do you want them to stay in here for this? It's your call."

"They can stay," she says in a shaky voice.

Mac nods. "She has a fractured skull and cheekbone, two bruised ribs on her left side, and one on her right. Her forearm has a small hairline fracture and she has three broken fingers."

I drag my hands down my face. *What the fuck did that piece of shit do to my girl?*

"She has some minor swelling in the brain, but I feel confident there won't be any permanent damage. Of course, we won't know for sure until the swelling goes down and she wakes up. However, I am concerned by the deep bruising on her neck that there could be some long-term damage to her throat, possibly her vocal cords. Again, we won't know for sure until the swelling goes down."

She was choked.

This is all too much. I can't.

Twisting myself out of my mother's hold, I turn and storm out of the room.

I need a minute to pull myself together.

My girlfriend almost died today.

I need to punch something. Or cry.

Rounding the corner of an empty hallway, I clasp my hands behind my neck and pace before pressing my back against the wall and sliding to the floor. My chest heaves until I can no longer fight against the ache buried deep in my soul and the reality that I could've lost her forever. With my arms crossed over the tops of my bent knees, I drop my head and let go.

WHEN I RETURN to Jay's room everyone is gone except for Emerson, Bass, and Lisa. Emerson is hysterically crying in Bass's arms. "He was on top of her... punching her... choking her." She hiccups. "I thought if I could just get to her, she'd be okay. It was like a bad dream. The faster I ran, the farther away from me she got. And then she... she just stopped fighting, B... she just...went limp...I thought she was dead!"

Bass eyes me over the top of Emerson's head. "Stop it, Em," he growls.

Gripping his T-shirt, she cries into his chest. "I'll never be able to erase the image of my baby lying there lifeless and bleeding. How could he do that to my beautiful little girl? Why? She didn't deserve this."

Nobody deserves this.

Especially Jay.

I'm wiping away my own tears when someone sniffs behind me. I look over my shoulder to see Cole walking out the door.

"Zach," Emerson says as she moves forward, wrapping her arms around me. She seems so small and fragile. "I'm so sorry. I didn't mean for you guys to hear that." Leaning back to look up at me, she asks, "Are you okay?"

Shaking my head, my gaze moves to the broken girl lying just a foot away. *My girl.*

"It's okay to be upset, Zach. What happened today was awful."

The door opens again and Special Agent Avery walks in followed by Jay's bodyguards, Troy and Levi.

"I'm gonna step out," Lisa says, heading for the door.

"Patrick, I'm so glad you're here," Emerson says. "How's Harper doing?"

"She's in shock, mostly." He runs a hand through his short hair.

"You have any idea why this happened?" Bass asks.

Agent Avery crosses his arms and leans against the wall with his foot propped up. "Because this is an ongoing investigation, I can only give you a brief summation. Two years ago, Kalista Rosewood—you know her as Kali Brooks—met Austin Boyd at a campaign fundraiser for Austin's father, Congressman Callum Boyd. They dated for nearly a year. Austin was a bit older, but he treated her like a princess. Behind closed doors, Austin was a bad guy. In fact, he was involved in some pretty shady shit, which I'm not at liberty to discuss.

"Long story short, he terrorized Kalista with physical and verbal abuse. He made threats against her family, using his father's political ties as a scare tactic and a way to manipulate her. After Kalista disappeared in the middle of the night, my team was hired by the Rosewood family to find their daughter. During our investigation, it was discovered that Kalista had disappeared to protect her family and most likely to save her life. She sought help from someone no one would suspect—Yolanda, the family's house manager. She knew Kalista was in trouble, so with the help of Yolanda and Mrs. Rosewood—unbeknownst to Mr. Rosewood—they helped her get out.

"It all sounds a little crazy and far-fetched, but Mrs. Rosewood wasn't sure how far Austin's or Congressman Boyd's political ties reached up the legal chain. Kali's been living with Yolanda's niece,

Stephanie Brooks, for the last year or so. I've had my guys keeping an eye on Austin and his buddies for a while now.

"A couple of weeks ago, photos of Kalista and a young man by the name of Lucas Wild showed up on social media. Austin followed the breadcrumbs and hopped on the first flight to Florida. They were already parked outside Kalista's place when Emerson picked her up this morning. Austin and Tripp followed the girls to the mall. The girls parked in the garage outside Nordstrom. Austin, the clever little fucker, parked in the adjacent garage and entered the mall. My guys parked a few spaces down and followed them. Somehow, Austin and Tripp managed to lose my guys and snuck into the Nordstrom garage. They were waiting for them when they came out of the mall."

"Persistent fucker," I mumble.

"So, what now?" Em asks.

"The Rosewoods are on their way. Austin Boyd and Tripp Daniels are in custody facing assault and battery and attempted murder charges. I'm sure Congressman and Mrs. Boyd as well as the Daniels' will be raising hell, but not even the Congressman can make this go away. We have a solid case against both men. Along with the security cameras, we have statements from the Martinez boys, Lexi, Harper, Mrs. Mackenzie, and yours," he says to Emerson. "I have to ask. Who taught her how to fight?"

"Why?" Bass asks and I laugh to myself. Jay's big teddy bear has turned into a grizzly bear.

Agent Avery shrugs. "Because she kicked Tripp Daniels' ass. Broke his nose."

Pride surges to the forefront. *That's my girl.*

"I'm sorry this happened to your family, Emerson. I've been assured she'll make a full recovery." He drops his foot to the floor and pushes off the wall. "Now if you'll excuse me, I need to go check on my daughter." He shakes his head. "That sounds crazy coming out of my mouth." He gives us a small wave on his way out the door and calls over his shoulder. "I'll be around if you need anything."

"Who's his daughter?" I ask.

"Harper," Cole answers from the doorway.

Well, I didn't see that one coming.

NEWS OF THE attack spread like wildfire across the globe and I swear the entire town of Heritage Bay is down in the waiting room. Because of the delicate situation, Emerson won't allow anyone to see Jay except for her closest friends and family. I still haven't seen Harper. Kali's room is on lockdown until her parents arrive, so none of us have seen her either.

Evan and Grayson stopped by and filled me in on what they could. I never thought the day would come that I'd be thanking Grayson Martinez. According to Grayson and Evan, they were at the mall and ran into Lexi and were walking with her, Emerson, and Mimi, to the parking garage. Then all hell broke loose when they saw a frightened Harper through the glass doors, running toward them, screaming for help and dragging Zoe and Willow by the arms. Grayson tackled Austin, beating the shit out of him while Evan went after Tripp. They held them until Troy and Levi showed up. Emerson had given them the day off, but luckily, Troy and Levi followed their instincts and stayed close by, parking in the adjacent garage.

Although Kali was the target, it's still not safe for Jay to be out in public without protection. Especially now that the public knows who *Jaybird* is. Troy and Levi were smart to follow their instincts.

Jay's family and friends have been in and out of her room all day. My parents brought me a change of clothes and a toothbrush, hung around for a few hours, and then headed home. I managed to go over to see Zoe before Logan took her home. Her legs were a little scraped and she was crying for Jay. Broke my heart in two.

Emerson and Bass are meeting with their security team and the detectives. So now it's just Alex, Eva, and me sitting here silently, staring into space, willing Jay to wake up and be her sassy self again.

The muffled sound of voices coming from the hallway has us all turning our heads toward the door just as it swings open and Lucas walks in. His red swollen eyes scan the room before landing on me. "Hey, dude," he says, shoving his hands in the front pockets of his jeans as he makes his way into the room.

"Lucas," Eva cries out as she pushes herself up from the sofa and rushes toward Lucas, throwing her arms around him and sobbing into his shoulder.

The door swings open again Andrew Wild walks in, followed by Tommy Stone and Chaz Vargas from Royal Mayhem and Eva's parents. Eva pulls away from Lucas and flings herself into her father's arms.

If Jay were awake right now, she'd be rolling her eyes at her best friend and calling her a drama queen.

Lucas turns to them. "There's too many of us. We're gonna get kicked out."

"Nah," Andrew says as he makes his way over to Jay's bedside and perches himself on the edge. "Mac Daddy knows we're a package deal." He gently takes her hand in his. "My God, sweet girl. What the hell happened to you?" He leans over and kisses her bruised cheek.

Lucas stands frozen at the foot of the bed and stares down at Jay. He doesn't hold back the tears. "She's gonna be okay, son," Andrew reassures him.

Andrew turns to Alex and asks, "How are you holding up, son?"

Running his hands over his face, Alex shakes his head and averts his gaze.

What the hell was that about?

"What about you?" Andrew asks me.

"I don't know." I rub the back of my neck and look over at Jay. "I'm still trying to wrap my head around all of this."

Liam Mackenzie storms into the room, his gaze immediately lands on Jay and he jerks to a stop. "Fucking hell." He blows out a breath as he makes his way over to Jay's bedside and bends to kiss her on the top of her head. "Where's my mom and my sister?" he chokes out.

"Em and Bass are with the detectives," Alex answers. "Your dad took your mom home to rest. She was pretty shaken up today."

"And they got the guy who did this?"

"Yes," Alex replies.

Without another word, Liam turns and storms out of the room.

The door clicks open again and I'm starting to get irritated by all the in and out, until I see it's Kali being wheeled in by a nurse, followed by an older man and a woman, I assume are her parents. Kali's face is bruised and swollen and her lip is busted.

Lucas sucks in a breath and steps forward. "Oh, we've a got a full house tonight," the nurse says. "I'll give you a few minutes." The nurse squeezes Kali's hand and leaves the room.

"I'm sorry for interrupting, but I needed to see her," Kali says. "These are my parents." She nods to the couple beside her. "These people are Jayla's family."

Andrew stands and walks over and offers his hand to Kali's father, then her mother, before dropping a kiss on the top of Kali's head. "How are you doing, sweetheart?"

"I'm obviously doing better than she is," she cries, gesturing to Jay.

Lucas shakes hands with Kali's parents then moves to crouch down in front of Kali with a pained expression. "Kali," he says quietly. "Jesus. I had no idea you were involved."

Kali shakes her head as a tear runs down her cheek. "This is all my fault," she cries. "She's here because of me."

"No," everyone says at once.

Kali turns to me. "Zach, I'm so sorry. I didn't think he'd ever find me."

What?

"Austin did this?" Lucas asks incredulously. "I'm sorry. I didn't know. I was on a plane and then we came straight here."

Kali nods. "He did." She points to Jay. "And he did that to her."

"Can you tell us what happened?" Andrew asks.

Kali looks up at her parents. Her father nods, giving her the okay, so she takes a deep breath and begins.

"Austin and Tripp were waiting for us in the parking garage. It all happened so fast. Tripp grabbed Jay by the hair and put her in some kind of choke hold. Austin punched me in the face several times and when I fell to the ground, he kicked me. I curled into a ball and played possum." She looks back up at her dad and smiles sadly. "That's what my dad used to say to us when we were kids and pretended to be asleep. I knew Austin was going to hurt her, but there was nothing I could do to stop him." She closes her eyes and lowers her head. "She was scared and crying. They were touching her and saying things."

Andrews lifts his brows. "Like what?"

"Touching her *where*?" Lucas and I snap at the same time.

Taking a deep breath, Kali looks over at me with regret. "Touching her... between her legs and her breasts. Austin grabbed her face and kissed her." There's a collective chorus of whimpers and growls around the room. "Then Harper walked up with Zoe and Willow. Willow called for JJ and Zoe started crying. Austin said something about it being his lucky day and that set Jay off. She told Harper to run and then she went apeshit. She kicked Austin in the balls and did some crazy move that I've only ever seen in movies."

I smile. *That's my girl.*

Lucas and Eva both laugh out loud. "What did she do?" Eva asks.

Kali snorts. "She stomped on Tripp's foot with her heel, threw her head back, and head-butted that fucker in the face. Then she popped him with her elbow, like bam, bam, bam," she demonstrates.

Laughter fills the room and once again, my heart fills with pride.

LUCAS WAITS FOR everyone to leave the room before turning to me. "Listen, dude, I'm glad you and Jay worked things out, but don't ever make her feel guilty about who she is. She's been struggling with it for a long time. She doesn't think I know, but I do. She doesn't want this life. She's doing what she thinks Uncle Marcus wants. The man wouldn't care if she was a server at Denny's because she'd be the best damn server Denny's ever had. She just needs to stop fighting it and do what she feels is right. She's beautiful, smart, and loyal as they come. She's forgiving." He narrows his eyes. "It might take a year or so." He smirks and I shake my head. "Don't get me wrong. She's a stubborn pain in the ass and she's got a fiery temper."

"Yes, I've seen it *many* times," I tell him with a shrug. "I think it's kinda hot," I admit.

Lucas rolls his eyes. "Oh, yeah, until she swings on you." He snorts. "That shit hurts." He pauses to mull something over before he says, "Is it fucked up to say I wish I'd been there to see her head-butt that guy and break his nose?"

I shake my head. "I would have paid to see that."

"Bet you didn't know she could fight like that, huh?"

I shrug. "I can't say I'm surprised. I figured with that sassy mouth of hers, she had to know how to back it up. She took on three girls at school with a fractured hand and a broken finger."

Lucas grins. "Years ago, Uncle Marcus hired these two guys—former MMA fighters—to teach her self-defense." He shakes his head. "That man was all about protecting his girl. Even with all that training, I don't think she expected that she'd ever need it. Not with all the security she's got. I can honestly say for the first time that I'm glad Marcus isn't around. Seeing her like this would break his heart."

I'm sure if he were still around she wouldn't be in the hospital. Or Heritage Bay.

Lucas stands up and stretches his arms over his head. "It's been a long day. I'm gonna go talk to Kali before I head over to King Manor. You staying here?"

"Yeah. I'm not leaving her side until she wakes up."

"Good to know. I'll be back in the morning." He starts for the door but turns to me with an afterthought. "Dad and I are going to hang around for a while. Even after she wakes up, she's got a long recovery ahead of her. I wish I could tell you this is going to be easy, but I know her and I've seen what she's capable of putting herself through."

"I know. I promise I'll do whatever it takes to help her get through this. I love her."

"I know." He smiles. "Uncle Marcus would've liked you."

I smirk. "So, I've been told."

THE NEXT DAY is more of the same with Jay's family and friends coming and going. Jay's nurses, Mia and Holly, have been taking good care of us. Mia even brought me one of those flavored iced coffees from Starbucks. Turns out in this small world, Holly is Olivia's older sister, and she knows Harper.

My phone has been blowing up with phone calls and texts from classmates. Chelsea called after she got the call from Justin. She and

Jay had been talking a lot over the last week and have become friends. Reagan even sent a text telling me that she was sorry to hear about Jayla and that she hopes she makes a full recovery. It's tragic events like this that gives us all a reality check.

Emerson is with my dad and Brick Manning, dealing with the media shitshow and Bass is organizing more security.

My mom has already been here with food and another change of clothes. Then she left to watch Zoe so Logan could come by.

Kali was released this morning. She and her parents are staying at the Heritage Bay Hotel. Kali refuses to go back with her parents until Jay wakes up.

Evan came by with Lexi, who is struggling. I've never seen her so quiet and withdrawn. Evan said she's hardly eaten or slept more than a few hours. And every time she does fall asleep she wakes up in tears.

Harper finally stopped by with Cole. She cried. A lot.

Cole thinks she's still in shock.

Jay told me Harper's sister died in a car crash and that they were very close. I can't imagine going through that all alone. I'm sure this stirs up a lot of bad memories for her.

I'm kicking back in the recliner, flipping through the channels looking for ESPN when the door opens and a woman walks in, dressed in a high-waisted black skirt, cream-colored blouse, and heels with the red soles. Her black hair is cut into a short bob, she has one of those beauty marks over her lip like Cindy Crawford, and her eyes are a bluish purple. *She's stunning.*

"You must be Zach," she says with a sad smile, holding out her hand. "I'm Doctor Jasmine Ramos. Jayla has told me a lot about you." She perches on the edge of the bed and lightly brushes her fingers down the side of Jay's swollen face before she turns to me. "I think it's time we get to know each other and talk about what happens after this sleeping beauty wakes up."

TRACK 60:
FINDING MY WAY BACK HOME
Jayla

"IT'S TIME TO go, Jaybird."

"I don't want to go, Daddy. I want to stay here with you."

"I know you do, baby, but you can't. You have to go home."

"I don't want you to leave me again. Come home with me."

"I never left you, Jaybird. I live in your heart, your memories, your thoughts, and in your dreams. You're a part of me, forever. And until it's time for us to be together again, I'll be here, watching over you, always loving you. I'll never leave you. Never. I promise."

"Daddy, please—"

"You're a King. What do Kings do?"

"Conquer."

"Go home, baby. Show everyone that my little Jaybird is strong, a fighter. And tell the big guy I miss him, too, and to stop blaming himself. This isn't his fault. Tell him I said thank you for taking care of my family. And tell Em that I'm proud of her and that I love her, always."

"I will."

"Tell Zach that I expect him to take care of you and to love you the way you deserve to be loved. Don't settle—"

"—for anything less. I know, Daddy."

"I love you, Jaybird."

"I love you, too, Daddy."

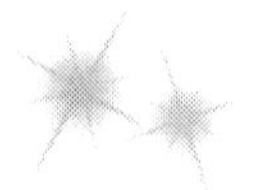

I BUCK MY hips, and kick my legs, trying to knock Austin off me, but he's too heavy and I'm fading fast. My lungs burn, begging for air as I switch between clawing at the hand around my throat and blocking the blows to my head, face, and ribs.

Beep. Beep. Beep. Beep. Beep.

"Jayla—shit! Go get the nurse. She's trying to pull out her breathing tube." *Mom.*

"Princess, hold still." *Bass.*

"Jayla, sweetie, it's okay," a female voice says soothingly. "You have a tube in your throat to help you breathe. You have to calm down if you want me to take it out." I feel her grasp my hand. "Squeeze my hand if you understand."

"Did she squeeze it?" Mom asks.

"Yes. It was weak, but I felt it," the female voice replies.

More commotion and other voices fill the room.

"Daddy, she's waking up," Mom says.

"Jayla, can you open your eyes for me?" *Mac Daddy.*

"Come on, baby girl, open your eyes for Mac Daddy." *Mimi.*

"Is she awake?" *Weenie.*

"Kind of," Mom says. "She was trying to pull out her breathing tube."

Another male voice breaks through the commotion. "Okay. I need everyone to clear the room for a few minutes so I can remove her breathing tube and check her over."

"I'm not leaving," Mom demands. "Eva, text Zach and let him know she's waking up."

Zach.

Zach

JAY'S BEEN IN the hospital for three days now and she still hasn't woken up. Her latest CT scans showed that the medicine used to reduce the swelling in her brain is working, but it's up to her body to decide when she would wake up. The doctors are still concerned about the damage to her throat, mainly her vocal cords, but that determination can't be made until after she wakes up.

Hopefully, it'll be soon.

I miss her.

I wanted to stay with her until she woke up, but, unfortunately, with only three months left before graduation, I can't afford to let my GPA slip and risk losing everything I've worked for. It's like running a marathon and collapsing three feet from the finish line.

As Mr. Baxter babbles on, my mind is on Jay. The images of her battered face and lifeless body lying in that hospital bed are something I'll never forget.

Cell phones aren't permitted in class, but Principal Avery gave me special permission to keep mine on me as long as I keep it on vibrate. Thank God for that because when my phone vibrates in my pocket and I pull it out to see a text from Evangeline, my heart soars. ***She's awake.***

TRACK 61:
CRUMBLING BENEATH THE SURFACE
Jayla

"HERE YOU GO, babe." Zach drops two pills in my palm and hands me a bottle of water. "I'm gonna run home for a little bit, but I'll be back in a few hours. Get some rest." He kisses me on the forehead. "I love you."

"I love you, too," I whisper. "Give Zoe a kiss for me."

"I will. Rest up like the doctor said and, hopefully, soon I can bring Zoe over to see you. Logan says she asks for you every day."

I nod as Zach turns and leaves the room. It's good to finally be home, in my own bed, after spending nearly two weeks in the hospital.

I've had a lot of visitors since I woke up, including the police. I couldn't use my voice yet and, honestly, I was relieved I wouldn't have to talk about it. I remember everything that happened that day. Every touch. Every sound. Every word. Every blow from his fists. The pain. The fear. But there are some things that are a little fuzzy.

Lexi, Harper, Cherry, and Olivia came to the hospital every day after school. Turns out Olivia's older sister, Holly, was one of my nurses and, she was also a friend with Harper's sister. Zach's parents, Logan, Principal Avery, my teachers, my friends, Juliette from the dance studio, Xavier, and the Mannings all came to visit.

Even Chelsea drove down from school. She cried when she saw

me. Thankfully, Zach and Justin knew how to handle her.

Lexi told me that the day Kali and I were attacked, Ashton showed up at the hospital and hasn't left her side, since. Ashton even brought flowers—ranunculus—my favorite. Which, to me, meant she was trying to make amends. She apologized for the way she treated me and asked for a second chance.

A wise man once told me that life is all about chances. Including second chances.

Judging by the by the expressions on everyone's faces, I looked like shit. I decided I didn't want to see my injuries, so I've avoided mirrors at all costs. Zach hung a sheet over the mirror in my bathroom—even though he says I'm being ridiculous—so I can't see my reflection when I brush my teeth or undress for the shower.

Kali came by the hospital and introduced me to her parents. To say I was shocked by her story is an understatement. *Holy shit.* What that poor girl has been through is unbelievable. Her parents want to take her back home, but she wants to stay in Heritage Bay until graduation. Mom finally convinced her parents to let her stay with us, where she'd be safe, especially since Bass hired more security due to the media camped outside the gates and Lucas is here to help take care of her. I know Kali carries some guilt over what happened to me, but the only ones to blame for this are Austin Boyd and Tripp Daniels—or as Zach refers to them, "the pieces of shit."

Dr. Ramos has been staying with me for the past week. She was there when I woke up at the hospital but left before I was released. When the nightmares started, my mom asked her to come back.

Zach is practically living with me. He refuses to let me out of his sight and I'm okay with that because I'm afraid to be alone. Mom didn't even bat an eyelash when he walked in with his bags packed and demanded he was staying. She even helped make room in my closet for his things.

Cam left for baseball camp a week ago and things still unresolved between him and my mom. Zach told me Uncle Liam found out about my mom and Cam and he was pissed. Liam swung on Cam. Cam fought back and security had to break them apart.

Bass is back staying in his apartment. And my amazing Grace, poor thing, has been staying in one of the guest rooms to be closer to me.

Harper has been staying with her dad at Principal Avery's house. I still can't wrap my head around that.

Slipping out of bed, I make my way out to my balcony. There's still a slight chill in the air in the early morning. I spot a familiar figure perched on the dock. Grabbing a blanket, I slowly make my way down the steps.

"Can't sleep?" I croak. My throat is still healing. I sound like shit.

Bass smiles at me over his shoulder and watches as I approach. He reaches out and grips my arm to steady me, as I ease myself down to sit beside him and pull the blanket tighter around me.

"You're supposed to be resting, Princess," he says. "I take it Romeo left."

"Yeah." I sigh. "I can't sleep, B. I'm afraid to fall asleep."

He wraps his arm around my shoulders and tucks me in to his side. "Tell me why."

I shrug. "I can still feel him. His lips, his tongue, his hands, and his fists." I shudder. Bass tries to cover the growl by clearing his throat. "Every time I close my eyes, I see his face, and I want to throw up. Sometimes when Zach kisses me or hugs me, I have flashbacks. I try to shut it off because I don't want to hurt Zach. He's having a hard time as it is."

He rubs his hand over his bald head. "Is that what your nightmares are about?"

I nod and he gives me a reassuring squeeze, but not too hard since my ribs are still healing. "I'm sorry this happened to you, Princess. I'll never be able to forgive myself for not being there."

"Oh, my God, B, stop that. It's about as much your fault as it is mine."

Bass stays silent.

"There's something I need to tell you."

"Hmm?"

"I talked to my dad." I smile and Bass lifts a curious brow. "He told me to tell you to stop blaming yourself and to tell you thank you for taking care of his family."

Bass just nods and lowers his head.

Zach

WALKING INTO MY house, I head straight upstairs to my room and fall face first into my bed. It's Saturday and I just need a few hours to myself. Jay's nightmares are becoming more frequent, which keeps me up half the night, taking a toll on my sanity. This past week I've had a hard time focusing and have been struggling to stay awake in class.

"Zach," my mom whispers as she walks into my room.

"Hmm?"

She sits down on the edge of my bed and runs her fingers through my hair. "What are you doing home? You okay?"

I roll to my back and look over at her. "Jay's been having nightmares." My mom frowns. "She's not doing well, Mom. She flinches every time I touch her or kiss her and I know it's because she's thinking of that piece of shit. She's wounded physically, mentally, *and* emotionally. Her doctor warned me this might happen. I just want to help her feel safe again."

"Zach, I don't think Jayla expects you to do anything except be there for her. I think just having you by her side is all she needs. Don't put that kind of pressure on yourself. Just be there for her. If it gets to be too much, then come home. I'm sure she'll understand."

"I'm not leaving her. I just need a couple of hours to myself. I'm exhausted."

She pats my back and stands. "Get some rest. I'll wake you in a couple of hours."

"Thanks, Mom."

She smiles, knowingly. "Of course." She bends over and kisses my forehead like she used to when I was little. "Get some sleep," she says as she turns and walks out of my room, shutting the door behind her.

TRACK 62:
BACK WITH A VENGEANCE
Jayla

OVER A MONTH has passed since the parking garage incident. I'm back at school and things are progressing. My injuries are mostly healed and, luckily, there was no permanent damage to my vocal cords.

Things are going well with the Project Mayhem students. Alex and I are working out some details so we can take them on tour as our opening act. We want the world to see the results of the Mayhem Foundation's first project. It's the best way to get the word out and bring in more donations to the charity. We're hoping to branch out into another school the year after next.

Spring break is upon us and tonight we're celebrating Zach's nineteenth birthday at Oceanside Grill. We reserved a private room for just our families and close friends, with security standing right outside the doors.

When the server brings out the cake, Zach tells me he wants me to sing "Happy Birthday" first.

When I was attacked by that psycho, I didn't think I'd survive. But I did. However, the probability of losing a part of who I was made me realize I had taken my talent and opportunities for granted. Just because I didn't want to be a rock star didn't mean I shouldn't appreciate the gift I'd been given. It's true what they say, "You don't know what you've got till it's gone." The whole table applauds and I catch Mom wiping her eyes.

After cake, I excuse myself to the bathroom and Zach insists he go with me. As we step back into the room, I catch the tail end of a hushed argument between Mom, Alex, and Evangeline.

"This is Zach's night. We can talk to her about it tomorrow," my mom argues.

"The longer you put this off, the more pissed off she's going to be," Eva says.

"He was my father, too, and barely in my life before he was gone," Alex barks out. I gasp but no one hears. Zach puts his hand on my back. "She's all I have left and I almost lost her, too. You're not protecting her—you're lying to her. You're all lying to her."

I charge further into the room. "You're my brother?" I choke out.

All three of their heads jerk in my direction, clearly shocked they've been caught. Evangeline gasps and covers her mouth. Her eyes instantly well up with tears. Alex nods slowly, gauging my reaction.

"Why would you keep that from me?"

I look up at Zach and he shakes his head. He didn't know.

My heart pounds against my chest as I scan the faces around the room. Some are filled with shock and others are filled with guilt.

"Jayla, listen to me," Mom starts.

I shake my head. "What the hell? You all knew he was my brother?"

My gaze moves back to Alex, taking in his features. I mean... yeah, I always thought he could pass as a young Marcus King, with his blue-green eyes, dark hair, physique, and even the way he performs on stage. It's been right in front me this whole time. He's Marcus Alexander King twenty years younger. *How did I not see it?*

"What's your full name, Alex?" I ask.

"Marcus Alexander Reyes-King," he answers in an apologetic tone.

A mixture of anger and disappointment grips my heart. My eyes fill with tears.

I look up at Zach. "I'm sorry, Z. I have to get out of here," I whisper.

Zach tugs me closer to his chest. “Then let’s go.” He takes my hand and we head for the doors.

“Where are you going?” Mom asks.

“Princess,” Bass calls.

I pause and turn around. “Excuse me if I don’t want to spend another minute with a bunch of liars. I’m not a baby, you know, I don’t know why you keep treating me like one. I’ve been through a lot in the last year. My own brother has been right in front of me almost every single day and none of you thought it was important enough to me to tell me the truth. I can’t be near any of you right now.” I turn on my heels and storm out of the room with my bodyguards right behind me.

Once outside, I turn to Zach in a huff. “I’m sorry I ruined your birthday dinner, Z. I promise to make it up to you. Would you mind going back to get my purse? I’ll wait here.”

“God forbid after that dramatic exit you should have to go back for your purse.” He chuckles and dodges my hand as he goes back inside.

TRACK 63:
DONE WITH THE LIES
Jayla

"IT'S YOUR MOM," Zach says, holding out his phone.

Taking his phone, I bring it to my ear. "Hi, Mom."

"Jayla," she breathes out, sounding relieved. "You're in St. Thomas?"

Call me impulsive, but I was pissed at my mom and the rest of my family. So, Zach and I drove straight to my house from the restaurant and grabbed our bags, which were already packed because we were supposed to leave the day after tomorrow. Luckily, George, my trusty pilot was available at the last minute. I feel bad for leaving our friends behind, but I need a few days alone with my guy. Zach called them from the airport to apologize and that I'll be sending the plane to get them.

"Yes. I just need some time alone, okay? And don't worry, Troy and Levi are close by."

"I'll respect that. We shouldn't have kept that from you. It was wrong. Don't blame Alex, though. It was my choice to wait. I thought with everything that's happened, it was too much and it would be better to wait until after you graduated. Unfortunately, someone got hold of the information and leaked it to the media before I got the chance to tell you. I hope you don't hate me. I—"

“Would you stop saying that? I told you before that I could never hate you. I have a lot of questions, but I need to wrap my head around this first.”

“I feel like I’m failing at this single parent stuff,” she cries.

“Mom, stop. That’s not true. You have been the best mom anyone could ask for. I love you and your craziness. Mean it.”

“Ha-ha. How’s Zach? Is he ready to bail yet?”

“Pssh. Please. Have you met Elizabeth Easton?” I laugh and Zach looks over at me with raised brows.

“Okay. I’m off to LA to meet with Chandler and our attorneys to see if we can get this story retracted. I won’t let the media ruin the reputation Marcus worked so hard to build. He and I loved each other and he didn’t cheat on me. And I won’t let them make Sophia out to be a home-wrecker. She’s a good woman.”

I sigh in relief.

“Two words, Mom. Miles. Townsend.”

“Hmm. I hadn’t thought of that.”

“Dad trusted Miles. He’s on our side. Alex’s article isn’t supposed to come out until next month. There’s still time. Let Miles help.”

“I’ll do that. Good thinking, Jayla. We’ll be going over some last-minute details for the tour, so please answer your phone when I call.”

“I will. I love you very much, Mom. Even though you baby me too much and piss me off, I know you only do it because you love me and want to protect me.”

“You’ll understand one day. I love you, baby. I’ll call you when I get to LA. And promise me that you’ll give Alex a chance.”

“I promise.”

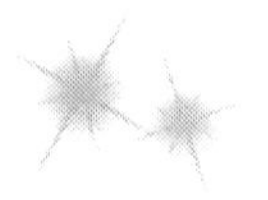

I WAKE TO the sound of my phone ringing, Dude LAW flashing on my screen. “Lucas, you’re lucky I love you,” I say by way of greeting.

“Did I wake you?”

“Yeah, but it’s fine. Is everything okay?”

“My dad just told me about Alex. I was calling to see how you’re doing."

"You didn't know?"

"Hell, no! There's no way I would go along with keeping a secret like that from you."

"Weenie did."

"Yeah, well, I can't imagine it was easy for her. She probably only did it for Alex. Where are you?"

"St. Thomas. We're on spring break."

"I know. You guys want some company? I really want to see you."

"You know I never turn down a visit from the *LAW*," I drawl, teasing.

He chuckles. "Funny. Kali and I will be there probably the day after tomorrow. Is that cool?"

"Sounds perfect. The whole gang should be here by then."

"Hold on a sec," he says and there's a muffled voice before it becomes louder once more. "You're on speaker, Jay. Kali wants to say hi."

"Jayla," Kali says. "I swear the hits just keep on coming. Are you okay?"

"Yeah. I've come to realize that this is my life and anything is possible."

Zach chuckles beside me.

"It'll all work itself out. Go back to sleep. I love you. We'll see you in a couple of days," Lucas says.

"Love you, Jayla," Kali says.

"I love you, too. Bye."

"JJ!" WEENIE YELLS as she comes bursting through the front door and slams into me.

Oomph! "I'm so sorry," she cries.

"Weenie, you're choking me," I say and Zach guffaws beside me.

"Hey, Jay," Alex says as he steps through the door.

Evangeline releases me from her bear hug and I walk into Alex's open arms. He hugs me as if his life depends on it. "How much do you hate me?"

I pull back and look up at him. "Why does everyone keep asking me that?"

He shrugs.

"Are you mad at me?" Evangeline asks.

"I am not mad at you. I just.... I don't understand why I'm the only one who didn't know."

"It wasn't my call," Alex claims.

"I know."

"Okay, you two. Zach and I are gonna leave you to it," Evangeline announces before she presses a kiss to Alex's lips and heads for the door. "Meet us down at the beach when you're done."

"Bye, babe. I love you," Zach says, leaning over to kiss me before he follows Evangeline out the door.

Alex and I each take a seat at the kitchen table, just staring at each other for a minute.

Alex tilts his head a little. "You can ask me anything, Jay."

"I don't even know where to start," I admit.

"Then I'll start." He leans forward with his forearms resting on the table. "I always knew my dad wasn't my real dad. My mom never kept it a secret. All I had to do was ask. But I had a dad who loved me. He coached my little league games, volunteered for school field trips, gave me advice on girls, bought me my first box of condoms—"

"Eww." I roll my eyes. "TMI, Alex."

Alex laughs. "He taught me how to drive, helped me pick out my first car and always made sure I had gas money. Every so often I'd think about my real father, wondering if he would've done those kinds things for me if he were around. Then I'd feel guilty, like I was betraying my dad. It wasn't until I was in college, when my parents sat me down and told me who my real father was. It's not every day you find out your real father is a famous rock star and the lead singer of one of your favorite rock bands. I laughed. I thought she was kidding. She went on to tell me that she and Marcus met at a diner, after a night out drinking, where she and her friends had stopped for "drunk food". It wasn't love at first sight or anything. She was a twenty-two-year-old girl with a crush and a once in lifetime opportunity to spend the night with a rock star.

"I asked Marcus if he was married when he and my mom met, because rock star or not, I would've lost all respect for him if he were. He swore to me that he hadn't met Emerson until later."

"I still don't understand why he didn't tell me," I add. "How did you even get in touch with him?"

"My dad had a lawyer friend who referred us to Mike Easton."

"Mike Easton? Zach's dad?"

"Yeah." He laughs softly. "Long story short, after my mom explained the situation, Mike excused himself from the room and returned fifteen minutes later to tell us that Marcus agreed to meet me.

"We spent the next year getting to know each other before he invited me to California to meet you. He was very protective of you, Jay. Even from me. But before I got to California to meet you, he found out he was sick. I don't know why he didn't want to tell you, but I suspect his illness was more than you could handle without the added drama of an illegitimate son from a one-night stand."

"Gross. Stop saying, 'one-night-stand'. No one wants to picture their parents having sex, let alone with someone who isn't the other parent."

"I have something for you," he says, pushing back from the table and making his way over to his bag, which is still sitting by the front door.

A few moments later, he sits back down at the table and passes me an envelope with the familiar handwriting addressed to Jaybird.

"What's this?" I ask with a shaky voice.

"It's from Marcus."

The man had a letter for everything.

"Have you read it?"

Alex frowns. "No. I would never do that."

"I didn't mean anything by it, Alex."

He nods stiffly as I open the envelope and pull out the letter.

Jaybird,

If you're reading this letter, then you know Alex is my son and your brother. I can only imagine what you

must be feeling and all the questions running through your mind.

First, you need to know that your mom is the love of my life and when you were born, it was the best gift she could've given me.

Alex's mother, Sophia, and I spent time together before Em and I ever met. We were at the end of our tour in Florida when I met Sophia. I missed my flight back to LA, but I was lucky to get a last-minute flight to LA from Tampa. That was the day I met Em, the love of my life, my soul mate and the woman who would become my wife. It was fate.

Your mother and I wanted to tell you about Alex. And we'd planned to. But before we had the chance, I got sick. It was just too much to dump on my baby girl all at once. I'm sorry if you're hurt, but I was only trying to protect you. Your mother wanted to protect everyone, including Alex and his family. They're good people and at the end of the day, he's still my son. And he's still your brother. He's still Alex.

Give him a chance.

Love you always,

Daddy

"Maybe I should be asking if you hate me?" I admit, setting the note on the table between us before swiping the tears from my cheeks with the backs of my hands.

Alex frowns. "Why would I hate you?"

"Because I had him as my dad for seventeen and a half years and you only got a few years with him before he died. I feel guilty for that."

"Don't feel guilty. I told you, I have a dad. He might not have been the man who gave me life, but he raised me and I love him. And besides, I had something that you didn't and that makes me feel a little guilty."

"What's that?" I ask, sniffling.

"Normal."

TRACK 64:
PIECE OF ME (PIANO VERSION)
Jayla

Jaybird,

Em tells me prom is the most important dance of the school year. I can only offer you the same advice as I did for your Homecoming dance. Have fun and make lots of memories. You have my vote for prom queen.

Love you always,

Daddy

P.S. Tell your date to keep his hands to himself.

I survived a vicious attack and the possibility that I'd never sing again and I'd almost accepted that as my fate, but every day I was reminded by the people who love me, that defeat wasn't an option. I'm going to get up on that stage tonight and show my classmates that I'm not only *Jaybird*, I'm a King.

We don't cower.

We *conquer*.

Zach

PROM NIGHT IS upon us and I can't believe it's already been a year since I was here with Reagan. I shudder at the thought. This year it will be so much better because I'm here with my girl.

Cherry approaches with caution, making sure Jay sees her before she reaches for her hand. Although Jay is doing much better and the nightmares are gone, she's skittish and startles easily. "You ready, Jay?"

"Are you sure you want to do this?" I ask.

"Yes, I'll be fine."

"I'll be right in front so you can see me. If you need me, just say the word and I'll get you out of here. Okay?"

She nods. "I'm fine, Z. Relax."

I pull her tight to my side and nuzzle her neck. "I love you, my beautiful, strong, stubborn girl." I pull back and she tilts her head and pushes out her lips. I press a kiss to her lips and smack her on the butt. "Go on before I change my mind, throw you over my shoulder, and take you back home."

Yes, home. I'm still living with her. I'm never leaving.

She rolls her eyes and snorts a laugh. "Horndog."

I hold my breath, watching as Cherry leads Jay backstage. "Hey," Cole says beside me, following my gaze. He shakes his head. "She's amazing."

"She's stubborn." I laugh. "And she doesn't like to lose." I remember her words from our first date.

"Where's Harper?" I look around.

"She's backstage with the other girls. Em's back there, too. They wanted to surprise Jay and have some girl time with her before she gets on stage."

"Are you guys back together?"

Cole shrugs. "It's complicated, but I love her."

"Yo!" Brad says as Evan grips my shoulder and smiles. "Is our girl gonna sing tonight?"

I nod, suddenly feeling an overwhelming wave of emotions.

Cole hooks his arm around my neck and leans in close to my ear. "You all right?" I nod. "It's okay if you're not. It's only been a few months. You might not have taken the physical blows, but that doesn't mean you weren't hurt, too. Everyone who cares about her has been affected in one way or another. Thank you for sticking by her and going through the motions. I know it hasn't been easy, but you have no idea how much my family appreciates it."

"You don't need to thank me. I love her. I'm never leaving her."

Cole smirks. "You signed?"

I nod. "You?"

Cole grins and tugs me closer. We're gonna be teammates again.

Sometimes you have to make sacrifices for the people you love. Football isn't forever but Jay is. I still haven't told her yet. I'm waiting to until after graduation to tell her the news.

The Gulf Coast University football program is fairly new compared to other universities. The football team isn't bad, but with Cole and me on the team, they'll be a whole lot better.

Principal Avery takes the stage with a few short announcements. He skips over the rules, telling us to just enjoy ourselves—but not too much, of course. The man hasn't stopped smiling since his son came home and they discovered Harper was their granddaughter. She'd been under his nose the whole time, just like Alex had been with Jay.

Things between Alex and Jay have been good. They laugh a lot and, now that the secret is out, it's obvious they're siblings.

The girls come rushing out and find us in front of the stage. "I'm so nervous," Lexi squeals.

"Why are you nervous? You singing tonight?" Evan asks sarcastically.

"Shut up, Evan. I'm nervous for Jay."

"She sang at Zach's birthday," he reminds her.

"She sang 'Happy Birthday.' This is different. You know everyone is curious to see if she's still got it."

"Is she nervous?" I ask.

"Doesn't seem that way," Harper answers and Lexi nods in agreement.

Ashton walks up hand in hand with her boyfriend. "Is Jay gonna sing tonight?" she asks.

A lot changed the day Kali and Jay were attacked. People, too. Including Ashton. It's like she had a personality transplant. I'm not used to her being so... tolerable.

"Yep. She's up first," Lexi tells her.

"Zach!" I look over my shoulder to see Kali squeezing through the crowd, making her way over to us while dragging Lucas behind her. I chuckle. He's gotta be hating life right now, but like I said, sometimes we make sacrifices for the ones we love.

I notice the curious looks he's getting, knowing it's only a matter of minutes before he gets mobbed by a bunch of high school girls.

He must be aware of it, too, because he says to Kali, "I'm gonna go hang backstage with Eva." He gives her a kiss, glancing at me over her shoulder and rolling his eyes. "I can't believe I'm actually at prom."

"Hey." She slaps his arm playfully. "You never got the high school experience either. At least now you can say you went to prom."

Lucas groans. "Let's just see how it goes for now. I'll see you in a few," he says before heading over to where Eva is standing with Alex.

"Do we know what she's singing tonight?" Kali asks.

"The one she wrote for Zach, 'Piece of Me.'"

I smile at that. *God, I love her so much.*

'Piece of Me' hit number one within the first week of its release and remained at number one for twelve weeks straight.

The lights fade out and the sound of a piano drifts from behind the curtain. The curtain pulls back and there's my girl sitting at the piano in her beautiful champagne-colored gown. Cherry and Olivia are singing backup.

'Piece of Me' blends into another song and someone elbows me. "I know this song," Lexi squeals. The girl is like a musical encyclopedia. "It's called 'Fight Song.'" When Jay sings about scars, she runs her finger across the scar in her hairline. When she sings about pain, she presses her hand over her heart. As the song comes to an end, my girl stands up, flexes, and points to the "Conquer" tattoo on her bicep, and the whole room erupts in cheers.

Eric walks out and takes over the piano and the music switches to "The Fighter" by Gym Class Heroes, and ends with "So What" by Pink. The whole place goes nuts and sings along. People love and care about her. It fills my chest with pride. When the song ends, Jay throws her arms around Eric and he swings her around and kisses her on top of her head. They turn, facing the crowd and when she smiles, I see her eyes are lighting up. When her eyes find me, she blows me a kiss and mouths, "I love you."

My girl is definitely back.

TRACK 65:
I LIVED
Jayla

I DID IT.

I graduated high school.

"I never thought I'd see this day," Mom says, her eyes filled with tears.

I know what she means, but I can't help it. She brings it on herself. "You didn't think I'd graduate from high school?"

She scoffs, wiping away her tears. "No. I never thought I'd get to see you walk across the stage and accept your diploma with the rest of your class. This is a big moment for me, too." She's been very emotional lately. She says it's hormones. I say it's just her being crazy.

Since our group has become so enmeshed, our graduation parties have been combined and are taking place at the Heritage Bay Beach Club. The security is so tight, even the President would approve.

Zach wraps his arms around me from behind. "Babe, I have a graduation gift for you," he growls in my ear.

"It's gonna have to wait till after the party, horndog." I laugh.

"I'm standing right here," Mom says.

"Oh." I snort at the same time Zach says, "It's not that. Come with me."

Zach leads the way through the French doors and out to the

balcony overlooking the bay. He reaches into the inside pocket of his jacket, pulls out a folded piece of paper, and passes it to me.

"What's this?"

"Read it."

Slowly, I unfold the paper and skim over the words "Letter of Intent" and at the bottom of the page is Zach's signature. "You committed to Gulf Coast University?"

He nods.

I was afraid Zach would choose Gulf Coast University because of the attack, but the letter is dated a couple of weeks before the attack happened.

"You did this for me?"

"I did this for us. We're a team. You said that once." He leans over and presses a kiss to my forehead. "Football is my life, but you're my everything, Jay."

His words are familiar.

I'd said something similar about my dad at his funeral.

Zach *was* there.

My eyes well up with tears. "You were at the funeral?"

He nods. "I was."

I press my hand to my chest. "I don't know what to say, Z."

"Say yes." He drops to one knee, pulls a ring from his pocket, and I burst into tears. "Jayla Mackenzie King, I love you. Every good decision I've made so far is because of you. You are the strongest, most beautiful person I've ever known, inside and out. No one has ever made me smile, laugh, or even cry as much as you have. You make me feel things that I only ever want to feel with you. I'll never forget the day I met you in your sparkly shoes and your princess shirt. When you kicked Logan in the shin and called him a punk, I thought you were the coolest girl I'd ever met. I think I loved you then. Our first kiss confirmed my feelings for you were real. And then that summer in St. Thomas, I knew without a doubt that you were it for me. You're my girl, Jay." Zach gets to his feet and wraps his arms around my waist. "Marry me?"

Tears of happiness are sliding down my cheeks and a smile is permanently etched on my face. "Yes, I'll marry you, Z. I love you."

"I love you, too, Jay." He presses a gentle kiss to my lips and slides the ring onto my finger.

Just after the most beautiful proposal, the collective sound of everyone's cell phones all chirping at once has Zach and me looking through the glass doors. Then Zach's phone chirps.

He pulls his phone from his pocket and swipes his finger across the screen. I watch as his eyes bulge before he passes his phone to me.

JAYBIRD IS OFF THE MARKET.

Jayla King, 18, whom we've all come to know as Jaybird, is off the market. A source tells us that the rising star married her longtime boyfriend, Zach Easton, 19, last month while vacationing in St. Thomas. The couple exchanged their "I dos" in a private ceremony on the secluded beach near King's villa. The source claims the two seemed happy and very much in love.

"Jaylaaaaa!" My mom's voice rings out from inside. *Shit.*

Zach smirks. "Let me rephrase the question. Will you marry me... again?"

BONUS TRACK 01:
SOUL MATES
Jayla

TO MY BEAUTIFUL JAYBIRD,

This is the hardest letter to write because it's my last. Today is your wedding day and as you stand before the mirror in your white gown (it better be white), know that I'm standing behind you with the biggest smile on my face. (Okay, I'm probably scowling a little, but on the inside, I'm smiling.)

After today, you're not just my little girl anymore. You're someone's wife. Someone's better half. And one day, you'll become someone's mother. These are the thoughts that are weighing heavily on my heart because your husband and future children are so lucky to have you.

I thank God every day for giving you to me and letting me be your dad to nurture and love. I do love you, my little Jaybird, with all of my heart and soul. I loved you before you were born.

Today as you walk down the aisle toward the lucky man whom you've decided is worthy of your

hand, I'll be walking beside you. Still scowling, but I'll be proud. No matter what, I'm always proud of you.

I love you always and forever, my beautiful sweet girl.

Daddy

Mom gave me this letter a week before my wedding and I'm thankful she did because it was like having to say goodbye all over again. It took me nearly the entire week to recover.

Zach

To the man who my daughter deems worthy enough to marry. And if you're still in one piece, it means that Bass approves.

If Zach is reading this letter, then this goes to show how well I know my little girl and that she followed her heart.

I'm sorry we never got to meet in person, but I've seen you, you know? I had to see the boy who had my daughter writing love songs since she was six years old. I went to one of your football games once, and I'll admit you're a talented young man with a promising future.

Today you need to be thanking God for giving you this unique and precious gift. I've done my job, as her father, to prepare her for life's ups and downs. Now it's your job, as her husband, to stand beside her and face those ups and downs as a couple. A team. A united front.

Promise to love her. Respect her. And to worship her every day. Make every single day count. Because every single day—every single

second of the day—is precious time.

Take care of our girl, Zach.

Marcus King

BONUS TRACK 02:
WHO SAYS YOU CAN'T HAVE IT ALL
Jayla

Five Years Later…

WHEN MY DAD passed, he placed the world at my feet and shoes too big to fill. I'd struggled with who I was and who I wanted to become. I was born with a talent; a gift. Something aspiring musicians paid money for had come naturally to me. I put so much pressure on myself to do what I thought was expected of me. When really, the choice had always been mine.

"Mommy," my babies, Alex, Bella, and Mackenzie, call from the other side of the bathroom door. Alex and Bella are three and a half and my little mini-mes. Mackenzie Grace is eighteen months, a spitting image of Zach and a daddy's girl. She reminds me so much of Zoe.

"Babe," Zach calls out as the door knob wiggles. "Why is the door locked?"

"Give me a minute, Z," I reply, biting down on my lower lip as the little pink lines appear in the window of the little plastic stick. *Jesus, it hasn't even been a whole three minutes.*

"You okay?" he asks.

"I'm fine," I lie.

I'm pregnant.

Again.

After the news spread that Zach and I eloped, my mom, Liz, Mimi, and Grandma Kate put together a real wedding for Zach and me. My only request was that they use my favorite flowers and for the wedding to take place before I left for the tour. Zach's only request was that he got to pick our song.

Yeah, that shocked me, too.

And they pulled it off. Zach and I were married on Saturday, June twenty-fourth at the Heritage Bay Beach and Country Club.

Zach chose "My Girl" as our wedding song.

On July Fourth, Royal Mayhem kicked off their Project Mayhem tour at the Gulf Coast University football stadium. Which was also where Zach had accepted a football scholarship. He made the formal announcement during our graduation party shortly after the news of our marriage had been blasted all over social media. Cole also announced he'd accepted a scholarship.

The Project Mayhem class joined the tour as the opening act for Royal Mayhem. The tour only lasted three months, but it was tough being newly married and away from my husband.

Shortly after Zach and I celebrated our one-year anniversary, I found out I was pregnant and, eight months later, I gave birth to Alexander Michael and Annabella Elizabeth.

Our families were thrilled. Except my mom, of course. She needed to warm up to the idea that her baby was having a baby. Or in my case babies.

I knew the odds were stacked against Zach and me from the beginning, married so young. He was in college and busy with football, but we fought hard to make it work. That's what we do. We make it work.

Mike and Liz were a good example. They had been together since they were in middle school. Sure, they've encountered a few bumps and scrapes along the way, but their love for each other was what helped them push through the rough times. If I learned anything from them, it's that relationships aren't always perfect. People make mistakes and it takes more than love to make a marriage work. Patience, understanding, compromise, sacrifice, and, in Mike and

Liz's case, forgiveness.

But what worked for Zach and me was balance.

Patience was something I didn't have a lot of, but once I found a balance between mine and Zach's chaotic lives, patience was easier to come by.

As far as my career, music is in my blood and will always be an important part of my life. I wouldn't trade a second of my childhood for anything. But life on the road isn't for me.

I still write music because it's what I love. I've taken over the Mayhem Foundation and I volunteer a couple of days a week in the Project Mayhem class at Heritage Bay Academy.

In the last five years, with help from my mom, Liz, Mimi, and Grandma Kate—because of their involvement with several charities and experience in organizing fundraisers—along with family, friends, and Zach's football connections, the Mayhem Foundation has raised enough money to extend the program and fund four more schools.

My involvement with the foundation and the ability to see the projects through from the beginning keeps me connected to my dad. It still breaks my heart that he isn't here to see how far we've taken his dream. But I know in my heart and down to my core that my dad is proud. *I'll always be proud of you, Jaybird.*

Zach graduated from Gulf Coast University and was snatched up by the Heritage Bay Storm.

Alex moved to LA and works alongside his father-in-law, Chandler, at King Records. Alex and I are equal partners of King Records, so all major business decisions still have to be discussed with me, but for the most part I leave it to Alex.

Evangeline retired, her words, from modeling to stay home with their two-year-old son, Alex, and is expecting their second child, a girl, any day. I'm not allowed to call her Weenie anymore. Zach put his foot down after the twins started calling her Aunt Weenie.

"Babe," Zach calls again, knocking harder on the door. "We're gonna be late."

Opening the door, I come face to face with my gorgeous husband and his mini-me, Mackenzie, perched on his hip. "Hi, Z."

He circles my waist with his free hand and he tugs me to his chest. "What are you up to in here? Why was the door locked?"

"Um..."

"Here, Daddy," a little voice says below me. I look down to see Bella holding up the pregnancy test to Zach. *The little stinker ratted me out.*

Zach takes the stick from Bella, looks at the results, then a smile curls up one side of his mouth. "Really?"

I nod. "Are you freaking out?"

He shakes his head but says, "A little." Then he presses his lips gently against mine. "Are you okay?"

I nod. "Are you?"

He nods and drops his forehead to mine. "I love you so much, Jay."

I slide my hand over the curve of his perfect ass and squeeze. "I love you, too, Z."

"Should we tell them?" he asks.

"Not yet. Remember when we brought Mackenzie home from the hospital? Bella cried for three days."

Zach rolls his eyes. "How did we end up with such a drama queen?"

"Your mother," we both say at the same time and share a laugh.

Do I have any regrets? Not a single one.

If I knew that all of the heartache, grief, and pain I'd suffered throughout the years, would lead me to my beautiful family, I'd suffer through it all over again. This might not be the normal I'd wished for; but it's so much more.

This is meant to be.

My destiny.

My karma.

My fate.

My happily ever after.

The End

JAYBIRD PLAYLIST

Heaven ~ Live
I Love You ~ Climax Blues Band
My Sweet Summer ~ Dirty Heads
Breath ~ Breaking Benjamin
Sympathetic ~ Seether
Life is Beautiful ~ Sixx A.M.
Hate To See Your Heart Break ~ Paramore
Gone Away ~ The Offspring
Broken ~ Seether (Feat. Amy Lee)
Rise Above This ~ Seether
If You Only Knew ~ Shinedown
It's Time ~ Imagine Dragons
Welcome To Your Life ~ Group Love
How You Get The Girl ~ Taylor Swift (Not available on Spotify)
The Chainsmokers ~ Roses
Somebody That I Used To Know ~ Goyte (Feat. Kimbra)
Hello ~ Adele
Shut up and Dance ~ Walk The Moon
Here ~ Alessia Cara
Send My Love (To Your New Lover) ~ Adele
Can't Stop The Feeling ~ Justin Timberlake
Stitches ~ Shawn Mendes

All About That Bass ~ Meghan Trainor
Wherever You Will Go ~ The Calling
Fine Again ~ Seether
Cut The Cord ~ Shinedown
We Will Rock You ~ Queen
We Are The Champions ~ Queen
Ain't It Fun ~ Paramore
Burning Bridges ~ One Republic
My House ~ Flo Rida
Kiss ~ Prince
Nobody Knows ~ Pink
Faithfully ~ Journey
I Hate That I Love You ~ Rihanna (Feat. Ne-Yo)
Give It To Me ~ The Deekompressors
Ho Hey ~ Tyler Ward Cover (Feat. Alex G)
Closer ~ The Chainsmokers
Try ~ Nelly Furtado
F**k Around (All Night) ~ Pepper
Blank Space ~ I Prevail
First ~ Cold War Kids
You're Going Down ~ Sick Puppies
24K Magic ~ Bruno Mars
Girls Chase Boys ~ Ingrid Michaelson
Love On The Brain ~ Rihanna
Animals ~ Maroon 5
Blow Me (One Last Kiss) ~ Pink
I Don't Wanna Live Forever ~ Zayn, Taylor Swift
Closer ~ Nine Inch Nails
Famous Last Words ~ My Chemical Romance
So Far Away ~ Avenged Sevenfold
Fight Song ~ Rachel Patten
The Fighter ~ Gym Class Heroes (Feat. Ryan Tedder)
So What ~ Pink
Scars To Your Beautiful ~ Alessia Clara
I lived ~ One Republic
My Girl ~ The Temptations

ACKNOWLEDGEMENTS

Thank you to all the readers out there who have taken a chance on me.

Thank you to thank my family, especially my husband, for keeping me caffeinated and hydrated while I'm writing.

Thank you to my boys. Mom loves you.

Thank you Martha Sweeney for your encouragement and for always taking the time to answer my questions. You're the best!

Thank you Becky, Donna, Carrie, Kristen, Mandy, Crystal, and Kolleen, at Hot Tree Editing.

Thank you Robin Harper at Wicked By Design for an amazing book cover. You pretty much nailed it on the first try.

Thank you Jessi Gibson, my writing coach, for your encouragement and praise. You've become a valued friend.

Thank you Kim Ingram Deister at The Story Tender for the final editing and proofing. You're my unicorn.

Thank you Nicole at Indie Sage.

Thank you Belinda Boring at BookishSnob Designs for the fantastic teasers and my adorable author logo. You are an amazing lady.

Thank you Angela at Fictional Formats for working your magic and for coming to my rescue more than once.

Thank you Lisa, my book girlfriend, who introduced me to

Christian Grey, which led me to Amazon One-Click and in turn, forced me to get a real job to support my reading habit.

Thank you Amy for your input on Zach and Jay's story.

Thank you to my bitches. You know who you are. I love you girls with all my heart. Thank you for being patient with me and not writing me off as your friend, when I've been too busy trying to meet deadlines.

Thank you my new author friend, Louise Evans for the additional teasers and for always including me.

And last, but not least, thank you Louise Rogers-Thomas for being the best damn PA, I could ever wish for. You make my world go around.

ABOUT THE AUTHOR

M.A Foster was born and raised in Tampa, Florida and currently resides in Land O'Lakes, Florida where she is suffering from empty nest syndrome with her husband and her crazy dog, Rocky.

When she's not reading or writing, she's searching for chocolate.

You can connect with her at one of the following:

Email: mafosterbooks@gmail.com
Website: https://mafosterblog.wordpress.com/
Facebook: https://www.facebook.com/AuthorM.A.Foster
Twitter: https://twitter.com/authormafoster
Goodreads: goodreads.com/author/show/16374121.M_A_Foster
Pinterest: https://www.pinterest.com/authormafoster/
Instagram: https://www.instagram.com/mafosterbooks/
Newsletter signup: http://eepurl.com/cEeb2T

Made in the USA
Columbia, SC
05 April 2018